Bruce Murkoff

WATERBORNE

Bruce Murkoff was born in 1953, spent many years in California, and now lives in Stone Ridge, New York.

WATERBORNE

WATERBORNE

A NOVEL

Bruce Murkoff

Vintage Contemporaries
Vintage Books
A Division of Random House, Inc.
New York

FIRST VINTAGE CONTEMPORARIES EDITION, FEBRUARY 2005

Copyright © 2004 by Bruce Murkoff

All rights reserved under International and Pan-American Copyright
Conventions. Published in the United States by Vintage Books, a division
of Random House, Inc., New York, and simultaneously in Canada by
Random House of Canada Limited, Toronto. Originally published in
hardcover in the United States by Alfred A. Knopf, a division of
Random House, Inc., New York, in 2004.

Vintage and colophon are registered trademarks and
Vintage Contemporaries is a trademark of Random House, Inc.

The Library of Congress has cataloged the Knopf edition as follows:
Murkoff, Bruce, [date]
Waterborne : a novel / Bruce Murkoff.—1st ed.
p. cm.
1. Hoover Dam (Ariz. and Nev.)—Fiction. 2. Dams—Design
and construction—Fiction. 3. Depressions—Fiction.
4. Arizona—Fiction. 5. Nevada—Fiction. I. Title.
PS3613.U695W37 2004
813'.6—dc22   2003058859

Vintage ISBN: 1-4000-3258-X

Book design by Anthea Lingeman

www.vintagebooks.com

Printed in the United States of America
10 9 8 7 6 5 4 3 2 1

For Suzanne

Raging rivers [are like] the power of the Lord;
They bring headlong those who despise him.

And entangle their paths,
And destroy their crossings.

And catch their bodies,
And corrupt their natures.

For they are more swift than lightnings,
Even more rapid.

But those who cross them in faith
Shall not be disturbed.

And those who walk on them faultlessly
Shall not be shaken.

From Odes of Solomon 39

THE
RIVER

*T*he river begins, squeezed out of rock older than the earth itself, high in the snowdriven streams and alpine lakes of the Rocky Mountains, running clear and bright through the clenched fist of granite peaks. Finding its course, feeding off tributaries, for two thousand miles it cuts and shapes, hews and contours, gnaws and seeps through rock and soil, this magnificent gash in the American West.

The river works, ever steady, carving a path through stubborn plates of shale and limestone, while the ground convulses and heaves, sending up rock sheets hundreds of feet tall. These walls rise, nicked and scarred, and the river pours between them, crimson in the dusky sunlight, the color of violence and birth. A roar thrums through these canyons, slick in their newness, only to fade and disappear as fissures heal and molten rock knuckles the ground, frozen in place, supplanted by the rhythmic slap of water on rock as only the river continues to move.

When evening comes, the river is a rich velvet, black as licorice. On clear nights the riffles are razorcut by moonlight, the surface phosphorescent; in the morning the water is milky, its edges patinated with algae; at high noon the sun radiates the surface with the warmth of a silver dollar; and as the sun sets the water dulls to tungsten, then to ink, as it keeps on flowing.

The river is fat with trout, their tails pushing against the driving current as they feed on drifting nymphs that tumble in the gravel rubble. Deer tongues shatter the glassy pools that crescent sandy beaches. Beavers build submerged dens on the cusp of faster water. Speckled hawks nest in the pocked faces of sheer cliffs. Rattlesnakes leave soft impressions in the crumbled sandstone that dusts the ever-changing shoreline.

The river ebbs and eddies, reacting to centuries of seasons. A flurry of high mountain snowflakes will cause it to run its banks on yellow plains below. Years of drought will encase silver-bellied fingerlings in crosshatched miles of rockhard mud. But rain will fall again, and underground aquifers, always cool with dampness, will refill and bleed into trickling creeks that will rise, tumescent and swift, to nourish a river that sustains itself on droplets and torrents, fog and sleet, a champion of its own drama.

For centuries the river remained remote, settled only by Indian tribes along its lesser tributaries and feeder streams. The Papagos built canals and irrigation ditches to cultivate their crops in the valley of the Gila, and wisely built their stone pueblos on higher ground. The Chemehuevis, near-naked wanderers between the forests and water, lived like poor relations on the banks of the Rio Virgen, and tribes of Utes lived in the canyons near the Paria, hunting mule deer on the plateaus and fishing for trout in rocky pools. The Navajo invaders lived in a canyon fortress near the San Juan, and peaceful bands of Shoshones built villages of boughs and rabbit skins on the banks of the Yampa, where they gathered roots and hunted for geese and elk.

The Spaniards came from Acapulco, dispatched by Cortés to find cities of gold in the northern territories. Brave men accepted the challenge, but it was years before a ship risked destruction at the river's frothy mouth in the Gulf of California, sailing far enough inland to allow its foolhardy captain to gaze into the hellish depths of the Grand Canyon before turning back. It took another two hundred years before the padres and fur trappers discovered the headwaters of the river, and a hundred years more before the United States government sent explorers and surveyors and a one-armed major to plumb its mysteries. And with the westward expansion came visionaries and fools, optimists and clowns, to investigate the river and what it might do to nourish the arid reaches of the New World.

Now engineers squatted on the high cliffs of Black Canyon with measuring devices and topographical maps, floating barges in the red water to test her flow. Now the canyon walls, already battered for centuries, are under attack by jackhammers and dynamite, and far below, water bubbles and explodes with the hard tears of demolition.

Unpredictable to its murky depths, the river bows but does not surrender.

The river never stops.

WEST
OF THE
MISSISSIPPI

1932

*H*e left Chicago after midnight and drove across the Nevada state line four days later, a few hours before dawn. He enjoyed driving through the night—the long stretches of deserted highway, a surrounding blackness invaded only by the nearly parallel bores of his creamy yellow headlights. The hours drifted by, endless and stark, allowing him to think of things beyond his last job or the one waiting for him in the Nevada desert.

Filius Poe took pleasure in being alone.

At four o'clock in the morning he stopped his Chrysler in the middle of the Rock Island Bridge. His white shirtsleeves rolled carefully above the elbow, he leaned on the pitted rail above the Mississippi and brought the silver lighter, a gift from his wife, up to the cigarette in his mouth. The smoke he blew out gusted back and trailed over his shoulder. He turned west to follow the river as it flowed, straight and wide, to the oily horizon. A row of squat tugboats were tied to the pier on the Moline side; a light was on in the pilothouse of the first boat, and Filius could see three men playing cards under the green-painted ceiling. A Canadian freighter long as a city street was waiting in the lock, its smokestacks forming an irregular outline above the factories and warehouses that stood solidly packed along the dismal riverfront.

An engineer himself, Filius never failed to marvel at the wonders of bridges and locks and dams, at the articulated brilliance of construction and design by which men conceived the great ribbons of steel and cable that tamed the open water, regulated the flow of rivers and harnessed the natural energy that cracked like a whiplash through the mysterious earth. It was exactly this manufactured amity between mind and nature that drew Filius to things mechanical and primary, that propelled him westward.

Startled by a sudden beam of light, intrusive as a push toward the rail, he turned, squinted into the harsh glare and made out the gold Iowa Highway Patrol emblem on the car parked behind his own. Two policemen leaned against the squad car, watching. The taller one had his arms crossed, and his hooded eyelids fluttered as if he'd just woken up; the other cop moved his flashlight beam from Filius's face to the fenders and trunk of his car, dulled by road dust. Both cops were young and stocky, healthy as corn-fed steer.

"This your car?" The shorter cop's voice was high and clipped, jangly from too much coffee.

"Yes."

The cop let his flashlight beam dip through the rear window and explore the interior. "It break down or something?"

"No, it's fine."

"You got a bottle on your hip?" The taller cop yawned as he posed the question, and Filius didn't understand a word he said.

His partner impatiently clicked his flashlight on and off, pulsing the beam off Filius's shoes as he stepped closer. "You been drinking, bud?"

"No."

"You maybe gonna jump?"

Filius didn't answer.

Their nerves stretched and loopy after a long shift, the cops giggled like farm boys because they knew they'd be home within the hour. The taller cop was anxious to be coiled beneath the sheets with his young wife, both of them naked and twitchy and only half asleep, while his partner knew that his bed would be made, sheets fresh and stiff from the line, and his mother would've left a tin of peaches on the kitchen table just for him. This was the joke, not this stranger, and they meant to let him in on it, to share in their fidgety ease. He could've had a fifth of bootleg gin in his pocket, or leapt off the bridge backward, they wouldn't care. But the stranger, not recognizing their gesture of camaraderie and goodwill, stood by the railing and didn't move. The cops settled down and saw only a tall, slender man, old as a big brother, standing there in his white shirt and khakis, his brown hair as washed out as his eyes, staring at them through wire-rimmed glasses, looking down his long wing of a nose, supposing they were really the fools they were acting, and now their pleasure was soured.

Filius couldn't see this, couldn't recognize their pleasure because he no longer recognized it in himself.

The cops straightened up, suddenly annoyed with the hot breeze coming off the river, sticky with the reek of dead fish and diesel.

The short cop shined his light in Filius's face and gestured to his car. "Move that heap out of here."

"This ain't a park," the other observed.

Filius looked down at the crimped shortness of his cigarette, a burning eye between his fingers. He flipped the butt over the railing and watched the wind carry it below the bridge, the last sparks fading to gray ash.

Thirty minutes later, the Chrysler picked up a nail in the road—the loud hiss of air giving the car a deceptive buoyancy before the thudding knocks of the flattened tire coasted him to a stop along the banks of the Cedar River.

Filius got out of the car and stepped to the edge of the empty highway. He couldn't see the river through the thick stand of pines, but he could hear the cool, chattering rush of shallow water over the stony bed a hundred feet below. He walked back to open the trunk, reached past the spare tire humped under a moth-eaten blanket, pulled out a small canvas satchel, his bamboo fishing rod, his bedroll, a battered tin coffeepot and a bag of oranges. Glancing up at the purpling on the horizon, he knew it would be daylight soon and time enough to deal with the tire. He bundled his gear together, slung the satchel over his shoulder and half slid, half climbed down the crumbly bank to the river beyond the trees.

He didn't so much dream as remember. That night he remembered himself as a small boy, standing on the end of a short pier on the banks of a great lake as a violent thunderstorm tore up the sky. Dark clouds, heavy and slow despite the screaming wind, massed over the water, bundled together like a bouquet of black roses. A roll of thunder ended with a bang he felt deep in his chest. The lake churned below; the water, as it slapped against the pilings, sent up streams that unfurled over the wooden planks, soaking his bare toes and the cuffs of his pajama bottoms. He pushed his shoulders closer to the wind and crouched like a boxer, wanting to feel the storm as it arrived. The thunder cracked again directly overhead and a crooked jag of lightning seared the night sky. In that instant, the boy saw the wind-pushed rain, blistering sheets of it, racing toward him across the water. He looked up into the black gloom—stunned by the noise of it—and the air turned liquid around him. He dug his toes into the slippery wooden planks as the scattershot of rain burst across the boards and peeled off his pajama top. Forcing himself to look up again, he could see only water and the welts of brightness that shattered the sky. He allowed himself to be lulled by the rhythmic pounding that beat in his ears and on his skin, and opened his arms to a tall gray wave, its crest sheared off by the wind, washing over the pier. It wrapped around him and for a moment he was swimming in air—weightless, dream-drugged—until suddenly he was lifted by two big hands that roughly clenched his shoulders and pulled him free of the lake's narcotic pull. It was his father, his long coat streaming with water.

He blinked awake and rolled onto his side. Pushing away his bedroll, he watched the cowbirds move through the brittle leaves near his campsite, flipping them over like playing cards, hunting for sow bugs and red worms. When he sat up, they lifted in an angry ruckus before settling in the boughs overhead.

Filius stood and looked at the river ten yards away: wide and shallow and fast, with calm pockets of flat water along both banks. A neglected pasture bordered the opposite bank, and a sparse stand of runt willows stood in the fetid muck, the lowest leaves nibbled into brown patches by watering cattle. In the broken morning sunlight, Filius made out a small stonefly hatch underneath the willows. He squatted on his bedroll and assembled his three-piece rod, broken-down and tied up with twine. He'd built the rod himself when he was sixteen, carefully wrapping each ferrule with green string and applying coat after coat of varnish until the cane gleamed like bronze. When he had finished, his father burned *Filius Poe, Madison, Wisconsin, 1915* into the thick shaft above the cork handle. By now the cane had lost most of its snap, but he'd come to like the new, lazy action. He reached into his satchel for the small Hardy reel his father had given him, and from a sheepskin sleeve, a Light Cahill he liked for this water. Still barefoot, he rolled up his pant legs and walked to the river, feeding out line even before he stepped in, listening to it whistle through the guides as he scanned the opposite bank. What he wanted was the big trout finning in the shade under the nipped willows across from him, and when he looked over his shoulder to adjust his back cast, he saw the girl and the baby.

Crouched naked in the shallow channel upstream, she looked young, maybe seventeen or eighteen. Her long brown hair, lathered with soap, hung over her shoulders but didn't hide her breasts, heavy with milk, the nipples large and dark as cherrywood. Washing the inside of her thighs, she looked straight at Filius without moving to cover herself, leaning forward until her nipples and then her forehead touched the surface, hair now swirling in the fast water. The girl remained still, poised over the calm oval pool that reflected the whiteness of her soft belly, and let the current strip away the soap.

On the shore, several yards back, the baby, a boy not even a year old, tottered between rolled-up towels on a green blanket, a scruffy wirehaired terrier sitting next to him. A two-man tent, army issue, the canvas faded almost white, was set up in the clearing next to a smoldering cookfire. Diapers and a woman's print dress hung from a sagging line, drying slowly in the muggy air.

The baby pointed at Filius, laughing, and the dog's tail twitched rapidly.

Filius jerked the rod tip and fouled his line. A great skein of knots fell in the water and drifted toward him. He looked down as the soapy water from the girl's bath swirled at his bare feet. The tiny bubbles formed a temporary bracelet, oily with color, around his ankle before bursting, one by one.

Filius felt his eyes go wet and turned away.

. . .

Addie McCabe pulled out the chair across from him and, before she sat down, lifted a small leather-bound notebook and a fistful of pencils from her worn leather bag. She opened the notebook, rolled the pencils in a row in front of her and said, "Filius. That's an odd name."

"I'm named after my grandfather."

"Paternal?"

Filius shook his head as Addie flipped through her notebook, densely packed with her small, tight handwriting, looking for a clean page.

"No," he said. "My mother's father."

"Was he an odd man?"

"I don't know. I never met him."

They sat at a round table on the second floor of the Wendt Engineering Library. Addie McCabe was a journalism major, sent to interview him for the *Badger Herald*. She wore a pale yellow linen dress with an intricate floral design hand-stitched into the rounded collar. On her head was a short-brimmed woven hat with a wide golden band. When she finally looked up from her notebook and pencils, her face was framed by the short flaxen hair that fell in bangs over her forehead and was cut straight across at her neck. In the March sunlight that fell through the window over Filius's shoulder, she seemed to have been sculpted out of raw honey.

Her eyes, locked on his, were glowing.

"Are you Italian?"

"Pardon?"

"Filius. Wasn't there a Roman politician called Filius?"

"That was Flavius."

"Pope Filius?"

He couldn't take his eyes off her. In his mind, he scrolled through the ancient history texts from his father's library. "Pope Simplicius. Pope Gelasius. Pope Anastasius. Pope—"

"Emperor Filius?"

"Claudius. Aurelius. Theodosius." He watched a smile radiate across her face, skin as cool and creamy as the ivory netsuke animals his mother collected. "No Filius."

"Maybe he was a gladiator."

"That was Demetrius."

"So you're not Italian."

"No."

"It's still an odd name."

He thought again of honey.

It was 1919, and the juniors and seniors returning from tank battles at Cambrai and the dark whorehouses of Paris were full of wisdom and swagger. Still enamored of their singular experiences, some sporting thin moustaches, they relished their victory by personalizing episodes of combat and liberation in the ruined towns of Europe, proud of their service and counting themselves lucky to be walking the grassy knoll of Bascom Hill instead of living on in name only, forever chiseled in granite at Memorial Union.

When Filius turned eighteen the war was already coming to an end, and instead of enlisting at the courthouse on State Street—still festooned with red-white-and-blue bunting, faded now and drooping—he studied engineering with his father at the university in Madison. The campus was populated now by girls in disproportionate numbers, girls in their prime who made beautifully wrapped bandages and pined and wrote letters to boyfriends and classmates overseas, those brave sons of Wisconsin–turned–adventurers in brass buttons and khakis. These girls treated the boys left behind— for bad hearing or bad hearts or for being born too late—as simply that: boys.

Filius kept to himself, more comfortable in his own company or the company of his parents and their friends. He had always looked mature for his age, with that proud flag of a nose that other boys found threatening or humorous, and that would take him ten more years to grow into. Filius used this time of invisibility to concentrate on his studies, specializing in pneumatics and hydroelectric energy. At nineteen, he was a third-year engineering student, already published in technical journals, courted by prestigious firms in Chicago and New York and by the Bureau of Reclamation in Washington, D.C. It was Addie's assignment for the *Badger Herald* to find out why, and this is what Filius tried to explain to her when she accepted his invitation to go sailing on Lake Mendota the first warm day of spring.

At seventeen, Filius had taken over his father's workshop and built himself an Alpha Dory, which he'd read about in an old issue of *Forest and Stream* magazine. Accompanying the article was a pencil sketch of the dory sailing on a reach, mainsail stiff in the lead-lined breeze, the dory itself sleek and heeling dramatically in the blurred chop of Massachusetts Bay. Filius wrote the designer to request a set of plans, and William Chamberlain, an Atlantic sailor who'd never imagined one of his boats racing across a Wisconsin lake, sent him a full set of drawings and a handwritten note wishing him luck.

For the next six months, Filius worked on his boat. He read Neison's *Practical Boatbuilding for Amateurs* and talked to Alf Kemp, who ran the small marina at Maple Bluff. Alf convinced him to build a scale model first, so he could see the lines properly and understand the layout of the planking. He built it in a week, working nights, and the morning after he showed the unpainted miniature to Alf, he cleared a space in the workshop and drew the baselines of the twenty-one-foot dory directly on the floor. Using Chamberlain's plans, he calculated the offsets and penciled them out on two long sheets of brown paper, getting the exact dimensions for the five planks he needed for each side. Then he drew the bottom of the boat on another sheet—from tapered bow to notched stern—and assembled the three pieces together, folding them carefully to create a full-sized dory in paper.

Filius constructed the bottom of the boat and the planking with white pine, as Chamberlain instructed, and used oak for everything else but the thwarts and risers that held the mast. He bought bronze Anchorfast nails, cut the wood and framed it himself, using galvanized metal clips on the bottom knuckles, and squared the transom by "horning" it—a method Alf learned from his grandfather, who'd built boats on the Maine coast. He faired the planks as the books taught him, pushing the plane with a gentle touch, cutting his shavings as fine as shedded snakeskin. The sixteen-foot mast and boom were Douglas fir, and the gooseneck and sail grommets, like all the other fittings, were bronze. Filius set the sailing rig to Chamberlain's specifications, and the only real change he made to the Alpha was the centerboard, which he set into a box with a wider pivot ratio, allowing for better maneuverability and speed. The last things he made were the oars: eight-foot pieces of the lightest pine he could find, which he cut to size and lathed himself.

When the dory was finished and the rains of April diminished to a soft wetness that dried out by noon, Filius rolled the boat out of the wide workshop doors onto the spongy lawn. He treated the outside of the dory with a rot preservative Alf had given him, and sealed it inside and out before painting it white and trimming the gunwales and hull below the waterline with blue paint he'd mixed with black. As the paint dried, Filius unwrapped the brass nameplate he'd bought with money earned cutting winter firewood and had ordered from a metalworks in Chicago that made the nameplates for the doors of the Senate chamber and the Supreme Court in the Capitol, ordered the same day he'd sent away for the plans. And on the first sunny morning in May, he attached the brass oval to the stern and christened her *Nightwing*.

Two years later, Filius guided the dory through the tempered wind at University Point, sailing at an easy reach in the bloomy dusk, watching the gray water roll back from the bow. Addie sat in front of him, her profile outlined against the mainsail, and pointed at the shoreline, at the rat-a-tat-tat of pintails and mallards taking flight, their mottled wings beating furiously, webbed feet trailing watery lines. He smiled as the ducks passed overhead, and let her take the tiller and swing *Nightwing* farther out into the lake.

On this, their first date, Addie told him about learning to sail on Lake Michigan with her father, a respected psychiatrist who taught at the University of Chicago and kept an office in one of the large buildings that rose like stacks of coins along Lake Shore Drive. In March he would begin to alter the schedules of his private patients so he could go down to the small pier at the end of Oak Street and start getting his boat ready for spring sailing. For her eighth birthday, he took Addie along on *Runaway*, a twenty-foot cat-rigged scow he'd bought new that year. Addie fell in love with her spear-headed lines, the shine of her mahogany gunwales and seats, waxy and redolent with fresh varnish, with the sights and smells of sailing before she even set foot on board, and when her father finally lifted her up and she stood bowlegged on the bottom planks, arms outstretched for balance, the wobbliness of wood on water, the slap of water against the hull gave her sounds to love as well. Addie cherished this memory, her father's hand on hers as they steadied the quivering tiller just outside the harbor.

They didn't talk much on those Saturday excursions, the occasional shouted command and the hollered decisions over the choice of sandwiches her mother had packed for them substituting for conversation. They caught up on talk and laughter back at the pier, after the ropes were coiled in circles alongside the cleats as Daniel had been taught and in turn taught his daughter. If the weather was fair they walked home along Goethe Street, or if it was dark and rainy they rode the trolley, going on about school or neighbors, local gossip, innocent and familiar, sometimes missing their stop and arriving home late for supper.

The boats of Addie's memories were watched over and maintained by Tommy Chipps, a friendly man as compact and broad as a tree trunk.

"When he laughed," she told Filius, "you felt the earth vibrate through the soles of your shoes, his voice was so rich. He had a dog, a stubby-legged little bitch, all scruff and whiskers, white with brown spots like somebody'd spit tobacco juice on her. She'd followed him to Oak Street one morning three years before and never left his side. Peppy he called her, even though she spent most of the day sitting with her back legs crossed in whatever patch of sunlight she could find, and every time you looked at her she'd yawn. She was the cutest ugly dog I ever saw, and every spring when we went down to the pier, she had a new litter of puppies, five or six. And they were always shorties just like her, little hairy things all mud-splattered brown-and-black, never taking on the characteristics of any dog but her, like the male dog didn't matter at all, even though Tommy did admit she did get out of his yard on occasion, and more than once he picked her up running with a pack of terriers in Douglas Park."

She turned away every couple of seconds, interrupted by wind changes or the sudden flap of the sail. Filius edged along the seat until their knees touched, and put his hand toward the tiller. Addie happily gave it up, turning toward him with her back against the gunwale and one leg tucked under herself, their knees still touching. She brushed loose strands of hair behind her ear before leaning forward, so close he could feel the bursts of her breath.

"Tommy kept the puppies in an old wooden apple basket with a red sign sticking out of it that said *Free Dogs*. Every April I fell in love and begged my father to let me have one. After two years and two litters, a dozen or so dogs that went off to other homes, to other children, he gave in. I ran over to the basket and stuck my arms into this squirming mess of pee-smelling puppies and I just couldn't pick out the one I wanted the most. She had six that year, all cute and nasty, the spitting image of their mother. They scampered and yipped and burrowed under my arm, but I still couldn't decide. The wind came up and my father called me and told me it was time to set sail and I could pick one when we got back. Tommy promised me they'd all still be there—he even took down the sign—so I grabbed the sheet and cleated the line when my father gave me the signal, and when I turned to wave good-bye to Tommy I saw one of the puppies jump out of the box."

As Filius watched, Addie's eyes and mouth and hands were in constant motion, pantomiming these events while he steered the dory in an ever widening circle.

"It was the littlest puppy and she jumped in after us, her bark no more than a squeak, all stiff-legged and surprised when she hit the water, and I saw her furry little head bobbing in our wake, no bigger than a muskrat. My father saw it, too, and came about as quickly as he could. I couldn't see the puppy anymore, so I scrambled to the bow and hung over until I nearly fell out, keeping my eye on the ripply water, afraid to look away because I'd forget where the puppy had been, and when we came around I stared straight down into the water and there she was, floating a couple of inches below the surface. When I felt my father's hands on my waist I reached in up to my shoulders and grabbed her from the ice-cold water, her eyes closed and her little body heavy as lead. I pressed her tight to my chest and she spit up a pint of Lake Michigan, breathing in gasps, but at least breathing. I kept her warm in my extra sweater, a sweater she slept on at the foot of my bed for ten years. I named her Grace and she came sailing with us every summer, playing with Peppy while we got the boat ready, both mother and daughter homely to everybody but Tommy and me. Peppy died when she was thirteen, just went to sleep one night and didn't wake up, and we had Grace until her hips ached too much and she couldn't climb the stairs anymore, up or down. We did the right thing, and I held her as she died. It was good, those ten years we had together, and I smile every time I think of her."

She was sitting close to Filius, their knees still touching. By now it was almost full dark, quiet except for the lapping of water against the hull and the snap of the luffing mainsail. Filius turned the dory toward the small dock in back of his parents' house on Livingston Street. He was aware of Addie watching him, and of the silence that drew them closer together on the narrow seat. The quarter moon emerged from behind a furl of tarnished cloud, silvering its edges. He hardened the mainsail and looked back, finding Addie's eyes in the darkness.

Three nights later, he took her up inside the Capitol dome—his favorite place in Madison, his architectural twin and part of his own history. At four years old he'd watched the first Capitol burn to the ground, gutted by orange-spiked flames that flickered through the smoke into a black, wintry sky. The morning after, his father took him to see the ruins, the marble façade singed black and surrounded by broken glass, the nearest trees blackened, the circles of melted snow on the walkways reflecting the gray sky like puddles of splashed mercury. Smoke still rose from the furniture heaped on the vast lawn, and the bitter smell of rot and smolder seared Filius's nostrils with a sting more penetrating than the February chill. The assistant fire chief, Tom Mooney, sat atop his big Morgan gelding in front of six towering Corinthian pillars that had withstood the blaze.

He was soot-smudged from head to toe, swaying gently in his saddle, fast asleep.

The Capitol's reconstruction became the yardstick that measured Filius's adolescence. He watched the crisscrossing of huge cranes from his bedroom window as he got ready for school; on his way home, he'd take a shortcut up Washington Street to count the great stacks of Vermont granite and try to figure out how many had been hoisted into position while he sat at his desk learning his multiplication table, and later, algebra and geometry. Over the next ten years he would note, on a daily basis, the accomplishments and delays, with a satisfaction his father found amusing.

Claude Poe, chairman of the Engineering Department at the university, served as a consultant on the project, and Filius often stood at his side, quiet and attentive, while the chief engineer and hired contractors unrolled great waves of blueprints on a long table and solemnly discussed tympanum and entablature, loggia and esplanade, the boy memorizing and luxuriating in the words. In the evenings he would ask his father to explain the terms, and Claude gladly let his coffee grow cold as he cleared space on the dining room table to illustrate the architectural embellishments he was describing. He patiently diagrammed and outlined the blueprints for his son, who slowly began to make sense of the nomenclature of design. He admired the Greekness of this new language and what his father called the "anthropology of form." By the time Filius was twelve and the building almost finished, his questions became more challenging and his understanding more keen, and these sessions evolved not only into a daily dialogue on territory and site and the human need to urbanize the spaces between, but also about Boston beating New York in the World Series, or Teddy Roosevelt's African adventures as they were serialized in *Scribner's Magazine*, or the sinking of the *Titanic*. Claude loved his son, and recognized that he had the intellect and the will to build great things.

As the years passed, the men who worked on the Capitol became used to Filius's presence and allowed him to wander the site freely. He stopped by most mornings on his way to school as the men fell into the rhythm of their day. He would watch the German and Italian immigrants work with the beautiful stone and marble in the great rotunda, sitting among them as they bantered back and forth in exotic tongues, picking up scraps of sentences and slang. As he got older he joined them for coffee around the trash fires they lit in winter to keep warm, and in summer to eat from their baskets of apples and pears. From these men, he learned to distinguish between Numidian marble from Algeria, butterscotchy and smooth, and that dug out of the wet earth in Hawkins County, Tennessee, and to appreciate the coolness of the granite walls, huge squares excavated from Marquette County, no more than a hundred miles north of where he stood.

His other boyhood pastime was scrambling through the Heat and Power Plant under construction on East Main Street. A simple brick building, plain and dumpy as a hatbox, it hid the underground guts of pipes and tunnels that supplied steam heat to the cavernous maw of the Capitol two blocks away. Twenty feet below street level, he stood among the workmen as they shoveled dirt, their wrinkled faces caked and patterned with grime, and watched as huge cylinders of concrete were lowered in sections, swaying gently on girdles of thick chains and throwing massive shadows in the scummy light of jaundiced lanterns. He stood shrouded inside these round, nine-foot cylinders as the men fastened them together, cloistered in a darkness echoing with hammers and pickaxes. He heard the men's curses, their gutter spew and raw affection as they cooed to their tools while bleeding from scraped knuckles and banged knees, and the tunnel pieces, a half mile of them, slowly came together in these warrens under the cobblestones.

But it was the Capitol dome that gave Filius the most pleasure, not so much the architectural peel of the outside, ribbed in giant blocks of Vermont granite over a terra-cotta skin, as the inner dome, two thousand tons of structural steel in a systematic configuration of T-irons and trusses. He would stand in the middle of the public hall and tilt his head back to look straight into the heart of the Capitol, staring at that wide neutral space between the two ceilings, dim as the inside of an eggshell, and watching the men on the catwalks and corkscrewing staircases that ran up to the steel platform holding the lantern in the fluted plug above the dome.

When he turned fifteen, his father took him up into the barrel of the dome. They went through the narrow, unmarked door on the fourth floor and climbed the stairs to the first exterior balcony, 150 feet over the city. Filius had been up this far before, and instead of gazing over Madison with its maple trees ablaze and its circuitry of streets crawling with wobbly Fords that spit smoke rings and scared dogs and small children, he leaned his back against the granite balustrade, gazed upward and studied how the dome curved out of sight.

Claude waited for the boy to blink, and said, "Come on."

Filius, his mind drifting, started walking down the hallway to the staircase that led back to street level, and then, hearing only his own footsteps, realized he was alone. He turned around to see his father standing next to an open door, and just past his father's smile he could see the circular black staircase that traveled like an artery up the interior wall of the Capitol and under the second skin of the dome itself.

Filius held that same door open for Addie and watched her eyes track the winding staircase into the darkness above them. A few minutes earlier, they had entered the Capitol and stood at the edge of the rotunda. He lighted the lanterns he carried, and in the burnished glow they saw their giant shadows rise along the wall. Happily spooked by her sudden enormity, Addie spun to face him, her eyes glowing as white as her blouse in the artificial light, and turned again to enter the massive room. Her low, hard heels clicked loudly on the floor, and in the moonlight falling through the glass panels arching over each of the four wings, she stopped to remove her shoes. The light sifted down to a faint shine that reflected off the marble floors and walls. Filius followed as she padded to the center of the room, where she tipped her head back and looked up at the mural in the dome above her.

Filius put down the lanterns and crouched to adjust the flame, the wavering light giving temporary life to the marble statues of women clutching falcons and wheat at the entrance to the hall. He looked from their chiseled feet to Addie's splay of toes, naked and fleshy, and when the toes curled he blushed and stood up straight.

"Ready?" he said.

They climbed to the fourth floor, where he guided her to the narrow, spiraling staircase that ran up the inner dome, holding the lantern behind him so she could see. He stopped at the halfway point, and when she came alongside, he could smell the lemony soap she used in her hair.

"Do you want to stop a minute?" he asked.

"I want to go to the top."

They came to the steep staircase that angled out over the bowl of the inner dome. Filius had been up here so many times he could climb the steps with his eyes closed, but for Addie's sake he did it slowly. At the first platform he turned to help, and her arms were outstretched to grip the rails on either side. She was suddenly aware of the height, and her eyes glanced electric around this immense hollow of granite and steel that belled around them.

Filius set the lantern down and helped her onto the platform, her fingernails seizing his arm as he led her to the waist-high railing directly under the mural.

"Bend your knees," he said.

As she did, Filius watched her face as his father had watched his, and he bent his knees, too, until they were side by side, leaning over the wide-eyed oculus and peering down, past the telescoping tiers of railings that marked each floor, to the lantern Filius had left burning in the center of the rotunda.

Addie held on, fingernails anchored into his arm, and caught her breath at the sight of the kaleidoscope of marble tiles that seemed to move, shadowy as wildcats, in the flickering light two hundred feet below them.

"Oh my."

"Are you okay?"

"I'm sick to my stomach." She laughed and threw her head back.

Filius quickly put his hand on her spine to balance her, but she let herself fall into him and they collapsed to the gridded platform floor. Addie stretched out with her hands behind her head and closed her eyes, laughing and gulping for air, with Filius's hand still on the small of her back. She didn't move, and neither did he.

"Dizzy," she said.

"That'll go away."

"I hope not."

Her long gray skirt was hooked up on her raised knee. Filius leaned back on his elbow and studied the slender lines of her exposed calves, following them up and down to the outline of her thighs. Addie's breath soon steadied and quieted, and he felt the muscles in her back relax under his spread fingers. She shrugged one hip and then the other, and Filius adjusted his fingers to the contours of her body. Addie didn't flinch, and he didn't move his hand away until she sat up.

"Let's go," she said, jumping to her feet and starting up the next set of iron stairs. Filius stood and held the lantern high to light her way. Addie reached the last spiral staircase and spun round and round as she made for the roof, her wide skirt throwing dark phantoms on the walls around her. When she pushed against the creaking door that led to the outside terrace, Filius put the lantern down and raced after her, whipping up the stairs and pushing through the unfastened door in one continuous motion. The shock of fresh air, pure as ether, paralyzed him. The night was cool and the sky moonbright, the pure blackness of it pricked with a million stars. Addie was leaning on the balustrade in front of him, gazing over the twin cups of lakes that defined the city.

"Filius."

She reached out to touch him without looking away from the strange and familiar landscape below them, and her fingers found his face, traveling along the dominant slope of his nose. She caressed his cheek and let her pinky rest at the corner of his mouth and her thumb on his jawbone. Slowly, so as not to startle her, he raised his arm and pointed. The moon seemed close, its craggy features as clear and sharp as pitted snow.

They walked around the circular balcony as midnight settled over the city. From their citadel high above the streets, they willed people to their beds, willed them asleep, willed them pleasant dreams.

They found a place to sit and stretch out, and spent the night on top of the dome. Filius had done this often, but never with anyone else. He covered Addie's shoulders with his sweater as a cool breeze began to blow and the stars lost their luster. An hour later they saw storm clouds band fatly on the horizon. Just before dawn it started to rain, and they stood to watch it come across the lake, hearing it on the water and the trees before it reached them. When the rain fell the heaviest, a red-tailed hawk appeared before them, wings tattered in the slash of water. It fought the rain and hovered over the balcony like a broken kite, fierce and thwarted by the two people sitting there. The hawk screamed once, its cry slurred and swallowed by the rain, and flew off.

At daybreak the sun came out. Filius and Addie were soaked. When they stood up, they found what the hawk was after: a loose, messy nest built between the two rails in front of them, packed tight with speckled eggs.

Filius kneeled down and counted the eggs—there were six of them—in the nest.

"Finches," he said.

Addie knelt beside him.

They stayed like that, dripping wet together. They never slept.

*L*ena McCardell left Oklahoma with her son and one suitcase. It was four in the morning when she woke the boy, his body salty sweet, his skin still spicy from the wild sage he'd run through behind the smokehouse on his way to the muddy pond where he spent the day chasing frogs around the crumbled edges of stinky muck and cattails. She buttoned him into dungarees and pulled a striped shirt over his head, blue and brown, tugging at the two holes he'd ripped on thorns, and cinched it all together with the boy's Indian-beaded belt. He yawned in her face as he started to wake up, and she signaled him with a finger to her lips to be quiet.

Lena took the boy's hand, his fingers curling like baby mice against her palm, and picked up the suitcase she'd packed in a hurry and without much thought. Mother and son stepped into the narrow hallway. It was already hot, a July of scant relief, and all the doors and windows were open to let in what cool moisture lingered from a storm that had lost most of its strength as it drifted in from Arkansas. The house was thick with the scent of honeysuckle that grasped the white trellises on both sides of the porch.

Lena didn't look into the living room as they passed it, but the boy did. A single lamp in the corner cast a weak yellow stain on the wall. The boy's father sat in the dark, his chair facing the open window, his back to the hallway. Cigarette smoke hovered in the air, as static and weary as the faded red roses on the wallpaper. The man didn't turn as Lena and the boy hurried past, shoes scraping the plank floor and suitcase ticking the walls, or when the screen door whooshed open, its hinges polished smooth by the fine Oklahoma dust.

The boy looked over his shoulder as his mother pulled him forward, his eyes still filmed with sleep, and saw not his father, but his father's shadow on the wall, just the profile of his face, the head swollen big and black and the nose pulled to a point at the edge of the windowsill. The shadow was as vivid as spilled ink. It was the impression of a man who wasn't there, a man real in his absence. It was the last time the boy would see him, and he knew it. He pinched his eyes shut and tried to remember his father's face, though all he could see was smoke and shadows. Lena yanked him outside and the screen door slammed. The boy almost tripped over the pile of dirt from a broken flowerpot on the porch, and when he opened his eyes to the hot night, the smoke and shadows were gone.

The bus station in Hugo was closed. After twenty minutes, the janitor arrived and let them in. He was the blackest person the boy had ever seen, so skinny his head seemed to be mounted on a stick. Lena thanked the man and sat on the hard bench facing the street, the boy's head in her lap, and waited for the westbound bus. The janitor moved slowly through the station with his broom, raising wisps of dust that settled slowly behind him. He turned on lights as he moved toward the lunch counter, humming a four-beat repetition with a voice as high and heartbreaking as a crying woman's, and the sound held in the air, rich and resonant against the tiled walls of the waiting room. Lena listened and watched the moths that clustered against the outside window, a dozen or more of them drawn to the white glow of the fluorescent lights, fluttering around the cracked o of HUGO and banging into the glass.

Lena looked down at the sleeping boy. She ran her fingers through his hair and moistened her thumb to work at the mocking smear of red juice in the corner of his mouth from the cherries he'd eaten after dinner. He squirmed under her touch, and the bulb of his elbow jammed into her thigh before he kicked and stretched out on the long bench, his head still nestled in her lap.

. . .

He was eight years old and named after her grandfather. At birth, his features had been as bland as rising dough; wrapped in a white hospital blanket, he lay in the crook of her arm, a small wheylike thing with shallow pocks for eyes and a soft nub for a nose. He didn't resemble anyone she knew. Not her garrulous red-haired grandfather, Burr McCardell, or, thank God, the bristle-faced men who romped and swayed in her husband's family tree. Lena went to sleep that first night with the fear that her baby had been switched with the son of Annie Jacobson, the grocer's wife, in the room down the hall, both babies delivered in the middle of the night by Dr. Marx, tired and cranky his entire sixty years, his lips drawn down from this duet of births fifteen minutes apart. Annie Jacobson had been chubby as a girl and was chubby still, all dimpled and bloated and pink like the little thing asleep in the crib by Lena's hospital bed.

The morning nurse, a wiry woman who smelled of pickling spices, laughed at Lena's concern. "He's yours, all right. But don't you worry. He'll be his own little man soon enough."

Lena scrutinized the baby's face every day, and when his hair came in the color of wheat instead of the fiery-tipped spears of foxtail millet that grew by the lake, and when his eyes stayed jet instead of green flecked with gray like everyone else in her family, she loved him for the surprises he gave her without even knowing it. She loved him as much as her heart would allow, and she knew she would never leave him like she'd left her husband, a man who'd left her long before she even realized he was gone.

Burr's eyes popped open, startling her. He kept his head in her lap as he scanned the low plaster ceiling of the bus station, following the cracks that spidered from corner to corner, and he remembered where he was. "I'm hungry."

"You have to wait for breakfast."

"When's that?"

"Sunup."

"When's that?"

"Soon." Lena knew he wasn't hungry, just confused.

He swiveled his head in her lap, hitching up her lightweight cotton print dress to her knees, as he looked around and sneezed out the moldy air of the waiting room. "Are we going to the café?"

"Yes."

"Can I get what I want?"

"Yes."

The skinny Negro still hummed mournfully as he emptied standing ashtrays into a metal bucket that he slid across the floor between his feet.

Burr closed his eyes and exhaled softly. "Cheese omelette."

The old man got on the bus in Ardmore a little after noon and took up most of the aisle. He was big, surprisingly tall for a man whose age should have robbed him of his height years ago. He walked slowly but steadily, back straight and arms held slightly out from his side for balance. His dungarees were faded and soft as suede. A paper sack was clutched in one of his oversized hands.

Burr watched him as the bus picked up speed again and lurched forward on a slipping clutch. The old man didn't stumble or trip or bang his knee on the iron-rimmed seats like some of the other passengers, red-faced and angry but too embarrassed to say anything to the indifferent driver. The old man, bowlegged as a sailor, rode the pitch of the bus with ease, and lowered himself into the aisle seat across from Burr.

He took off a Stetson hat the color of mud, reached up and placed it carefully on the shelf above. His bald ivory knob of a head was splattered with freckles. He opened his paper sack, pulled out an apple, and got an abalone-inlaid penknife out of his pocket. Burr stared at the knife, the handsomest one he'd ever seen, and watched the old man slice a narrow wedge out of the apple.

The slice, beaded with juice, clung wetly on the knife blade as the old man reached his hammy fist across the aisle and offered it to Burr. "Go on."

Burr hated to be caught staring. He looked up and the old man was smiling, his teeth big as skipping stones, white as chalk.

"Take it."

Burr looked at his mother. She was asleep, her head resting on the window, the Oklahoma flatland a brown blur behind her. Burr could smell the cut fruit over the harsher odors of flesh and exhaust.

He looked at the apple again.

"Got a whole bag full. Take it before I drop it."

Burr slid the wedge of apple off the knife blade and stuck it in his mouth, chewing slowly, making it last. The old man offered him a second piece before he even had a chance to finish the first.

As the bus crossed the Red River to pick up the highway east of Vernon, Lena woke up. Her forehead banged on the glass and she looked out at the cotton fields that straddled both sides of the Texas border. It was morning, a half hour after sunrise, and they had been riding on the bus for a full day. A light breeze bent the tops of spindly prairie sumac, occasionally bent further still by the weight of marsh hawks, hunch-shouldered as priests over breakfast, as they scouted the dips and washes by the side of the highway for rabbits and field mice. An unending sheet of clouds pleated the sky.

Most of the passengers were still asleep. A middle-aged man in a brown suit looked over yesterday's Tulsa newspaper, folded open to the employment pages, already heavily penciled by the last reader. A woman near the front washed her face with water from the dented canteen in her lap as her seatmate brushed his teeth with a vigorous finger. Burr was curled up next to Lena, sleeping with his mouth open, a single fly flitting around his apple-sticky thumb.

She inhaled deeply and caught herself, the air foul with the lingering, pungent smell of hard-boiled eggs, the simple dinner the young man and wife in front of her had shared the night before, their heads together now and both of them snoring. She looked about fifteen, and he not much older. Lena cracked open the window and pressed her cheek along the cool glass, breathing in the scent of the fresh-mown timothy grass that rolled off the plains.

She was overwhelmed with exhaustion. Thoughts of her husband and their confrontation three days ago invaded her sleep like the hairy men and wolves that had tormented her childhood dreams.

Every time she closed her eyes he was there. Even the lulling vibrations of the bus couldn't trick him away.

She had met Frank Mullens ten years ago when she was eighteen and he was twenty. A salesman for a publisher of religious literature out of Knoxville, Tennessee, he had an appointment in Hugo that afternoon to promote a new series of children's Bible stories at the biggest Methodist church in Choctaw County. Lena wasn't Methodist but her best girlfriend, Fanny Kruger, was. They'd ridden their bicycles to the church that day so Fanny could ask her mother, a Sunday-school teacher, to lend them the family car so they could drive forty miles to hear Henry Simms and the Bottom Boys play at the Grange Hall in Idabel.

Lena waited for Fanny on the front steps, sitting on her schoolbooks so she wouldn't get the back of her dress dirty, and looked down at her legs, stretched out on the brittle grass along the walkway. They were long and firm, polished dark by the summer sun, and much admired by boys and men. She remembered her cousins Jake and Buddy, brothers a year apart and a couple of years older than Lena, who would challenge her to foot-races and let her get ahead just so they could run behind her and watch her skirt fill with wind, curling up around her thigh and showing maybe a quarter moon of underwear before she slowed down. Lena knew what they were doing and didn't care. They were almost struck dumb by their esteem for her body parts. Lena didn't realize until a few years later that their reverent shyness was simply guilt for lusting after a relative, a girl they had to see almost every day in school and after church and at family dinners every other Sunday, where she sat between them, barefoot and careless, and drove them silently crazy. The cousins would go to bed at night and try not to picture her naked, but her image would loom large in the darkness and they'd give up, facedown on damp sheets with hands busy and minds racing.

Lena didn't think about any of that. She saw only her imperfections, the too-large feet and the long pink stripe of the scar that ran down her shin to her ankle, a scar she'd earned herself in a bike-riding joust with those same derelict cousins. Lena saw what she wanted to see, and let others see what they wanted.

Frank Mullens drove up slowly, his stovepipe Ford bouncing through the thick dust of the parking lot that wouldn't be wetted down until services on Sunday morning. Lena watched him park in the shade of the sugarberry tree, its broad branches filled with abandoned robins' nests. The Ford was softly crusted with dirt, and on the passenger door were small handprints next to the childishly scribbled words SHIT and FUCK. He got out of the car, his back to Lena, and stretched, looking out over the vast flatland of broken stalks, detritus of the season's first cut, that surrounded the church. He had the stub of a Sweet Caporal in his mouth, and lit a new cigarette before flicking it away. Then he grabbed his black suit jacket off the seat and stepped around the car.

He was dark, the color of wet clay, and he was the first man Lena ever saw outside of magazine pictures who wore sunglasses. He hadn't seen her yet, hadn't even glanced at the church. His attention was focused on the obscenities scrawled on the car door. He pulled a faded yellow handkerchief out of his pocket, neither angry nor amused, and rubbed until the handprints and mischief had disappeared in a large oval that shone like polished onyx.

Frank Mullens turned around, put on his suit jacket and finally saw her. He smiled, sure of himself. Although he was only two years older than Lena, he was already a man. She didn't smile back, but didn't look away. She knew that they wouldn't be needing Fanny's mother's car to get them to Idabel anymore.

Thirty miles west of Tucumcari, a gasket on the oil reservoir had given out, throwing oil through the vents on the metal hood and splashing the windshield like black rain. It was one o'clock in the afternoon, ninety-five degrees, and it was so yeasty and hot inside the bus that it was hard to breathe even with the windows open. Burr had the window seat now, and was careful not to lean too close to the glass, because the steel frame had already burned his elbow once. He sat up straight and stared across the desert. Anvil-headed thunderclouds, as deeply colored as bruises, hung in the sky over New Mexico.

The driver pulled over and got out, muttering a stream of curses as he slammed the latch to release the hood. He climbed onto the rim of the big tire and knelt on the wobbly fender, peering at the engine. Sweat turned his blue shirt purple, dripped off his crooked nose onto the radiator and sizzled away in puffs of steam. The driver swore in a language stressed and inarticulate. He jumped off the tire, sat lightly on the heated running board and started pulling off his shoelaces.

Burr looked over the desert that spread evenly to the southern horizon. A Ford panel truck, long abandoned, sat ten feet off the highway, its exposed rims buried halfway in the sand. The tires, windshield, steering wheel, seats and wood panels around the truck bed that weren't splintered and warped had been scavenged. What was left of the body was pimpled with rust. The broken skeleton of a steer, the bones of its bleached rib cage curved into the ground like the tines of a plow, lay in front of the truck, one horn buried in the sand and the other puncturing the exposed, crinkled radiator.

The driver climbed back on the fender and tied his shoelaces around the oil lid as firmly as he could. He drove on, slower now, with his small head cocked over the steering wheel, listening for clanks and whistles in the engine, cursing in that brayful tone for every single one of the 150 miles it took to get to Albuquerque for repairs.

They pulled into the bus station at about six o'clock, and a mechanic was waiting there in the grease-stained bay, sitting on a stack of bald tires with a china bowl balanced on his left thigh, finishing an early supper of tortillas and creamed corn speckled with chile peppers. The driver conferred with the mechanic, who wiped his bowl with the last of his tortilla and nodded. He ran a thumbnail through the gap of his front teeth and turned to the passengers milling around the front of the bus. "This'll take about an hour, folks," he announced. "Guadalupe's is right across the street and the food's good. Just tell 'em Ollie sent you and they'll set you up just fine."

Lena took Burr's hand and started for the restaurant. The sky was deepwater blue, and cool air rolled off the San Mateo Mountains to the west. She tugged at the boy's arm as his eyes skimmed the streets and plazas, sucking in the sight of trucks pulled up to hitching posts and men in cowboy hats slurping ice cream cones. In front of Guadalupe's, Pueblo Indians sat on dusty blankets and leaned against the wall under the sagging veranda. Their long, braided hair rested heavily on their shoulders, and they wore pearl-buttoned shirts and stiff indigo dungarees cuffed over cowboy boots. Arranged on the blankets in front of them were turquoise jewelry and silver conchos and pottery banded with black triangles in a slip glaze, and hanging from a sagging rope above them were tightly woven water baskets covered with dense pine pitch that had hardened and crackled into resin diamonds. Burr paused in front of a board, propped up outside the door, that displayed silver earrings of jackrabbits and roadrunners with tiny coral eyes. He reached out to touch one but his mother yanked him away. An old Indian woman, crooked as a warped post, smiled at him, her mouth a gummy hole of empty spaces.

The old man from the bus joined Lena and Burr at one of the small round tables inside as the restaurant quickly filled up with bus passengers and cowhands from the surrounding ranches. The waitresses, wispy blondes in their mid-forties with hips that bulleted out from their narrow, belted waists, seemed annoyed by the sudden rush, and took orders with impatient clicks of their tongues, and cheered up only when they could inform diners that the "stew of the day" was no longer available. Between tasks they perched on stools at the lunch counter, bookending the locals, ageless men bent over cups of coffee and hand-rolled cigarettes, and watched the cook flip hamburgers on the hot shine of the grill, letting the meat fall back in bursts of flame.

Lena liked the old man because of his kindness to Burr. On the bus he'd shared his bag of apples and listened to the boy tell stories about catching bluegills with live crickets in the lake behind their house, and in turn kept Burr awake and busy with his own tales about spooning for monster jackfish in the muddy twists and turns of the Little River across the border in Arkansas. He also told him about his days as a Rough Rider, when he'd hunted jaguars in the Cuban jungles with Teddy Roosevelt after the battle of San Juan Hill; that he'd been a wrangler for Buffalo Bill's Wild West Show and spent a year in Japan playing cowboys-and-Indians for a race of people who didn't understand a word of English; that he'd seen Andy Bowen and Jack Burke beat each other up for more than seven hours in a boxing ring in New Orleans before the turn of the century. Best of all, the old man had let Burr handle the penknife he'd bought from a seasick Texan on a trawler off the coast near Colima, and on those long, tedious hours on the bus he'd taught him how to sharpen it with a whetstone and spit.

At dinner he said his name was Charlie Chivers. He was seventy-two years old. His wife died last spring and he lost his chicken ranch to the bank.

"It was my father's business, chickens, and his father's before that, so I just grew up with it. Been in the family since before the Civil War. Have to admit I didn't much like chickens when I was Burr's age, all that stink and cackle, and I walked away from it a couple of times, especially when I was a boy. Then I got married, got older, and came back in oh-five. My father died the next year and I inherited the ranch. My own boy never took to it, though, and I didn't push him. Just as well, I imagine."

Charlie sipped his water and refilled his glass from the pitcher on the table. "When the banks fell, we lost our trucks and couldn't deliver any more eggs. They were just piling up and we ended up giving 'em away so they wouldn't go bad. No money coming in and we had all these chickens, two thousand of 'em. When we started running out of feed, we butchered 'em. Me and my wife and a Mexican feller been with us for years. Worked all day, air full of feathers, selling them four for a nickel until the nickels ran out. Gave 'em away after that. Then the Mexican feller moved on, no hard feelings 'cause he had a wife and baby to feed. Went way up north to Maine to hoe potatoes. Then Peggy died, fast, in her sleep. Heart just stopped keeping time. And the ranch got foreclosed right out from under me, it seemed, so now I'm back on the road, just like the old days."

He coughed into his handkerchief as their waitress appeared at the table, balancing three plates on her chubby arm.

"Two hamburger specials and mutton stew." She banged the plates down and moved on. Burr and Charlie reached for the hamburgers, and Lena took the mutton stew, a dish she'd loved as a child but that no one made anymore. This portion was huge, with long slivers of fresh green chiles floating in a broth thick with meat and tomatoes. The heat from the chiles, along with the memory of her grandmother tenderizing the tough mutton with a wooden hammer, made her eyes water.

Charlie dusted his hamburger with pepper and poured a little ketchup on the side of his plate for dipping. Burr watched him and did the same thing.

"Hey, Burr, you know what animal's dumber than a chicken?"

The boy shrugged.

"A two-headed chicken!"

Charlie laughed with a soft wheeze, and Burr almost expected a feather to blow gently through his teeth and float in the air between them. The old man took his first big bite, almost a third of his hamburger, and chewed it slowly. Burr caught up to him by the time he swallowed.

"My son lives in Flagstaff. That's where I'm heading. Got a house in the mountains that I've never seen, my wife neither. Too bad, those chickens kept us so busy right to the end. Bill says you can see snow in the mountains even in the heat of summer. Humphreys Peak, I think he said, biggest mountain in the state." He dipped his hamburger in the pool of ketchup and winked. "Mountains are surely lacking in Oklahoma, isn't that so, Burr?"

His mouth full, Burr nodded. He liked it when Charlie asked him questions, and he hated not being able to answer.

"Bill's got two trucks, used to do long-distance hauling to Los Angeles and San Francisco before the pinch. Since hard times, he keeps one truck in the barn and just does local jobs, mostly for the bank, repossessions and all. Folks look at their shoes when they see him coming, neighbors especially. One woman spit in his face when he went to pick up the dining room set she couldn't pay for, but she apologized later. Bill's an honest man and they know it. He doesn't like that part of his job, and he's been known to leave a couple of dollars behind, a loan he'll never see again, just so he won't have to come back for something the next week. He's got an extra room in his ranch house—in the back, he says—and I'll be staying there. Spend time with my granddaughter, Sarah, who I haven't seen since she was a little bit. Figure I can raise some rabbits for meat, maybe keep a few chickens in the yard. Earn my keep."

He sopped up the last swirl of ketchup with a piece of his bun and looked at Burr, who'd stopped eating so he'd be ready this time. "You like rabbit, son?"

"I like it fried."

"Me too, with milk gravy and biscuits I could eat it three times a day."

"Me too."

"We'll do fine in these lean times, won't we, Burr?"

"Yes sir."

Charlie grinned and wiped his big hands. When he lifted his water glass to drink, the waitress slapped down the bill in the puddle left by the sweating glass. Burr stared as the ring of water seeped up and followed the fibers of the cheap paper like blood through a vein, washing over the inky numbers and turning them as indecipherable as Chinese calligraphy.

"Where you folks headed?"

Lena was thinking about her father, Oren McCardell, who had worked twenty years for the tractor yard in Hugo. He traveled a lot, too, mostly overnight trips to Tulsa or Oklahoma City, filling orders for Case tillers and Farmall blades. Sometimes, on a job to Houston or Little Rock or Wichita, he would ride the train, and from every city he spent a night in, he'd bring Lena the morning paper. He wanted her to see the world beyond Hugo and the thousands of acres of cotton that surrounded them there. A world greater than the stockyards and feedlots on the edge of town, where cows stood in metal pens waiting to be slaughtered or shipped out, up to their hocks in winter muck or the summer slime of rain and piss. Greater than the smell of honeysuckle that grew thick and tangled by the river. Even greater than the smell of pigshit when the spring wind shifted.

Her father had opened a door and hoped that Lena would peek outside. She was first-generation Oklahoman, born a few years after statehood to a family of Scottish immigrants long after the original territorial expansion that had settled this land. Oren and his wife,

Clare, were accepted by the town when they arrived; he'd become a salesman and a Mason, and Clare baked rhubarb pies for seasonal fairs and church functions. But Oren knew he would always be an outsider—first in New York, when he got off the boat, and now in Oklahoma. He was devoted to his wife and daughter, and proud of his place in the community, though he also relished his estrangement, having lived a life or two before this one, because it gave him an openness of mind he hoped to pass on to Lena. He'd wanted to lure her with possibilities, to dangle the entire American experience in front of her wide eyes and entice her with the prospect of a daily existence different from their own. He was enticing his daughter, his only child, to run away.

Lena knew he loved her, and she loved him back. The morning after her father's return, she found the newspapers at the foot of her bed, folded as neatly as if they'd never been read, and devoured them from front to back—the stories of murder and passion, the gossip of the society pages, the articles about faraway wars in Finland and Russia, about Ernest Shackleton's great Antarctic adventure and fast girls who bobbed their hair, about Douglas Fairbanks and Knute Rockne and Kid Ory and Dixieland jazz. The hugeness of the world delighted her, but it would have to come to her because this was as far as she intended to go. Hugo was the only home she wanted and she swore she'd never leave it—even after her parents died in a freak railroad accident when she was seventeen, even when relatives offered to take her to Baltimore and put her through college. Lena stayed and finished high school in Oklahoma, got a job at the tractor yard where her father had worked and kept the house. And she kept getting newspapers, seven-day-old deliveries from Dallas and Tulsa that were dropped on her doorstep in tightly squared bundles. She read them as she always did and dated the sons of farmers, local boys with little education and round faces baked red from working the fields. And then she married Frank Mullens, a traveling Bible salesman. She had a husband and a son, and was inquisitive and happy until the day she found out that Frank had another wife and family in Shreveport, Louisiana. That's what it finally took to make her run away.

Lena put down her spoon and gazed over Charlie's wide shoulder. The sun was going down and the bus was parked out in front of

Guadalupe's now, engine running, the restaurant reflected in its row of shiny windows, the driver leaning in the open doorway of the bus and waving at the passengers to hurry up.

Charlie stood and laid some bills on the table. "Where you heading, Lena?"

"We're going to the dam."

*H*e was squatting in front of a row of lockers in Central Station, going through his duffel bag, when he glanced up and spotted the woman through the steady flow of legs that scissored past, hurrying to and from the trains. She was carrying a suitcase and walking away from the tall, rounded arrival gates set like cathedral windows into the far wall. He hadn't yet seen her face, but didn't have to. She was small, small as a girl, smaller than Lew, and that's all he needed to know. He bounced to his feet, the duffel between his knees, and kept an eye on her. In the big station, the sounds blended—voices and movement, laughter and shouts—into a sturdy drone, a human murmur. Only a baby's insistent cry, high and sorry, echoed off the high cupola and rained back down, inescapable.

Lew watched the woman walk toward the main entrance, where outside light flickered through the revolving doors, and for a moment she seemed to be stepping onto a movie screen as she was propelled toward Central Avenue. On the sidewalk, she stopped for a moment, startled by the sharp Los Angeles sunshine, and Lew saw her profile when she put down her suitcase to light a cigarette. She was dark, maybe Italian, maybe Greek; Lew didn't care. Her hair was black and thick, loosely plaited down her back. She was a little on the plump side, and although she hid it well under her clothes, Lew could see it in her face and in the way her suit jacket pinched her upper arms. She must've been close to thirty, a few years older than he was, and when she lifted the cigarette he saw a simple wedding band on her finger.

The woman inhaled deeply, then took off her short navy jacket before picking up the suitcase and heading north. To the Fourth Street bus, Lew figured. He grabbed a couple of ladies' watches out of his duffel bag, squeezed it back into the locker, put the locker key in his wallet and slipped the watches into an inside pocket of his jacket.

Then he stood, tall as he could, to follow her.

He'd grown up only a few miles away, across the river in Boyle Heights. His family had a house on a bluff over the First Street Bridge, and Lew could sit in the window of his parents' bedroom on the second floor and look over the Los Angeles River, past railroad yards and brick warehouses black with soot and into the city itself. It was a wonderful thing, he thought, to sit there and watch the city grow. His father called it progress and would sometimes sit with him in the window, his strong hand on the boy's shoulder, as the city took shape, big-boned and dark, before their eyes. And soon all the remaining squares of green were spread thick with concrete, and where grass once sprouted, now buildings emerged—sometimes, it seemed, overnight—to compete for space in the erratic skyline, as if the sun itself had drawn forth these tall, streamlined constructions of mortar and steel.

In those days, Boyle Heights had the feel of a small town, the perfect place for Isadore and Esther Beckman to settle and start a business of their own and raise their young son, Louis. For five terrible years they had lived in a Carroll Street tenement in Brooklyn, working long hours in the humid stink of lower Manhattan butcher shops—their weekly life defined by the pale, dreary hours between dawn and dusk, devoid of sunlight and leisure, their waking hours at home interrupted by the rude laughter of Negroes who played cards in open windows and on corner stoops and never seemed to sleep, and the harsh demands of Hassids from Polish farm country, former oxcart drivers and ragpickers who beat their wives and children with sticks in full view of the same cackling Negroes on Albany Avenue. The Beckman journey out west was not the whim of pure adventure that Louis liked to imagine, but an act of common sense and salvation. When they arrived in Los Angeles, Isadore opened Beckman's Kosher Meats on Soto Street, not far from Hollenbeck Park, and in the early days Esther worked with him in the shop, carrying Louis on her hip as she helped customers choose from the chickens that were displayed in the front window, swinging by their feet in the sunny sparkle of dust, plucked and forlorn, yellow as wax. The boy would sometimes sit under them in the window, listening to the familiar banter of Yiddish and German and English, his father making jokes and the men laughing, and his mother sometimes bringing him a glass of milk and a macaroon for an afternoon snack. And he would watch the people walking by on Soto Street, his face to the glass, underneath one of the gold-leaf Stars of David painted on the windows on either side of the front door, and feel contented enough to fall asleep, curled up like a cat in the rectangle of light, as ordinary life ticked by.

But as little Louis got older, things changed and didn't change. He didn't grow as fast as the other children, and when they teased him—*LittleLew*—he ran to his mother and she held him and told him that's what children do, they tease, and that he'd grow. When Louis turned twelve and stood four feet seven with his back held so straight it hurt, he knew he'd never catch up. But his mother told him that he, like his father, was special. Then when he was fourteen, someone threw a rock through the window of the market, shattering the glass and the gold-leaf Hebrew letters, and neighborhood children started calling him different names: *LittleLewLewtheJew-LittleLewLew*. And Louis got into fights with boys like Danny McHugh, who hated Jews because his father did, and eventually was suspended from school with blood on his shirt and knuckles. His father demanded that he not fight again, and Louis kept his promise to hold his temper—until one night after the market closed and he was delivering a package of meat and cheese to Mrs. Seidel on Inez Street near the park. It was just getting dark, the sky a gray flannel, and Louis pedaled his bike onto Breed Street, coasting down the cracked sidewalk on this rougher shortcut, anxious to get home. He was picking up speed when he heard Danny McHugh yell "Dirty kike!" from an alley near the corner. For once Danny was alone and Louis couldn't resist. He spun his wheels, skidded and rebalanced himself on scuffed shoes, and raced the bike furiously into the alley, straight at Danny. He caught only a glimpse of the stick that speared his front spokes, and as he flew over the handlebars he saw the tumble of arms and legs of the three boys who rushed him from the shadows. When he tried to break free they punched him in the face and his nose was broken for the first time. He kicked at them, but they pounded his legs and thighs until they were numb and heavy and dragged on the ground. Two boys twisted Louis's arms behind his back while Danny yanked off his pants and underwear, and when he looked up, his eyes full of rage and pain, he saw Jennie Carter and three other girls giggling in the spotty gray light at the end of the alley. Jennie was Danny McHugh's girlfriend, and he called them over. "Look at the Jewboy!" And Jennie sidled closer, her fourteen-year-old breasts barely visible under her sweater and her freckled legs lean under her woolen skirt, legs that Louis often thought about in school, and she kept one hand over her shy, laughing mouth, with her eyes wide open. "Look at the fucking Jewboy!" Danny shouted, and the girls looked. Louis glanced down at his circumcised penis, sleek as a porpoise, with Jennie kneeling not two feet in front of him, staring at it, and Danny, red-faced and laughing, urging her, "Go on, touch it! Go on, Jennie!" The other girls twittered stupidly behind her, brainless as hens, as she bit her lip and Louis tried not to think. He held his eyes shut but the tears still came, burning down his cheeks. When he opened them he saw Jennie's hand approaching him, and for a second their eyes met and like a separate entity his penis became erect, slowly rising to meet her shaking fingers. She screamed and skittered away, the other girls screeching with her in a broken chorus as they ran back up the alley and disappeared into Breed Street, their voices fading in the air. Danny kicked Louis in the testicles, and the boys holding him threw him to the ground while another urinated on the wad of his clothes. Danny grabbed the parcel meant for Mrs. Seidel and threw it high against the brick wall; butcher paper exploded in a splatter of beef liver, a string of sausage dangling from the fire escape. After heaving Louis's bicycle against the wall and slashing both tires with penknives, they all left. And Louis was alone, holding himself, unable to cry, as an old man in a third-story window lowered his shade against his shame. Louis never reported the boys to the police, no matter that his mother had cried and his father invoked biblical justice and screamed revenge for the first time in his life, demanding that the authorities exact an eye for an eye, a broken nose for a broken nose. But Louis shut his own swollen eyes and refused to listen, refused to give names. Danny thought he was too afraid to tell, and in his contempt for the little Jewboy, left him alone.

Five months later Louis, now seventeen, sat in the seventh row of the Golden Gate Theater on East Whittier and watched Charlie Chaplin in *The Kid*. Danny McHugh and Jennie Carter sat three rows in front of him, and when they laughed at the Little Tramp, he did, too. Most of the people Louis knew were in the theater that night, including his parents, and everyone laughed together. After the show he told his parents that it was a nice night and he wanted to take the trolley home with his friends. They knew he didn't have any friends, but allowed themselves to believe him anyway, always looking for the good, pretending there's no bad, especially in their own son. On the trolley, Louis sat in the first seat, drinking from the bottle of Coca-Cola he'd bought at the movie. Danny and Jennie walked past without noticing him and sat in the back. At Soto Street he was the first one off, and he walked ahead of the other kids as they split into groups, dissolving into the indistinguishable neighborhoods of Boyle Heights. Louis slowed only when he came to the high school, where he leaned against a streetlight like the Little Tramp himself and sipped his Coca-Cola and stared at the dark building that was witness to his many humiliations. When he heard footsteps behind him, he pushed off the post and ducked out of sight behind a maple tree. Danny McHugh had his noodly arm around Jennie's shoulder, walking her to her house on Eagle Street, when Louis slipped out in front of them. Danny looked down and smirked, "Ain't it kinda late for a little kike to be"—and Louis aimed at the smirk with the bottom of the Coca-Cola bottle, and three of Danny's teeth flew into the darkness, white as stars, before he collapsed at the base of the maple. Louis quickly stripped his clothes off and scattered them around the school yard, then kicked his arms and legs open and left him naked and gurgling under the tree. When he turned to Jennie Carter, he could hear her breathing through her mouth. He could smell the peppermint and fear that hung in the air between them. They stared at each other, and Louis never said a word. Jennie slowly took off her sweater, but that wasn't enough. She took off her blouse, but it still wasn't enough. She took off her bra, and Louis watched her nipples turn hard and white, almost shriveling away in the coldness, and yet this wasn't enough. The laughter of Jennie's friends and schoolmates seemed to echo over the neighboring streets. Danny McHugh moaned and tried to sit up. Louis kicked him hard in the temple and he collapsed again, his bloody mouth shiny in the moonlight, his breathing shallow and his penis tucked between his crossed legs. Louis faced Jennie and she undid her skirt and let it fall to the ground. When she started to turn around he shook his head and she stopped, holding the waistband of her white panties. Jennie waited but Louis waited longer and she let the panties slip past her knees to her ankles. Louis saw the goose bumps rise like a rash beneath the freckles on her skin, and the pale twisted hair and dark line of divided flesh between her legs, before she cupped her hands in front of her. And then he said, "The shoes." Jennie didn't understand until he spoke again. "Take off your shoes." Jennie kicked off her shoes and stepped out of her panties, shorter now; Louis could look her in the eyes. Kneeling in front of her, he gently forced her hands apart until her tight fists were locked against her thighs. He looked up and saw her trembling in the cold, and when the wind blew the hair from her face he imagined he saw her smile, so he smiled back. He didn't run away after he touched her, hoping that someday she would remember this kindness.

When the bus stopped at the corner of Alameda Street, Lew pushed ahead of the woman, almost knocking her over, then turned casually on the step and looked down at her, smiling. She looked back at him, knowing he was short no matter which step he stood on; but she could tell he was strong and fit in his suit, the pants riding high and the jacket pinched tight at the waist, and his pale blue shirt, its collar flat under the lapels, showed off his tan neck and throat. He was a little flashy, but so was she. It was something they had in common and sometimes that's enough. She liked his hair, thick and brown, and the broken, angular beauty of his nose. She smiled at him.

"You want help with that suitcase?"

He took her bag before she answered and carried it aboard. Two soldiers sat up front behind the driver, fanning themselves with rolled-up newspapers. Lew walked to the back, where it would be quiet and he could catch the breeze through the open windows, and the woman followed him. When Lew heaved her suitcase onto the rack above their seats, the bus pulled away from the curb and the woman fell against him. He caught her easily and felt the dampness against his hand as he held the roll of soft fat above her tight waistband.

"Where you headed?"

"Los Feliz."

"Me, too." Lew stepped to the side and offered her the window seat. "What's your name?"

"Mary."

Marie. Maria. Lew knew she was probably lying. He sat down next to her and offered his hand.

"Lew Beck."

He had spent the last ten years drifting, getting work when short of money and living light between jobs. He'd set bee boxes in the flower fields outside Lompoc, picked grapes for the Swiss Colony Winery in Asti and packed raisins for Sun-Maid in Fresno. And he'd fought. His nose was broken twice more before he learned how to keep his eyes open and dodge a punch instead of rushing into it; he'd learned not to throw his whole weight behind a punch, to check his balance and shield his ribs with his elbows. He also started to use his size. While other men went for the face, throwing hard, looking for the easy damage and quick end, Lew jabbed at kidneys, sharp blows to both sides, until his opponent was on his knees, coughing up dry air and forcing spit, and that's when he went for the face, the easy damage, the quick end.

LittleLew LewtheRunt LittleMonkey Tough Monkey.

He was still a teenager when he left California and took a job on the Luhrs building in Phoenix, Arizona. The ten-story steel frame

was already under construction, three stories above the once prominent Heard building. At the time, Phoenix was intent on inventing
itself as the city "where winter never comes," a playground of fine
hotels and guest ranches for prosperous men in white suits and their
lovely wives, women pale as linen, their faces hidden under the hats
they wore to protect themselves from the sun they'd come to wor-
ship.

The Luhrs building was Lew's first construction job and he
worked with the bolters' crew high above the site. Once the raising
gang had finished placing the beams—black lines of steel penciled
into the sky—it was up to Lew and the two other bolters to climb
the uppermost reaches, spud wrenches dangling from thick leather
belts, and tighten the single, bracketed bolts to secure the frame.

Lew was small and strong and liked working on this soaring web
of steel. He discovered the exhilaration of height, the bursting awe
that clenched his lungs and numbed his skull every time he stepped
onto the highest girder and walked that straight line into the crys-
talline sky. Buoyed by youth and the thrill of misadventure, he
amazed himself with his total lack of fear.

The first moments were the best, as he overcame the feeling of
utter weightlessness with perfect balance. Lew would take a deep
breath and suddenly all his senses became keener. He would collect
himself on a beam and slowly straighten up, light but grounded, and
then pause, believing he could hear men on the ground, seven stories below, whispering in homage to the prowess of Lew Beck, the
young prince of steel. With his head full of wonderment, he would
look out at the desert horizon, edged in a sharpness of red stone
against blue sky.

He woke every morning in a glaze of perspiration, ready for
work. He threw off his sheets, gritty with salt and dirt, and catapulted out of bed, wide awake and whistling as he put on water for
coffee. Speed Owens and Henry Faulk, the boys he shared a room
with in a motor camp on Van Buren, would buckle their pillows over
their heads and moan when Lew reached over their cots to open the
window onto a violet dawn.

Lew bathed at the sink, too young to shave, and put on the damp
underwear he'd scrubbed the night before, still itchy with the powdered soap he could never fully rinse out. And while Speed and

Henry cursed him for his good humor and energy, Lew was already out the door and walking to the job site downtown.

Always one of the first to arrive, he stood each morning and marveled at the tall black skeleton of the building, stepping around the idle bulldozers and earthmovers to get a better view. Then he squatted in front of the tin work shed and drank a cup of murky coffee with the foreman's assistant, a pimply-faced boy who ran errands all day without saying a word. Lew would rock on his heels and watch the other men arrive, Speed and Henry among them, shifting side by side like penguins as they shuffled past.

"Morning, Beck."

"What do you say, Lew?"

He liked it that other men noticed him in the morning and later stepped aside when they heard the jangle of nuts and washers in his deep pockets, as fine a sound as change to a gambler. He liked the way their looks gave him a boost as he pulled himself onto the highest beam and went to work, straddling a narrow flange in the windless air over Phoenix.

For two weeks, this was Lew's favorite place on earth—the West of his imagination, full of rangy cowboys in Stetsons and dungarees bleached by sweat and sun. They'd come to town from the northern ranchlands in pickup trucks hauling stock trailers full of skinny cows whose muzzles were a blur of flies feasting on the crusty tears that caked their eyes and nostrils. Lew saw them on his way to work, usually the same men every day, as they gathered in a vacant lot at the edge of downtown, their back pockets imprinted with the bulge of a dented flask, ignoring the moans of their starved cows, drinking instead and complaining about wives and banks and the hand life had dealt them. They were not the Hopalongs and Hoots from the serials Lew saw in the cinema palaces of Los Angeles; they weren't even the sun-damaged ramrods who sat in the background on horseback or rail fences. The faces of these Arizona cowboys were burned red from homemade whiskey, and the lines that creased their faces and necks were the ugly scars of lifelong embitterment. They were old men out of place in the growing cosmopolitan sprawl of the Southwest, blaming their woes on Jews from Chicago and New York queers who threw their money around and watered the desert ground with the green ink of their paper currency, turning it into lush golf courses they could view from their hotel windows while fleshy mistresses and young cabana boys knelt between their fat legs and paid them honor. The cowboys felt crowded out and foreign, and they hated it.

After a week on the job, Lew bought his first pair of cowboy boots from a pawnshop near the Capitol on Van Buren. They were cowhide, dyed a dark brown and buffed to the gleam of dried blood, with white stitching up the front that flamed out like eagle wings along the sides. He loved these boots, the tannic smell of leather and the pointed toes that didn't hurt his feet, and kept them in the original box under his bed. Every night he polished them with a chamois he'd bought from a shoeshine boy outside the Woolworth store, and then slipped them on for a moment, alone in his room, twisting his feet in front of the mirror to get a reflected view before putting them away.

On weekends, Lew went with Speed and Henry to the speakeasies and whorehouses in south Phoenix. He'd wear his new cowboy boots and strut along the midnight streets, the inch and a half the boots added to his five-foot frame giving him a confident swagger. Lew and his friends entered Moe's Place through the side door of Wong's Laundry and moved past tables full of men and women laughing and drinking and playing cards while a fat Negro sat at the piano under the stairs, facing the wall as his pudgy fingers rolled over the keys, plinking out a repetitive rag. The young men went right to the bar and drank enough warm beer to settle their stomachs before entering the next room, wavy with smoke and dark as a funhouse, to pick out a girl from the group leaning against the side walls, pinned there like wilted specimens in the hard, chromium light. Speed and Henry ignored the older women—old enough to be aunts and mothers, foulmouthed ladies with down-turned mouths and brittle, peroxided hair—and went straight for the younger girls, fourteen or fifteen years old, Negro or Chinese, they didn't care. Lew always went for the Navajo girls on the other side of the room, moonfaced and mute as stone. While Speed and Henry pinched and flirted, Lew immediately pointed to the girl he wanted, usually the shortest one who refused to look at him. He stood there with his finger in her face until she pushed off the wall and led him up a short flight of stairs to one of the small rooms overlooking the alley. Watching her wide hips sway under the long skirt, Lew had an erection even before they reached the landing. The girl quickly shut the door behind them, turned off the light and reached for his belt buckle. But Lew stopped her and turned the light back on, then eased her backward onto the thin mattress and raised her skirt and spread her legs with his hands and buried his head between her thighs and breathed in the dust and sweet chocolate of her skin. When the girl moved again to turn off the light, he stopped her once more, taking the shade off the lamp and undressing her in the unforgiving brightness of the bare bulb. He told her to tie up her thick black hair and gnawed her small breasts while her hands were busy. Only when she was naked and sprawled across the bed did he remove his own clothes, lifting her chin to make her wide black eyes meet his every time she tried to turn away. She was ashamed of their nakedness, and her eyes were scared but she didn't speak, and Lew appreciated that as much as he did her dark body, doughy with fat, her thighs and upper arms decorated with bruises from the hands of other men. He turned the girl over onto her hands and knees, and climbed on the bed behind her, probing her body with his fingers and tongue, keeping her close to the harsh light, and then he climbed beneath her and made her do the same things to him, guiding her hands over his short torso and around his erection, varying positions until he could taste both of them in the stifled air of the room. He wiped the sweat from his eyes and saw their reflection in the windowpane, his face over her bent back, and then he entered her, locking her legs with his, pressing her into the rough mattress as he came, stuttering, and the room went quiet enough for both of them to hear the single fly that buzzed and pinged around the glowing lightbulb. Lew wrapped himself in the single sheet and stood up to dry himself. As he dressed, he watched the Indian girl on the striped mattress, staring up at the gray ceiling, her breasts flat on her chest, the dark nipples lacquered with sweat, her pubic hair mossy and black. She lifted one leg to relieve a cramp, and Lew saw his milky dampness clinging like syrup to the inside of her thigh. He put on his boots and took out his wallet, leaving five dollars on the table. Then he unfurled the sheet, so thin he could see the girl's fetal outline in the opaque blur of cotton as it wafted down over her. He turned off the lamp and left.

. . . .

Lew ordered another beer at the bar, waiting for Speed and Henry. Tipping his head back, he drank deeply. He could smell the Navajo girl on the hand that held the brown bottle, and when he shifted his weight, he could feel his penis sticky and cool against his leg. The beer coursed through his body, rising lightly through his own fluids, back to his head. It was Friday night and he found himself thinking about work on Monday, anxious for it, and he smiled.

The arm hit Lew in the back of the head while he was taking another gulp, and the upturned rim of the bottle smashed against his lower lip. He turned around, his mouth filling with blood and spit.

"Sorry, kid. Didn't see you."

A tall man grinned down at him, his face a starburst of broken capillaries above the yolky yellow of his rayon shirt, his wide arms pink and dimpled below rolled-up sleeves. His whole body seemed swollen with muscles that ballooned like tumors.

The bartender silently put eight beer bottles down in front of the tall man and clawed the two crumpled dollar bills he'd tossed on the wet plank. Effortlessly, the tall man picked up four bottles in each hand, clanking them between stubby fingers, and winked at Lew.

"Lip's bleeding, Shortstuff."

Lew watched him walk back to a table next to the piano player where two women and a man were sitting. The tall man pried off the caps with a church key and said something, his voice muffled in the crowded room. His friends laughed loudly, off-key with the insistent swing of the piano, as he passed the bottles around.

Lew turned back to the bar and wiped the blood off his lip, digging his tooth into the shallow cut, letting the pain offset the anger. He felt an ache in his feet and realized he was ramming his toes into the points of his boots. He swilled the few remaining drops of beer, letting them sting his split lip, and then sucked the air out of the bottle until he couldn't breathe, his heart pounding with the hate that ran like quicksilver in his shrunken veins.

"Drunk." The bartender wiped down the surface in front of him, his pockmarked face and neck as gray as the moon. Lew felt like jabbing his fingers into the pitted skin until he realized he'd meant the big man. The bartender eased the empty bottle out of Lew's hand and pulled a fresh one out of the galvanized tub behind him, and when Lew reached into his pocket for change, he waved him off.

"Forget it." He popped off the cap with the metal opener around his neck and moved down the bar.

The room smelled of cigarette smoke and bleach. The piano player picked out a dreamy blues number, repeating the phrase, letting it hang in the air before being swallowed up by the next roll. Holding the wet bottle in his hand, Lew looked toward the back stairs for Henry and Speed. He was ready to leave.

He tilted the bottle for a swallow and felt a sudden tightness encircling his chest. For a moment he was weightless, spinning in the air. It wasn't an entirely unpleasant experience until he looked down and saw the shoes of the tall man moving in and out of view on the floor. He struggled, and the arm that gripped him squeezed harder. The blood rushed to Lew's head and filled his ears, turning everything blue. Arms and legs dangling, he watched the floor sway beneath him, a greasy mosaic of cigarette butts and broken glass ground into the linoleum, then felt himself being lifted higher and revolved through the air like a wooden puppet, involuntarily jerked and joggled until his feet thumped down in the middle of the crowded table by the piano player. He looked into the holes of their laughing faces, blinking like a newborn on wobbly legs. "Look at him! Like a little doll!" The tall man steadied Lew as he would a priceless vase and stepped back. Lew stared at the woman across from him, rocking back in her chair, her face the color of a watermelon rind. She was laughing at him, hiding her overbite behind her hand. They were all laughing. The room resounded with it.

Lew straightened up and turned to the tall man, who was entertaining the room, pointing at Lew over his shoulder, his boozy laugh drawing more attention. Lew saw Henry and Speed standing at the bar, the only ones in the place who weren't laughing, and that made Lew feel like laughing. When the tall man finished his rotation he flashed Lew a low-wattage smile, as if they were a team, like Laurel and Hardy or Gosden and Correll. And Lew smiled back, warmly, a man who could take a joke, a forgiving man, a man like the rest of them, before he grabbed the tall man's head and pulled it down against his raised kneecap, and that veiny nose as overripe as a summer berry exploded on impact, the soft tissue and cartilage reduced to a honeycomb of mucus. When he yanked the man's head back, a parabola of blood arced through the air, as if Lew were a magician who'd just pulled a bright red scarf out of his assistant's mouth, but the drops splattered the faces of the screaming women at the table and dissolved in their glasses of beer. Lew held the man's head with both hands and slammed it down between his legs in the center of the felt-covered table, and the two of them collapsed on the floor in a shatter of splintered wood and broken glass. Feet and hands searched for Lew, who was able to punch a man he'd never seen before in the eye and kick the horse-faced woman in the shin before he saw Speed and Henry throwing punches as they were pushed out the front door. Three men subdued him and beat him senseless in the alley before the police hauled him to the Maricopa County Jail and threw him in a filthy lockup where the smell alone was enough to make him vomit. Before morning he got into two more fistfights, and the cops decided to hold him over the weekend. And when the new drunks arrived after their Saturday-night binge, mean and broke, two men held him down while a third tried to steal his boots, and Lew beat him until he wept and stopped weeping, and his own hands came away sticky and numb when the cops finally pried him off and decided to hold him a little longer. When he reported for work at the Luhrs building on Wednesday, he was out of a job. The foreman gave him the money he was owed and an extra ten dollars.

"You're a good worker, Lew," he said, "but you're nasty. Plain nasty."

Lew nodded. His knuckles were still swollen and he was sore all over. He looked up at the unfinished building, the top floor of the frame poking into the sky. He liked it up there and knew he'd miss it, but he shook the foreman's hand, stuffed the money into his pocket and stepped onto Van Buren Street with his thumb out, walking backward, heading west to California.

*B*y Bayard, Iowa, he'd been traveling for hours on back roads that cut through the level prairie dissected by the three Raccoon rivers. Here the earth possessed a chronic flatness as it stretched through Guthrie, Audubon and Shelby Counties, straight through to the Nebraska border and beyond. The road outside Kirkman was bordered by dry clumps of wild roses and greasewood, and Filius saw a long-eared owl, massive in its own shadow, swoop low for skunks and marmots, feeding on the pulpy flesh of carrion flung to the roadside by spinning tires.

In the long hours of the night, mile after mile of sameness and solitude, the radio picking up only static between snippets of market reports in Omaha and the warbling euphony of the Happiness Boys, he was able to lift his eyes from the empty road and track the constellations in the northern sky. Triangulated between the three brightest stars above the straight-edged horizon, he saw Arcturus, Vega and Capella. He remembered the cool nights in May when he was eight or nine and his mother had taught him how to read the sky. They lay on their backs side by side on the sloping lawn behind the house in Wisconsin, Filius's head leaning against his mother's warm shoulder as she held his hand directly overhead and pointed at the stars. Together they traced the geometric patterns that formed celestial pictures, and Alice told him stories that brought the pictures to life. Their fingers moved over the humpbacked cluster of Cassiopeia, the beautiful "Lady of the Chair," banished to the night sky by sea nymphs to learn humility.

"She was a brazen thing."

"And that's bad?"

"In a queen it is."

His mother shifted fingers to the right and outlined the stick figures of Gemini, anchored by the bright Orion in the galactic swarm of the Milky Way. "See the Twins?"

Filius squinted hard and saw arms and legs take shape between the stars. "Yes."

"They're holding hands. First is Castor. And then Pollux."

"Pollux is bigger."

"That's because he's immortal."

Their hands moved crablike to the familiar constellation of the Big Dipper, forever hanging in the center of the sky.

"The handle makes the tail, and if you follow the stars you can see the snout and legs of—"

"The Big Bear!"

Alice pointed to Arcturus at the apex of the stellar dome overhead and traced the pattern that extended below the icy star.

"And who's that?"

"Boötes. The Bear Driver."

Filius knew what was coming next, and moved their fingers to the two dim stars that hovered near the great bear's tail. "The Hunting Dogs!"

The dogs were his favorite, and he stared until the stars blurred and he saw Boötes set his bony hounds, howling and slobbering, after the bear, nipping at his tail as he loped unafraid through the heavens.

"Canes Venatici," his mother said.

"Canes Venatici," he repeated.

On clear nights they stayed out past midnight into July and August, young mother and boy, watching the stars' rotation above them. Sometimes she fell asleep beside him, and Filius watched her and listened to the night sounds by himself: the hiss of wind through dry leaves, the echoes of a dogfight below Dayton Street, the wet sweep of ducks landing on Lake Mendota. When she woke, her eyes quick and alert, it was time to go in. They lifted themselves off the soft, dewy lawn, the blades crinkled where they had lain, and while his mother took his hand, Filius looked over his shoulder to the bodyprints they had left behind.

. . .

He glanced down from Regulus, at the foot of Leo, and spotted a big porcupine ahead in the middle of the road. He had enough time to swerve, but in a panic the animal turned its rear to the bright lights of the car, its spines erect, and backed directly into his path. Filius felt the front wheel thump beneath him, then stopped and turned the car around, his tires chipping at the rim of cracked asphalt. He got out where he thought he'd hit the animal and scanned the brush around him, breathing in the hot turpentine stink of broken sage, but there was no sign of it. The radio was still playing, and through the open window Rudy Vallee sang "I'm Just a Vagabond Lover," his voice clear as the breezeless air that settled over the black-and-gray plain.

He squatted down by the front tire on the passenger's side and pulled four porcupine quills out of the treads. Held up in the headlights, they were long and thin, translucent as fingernails.

The house Filius had grown up in was built the year he was born, a large, angular house of brick and wood, prairie style, at the end of Livingston Street, where the lake lapped up against the grassy shore. It was a serious house, heavy and permanent, with roofs and eaves that loomed over wide porches front and back. The walls were fitted with tall, narrow windows decorated with lead stencils of sugar maples in leaf, the green-and-orange glass allowing sepia-toned views of the water from almost any position inside, part of what the architect called the "simple rhythm of a landscape unobscured." The house was designed around five great fireplaces, deep and shadowy, and in the coldest months each room was flavored with wood smoke from enormous oak logs. Claude Poe would not cut down a tree for wood, and used only deadfall from the forests around Shawano, casualties of windstorms and lightning strikes.

Filius's bedroom was on the third floor. Overlooking the lake, it was a boy-sized room, defined and shrunken by the severe angles of the roof. He spent the winter months in this architectural nook, his bed toasted by his father's aging English pointer, Amos. Wrapped in striped woolen blankets worn thin around the bottoms from his habit of walking on the edges to keep his feet warm, Filius'd curl up for hours in the deep window seat, concentrating on the pellucid sheen of the lake, waiting for it to freeze. As the temperatures dropped through November it began to breathe with steam, low whiffles that would swoon and evanesce as the morning sun rose through the cold blue air, and the liquid surface soon became skinned with ice. Through this opaque cap, thick as the bottom of a milk bottle, Filius could see the green aquatic grasses, pondweed and stonewort, bent and scrolled under the surface like lines drawn in the Celtic hand.

His parents insisted that he stay off the ice until it was at least three inches thick. Every afternoon, after he'd walked home from the university, Claude Poe would take his son out to the small pier at the end of their property, each walking stiffly in jackets of fleece and wool, and drill into the ice with a small handheld auger, letting Filius take the measurements. At night Filius dreamed of the water under the ice, the current warped in slow motion, the green water turning white, frigid, trapped by the tremendous weight above it.

After Thanksgiving, in the cove off Henry Street, men used mules and horses to drag their ice-fishing shacks across the crusty snow on wide wooden skis. They gathered every morning, doctors and farmers, lawyers and layabouts, all passing around a flask and blowing over their mittened hands with whiskey breath, impatient as Filius for the lake to harden.

At the end of the first week of December, Claude stood on the pier with his small auger, brushed the snow from his knees of his pants and nodded his head. Filius immediately laced on the skates he'd slung over his shoulder and raced across the sterling ice, gliding over bumps and windblown grooves, tucked low, riding on blades he'd been sharpening for a month, his face raw from the wind and the cold, the pointer Amos running at his side.

Sometimes his mother skated with him, navigating the shoreline in long, expert strides, more concerned with form than speed. Filius thought she looked beautiful on the ice in her long black coat and sealskin hat shaped like a cupcake—especially from a distance, where her every movement appeared balletic and natural, radiated by a winter sun that turned the ice she kicked up into blue sparks.

On weekend mornings, Filius rose early. He wiped the snowfrost from the windows and peered out at the arctic dawn, an overwhelming whiteness marred only by the black scratches of Norwegian maples and the vague recollection of a horizon somewhere in the distance. After a moment, he saw the thin spires of dark smoke etching through the fog and he knew that the fishermen were already on the ice. He tumbled into his clothes, pulling his sweater over his head in the blind dash downstairs, where he hauled his skates out of the wooden box under the coatrack and banged out the back door with Amos, both of them running toward the dock, leaving repetitive impressions, in twos and fours, in the fresh, nightfallen snow. He would sit on the end of the dock with his mittens in his mouth, tying on his skates, the tip of his nose already red and runny, while Amos lifted his leg against the old hackberry tree on the side of the house, pumping out yellow squirts that seeped into the glaze of snow. Then he'd whistle for the dog and take off across the lake, toward the smoke trails, the fog wrapping around and dematerializing him.

The shacks, clustered in a pattern handed down for generations, arose out of the morning mist like a primitive village, rickety constructions of leftover wood and tar paper, designed for two to four men, fitted with cast-iron stoves, shelves for canned goods and brown liquor bottles, plank pallets covered with sleeping bags and blankets. Long, stiff saws with ragged teeth dangled from hooks by the door. Men would take turns cutting through the ice, removing a circular, manhole-sized plug six inches thick and rolling it like a wagon wheel into the corner. Pulling up chairs around the hole, they dropped weighted lines into the water, the large treble hooks baited with raw meat and Wisconsin cheese, and threw chunks of oak and pine into the woodstove and leaned back in this neutral warmth, listening to the wind whimper through the chinks and waiting for the lunkers to strike.

Filius loved the extra life these men created in winter's shortened days. He loved to hear them talk about neighbors and wild turkeys so stupid they'd run into trees. He loved the sweet brandy fumes in the air, the pipe tobacco mingling with the smoke and splatter from the blood sausages sizzling in the buttered skillet on the stove top, heavy with crushed red pepper and fat as puppies. Most of all he loved the fish they pulled out of the jagged holes: brassy walleyes and muskies up to three feet long, splashing and twisting their lean, zebra-striped bodies, gills working like bellows, angry eyes huge and unlidded, lips parted as if to scream. The men would gaff the fifteen- to twenty-pounders and drag them onto the ice, yanking out their hooks with the bait still attached. Careful to stand clear of the slapping tails and pointy snouts full of teeth, they dropped their hooks back into the lake, feeding out line from the big reels, while the huge muskellunges thrashed and died in the corner, spraying droplets of water pinkened with blood.

Filius sat with the fishermen for hours, laughing with them and eating their eggs and meat, running a crust of bread or a finger through the salty grease left on the plate, watching the fish pile up like timber, the sun burning away the morning fog as it rose above the Capitol dome, and he stayed on the ice until Freddie Clarke—a failed lawyer and hunting companion of his father's—wrapped up a four-pound center cut of pike for Alice to roast for supper that night, and sent him home.

With the arrival of spring, once Filius was old enough, Claude would take him and Amos to his hunting cabin near Mount Horeb on the north side of the old Military Ridge. They'd spend a week together exploring the rocky summits and fishing for brook trout in the high-rising streams and creeks, silver with snowmelt, flowing down from the scraggly line of hills to the Wisconsin River.

On one of these trips, they stopped at the Sammett place outside of Blue Mounds, just as puckered clouds appeared and the sky took on a greenish tint. A dog breeder, Jack Sammett had sold Claude's father a champion pointer, and then, ten years ago, that pointer had sired Claude his own dog, Amos. Filius helped Jack's wife, Peg, put up the horses, tossing them loose oat hay from the crib in the barn, and watched Amos play with a litter of pointer pups in the side yard. When the rain started to fall, Peg called him inside for supper. The dogs whimpered and yowled and scratched at the door until Jack turned and whistled sharply through his teeth. The puppies immediately stopped their whining and scampered off to the wooden shelter under the hickory trees, Amos with them.

That night they ate roasted venison from a buck Jack had shot out of season because its hind leg had been caught and broken in a sandstone wedge on a birch-covered slope east of the gap. Over a dessert of dried apple cake and, for the men, Claude's brandy, Jack told them about the prize dog he was working who'd held point for three hours in the field, through thunder and hail, until he released it with a click of his tongue. Claude and Filius slept on their blankets in front of the fire while the rain fell steadily all night, and when the boy woke up in the pitch-darkness, he could hear big droplets of water fall down the chimney and sizzle on the pine logs still glowing in the hearth.

The morning was clear and Filius was out of bed before dawn. He set out the leftover deer meat and bones Peg had put aside for the dogs, and filled their low trough from an oak bucket heavy with rainwater. He helped his father tack up the horses and tie down their gear on the back of their saddles, and after a breakfast of eggs and potatoes under a corn-bread crust, they set off.

Amos dug his nose into every culvert, snorting out squirrels and chipmunks, while the Poes rode their horses along the dirt road, Claude on Jimmy, his tall, prancy gelding, always keeping a tight rein and hard leg on his flank, and Filius on Potato, a short, stocky, twenty-year-old chestnut mare with a back broad enough to sleep on.

A tubular band of fog hung thick as cream in the valley, and they had to dip into it before hitting the high road to their cabin on the ridge. Filius rode close behind, keeping an eye on Jimmy's swaying rump because his father's back was soon lost in the misty wetness that obscured the valley. Climbing up the slope, through the scrimming haze, Filius could make out the trunks of evergreens that became a picket, then a forest, and finally they were above the fog, drenched but warm in the morning sun that blazed in the cloudless sky.

They arrived before noon at a square, one-room building constructed of logs hewn from the white oaks growing on the slope behind it. Claude opened the cabin door and stomped his feet to run off the mice, and they unloaded their provisions and put away their saddles before Filius let the horses loose in the fenced pasture. He stood on the bottom rail and watched them walk with lowered muzzles through the prairie grass and drink from the creek that wiggled through the meadow, then ran back to the cabin.

As Claude dumped firewood in the box, he told Filius to see if the Martins were in their cabin. "If you can't see their horses, look for smoke in the chimney. If they're there, we'll walk over tomorrow and fish below the falls."

"Can we swim?"

"It'll be too cold."

"If it's not?"

Claude smiled as he brushed leaves and wood dust from his sleeve. "If it's not."

Filius bolted out the door, with Amos at his heels, and ran up the deer path that cut almost a straight line to the top of the ridge. He jumped over clumps of blue lupine that grew near the track and Amos hopped over mounds of puccoon, all four legs collected under his deep chest as he sprang up and down, trying to ferret out rabbits, real and imagined, that hid in the brush. They climbed higher, passing a grove of basswood trees just starting to flower, which Filius knew would be swarming with bees later in the summer. He reached the sandstone shelf he remembered from his last trip and stopped to rest. Taking off his sweater, he looked down at the cabin, where his father was splitting oak chunks with a red-handled axe. Amos darted out of the brush, a black-and-white blur, then cut into the thicket on the far side of the deer path, gone again.

Filius pushed himself off the ledge and up to the summit. He put his hands on his knees and caught his breath, looking over the plains that stretched below him, and thought he could see the Wisconsin River, miles away, a green pulse on the horizon. Turning to the western meadow, through the sparse tips of the cedar tree, he saw the Martin horses below him, rollicking around the small corral, and smoke wafting out of the stone chimney.

Filius breathed in the scent of pine needles and spring grass, closing his eyes and thinking of this wide valley being underwater, as his father told him it was millions of years ago. He imagined the Blue Mounds poking out of the water like two turtle backs, and ichthyosaurs with long tail fins and webbed feet and razor teeth, swimming in the muddy depths with shovel-headed fish-lizards, crocodile kin, that coasted just below the surface and waited to slurp down long-ago birds that paddled within the bull's-eye of their clouded vision. The diorama of ancient Wisconsin scrolled against the black screen of his closed eyes. He saw the mastodons and saber-tooth tigers of his schoolbooks roaming the top of the ridge. He could hear the primordial lapping of the great lake at his feet, and the beating of pterodactyl wings as they wheeled overhead through a bloodshot sky.

The sound grew louder, a dog barked and Filius opened his eyes.

Straight down the deer path there was a rustling in the brush, and a big doe, her tawny coat the color of the hills, burst out of the lupine with Amos right behind her. The doe charged forward, weaving around rocks and bushes, staying close to the hardcut trail. She twisted her body, anticipated her footing, suspended in the air as if forever, as the dog crashed and flew behind her, ten feet back now, big paws snapping the tops of wild indigo, eyes riveted on the white bristles of her flag.

Filius stood at the top of the path and the deer came right at him. She was huge and frightened, and in her terror, he was invisible. When the boy moved, the doe moved with him; they dodged together, locked in each other's way, and even as the moment stripped him of his breath, Filius knew he was choreographing something magnificent. He could hear the doe's short, panicked gasps and the click of her hooves on stones as she ramrodded up the steep path, and he wondered if she could hear the tom-tom of his heart. His body trembled and his eyes wouldn't close and suddenly the deer was upon him. All he saw was her massive chest, bramble-knicked and tufted, and the bony knobs of her knees as her legs gathered below her and again she was airborne. Filius looked up as her body rose, gazing at the blackness of her nose and the brown clarity of her eyes, smelling the damp musk on the updraft she created, feeling her feral breath in the narrow space between her belly and the top of his head. He didn't turn around as she soared over the ridge, didn't try to stop Amos as he ran after her. He blinked his eyes and heard his father call his name, which echoed through the valley, then blinked again, harder and faster, trying to remember and hear and smell every fractured second of the wonderful moment he'd just lived.

. . .

In the summer of 1921, Filius and Addie took the night train from Chicago to New York and sailed to France for their honeymoon. They traveled first class on the great Cunard liner *Minnewaska*, the tickets a gift from her parents, and rented a Ford runabout for three weeks of touring the French countryside, a gift from his.

They spent five nights in Paris at the modest Mont-Thabor Hotel so they could splurge like young Americans and drink champagne at lunch and again at night to accompany the plate of pig tails and snouts they shared at Chez Paul. They sipped aperitifs at the Deux Magots, surrounded by workers who smelled of damp coal and sour wine, and who admired Addie when she laughed at their crude jokes and grinned when she translated them for Filius. In the evenings they dressed in their pressed linens to eat lobster at Restaurant Michaud two nights in a row, and during the day they dutifully toured the ancient churches, strolled the Boulevard Saint-Michel, visited the Musée du Luxembourg to view the Cézannes and Manets displayed in natural light in those drafty halls, walked along the Seine and bought used books in English in the stalls of the Latin Quarter. At night Addie made him dance with her at the Bal Musette or listen to slick jazz in the crowded bars along the Rue Bonaparte. In the still dark mornings they would return to their room exhausted, and sit up young and naked and unashamed, drinking Pernod and water and talking and making love as the sun rose and light shimmered down the narrow street like something presented to them on the blade of a knife, and finally they would sleep. Holding Addie, stretched on top of and then inside her, never felt awkward to Filius. There was a first time, of course, but even then it hadn't felt like one. Lying together on that bed in Paris, Addie warm and close, all honey skin and honey hair, aroused him quickly.

Addie saw this and smiled. "You're happy, aren't you?"

Filius didn't answer, as she knew he wouldn't, but she stroked him and moved her legs to make room for him. When they were finished and lay together almost asleep, he turned and whispered, "Yes."

On a warm, rainy afternoon they picked up their Ford, a two-seater with a crimped right fender, and drove to the forests of Saint-

Germain, where the wildflowers were just coming into bloom. From there they made short day trips, stopping whenever they felt like it, skipping the cathedral at Rheims and heading for the Swiss border, where they stayed at a small hotel under the great mantle of mountains and borrowed fishing rods from the innkeeper's son to fish the small cold streams near Chamonix. They drove south and spent three days in Nice and three more driving along the Mediterranean coast, stopping in sun-bronzed towns and eating fresh sardines and pan-sized loups, gutted and grilled over charcoal braziers by vendors along the beaches of Saint-Tropez, spending the late afternoons swimming in the azure waters and reading English newspapers until the sun went down. A week before their boat was to depart Le Havre, they headed north again, along the Rhône, to see the great Furens Dam.

They stopped first in Saint-Étienne to explore the small villages nearby, and at sunset drove up the Guizay hill and gazed over the lush moors and meadows in the valley below. Returning to their small hotel on the Grand'Rue, they found it crowded with Englishwomen, twenty of them on their way to Avignon to visit the graves of their sons. They shared their after-dinner sherry with Addie and Filius, telling them stories of their families before the war, laughing over their boys' pranks and accomplishments, an ode to dead sons practiced and repeated as the women picked up drifting thoughts and filled in for one another, never allowing a lapse to call forth the empty parts, the holes deep and permanent. They poured sherry until after midnight, making sure to keep Filius's glass topped off, mothering still, and when the concierge switched off the lights in the dining room, they burned candles from the fireplace mantel and talked until two. In the morning Addie went down early to take tea with them, but they'd already pressed on.

At nine o'clock, Filius and Addie left for the Furens Dam, driving south through the foothills of the Pilat, the air already hot and sweet with the scent of rotten lemons that had fallen from trees on the craggy slopes above the road. Outside the town of Rochetaillée, they picked up the Furens River, and followed it higher into the hills, where herds of Charolais cattle grazed in the deep highland grass and the mountains grew more stark and forlorn, ravaged along this cut by iron-pyrite mines.

The road looped along the lazy river, and when they turned that final bend and Filius saw the dam for the first time, he eased to a stop and fixed his eyes on the sheer face of stone that curved gracefully away from the mica walls on either side of the narrow gorge. He'd studied the dam in Wisconsin, memorizing the statistical facts and structural dimensions of its construction almost seventy years ago, but still wasn't prepared for its simple beauty and unaffected elegance. It was an engineering feat and it was architecture, from its slim profile to the long row of corbels and the twin parapets that suggested the severity of a medieval fortress.

Filius stood by the roadside and took Addie's hand. More than just seeing the dam for the first time, what excited him was the knowledge of the thing itself, of how it worked and how it was built, from its circular crest to its foundation trench embedded twenty feet below the river. And because he understood its very core, it was something he knew he could do, and he rejoiced.

Following a stone footpath to the top, they stepped onto the narrow roadway of the dam itself as an old man emerged from a concrete hut built into the rocks above the huge reservoir behind the dam. He wore a raggedy sweater despite the heat, and the cuffs of his khakis trailed in the dirt. Spitting French, he looked up only when he was a few feet away, stopped and peered at Filius over a nose every bit as proud as the one across from him. The men faced each other on the dam like centurions honored on a pair of Roman coins, and the old man unclenched his fists and smiled.

His name, he said, was Jean-Yves Ferrand. They sat at his table in the concrete hut and brushed away flies as they drank the local Carignane, sweet and strong, and when that was finished he took them onto the dam. They walked its bowed length, the two men leaning over the short guard wall to observe the projecting stones on the steep vertical face. Addie interpreted as Filius asked questions about the durability of the Vasay cement used to coat the stone where it met the rock cliff, and the adequacy of the two lateral tunnels that supplied water to Saint-Étienne and eased pressure on the dam. Jean-Yves had worked here for forty years, a job he'd inherited from his father, and he insisted the structure was as watertight as the day it was completed. Even in times of heavy rain, the reservoir never overflowed—unlike the days of horror in 1849, when the Furens

River, unimpeded, tore angrily down the valley. The afternoon sun was fierce, so Addie decided to return to the stone hut and her journal while Jean-Yves opened the heavy iron gates leading to a diversion tunnel that channeled the river so the dam could be built. Stooping in the gripping dark, Filius walked the length of the cool, smothering corridor alone, aware of the enormous weight of the earth above him. Blacker than inside the tunnels below the Capitol in Madison, blacker even than a starless midnight, it forced him to stop near the center, at once excited and overcome by a humbling dizziness, and he sat down hard, his back against the cut stone walls. He let the dampness saturate his clothes, seep into his skin, and he inhaled the taste of stone until he felt calm again, restored. For a long time he lingered in the deep void, bone cold and shivering, his ears slowly picking up a vibration from deep within the thermal earth. He sat stock-still and heard in himself a similar, fundamental tone, and felt for a moment that perfect solitude he both needed and feared, and he knew then that this was where his life would take him, this was where he belonged.

A month later Filius was earthbound again, working forty feet below the city streets for the Chicago Tunnel Company. As superintendent, he spent eight hours a day inspecting the sixty miles of narrow-gauge railroad tunnels that formed a honeycomb of thriving enterprise beneath the urban crust, where motormen transported coal and merchandise to downtown basements, steering their miniature locomotives along one-way tracks and, uncannily aware of approaching trains, able to brake or slow down at busy intersections without looking at the electric warning lights that so often failed. Filius fell easily into the pace of this underground city, entering the tunnels each dawn from an elevator on Hubbard Street, and opening the heavy metal door at the bottom to find Eddie Zigler already waiting for him. An old-timer at twenty-eight, a motorman with ten years' experience, Eddie was a soft, balding man with squinty eyes and skin that took on the dull shine of a cut potato. Every morning Filius would ride on the flatcar behind Eddie's locomotive and get off at Randolph Street to walk the tunnels on both sides of the

Chicago River. He learned to bundle up against the current of cold air that moved through these lower depths, and in time his ears grew numb to the unceasing clang of freight trains that accompanied the chilly gusts of wind and soot. Armed with his flashlight and extra batteries, he'd phone the dispatcher on the hour from various checkpoints. At noon Eddie would pick him up, and they'd ride to the Dearborn intersection and eat a hot meal already delivered to the elevator shaft from a chop suey restaurant above them, or for a change they'd have one of the company boys, dirty street kids permanently absent from school, fetch them thick ham sandwiches and macaroni salad from Good Meals luncheonette on State Street. As the days went by, Filius grew accustomed to the smell and taste of diesel and the fungus-slimed walls. He learned to eat while the trains moved around him, lounging on a pile of boxes destined for Marshall Field's, and spent the hour listening to Eddie talk about the illegal cockfights that Leon Rice, a big Negro who loaded mail sacks at the Federal Building, ran out of his backyard on Forty-seventh Street.

Filius especially liked the quiet, early-morning hours during the week, Tuesday or Wednesday, when he'd get Eddie to haul him to Thirteenth Street and switch onto a little-used spur that led to the basement of the Field Museum, near the lake. While Eddie read the morning *Tribune*, Filius would hand the museum watchman a quarter and enter the dark building to walk the empty halls alone, strolling through the ribbed shadows of dinosaur skeletons before ending up on the upper balcony, in front of the enormous windows, as the sun rose over the outside world.

When they returned from Europe, Filius and Addie moved into her parents' apartment on Goethe Street and unpacked their honeymoon bags behind the closed doors of her childhood bedroom. Daniel and Edie McCabe had offered to clean away the frills and childish debris of her bountiful youth, but she told them not to bother. It wasn't the pile of books and audience of dolls she couldn't part with, it was the bed; she wanted to share that private space of her girlhood years with her new husband, to lie together on the mattress that had been sculpted over the years by her own body, dimpled by the flare of her hips, smoothed by her lengthening calves. She wanted Filius to become part of the memories that were formed here, that formed her, and for this room to become the juncture where her past and future would begin to coexist.

After breakfast with Filius at five-thirty, she'd go back to the article on postwar France that she was writing for *Chicago* magazine. At eight she'd have another cup of coffee with her parents, and on dry mornings would wrap herself in a woolen coat and walk her father to his office. Overlooking Lake Michigan, it was the same office he'd occupied when Addie was a girl, and she remembered the lean years after her father had become an acolyte of Sigmund Freud and lost most of his patients by pledging allegiance to the God-denying Viennese Jew who promoted sexual immorality. In those slow years before the war, Daniel made ends meet by teaching full-time at the university and splurged only once, when he went to London to be analyzed by Ernest Jones, the prominent Freudian. By the time he returned to Chicago, Freud's theories were attracting more interest, and he was able to rebuild his practice with more open-minded, if still suspicious, patients.

On their morning walks, Addie and her father talked with the same ease and casualness they enjoyed years ago while sailing on Lake Michigan, and Daniel realized how very much alike they were in politics and human concerns, and on these morning walks he found himself slowing down as he approached his building, unwilling to end this privileged time with his daughter, so pretty and vibrant at his side, unafraid of life and blessed with humor.

Until they talked about Filius.

"He doesn't sleep much, does he?" Daniel prodded.

"He doesn't need to."

"Every time I get up in the middle of the night for a glass of milk or tea for your mother, he's sitting in the parlor with a book in his hand."

"Better that than a glass of bourbon."

"Perhaps the bourbon might help him sleep."

Addie let go of her father's arm and buttoned the top button of her coat, walking faster now, and Daniel was forced to keep up.

"Addie. Stop."

"Do you try talking to him?"

"Every time we bump into each other in the dark."

"Do you find him dull or stupid?"

"Of course not."

"Do you find him lacking in integrity or character?"

"No, just sleep."

"His inability to sleep has nothing to do with how he loves me."

"I know."

"And I love him very much."

"I know that, too."

She slowed down, and Daniel gladly took off his hat, flushed and damp from the sudden exertion.

"There's a certain distance to the young man, that's all."

"Not with me."

"And that's what matters."

"To me, yes."

That weekend Daniel took them onto Lake Michigan for what was to be the last sail of the season, the sky frosty and the water a constant chop. Most of the sailboats were already heading in, beaten back by the unsettled conditions and the threat of rain. When Daniel considered turning back, Filius asked to take the tiller, and then guided the *Runaway* out past Navy Pier, where the open water immediately slapped and drenched them as it rushed over the side, but he watched the telltale and found the wind when he needed it, riding the hard, short swells at a high angle that forced them all to the same side of the boat. Daniel—heart kicking and his skin frozen to his bones—watched his daughter balance herself in front of him, one knee planted on the mast bench and the other on the floor-boards. As she tightened the main, the spray of water plastered her short hair into a single wing at the back of her neck. He turned to look at Filius in the stern, one foot hard on the gunwale that nearly dipped into the popping water, seemingly walking on water, his hand steady on the angry tiller. At that moment, as the boat stood up and the horizon was lost in a veil of water, Daniel trusted them both. Filius reached past him and touched Addie on the shoulder. She eased out the jib and the boat slowly righted itself on the churning lake. Five minutes later they slalomed back into the calmer waters of the harbor, and Filius gave up the tiller to his father-in-law just as it started to rain.

The storm followed them home, where they took hot baths and had whiskey before dinner. Daniel couldn't sleep that night. Edie kicked and sniffled beside him, and at two o'clock he finally got out of bed, slipping on his robe but ignoring the slippers he couldn't find in the dark. Without looking in the parlor, he walked to the kitchen and boiled some water for tea, pouring two cups he then sweetened with generous amounts of brandy, and carried them out and took the chair next to Filius.

"It was a good day."

"Yes sir."

They drank their tea in silence. The rain streaked and slashed the window in front of them, the lightning burning through the clouds over Oak Street Beach as the storm moved east.

Daniel didn't probe or speculate or ask a single question that might stir a thought repressed, but simply said, "You're a sailor, Filius."

"Thank you, sir."

"Maybe if the weather breaks this week, we can go out one last time."

"I'd like that."

It was enough to sit here and watch the rain, in this house where his wife and daughter slept, with a young man he barely knew. Breathing in the brandy fumes from his empty mug, Daniel marveled at how many choices were available, yet how easy it was to welcome the consequences once a decision was made.

A month later, Filius got a letter from A. J. Wiley in Turlock, California, offering him the position of supervising engineer on the Don Pedro Dam, where construction would begin in July. Accepting without hesitation, he worked for the Chicago Tunnel Company through the spring as Addie finished her article, and in April they bought a new Essex sedan with their savings, loaded the car with suitcases and a tent and headed west.

Ten years later, Filius again was heading west. He crossed the Missouri River on the Omaha Bridge, and stopped outside of Waterloo,

Nebraska, to smoke a cigarette and stretch his legs. The night sky was a solid blanket overhead, and at three in the morning the air was finally cool, but he knew it wouldn't last. Looking around, he saw the outline of a distant farmhouse, caved in and abandoned. He stepped into the short grass, flushing out a family of prairie chickens that cackled and burst off in all directions. To the east, on the flat horizon, the faraway lights of Omaha were dim as the dying embers of a campfire.

Filius thought about all the years he'd spent traveling, first alone with Addie and then together with their son, driving cross-country from one dam job to another. But now everything was different. He dragged on his cigarette until the paper sizzled and burned his fingers. He got back into his car and, tired or not, drove on.

*F*rank danced with both Fanny and Lena at the Grange in Idabel, sliding them smoothly across a dance floor that felt like glass underfoot as Henry Simms and the Bottom Boys worked through "The Arkansas Traveler." Henry, the fiddle player, was a woefully skinny boy of sixteen, all knobs and protuberances, ears and hips and elbows. Beyond pale, an Ozark native who might've been carved out of soap, he held his fiddle close to his chest like an old-timer and kept his head down as he played, modest about his capabilities. He left the singing to the Bottom Boys, stern uncles and cousins whose voices were as high and lonesome as the wind fluting at the base of Taum Sauk Mountain.

It was a hot night, the hall feeling closed and musty even with the doors wide open, the air so wet it shined on the walls. Between songs, Lena sat by a crowded window gulping fresh air and sipping dandelion wine spiked with grain alcohol from a flask that Lester Hobbes Jr. kept handy at his hip. She stood cross-armed and watched Fanny dance with Frank, the band fiddling and strumming through "Turkey in the Straw." As farmers dipped and swung their wives around the hall, Fanny looked into Frank's eyes and trusted his lead, breathless and flush, holding his elbow and wrist with just enough pinch that Lena knew her friend was flirting.

Frank twirled her, his eyes searching the room over the whip of her blonde hair, and found Lena standing in the crowd. He smiled at her just as Fanny came out of the spin and leaned into his arms. She saw Lena watching and smiled, too.

. . .

Fanny was the daughter of Hans Kruger, a German immigrant who was swept into Indian Territory during the first great land rush, laid claim to forty acres of blistered prairie and let loose the six Hampshire pigs he'd bought from a trader in the boomtown of Guthrie. He dug a well, built a sty and cleared out a horseshoe of loblolly pine, using the timber to build a small house, leaving just enough trees to provide shade and a decent break from the dry wind that blew up from Texas. He attended Methodist services every Sunday at a tent set up on Boggy River and stayed for supper, hunched over the plank table with the rest of the congregants as the wind threatened to blow their plates into oblivion. It was at one of these suppers that he met Freda Zimmer, the minister's daughter, and they were the first couple to be married in the new church built outside the small town of Hugo. Two years later they had a son, Otto. Two years after that, in the fourth year of the new century, Fanny was born.

Fanny was a pretty girl, inheriting the sharp, Teutonic features of her father, but in her face the planes and angles were tempered by a plumpness she inherited from her mother. At ten years old she started working with the pigs, dragging sacks of corn and barley to the feeders, herding the frightened gilts into the farrowing house. It was her job to monitor the newborns, making sure they weren't crushed in the birthing frenzy and watching for signs of whipworm; in late spring she spread pine tar on the corner joints and windows of the sty to keep the blowflies under control. She liked taking care of the pigs and being outside with her father, especially during planting season, when he'd put fifteen acres in corn and she'd follow behind him, dropping peanuts between the rows. In the fall they let the breeder pigs loose in the fields to hog off the remaining stalks and root for the soft-shelled nuts, and Fanny and Otto would check the fence line at sunup and dusk every day, Otto carrying his father's .22 and Fanny looking for slack in the barbed wire and making sure the pigs were safe from wolves and wild dogs.

The boys always liked Fanny. She was the only girl who went swimming with them in the soupy pond at the end of Murphy's Road, and some of the other girls swore she swam naked as the boys did, letting them grope her in the green water and groping them back. Lena admired Fanny for her mocking, teasing ease with the boys, how she'd play baseball with them, and then, after the game, sit among them in the shade of the gum tree in the school yard, her knees grass-stained and bloody with picked scabs. Lena would pass them on her way back to class, smelling their collective sweat, pungent as vinegar, and be envious.

The girls didn't become friends, though, until they were three weeks out of school. It was a hot, dry day in June and Lena was indoors, practicing minor chords on the spinet in the McCardell living room. All the windows were open and the late morning sun streamed inside, throwing overlapping squares of light across the wooden floor. Lena pecked out a Chopin étude, playing it slowly, her fingers thick and uncooperative. She barely looked at the yellowy sheet music, too lazy to follow the cascade of black notes and bars. The parched air that collected in the house deadened the piano's tone and Lena could hear the notes fading away in the heat.

Outside, chickens jerked and pecked freely in the side yard around the doghouse, empty since her cocker spaniel had been killed by a stray hound in March. Lena glanced up at the window and saw Fanny Kruger riding her bicycle in front of the house, wearing a sleeveless blouse and shorts that showed off her strong arms and legs, already tanned the color of weak tea. She nibbled at an apple as she glided by in ropey loops, sending up a rooster tail of dust that seemed to evaporate behind her. Something was moving under the plaid cloth in the wicker basket between her handlebars, and a little black-and-white terrier ran alongside, leaping into the air every time Fanny took a bite.

Lena watched her toss the apple core into the side yard. The little terrier yapped and took off after it, scattering the chickens and tearing into the core as if it were a dead rodent. In their panic, the chickens cackled like idiots and ran into one another. Lena dashed out of the house, the door slapping her heel, and was about to scold the dog when she saw Fanny in front of her, leaning over the handlebars, her bare feet planted firmly in the gravel in the McCardell driveway.

"Come here."

Lena hesitated.

Fanny grinned, and her chubby cheeks took on a red shine. Her short blonde hair, darkened with sweat, stuck to her forehead and neck. "Closer. I want to show you something."

Lena could see a lumpy mass under the cloth in the basket, and moved next to the bicycle to peer over the handlebars. Fanny removed the cloth to reveal a little pig, maybe two weeks old. It was the size of a newborn human baby, fetal and pink and raw.

"You can touch it."

Lena did, grinning widely, and cradled it in her arms.

Lena was swaying, dancing.

"Mom."

The fiddle music was faint, strings singing in the distance.

"Mom. Wake up."

Burr pushed on Lena's shoulders and she opened her eyes. It was the middle of the night and they were still on the bus. Lena's face rested against the window and she looked out at the dark peaks of the Arizona mountains and the stars that shone like rivets in the coal black sky. She straightened up and studied the passengers around her, their heads bobbing in sleep, loose-limbed as marionettes. The bus smelled strangely fermented, edged with exhaust. Burr pulled on her sleeve again and Lena, turning to him, realized her neck was sore.

"Mom. Look." Burr pointed across the aisle. In the dim light, Lena could see Charlie Chivers in his aisle seat, fast asleep, his big arms dangling at his side, his chin bouncing on his chest.

"He's sleeping."

She took a deep breath to clear her head, then recognized at once the metallic smell and saw the dark stain on the front of Charlie's pants. The odor in the closeness of the bus was almost tropical.

The man sitting in the window seat next to Charlie was sleeping peacefully, and as the bus banked around a sharp curve his head was thrown back against Charlie's shoulder. He yawned and coughed, then looked down at his hand, which had fallen against Charlie's damp leg.

"Jesus Christ!"

Charlie snuffled through his nose and Lena leaned over her son, trying to reach Charlie's shoulder across the aisle.

"Charlie. Wake up."

"Driver! Stop the bus!" The man's voice was high but not very loud. The few people sitting nearby began to stir, and as the bus bounced, Lena's fingers skittered Charlie's arm.

"Charlie."

"Driver!" the man called again, now shouting. "Stop the bus, dammit!"

The driver slammed on the brakes and Burr could smell the smoky rubber left on the pavement as the bus jolted to a heavy stop. Everyone was awake now, confused, alarmed, sniffing something vaguely familiar.

Even Charlie was nudged out of his deep slumber. He blinked his eyes and yawned, rubbing at the short white hairs that tufted out of his nose. He winked at Burr and Lena across the aisle. "What, we hit a deer?"

Charlie shifted his weight and Burr saw his face go soft as he felt the liquid that saturated his lap.

"Oh my," he whispered.

Lena stepped over her son and crouched in the aisle next to him.

"It's okay, Charlie."

He stared down at the dark stain, his palms upturned on his thighs.

Passengers hung over their seats and hovered in the aisle, staring at him as the bus driver stalked down the aisle, pushing them out of his way. Standing over the old man and the woman crouching next to him, he saw the sneaky runoffs of piss winding through old dust trails and candy wrappers on the floor.

"Look at my goddamn bus."

"It's everywhere," whined the man sitting next to Charlie. "Where am I supposed to sit? What am I—"

"Shut up." The driver reached down and yanked on Charlie's arm. "Come on, you."

Charlie, his eyes watery red, didn't budge, even when the bus driver gave his shoulder a rough shove.

"Get up, you goddamn baby!"

Lena abruptly stood when the bus driver made another move toward Charlie. "Don't you do that again."

"He's getting off my bus!"

"Not like this, he isn't."

Her voice was clear and calm, but Burr knew she meant business. So did the bus driver, who took a step back from the puddle on the floor.

"Get him off my bus."

Lena gently eased herself in front of Charlie. When he lifted his head, Burr saw the grizzled swipe of day-old beard on his chin and cheeks. His mother smiled and rested her small hand on the top of his meaty fingers. "Let's take care of this, Charlie."

When Charlie nodded, Lena stood up straight and looked at the faces around her.

People moved back without being told as she helped Charlie out of his seat. He looked old now, Burr thought, all bent and bow-legged. Charlie reached up for his Stetson, angling it low on his head, and allowed Lena to lead him down the aisle. Burr looked down at the wet tracks Charlie laid out on the floor—left foot, right foot—then his mother caught his eye.

"Get his bag, Burr."

He leapt across the aisle, agile as a monkey, and from the overhead rack grabbed the suitcase he'd seen Charlie bring onto the bus. It was heavy, and he balanced it on the armrest. He could see the man sitting by the window glaring at him, as was the driver, his lips thin and tight. Everyone else on board was watching Lena and Charlie. Then he noticed the pool of urine directly below him and jumped straight down into it, sending up a spray of piss that went everywhere.

"Hey!" the driver snapped. "Watch it!"

"Grab that kid!" said the man by the window.

Burr raced down the aisle, propelled forward by the weight of the suitcase. His mother and Charlie were inching down the bottom step of the bus, and he had to grab the metal post to keep from banging into them. He felt footsteps pounding behind him, and jumped to the ground just as the driver swiped at the back of his neck.

He stood there, breathing in gulps, at the top of the steps. "Look at this goddamn mess. You know who's got to clean it up?"

Lena never looked away from the driver's face. Charlie stood at her side, not looking anywhere.

"Goddamn schedule's all shot to shit—"

"The boy," Lena warned him.

"—all shot to hell, and—"

"The boy, I said."

"—the goddamn bus stinking of piss. Stop in Flagstaff and I got to spend all my time on my knees bleaching the floor."

"Watch it now." Lena's voice was patient and firm.

"Me cleaning up after every sponge and whore's got fifty cents to board in Memphis, ride to destination unknown, and I am just plain sick of the crying and lying and them touching me with their hands, grabbing my sleeve like the stink rising off of them ain't already got my full attention."

"That's enough, I said."

"But at least I got a job, right? That's what my wife says. 'Shut up, mister, you got you a job. You get you a check every Friday, we eat bacon every Sunday, got a house to eat it in, don't owe a cent to nobody, so quit your complaining, 'cause all's you got to do is drive a bus.'"

"Your wife's right." Lena tried to keep her voice low. "Shut up."

"That ain't all I do, goddammit, that ain't all!" The driver pointed at Charlie's back. "Him. Goddamn pig!"

"You're a goddamn pig!"

"He's—"

"He's old!" Lena canted toward him, close enough to knock his knees. "He's just old."

The driver watched her, panting hard, and backed up the steps. He slumped down behind the wheel, sitting sideways, and glared at them.

Lena took the suitcase from Burr and set it down next to Charlie. "Why don't you go into those pines and put on something dry? Me and Burr will wait for you here."

Charlie bent his knees, picked up the suitcase, and walked slowly toward the trees. Lena put her arm around Burr and turned him away, pointing up at the stars fading in the incandescent wash of night.

"It'll be light soon," she said.

"I'm hungry."

"Me, too. We'll get something to eat in Flagstaff. Maybe even change buses." Lena squeezed her son's hand and looked down at him. "You don't mind waiting for the next bus, do you?"

He shook his head.

"No. This bus stinks."

She smiled. Burr knew she was feeling better now, and again he looked up, trying to locate the last star in the sky, but it had already disappeared into the dawn.

"Hey, lady." The driver, standing at the top of the open doorway, kicked Lena's suitcase down the steps and it bounced end over end onto the gravel. Then he closed the accordion doors, jumped back up into his high seat and put the bus into gear. Lena ran up and banged on the glass.

"Stop it. Stop!"

The driver pushed his hat back on his head with one hand and slowly turned the wheel with the other, giving the bus some gas. Lena walked alongside, staring up at him, but he only glanced once over his shoulder, as if to look for traffic, and pulled away. Passengers lined the windows, staring out with vacant eyes, as Burr ran to his mother's side and together they watched the taillights disappear around a bend in the road. The pines swallowed all sounds except for a quick flutter of pigeon hawks as they flew from tree to tree.

Charlie stepped up beside them. He wore fresh jeans and a clean shirt, and carried his suitcase in his right hand and Lena's in his left. He looked back down the road to Winslow, jutting his chin toward the east.

"Sun's up."

Burr saw a low hump of pale light on the hills they'd just passed through. He smelled pinesap in the cool air and his stomach grumbled. Two yellow lights flashed along the highway, heading their way, passing in and out of view as the car negotiated the curves at the bottom of the mountain.

Charlie put the suitcases down and walked to the edge of the road, lifting his big hand to wave the car over long before it ever reached them.

*F*rom Arizona he had gotten a ride on a hay truck that took him straight through Nevada. The desert was hot and monotonous, sheets of yellow earth, bloodshot at the edges, that stretched on forever. Lew's window wouldn't open, the handle spinning uselessly on stripped gears, so he sat there in a stale, oily pocket of his own stink, yearning for the breeze he couldn't reach, later waking to the same anthilled landscape of sandstone, the sun a white hole blown in the sky, maybe lower than it had been but just as bright, and only the torturously slow ticking of his watch proved that time was passing.

He felt anxious, almost giddy, when the Sierra Nevada Mountains appeared in the distance, cloaked in forests that seemed to drip like green jelly through the thrilling heat into the valley below. The driver dropped off five tons of oat hay at a cattle ranch outside of Carson City and gave Lew a dollar in exchange for helping unload the wired bales from the back of his Pierce-Arrow flatbed. They made a delivery to a ranch on the Truckee River, then another in Baxter, and made it as far as Auburn before the trucker pulled over and staked Lew to a room and breakfast. Over eggs and ham steaks he offered him a job, but Lew didn't like being cooped up in a hot cab all day long. The next morning he got off in Sacramento, and the truck, empty now and full of speed, headed down to the fields around Stockton to pick up another load of hay.

Lew walked to the main highway, passing rice fields that spread out from the delta and covered hundreds of soggy acres. A group of Japanese workers was coming out of the fields, men and women small as children, small as Lew, bent under heavy burlap but still laughing and talking, heads bobbing back and forth, consonants clicking like ball bearings between their teeth. When they saw Lew up ahead they abruptly fell silent, letting their feet drag through powdery brown eddies, acting as they were supposed to. They lowered their eyes and angled their heads away from Lew as they came closer, and he knew this show was for his benefit.

Once they passed him by, their laughter and talking resumed. Lew glanced over his shoulder and watched them again straighten up under their loads, hefting their burlap sacks of grain as if they were filled with air, their feet light and their voices high and overlapping, sharp as birdsong, mocking him in a foreign tongue. Suddenly enraged, he picked up a flat rock, its edges made jagged by the crunch of heavy tires, and threw it. It sliced through the air like a wing, hitting an old woman just as she turned to her neighbor to cackle an indecipherable joke at Lew's expense. The rock clipped her ear, and she fell to her knees and let out a wail. For a moment Lew thought she was laughing again, but it was only a gasp of pain. She looked at Lew through the salty tears in her eyes, holding her split ear as the blood ran through her fingers and down her arm. A young man kneeled at the old woman's side and wrapped her head in the soiled bandanna he wore around his neck.

"Is that funny? Is that so goddamn funny?" Lew shouted at them as they shuffled away. He picked up another rock and threw it. It bounced in the dirt, skipping three times before just missing the ankle of a man in the rear. No one even looked back. He stood there until they were almost out of sight, swallowed by the gently dipping road, until the heat made it impossible to stand still a moment longer. Then he walked onto a bridge over the American River and smoked a cigarette, the lazy water below creamy with silt. On the distant highway cars floated off the ground, riding high on the shimmering heat. Most of the traffic was heading south, and Lew knew that would be the easiest direction to pick up a ride.

In 1923 Lew Beck was back in Los Angeles. He was nineteen years old and needed to shave three times a week to clear the shadow that smudged his chin and upper lip. He found an apartment in Sunrise

Court, a run-down complex of lopsided bungalows in Highland Park, and paid by the month, cash. He'd read the early newspaper, comics and the want ads, on the stoop facing the courtyard, and sit alone smoking cigarettes and listening to the neighborhood women scream at their scabby children and dour husbands for being late for work or school, their tired morning harangues dulled by concrete and plaster, by their four-cornered urban existence here on the citified edge of the desert.

Lew found work at the alligator farm on Mission. Every morning he wrangled a ride with his neighbor Pete Scully, a quiet widower with two kids and a good job as a driver for the Coca-Cola Company on South Central. Lew bought him a weekly tank of gas in exchange for daily transportation to the Alameda Street bus that took him to the farm on the outskirts of Alhambra. They left early each morning, the sunrise a silhouette of fire over the downtown horizon, and Pete would complain about his son, a baseball fanatic and chronic delinquent who'd been suspended from high school for beating up his coach because he'd taken him out of a championship game against Monrovia, and now Pete Jr. spent his days bouncing a rubber ball off the side of the building and driving his father crazy. And his teenage daughter, Meg, was going with a man twice her age, an Italian who stood in for John Gilbert in the movies. Lew eased back on the seat and closed his eyes, tuning Pete out like a husband does a wife, and most mornings was dead asleep by the time they got downtown.

The first thing Lew did at the alligator farm was change into his green uniform, his name stitched on the pocket over a woven emblem of a gaping alligator curled up under a palm tree. By seven in the morning the alligators were waking up, their empty bellies scraping the concrete as they swished and slithered through their greasy shit and piss, looking for the fatty chunks of horse meat that the keepers had thrown over the fence. Lew's job was to clean out the concrete pools in front of the cages, draining the murky green water and attacking blue-painted walls with a long stiff-bristled broom while the gators watched him through the bars, chomping rancid flesh and waiting to be let out to bathe like ladies in a harem. Lew then filled the pools with fresh water, often hosing down the alligators just to watch them snap and hiss, some of the old-timers with broken teeth and moss on their backs. There was a young one who gnawed at the metal barrier every morning, gimping around on three legs, his fourth a wizened stump. Instinctively ferocious, always fighting with the other juveniles, scrappy and deformed, he was Lew's favorite. And once the alligators were finally let out to swim, floating like logs to scare the tourists and earn their keep, Lew moved inside the caged area and played the hose over the narrow channels cut into the concrete, the filthy waste pouring out the back of the cages into a long culvert encrusted with lime.

After two months, Lew asked Pete if he could borrow his car. It was early Sunday evening, and the sun was buoyed above the city in liquid mugginess. They were sitting on the front step while Pete Jr., a big boy with short blonde hair, bounced his ball off the wall, the *pock pock pock* steady as a woodpecker. Pete wore a sleeveless under-shirt that bagged around his skinny chest and his knees banged together each time he heard the ball hit. Lew handed him one of the two cold bottles of beer he'd carried over, and Pete held it between his legs, willing his knees to stop knocking as he considered Lew's request.

"Damn kid's giving me fits. Landlord says I have to paint that wall again and I already repainted it once. Next I'll have to fix the broken boards, another couple of bucks and a wasted Sunday."

He drank half of his beer, his Adam's apple working like a piston, then reached into his pocket and pulled out a clattering of keys. "You'll be careful, right?"

"Sure, Pete."

"No sex. Not even in the backseat." Pete grinned and tossed Lew the keys. "Park it where you found it. Have the keys with you in the morning."

Lew nodded quickly and turned away. The heat aroused him, prickly on his skin. He wiped the sweat from his forehead with the cold bottle of beer, letting it drip down the amber glass, over his hands, over his wrists. The hot breeze was percussive, ringing in his ears.

. . .

Driving into Boyle Heights, he saw the clouds that towered over the western horizon, great flat-topped ledges banked over the ocean, dense as stone. They filled the sky with damp air the color of dishwater, and Lew knew that it would rain that night and the streets would still be wet in the morning, the roads slick as snail tracks. He turned onto Soto Street and saw that nothing much had changed. Mendel's Hardware was now Mendel and Son. Hy Kaminsky still struggled with the metal gate in front of his pawnshop, kicking the rusted and bent iron until it rattled and sang. The streetlamp on the corner of First Street flickered dimly, and young men backed up against the slender pole without talking, smoking in a Chesterfield haze.

He parked across the street from Beckman's Kosher Meats, rolled down the window and stared at the familiar façade, unable to reconcile his past, feeling like a stranger in another man's car. The last gasp of sunlight glinted in the twin Stars of David, turning them bronze. Two old men in long black frock coats and *payes*, crooked and sinister as crows, walked out of the market—Hassids from Odessa or Brooklyn or Sioux City, carrying chickens wrapped in butcher paper under their arms. Through the open doorway Lew could see his father behind the meat counter, standing at the deep porcelain sink to wash his hands, letting the strings of chicken veins swirl around the clogged drain. The set of his father's shoulders was a little wider, his spine a little more bent. His hair was still dark and thick, a last youthful flicker on a body grown compact and aching with years. Then his father moved into the back storeroom and the front door swooshed closed; the lights in the window were turned off, and the Stars of David faded to black; signs of faith and commerce extinguished.

Lew got out of the car and crossed the street. He had no plans or desires other than to see his father. After more than two years of silence.

He had left in the middle of the night while his parents slept, his father dreaming of dirigibles amassing like bubbles over the Los Angeles River, his mother dreaming of bathing in a bathtub of cool milk, oft-repeated dreams brimming with promise and comfort that would be forever altered upon waking the next morning. Lew was missing. A boy was in the hospital and a girl was sent away to relatives in Albany, New York. Just children, Lew's schoolmates. The police had come around, asking questions. They had been gruff and tired, unsympathetic to Esther's fumbling English and Isadore's thick accent. Jews. Neighbors started rumors, and rumors became legend.

When Lew pushed the door open, the little bell chimed weakly over his head. He could smell garlic and allspice rising like spirits from the pickle barrel by the counter, blood and ice and meat from the freezer, almonds and sugar and shredded coconut from the macaroons under glass. In his mind he could smell the flour on his mother's hands and the starch on his father's apron, pink with bloodstains no matter how many times it was bleached. The smells levitated and tethered him, made him feel safe and afraid; they were the memories that he had not forgotten.

"I'm closed."

Isadore shambled out of the back room, his coat draped over his shoulders like a cape, seeing only another neighborhood kid coming for the salami or eggs his mother had forgotten, maybe salt or bread. They always came at closing time, these *pischers*—never the parents who knew Mr. Beckman would shake his head and turn them away once the lights were out.

Lew heard his father sigh, a hushed Kaddish full of dried tears. Isadore Beckman was about to become momentarily inconvenienced and five minutes late for his own supper. Lew listened to the sigh as it coursed through the store, rising to become caught in the cobwebs that hung like silk from the rafters, squirreling along the floorboards to find its way into mouse holes, seeping into the walls and wiring, there to keen forever, and Lew shuddered.

"What do you want?" The old man's eyes were clouded, and Lew, whose sight was perfect, saw his father's cracked lips part to expose his upper teeth, brown and white and broken.

"Speak. Minds I don't read."

Lew loved this man who'd spent half his life in America but only a blink away from the Pale; Krakow to Berlin to London, this wandering Jew who with his wife had cartwheeled in a migratory wind from Brooklyn to Cincinnati to Boyle Heights, three years learning

English from newspapers and insults, knowing their own and finding them in urban shtetls, comfortable slums with a rabbi, a Talmud and a kosher butcher shop like this one on Soto Street, making a life in neighborhoods on the outskirts of tolerance, with storefront synagogues where ten men sat in the gravy light of dusk to dip and daven and pray, each offering an off-key modulation of the same Hebrew prayer, some warbling high and others low, voices somehow blending together with an "amen" as beautiful as rain falling on water.

His father: five inches taller, an expert with knives, an artisan of loins and limbs, promising to save the feet and bones for Mrs. Steiner's stockpot, and the *pupik* for Moe Levine, who would dice it up with gristle and onions in a brown sizzle of butter and salt, then eat it with his scrambled eggs every Sunday morning.

A boy of eight, Lew had sat on the narrow stairwell in the front hall of the Beckman house, crouched on the landing where the staircase turned at a right angle and ascended to the second floor, his back against the oak newel under the leaded glass window that let in the orange shafts of the setting sun. He sat quietly as his parents' friends arrived for Sunday dinner, the women with platters of cod balls in aspic and dishes piled high with crisped potato kugel, while their husbands carried jars of pickled green tomatoes and chunky bottles of slivovitz. Lew watched as his parents greeted their guests and helped the women shake out of their coats while the men removed their hats, leaning them like horseshoes on the crowded rack by the door. And if no one had spotted him by that time, he'd move purposefully into the light and rock back and forth, throwing a shadow to offer himself up for their attention. Mr. Kipl saw him first and roared his giant laugh, then raised his arms and reached up until Lew felt his strong fingers snake under his arms, letting himself be hoisted over the railing and into the air. He looked down on Mr. Zwetchkenbaum's oval bald spot, shining like a coin on his tufted dome, and on Mrs. Steiner's open smile, framed by red lipstick that was applied so thickly it cracked, and on his parents, the pleasure in their faces obvious even though his mother tried to hide hers behind spread fingers as Mr. Kipl spun him through the air in a gentle reel of dips and glides. When he was lowered to the Persian runner in the hallway, he caught his breath and inhaled deeply, finding himself in an effluvium of toilet water and cinnamon, fenced in by dimpled knees and baggy tweed. Mrs. Kipl squeezed his cheek, mewing, *"Mayn kleyn moyz"*—and Mrs. Zwetchkenbaum pinched his other cheek harder and chirped even louder, *"Ya, ober zeyer gesundt. Zaftik vi der kotlet."* While Lew laughed and fidgeted, Mr. Levine pressed a copper penny into his hand as he always did—Lew counting on the money as much as he counted on the touching and the clucking that preceded it. His mother leaned down to kiss Lew on the forehead and told him to go outside and play, then his father spread his big, strong fingers across Lew's back, shoulder blade to shoulder blade, and whispered, *"Gut* boy," his voice feathery and ticklish through his mustache, "be home in an hour," and cupped Lew's backside in his hand to propel him through the door, and his son gladly went outside, clenching the bright penny deep in his pocket so it wouldn't bounce out, listening to his parents' friends laughing behind him, knowing he was being watched, the happiness rising in his throat so overwhelmingly pleasant that it could scarcely be contained in his eight-year-old frame.

Lew ran down the steps and across the street to the empty lot on the corner, where the neighborhood kids were playing tinball, batting dented tin cans with broken broomsticks and splintered pieces of wood, trying to arc them over the fence. He grabbed a plank, not too thick and warped just right, from the pile by the sidewalk and got into line to take his turn. Jimmy Swerdin, in front of him, was twelve years old, a skinny kid, all pimples and bone, who swung his stick, a broken baseball bat, and missed every can that Augie Paris pitched his way. Then Jimmy turned toward Lew and hacked up a great gob of spit that caught the light like blown glass before snapping off and splattering his own left shoe. And Lew laughed. He held the new penny in his pocket, his cheeks still flushed from the pinching, and he laughed right in Jimmy's dirt-streaked face. He couldn't stop laughing—not until Jimmy grabbed the back of his neck and slammed him face-first into the ground. Jimmy knelt on Lew's back and rubbed his face in the dirt as the other boys stopped playing and crowded around, but Lew couldn't hear their whoops and hollers, just the scraping of his skin against dirt and gravel, and he fought back only when he felt a piece of glass cut his cheek. Jimmy finally stood up, and Lew rolled over on his back and blinked, his mouth caked with grit. Jimmy wiped his own face with the back of his sweaty hand, leaving a swath like warpaint on his pimply skin, and sneered, "Laugh now, little Jewboy."

Lew felt the blood on his face and the tears about to come, and he scuttled at him, kicking Jimmy's ankles and knees before the older boy was able to reach behind him and grab his broken bat off the ground. Lew clambered to his feet, thrusting his body forward and windmilling his arms to catch his balance as he raced across the empty lot, not drawing a breath until the broken bat spun past his head. As the boys laughed behind him, he watched the bat dance end over end into the street, bouncing high off the curb and smashing through the windshield of the Ford flatbed parked in front of Mr. Kreiger's house. Suddenly, the boys scattered and Lew kept running, right across his yard and up the front steps into the hallway, where he ran into Mrs. Kipl coming out of the kitchen. And kind Mrs. Kipl knelt down, staring at his dirt-crusted face in horror, and when she reached out to wipe the already dry starburst of blood from his cheek, Lew slapped her hand away and pushed her backward and she thudded down on the Persian runner, her white cotton slip bunched around her chubby knees. Isadore screeched his chair away from the pinochle table in the sitting room and dashed into the hall to snatch Lew by the shoulder and drag him back through the doorway. The cardplayers froze and the women put down the teacups, all of them staring at Lew as if they'd never seen this wild boy before. Isadore demanded that he apologize, but Lew squirmed and refused, so Isadore squeezed him harder. This was the first time he ever laid hands on his son in anger, and he didn't know how strong his fingers were, how they tore into the boy's soft muscles like the claws of a hammer. Feeling the pain sear through him, Lew found a hard spot in his booming heart and punched his father in the chest, and when he still didn't let go, bit his hand. When Isadore saw Lew's teeth clamp down on his thumb, he slapped him hard in the face with his other hand. The boy's head snapped back, and Isadore let go of his shoulder. Lew swayed there in front of him, sucking on blood from inside his mouth, his eyes dry but the inside of his head screaming. Mrs. Kipl still sat on the floor. Esther rested a hand against the tea cart, looking around as if she'd forgotten where she was going.

"Are you sorry?" Isadore's voice cracked, because he was afraid of the answer.

Lew let the blood run down the back of his throat, and in the silence that followed, swallowed it.

"Go to your room," Isadore said, looking at the floor and hoping his son, the first Beckman born in America, would throw himself into his arms and plead to stay. Lew turned and walked slowly out of the sitting room, passing Mrs. Kipl without acknowledgment and climbing the stairs to his room without responding to the friendly, disbelieving stares he felt on his back. He shut the door behind him, the clicking of the mechanism as loud as if he'd slammed it, and sat on the end of the bed in front of the mirror. The dirt had flaked off his face where his father slapped him, and he could see where the ground had scratched his cheek. The glass cut on his other cheek had reopened, the blood welling up, but he didn't feel any pain. He leaned forward and shifted his body so he could dig deep into his front pocket. His penny was gone.

Isadore Beckman scowled from behind the butcher counter. "I'm a busy man. What do you want—for the second and last time?"

"Pop." He saw his father's whole face squinch up in the gloaming light, and heard him inhale sharply, just once, as if smell was the keenest of his senses.

Lew moved in front of the window and stood opposite him. "Papa."

Isadore shook his head, as if to clear it, and Lew saw the heaviness in his face.

"It's Lew."

"*Ver?*"

"Louis."

Isadore shuffled forward, his hard shoes brushing the wooden boards like house slippers. Although he had the carriage of an old man, Isadore grew taller as he approached, and Lew once again found himself looking up into his father's face. A car passed on the street outside, the headlights flaring into the store. For a moment, the gold-dipped Stars of David in the window caught fire, like oracles from God, and Lew thought he saw a reflected glimmer in his father's eyes, a light of forgiveness or responsibility. Then the car turned the corner, and the moment was gone.

"Du brechen di mitter's harts."

It took Lew a moment to understand what his father was saying.

"Mamzer."

Isadore raised his hand high in the air, and as Lew glimpsed it, he remembered a hawk in flight over the desert basin outside of Tulare, the way it spiraled down on the dead carcass of a calf, its belly already hollowed out by coyotes and its front hooves tangled in barbed wire. Lew remembered how the hawk blocked out the sun as it swooped lower, its dark wings menacing, and when his father's hand came down to slap his face, Lew grabbed it and clenched his fingers between his own. Isadore fought him and Lew gripped him even harder, and wouldn't let go when he tried to break free. Isadore's hands were still meaty and strong, but Lew was younger and stronger. He drove his father's arm down against his side. Then he bent the hand back, the same hand that once brushed his hair and cupped his shoulder, and applied enough pressure to force his father to lower his head until it was even with his own. Isadore's lips were compressed and he breathed through his nose to control the pain, but the braver he was, the harder Lew squeezed, standing straight and unflinching as he drew his father down to him. He put his cheek against the old man's, closed his eyes and whispered in his ear.

"Papa."

Lew kissed his father's jaw and broke two of his fingers, the sound of snapping bones lost in his father's gasp. Isadore sank to his knees and Lew gently let go of his hand and walked out of the store, the little bell chiming as he pulled the door shut behind him.

*T*hey got picked up off the mountain by the first car that came along. George Percy stopped his big green Chevrolet and made room for them amidst his baggage and kids. He'd driven through the night from the Chino Mines near Hurley, New Mexico, and was glad for the company. For the last two years he'd worked on the mine trains, transporting ore to the railhead in Silver City, but when copper stocks started dropping in '29, refinery output slowed, and the layoffs that started immediately finally caught up with him.

"Twenty-eight, that was the year. Prices were high and it seemed like the blasting never stopped. Slept on Sundays if I was lucky, we were that busy, working so hard there wasn't even time to spend the money I picked up every Friday. Let it fill the mattress. Good thing I did."

He was heading to the Bagdad Mines, forty miles west of Prescott. Having heard they were hiring drivers to haul ore over to the Santa Fe railroad in Hillside, he was hoping to make it to the company office before the gates opened that morning. The day before, he'd packed up his kids and what little they had and hit the road.

George was a small man, his face rough with stubble, and from lack of sleep and conversation he babbled without periods or pause, his knees banging as he drove.

"Worked copper since I was twelve, growing up in Pennsylvania, my daddy got me started, he worked copper too, for the Bethlehem people in Lebanon, easy to get to from our place in Sand Hill, easy enough for me, too, when I got old enough and big enough. Good company, Bethlehem, stayed on till I was seventeen, no school for me but I can read and write, add too, figured I had enough in my head and it was time to make some cash, course it got so I liked to have my pockets full, wiseguy that I was, buy a beer for me and anyone else who wanted one, kind of guy my daddy raised, stand a man to a cold glass, friend and stranger alike. Met Heddy Baxter at a company dance in Mount Zion, her folks was copper people too, married her and had Turnip, moved on to the Mary Mines in Polk County, Tennessee, had us a little gem of a cottage in Ducktown that Heddy fixed up real nice, two bedrooms and curtains in all the windows, and then we had Pea."

Lena and Charlie sat up front with George, and Burr was crowded into the backseat with his two little children, who were snuggled under the bags of clothes and suitcases that were piled to the roof of the car. Burr couldn't see them under their blankets—only an occasional pudgy toe or fist or wisp of colorless hair—and couldn't tell if they were boys or girls or one of each.

"After Pea, Heddy developed a soreness in the joints made her seize up in the winter, cold and wetness caused her awful pain, made it so she couldn't move without crying, even suckling Pea brought tears to her eyes, hurt her arm so much to hold her baby, and I did all I could, course it was hard with my shift and all, sunup to sundown. Neighbors helped me much as they could, her mama come down from Mount Zion for a while, but she was getting on in years and bone tired, too, sort of a humpbacked old thing, nice, though, prayed a lot—and the company doctor said it would be best if we headed south, where it was warmer. Boss in Tennessee squared me a job at Oak Knob in the Appalachians, but it wasn't south enough, fog in the air all day and a cold rain that would get under your skin, felt clammy even in your sleep, a bad, nasty place, dreary as a graveyard, and poor Heddy suffered for it. Didn't work there two months before we lit out for the Chino Mines in New Mexico, but the chills was already shaking poor Heddy so much she couldn't eat or sleep, so I stayed up with her in the car while the kids slept in the back, good as could be, quiet and all 'cause their mama was sick, and we'd talk about the cactus and buffalo and all the Indians we was going to see, how the sunshine and heat would make Heddy strong again, and it was good talk but talk was all it was, 'cause the pneumonia set in just like they warned us it would, and Heddy succumbed in

Natchez, Mississippi, God bless her, just me and the kids with her, never even made it to the hospital it happened so quick, and I broke my promise of gettin' her west of the big river, though I don't think she'd hold it against me."

Lena wasn't sure if he was done talking. Charlie straightened in the seat next to her.

"That's a sad bit of history, George," he said. "I'm truly sorry."

"We had our ups and downs, of course, ups mostly, with the kids and all, and we managed four good years before she got sick, and I know that's what she was thinking about when it got bad, me too, those four good years."

Burr saw George's face in the rearview mirror, as narrow as the rest of him, and although his eyes were on the road, they were somewhere else, too.

"Bus up ahead," he said.

Burr popped forward, gripping the seat back to get a better view between his mother and Charlie. It was the same bus. There were dents on the back hatch, and the bumpers were rusted and warped, tied on with baling wire. "Can't stand to follow a bus," George said. "The stink, I mean."

He eased over the center line to get a better view.

"Hold on," he said, and pushed down the gas pedal. The car picked up speed as naturally as a stone rolling downhill.

Lena didn't move, but Charlie stuck a big hand out the open window and rested his elbow on the sill. Warm air fluttered the blanket on the backseat and George's kids pulled it back down over them. Burr held his face in the window, and when they came up alongside the bus he saw the driver, his hat pulled low to block the sun and his hands curled around the wide arc of the steering wheel. Charlie ignored the bus. The only thing that moved was the hair on his arm, blown and twisted by the wind rushing through the open window. Burr could see his red neck stretched out and unpleated and showing white stripes where the sun hadn't gotten into the folds. He could see the thick muscles and loose skin and the tufted white hair that sprang up from below his collar.

George passed the bus and eased back into his lane. "What're you planning to do in Flagstaff, Charlie?"

"Got my son there." Charlie's voice was softened by the breeze.

"Visiting?"

"For a while, maybe. Maybe longer."

"Nice you can do that. All my relatives is back in Pennsylvania, lots of them, and Mom still in the house in Sand Hill, Dad dead now two years, but she's got brothers and sisters all over the state, so loneliness ain't an issue even if she wanted it to be, especially with my little sister, Honey, and her brood, just over the county line in Mount Joy. And I got a brother, Joe, a merchant seaman somewhere in the Pacific with an address in San Francisco, a rooming house near the pier he says, views of fog and bridges. I ain't seen or spoken to him since before we got married, but he's still my brother and I think of him now and again. Like the kids to meet their uncle Joe sometime since we're close now, miles-wise." George took his left hand off the steering wheel and stretched his fingers. "What about you, Lena? You got folks in Arizona?"

"No, I don't."

"Where you headed?"

"Boulder Dam."

"Looking for a job?"

"Got one."

"Good for you. Heard a lot of people looking for jobs out there, living in tents, hoping for a chance to work, like a fellow I know, Harry Book, got a job mopping floors at the cook shack, and it was hard work, Harry said, temperatures up to a hundred and twenty degrees, coolest time of the day was five in the morning when it dipped below a hundred and he'd sit outside his tent with his feet in a bucket of ice, but Harry made sixty dollars a month with food and board until the heat got to him and the doctor made him quit."

Burr fell asleep, soothed by the unending rhythm of George's voice, not even trying to follow the looping sentences, and he woke when the car eased to a stop in front of Mickey's Diner just off the highway. He looked up at the town clinging to the face of the mountain, the houses like sparrow nests built into the hillsides.

"Flagstaff," George announced.

They climbed out of the car, and Charlie glanced at the telephone booth in front of the diner. He pulled a small leather pouch out of his pocket and shook out two nickels and a folded square of paper with a telephone number scrawled on it. "Reckon I'll call Bill. Then we'll have us some breakfast. You hungry as I am, Burr?"

"Yes sir." Burr was glad to see him smiling again.

"Good, 'cause there's nothing better than bacon and eggs to settle an empty stomach. And fresh biscuits and strawberry jelly. You like strawberry jelly, Burr?"

"I like grape."

"Then get inside and order some. And order strawberry, too, 'cause I like 'em both. And I'm buying. Bacon and eggs all around, over easy for me with a short stack on the side. Can you handle a short stack, Burr?"

"Maybe."

"Then get us a couple of stools while I ring up my boy."

Charlie shook George Percy's hand and extended the invitation to him and his children, but he hadn't even switched off the ignition, anxious as he was to get back on the road. Burr grabbed his mother's suitcase. He dragged it behind him and suddenly remembered something. He spun around just as George Percy's Chevrolet pulled away, and saw Turnip and Pea looking back at him through the rear window, all blonde hair and pink mouths, laughing behind the glass. Girls.

Bill Chivers pulled up out front of Mickey's Diner two hours later, having spent a long morning hauling farm equipment to a bankruptcy auction in Williams. He'd been up before dawn, collecting disks and harrows from farmers unable to keep up their payments, listening to their whispered curses as their wives, their faces pinched with hatred, stood watching in doorways or behind windows. Bill loaded all the implements himself, with a tractor he towed on a flatbed behind his truck, and knew that Matt Carew, the local tractor dealer, wouldn't be happy when he saw how the returning equipment had been abused by the farmers, once they'd known for certain it was going to be collected from their yards and barns. Bill, who'd known most of them for years, couldn't blame them. He kept his mouth shut when he did his job; he didn't commiserate and he didn't condemn, and often offered ten dollars in recompense. Some would take it, and some would crumble up the note and shove it back in Bill's shirt pocket, but he wouldn't say a word either way, just walk to his truck and leave as fast as he could. He made two trips to Williams that morning, and the only real trouble he'd had was from Ferris Lane, a seventy-five-year-old widowed rancher with no sons and a falling-down place in the foothills of the San Franciscos who'd thrown airy punches that didn't connect after Bill took away the axe handle the old man had been trying to bash his skull with.

When he finished his job and dropped off the flatbed at Carew's dealership on the other end of town, Bill stopped off at the pool hall for a couple of cold beers to calm his frazzled soul before driving on to Mickey's to pick up his father.

His elbow nearly caught Lena in the ribs as he downshifted his wobbly truck before the road whipped like a serpent's tail around the next bend. She rocked against Bill Chivers and could smell the heat on him, the dry sweat. The tires, smooth as rubber bands, bumped along the edge of the steep and brittle mountain road, rutted by snowmelt, and the cramped cab shook like something palsied and about to bust. She pushed away from him and moved closer to Charlie, who slept on the soft folds of his arm as it hung across the open window. His lips were parted and his breath whistled through his nose, and she could smell an exhalation of the piñon nuts he'd been chewing, woody and sweet in the still air of the cab. She dug her haunch into the cracked seat, unable to sleep or rest. The smell of her own body was making her sick.

Burr slept in the truck bed with a pair of spotted mutts, Ev and Chester, curling up with the dogs on a mound of burlap sacks filled with corn and alfalfa molasses that Bill was hauling first thing in the morning to Joseph City. The tarp above and around him flapped and snapped, but he never woke up, snug in the fermented warmth of grain and sugar, cushioned by dogflesh that smelled faintly of dirt and old manure.

Above Flagstaff, the steep and rocky hills were bare except for bristlecone pines corkscrewing out of the unforgiving ground, their ancient limbs gnarled as dwarves. The shaggy peaks of the San Francisco Mountains softened in the hazy afternoon sky. Lena could hear the changes in Bill's engine as the hills flattened and wide expanses of alpine meadow spread out on either side of the road.

"Mule deer," Bill said suddenly, pointing at where they grazed in the green-and-brown grass. These were the first words Bill had spoken since pulling away from the diner, and they startled Charlie out of his sleep.

He sat up blinking. "What's that?"

"I was showing the lady the mule deer."

Lena had recognized Bill immediately when he came to pick them up at Mickey's. He had the same big bones and big head as his father, not quite bald yet but getting there; and both men, without asking for it, filled whatever space they occupied. There was a distance between them, a gap as defining as the curved field of resistance between two magnets.

"Shot an elk in this meadow last winter," said the son.

"Did you?" asked the father.

"Big buck. Took two shots to bring him down."

"Miss him the first time?"

"Nope. Hit him twice in the head."

"One shot should've done it."

"Didn't."

Bill pulled his dungarees up and scratched where his work boot chafed his shin.

Charlie had his face turned away, watching the meadow drift by the window. Lena tried to shift her weight but her leg was asleep, and she gave up any thought of comfort.

"How big was this elk?" Charlie finally said.

"Had a rack on him wide as a hay rake. That big. And he was winter fat. I couldn't even budge him, had to cut him up where he fell. Took six trips through the snow to carry all that meat down to my truck."

Charlie turned toward him. "You save the rack?"

"Sold it."

"Too bad."

"Got some meat left. Betty salted it away. Says it's good with eggs if you're hungry. Good almost anytime, you ask me."

"Would've liked to have seen that rack."

Bill held his tongue. Lena didn't hear contempt or bitterness in Charlie's voice, only something unresolved.

"And your mother," he added, "sure would've liked these mountains."

"She get the pictures I sent?"

"Propped them up on her bureau." Charlie refitted the Stetson on his sun-freckled scalp and put his hands on his knees. "I got them now."

Lena looked down at those big hands, scarred and toughened by years of work.

Bill bent forward and glanced past Lena so he could see his father, who was staring ahead, riding out the bumps in the road, his eyes focused on the mountains that bolted skyward in the distance.

"Wish she could see it like I'm seeing it now," Charlie said.

"So do I," Bill answered.

Lena relaxed in the sudden quiet, her body cool in the dry air, the altitude making her almost giddy. She shut her eyes, settling back and thinking about Burr and Frank and her own parents, wishing she could laugh but knowing it wasn't funny, this glue of disappointment that held families together despite every expectation, the things left unsaid and the unspeakable.

The air was transparent, so clear it broke her heart. She opened her eyes and said, "So do I."

When Bill downshifted into second gear and turned onto a long dirt road bordered by Douglas fir, Burr woke up and watched the tall trees fan by. Holding on to the rusted frame where the canvas tarp was tied back, he spotted a red-tailed squirrel foraging for loose seeds in the chambered husks of fallen cones. Then the road dipped into the muddy wash of a seasonal creek, and he saw a bloated dead cow lying on its side, legs sticking straight out, its neck garroted between two strands of barbed wire from a snapped fence post. Four turkey buzzards pecked and rested over the corpse, taking their time under an afternoon sun still high above the shredded clouds.

The dirt road broke into an open meadow vibrant with Arizona bugbane, the yellow flowers luminous as gold dust, following a fence line to a windbreak of aspens. Behind the trees the Chivers ranch house was two-storied and weathered gray, with a covered porch along three sides. A jumble of sheds and outbuildings stood where they were needed for chickens, hay and equipment.

Bill pulled the truck up front and Burr heard a thumping on the porch and saw a girl sail over the railing in a cotton dress, her legs tucked and red hair flaming upward. She hit the ground running and jumped into Charlie's arms. He flung her high, and Burr heard her giggle and noticed the freckles on her arms and legs, copper blotches as round and shiny as new pennies.

Sarah Chivers was Burr's age. When Bill introduced her, the girl was hanging upside down from her grandfather's shoulders, a little chimpanzee, her long red hair brushing the ground. She smiled at Burr, who couldn't get over her freckles—not pale and worn like Bill and Charlie's, but bright, almost alive, like something that had crawled onto her that morning and decided to stay. They ran into her hair and under the neckline of her dress, and Burr thought they were probably warm, maybe even hot to the touch, and he stared at a scratch that ran down her arm, connecting the freckles into a fractured A, or the steeple of a church, and at that moment Sarah was the prettiest girl he'd ever seen, even as she stuck her tongue out at him, squeezing it, tiny bubbles and all, through the gap of her missing front teeth.

Betty Chivers stood on the top step, arms crossed and barefoot like her daughter. She was young, younger than Lena, but the skin around her eyes and nose were chafed and her long hair, paler than her skin, was pulled back from her scalp in a ponytail of dying wheat. Her arms were stringy and strong, and her knuckles were red and blistered, her fingernails worn into yellow nubs. But her figure was still soft and girlish, and she scratched at a bloody mosquito bite on her calf with the nail of her big toe. Her dress was cut from the same cheap material as Sarah's, hand-stitched, no more complicated than a potato sack, and tied around the middle was an apron with a faded map of Texas on the front, the letters spelled out with a cowboy's lariat.

"Supper'll be ready soon," she announced.

Sarah grabbed her grandfather's forearm and twisted herself into an awkward somersault, landing on her rear end but bouncing to her feet as if she were made of rubber, then grabbed Burr's wrist and dug her bare feet in the dirt and pivoted toward the barn.

"Sarah!" her mother called.

Sarah ignored her and started running, with Burr alongside.

"Soon, I said!"

They were walking now, along a creek bed that had been dry for years. Ev and Chester ran up ahead, scampering in and out of the ravine, their swishing tails rustling the dead stalks of cattails. The children followed a row of new telephone poles, still oily with creosote, that ran for half a mile to the Flagstaff road, stepping carefully on the shadows of the double row of sagging telephone lines hanging above them, side by side, one foot in front of the other, like high-wire aerialists. Burr was barefoot, too, his laces tied together and the shoes slung over his shoulder. He couldn't keep his eyes off the freckles that covered Sarah's feet.

"I had a cat last year. Took her out of the barn when she was about to have kittens. She was tiny, pretty much a kitten herself, all bony except for a belly full of little ones you could see rolling around when she sat still. So I took her in and fed her table scraps and let her sleep on my pillow, and I named her Pretty 'cause she woulda been if she wasn't so darn skinny. You ever have a cat?"

"No. I like dogs better."

"You would."

When the sun went down the shadows of telephone lines vanished and they walked freely, the cool dust they kicked up feeling good underfoot.

"There's a big dip back in the last pasture behind the barn that fills up when the snow melts in the spring and it gets full of frogs. I catch as many as I can until it dries up in the summer and they all disappear. Never could figure out where they went."

"In the mud."

"That's stupid." Sarah jerked Burr to a stop and squatted in the road. She tucked her dress above her knees and looked up. When she squinted, the freckles around her eyes collected into a mask. "You ever see a hawk dive so fast for a snake it ran itself right into the ground, dead?"

"Nope."

"Me neither."

She held on to his hand as she peed in a neat, steady stream. Burr looked down and couldn't see anything except the thin, silvery line that inched along the dry ground. Sarah sighed, squatting there, and looked over the yellow meadow.

"We got Indians here. Lots of them."

"We got Indians in Oklahoma, too."

"Not Navajos."

"No."

"I didn't think so." Sarah rubbed her nose and sneezed. "Navajos and Hopis, that's what we got."

"Chickasaw for us."

She stood up and let her dress fall back around her knees, then cocked her head and stared him straight in the eye.

"Chickasaw? Sounds like a kinda bird."

"It's an Indian."

"If you say so."

Chester and Ev came bounding up from the ravine and sniffed at the blotch of urine at Sarah's feet, and when Ev put his paw in it, she kicked him. "Shoo! Shoo, you filthy dogs!"

The children turned around and headed back to the house. The sun had fallen behind the tall mountains that ringed the valley, and the orange glow on the ridges brightened like Sarah's hair.

Betty had a huge cast-iron stew pot going on the stove and was scraping carrots, parsnips and onions, still clingy with dirt from the garden, when Lena entered the kitchen through the back door.

"Anything I can do?"

"Nothing needs doing." Betty sniffed, her eyes and nose running from dust-blown alfalfa and snakeweed, then angled a long fork into the pot and pulled out the hen. Lena stood in the doorway and watched her slice the rind of fat away from the meat and separate it from the bone before cutting the stringy flesh into smaller pieces and shoveling it all back into the pot.

Bill came into the kitchen from the hallway and took down a glass from the papered shelf over the counter where Betty worked. He bent over his wife so as not to disturb her, leaving a space between them, a space Lena recognized, and turned on the tap at the deep porcelain sink.

"I just had Joe Kenny on the telephone," he said to Lena. "Said he'd be happy to drive you and the boy to Nevada."

"Thanks, Bill."

The water fizzled in the glass, well water, murky with minerals that disappeared after Bill took a long gulp. "He's going anyway. Wife of his, Selma, makes lingerie out of the house. Pretty stuff, ain't that right, Betty?"

"Don't wear lingerie."

Their backs were almost touching, but not quite.

"There's a shop they cater to in Las Vegas, small, but it's worth the gas money, so Joe says anyway. It's a good business they got. Making ends meet in these times, more so maybe, judging by those colored ties Joe fancies."

Lena smiled. "I don't mind a man in a loud tie. We're just happy for the ride."

Bill poured himself another glass of water as Betty pushed the carrot tops into a tin bucket for the chickens.

"Said he'd pick you up here, seeing as how I got to haul feed to Joseph City and can't just leave you on the road. Joe's got a smooth mouth, so watch yourself."

"I've heard it all before."

"I suspect most women have, except maybe Selma." Bill grinned at Betty, who kept her back to him as she stirred the big pot. "You'll be all right, though. Joe may have a lazy eye and a sweet line, but he's got a nice Chrysler." He shuffled closer to Betty, trying to get a look at her face. "Anything I can do, honey?"

Betty put her hands flat on the wooden counter and Lena saw the muscles bunch up in her neck. They stayed that way, until she rolled her shoulders and started working again. "Nothing needs doing."

. . .

Lena added some bath oil under the rushing tap, and as the tub filled she tied up her hair and took off her clothes in front of the open window. She hurriedly hung her soiled dress on a hook over the mirror so she wouldn't be tempted to look at herself, and then, as the water steamed and the smell of lilacs grew stronger, she lowered her grateful limbs into it.

Tentatively, she raised her toes out of the water. Three weeks ago she'd polished the nails a crimson red, deep and bloodrich, knowing that Frank, who was on the road, would like the lurid brilliance of it, but not knowing that while she sat there in her bedroom with the cotton balls between her toes, blowing on the polish and listening to Ruth Etting on the radio, the surprise was going to be hers. The color was almost worn off now, shrunken and cracked around her cuticles, miniature red mosaics waiting to be redone. She placed both feet against the far edge of the tub and raised her legs out of the water. Droplets adhered to the bath oil that coated her skin, running in drowsy rivulets back into the tub. Her legs above the knee were firm and brown, and she could see the indentation of muscle on the inside of her thigh. She spread them further and examined her calves, admiring the slender line from knee to ankle, and the pink ribbon scarring her left leg. Lena knew she was vain about her legs, but thought it was a harmless indulgence, as fleeting as a sideways glance in a storefront window, or an appreciative gleam in a man's eyes. She spread her knees until they touched the cold rim of the tub, and looked at her pubic hair, brown and thick and wavy in the cloudy water. Lena reached down and pulled her fingers through its pondweed tangliness and back up to her stomach, the flatness of her skin oily and smooth, then slowly traced the gentle wing of her pelvic bone and ran her fingertips down her leg and up again, following the hard, giving tendon that ran along the inside of her hip. She let her hand rest there, kneading herself, floating, and she remembered how Frank used to touch her with such kindness and intent, and her fingers lingered until she shivered, the water suddenly cold.

She climbed out of the bathtub and wrapped herself in the towel that Betty had left out for her. Nubby and thin, it quickly absorbed the moisture from her skin. She could hear people moving below her, their feet heavy and deliberate as they set the table in the large kitchen. The unnecessary thud of plates and glasses was unmistakable, and silverware clanged together like crossed swords.

"I don't have a choice."

"More'n me!"

"He's my father!"

"He ain't mine."

"Your daddy's dead."

Lena dried her hair and walked softly to the window. Charlie was sitting on the porch step below her with his abalone-shell penknife in hand, whittling a chunk of alder wood, aiming the beige shavings into the upturned Stetson between his knees.

"You out hauling hay all day or working for the bank, and me turning cows out in the morning and bringing them in at dark, running this place and keeping that little girl out of trouble—and now I get this."

"What the hell does that mean?"

"Being here. Alone. Just me and her and him, while you're out in that damn truck, getting the run of the world."

"You don't think I'd rather be here?"

"No, goddammit, 'cause I don't!"

The sudden silence seemed to suck all the air out of the house. Lena trembled when the door slammed, and Charlie, except for his hand guiding the penknife, never moved. She heard Bill start up the truck at the side of the house, and dust rose in the yard as he swung it around to the barn. Lena stared out the window at the enclosing mountains, flinty in this dusky light, the moon rising behind them, tinting the wavering clouds above them lavender and green, incandescent as the inside of a flame. It was as if the world were about to catch fire.

Sarah's room was in the upstairs corner of the house, and her bed was angled under the pitched roof between the two windows that were open to the breeze. A three-quarter moon burned in the sky, and she and Burr sat at the windowsill watching Ev and Chester snap at fireflies in the yard below, laughing as the dogs twisted and flew through the night air like goblins, their teeth bared and shiny. When the fireflies drifted upward from the branches of the alder tree in the front yard, the children gazed at the intermittent flare. Their mothers turned off the light at nine and they got ready for bed, giggling at each other and pointing at the underwear they slept in, glowing white in the cool moonlight. After climbing under the covers, Burr positioned himself behind her, unable to take his eyes off her dappled skin, counting the multitude of freckles on her back, losing track and starting over, and he fell asleep counting them, his hand on her spine as they began to breathe together and the night grew darker and fireflies blinked outside the window, drifting through the branches like sparks or dying embers.

*I*n the early evening, when the sun simmered in a white sky over the wind-seared farmland east of Kearney, Nebraska, he passed a handmade sign propped up against a half-buried fence row whose faded yellow letters read: SAUSAGES FOR SALE. A hundred yards ahead an old Dodge coupe was parked on the roadside, powdered gray with drought-stricken soil that refused to produce corn or wheat. Dark smoke billowed out of a capped metal pipe poking through the roof of the car, and another hand-painted sign, SAUSAGES HERE — COOKED OR PACKAGED, was leaning against the rear fender. Filius had the windows rolled down to circulate the unbreathable air, and the sudden aroma of spiced meat grilling on a wood fire caused his mouth to fill up with spit. He couldn't remember the last time he'd eaten, so he eased his foot down onto the brake pedal.

A young man wearing a blue work shirt was sitting on a small wooden crate by the side of the Dodge, chipping a thick length of dried hickory with a hand axe, swinging it steadily with his right and only arm. He held the wood upright between his feet, keeping it balanced with the heels of his round-toed boots. His empty left sleeve was neatly pinned up at the shoulder, and the right was rolled above his elbow.

He squinted up at Filius. "Hungry, mister?"

He spoke in a clipped drawl that sounded Midwest German. Filius smiled.

"Yes, I am."

"Good." He smiled back over the shoulder of his missing arm, his thin face retracting from his gleaming white teeth. "Got sausage cooking. Done by now, I think."

He stuck the blade of the hand axe into what was left of the log and gestured to the rear end of the Dodge. "Come on inside."

The backseat had been removed and a straw mattress was rolled out under the rear window. Burlap sacks hung from an iron rod, curtaining off the front seat, against which sat a small cast-iron stove where three sausages cooked slowly on the griddle. A coffeepot and a couple of pans hung from hooks that studded the car's headliner around the vent pipe welded to the roof. Filius grabbed the open door handle, climbed inside, and sat on the edge of the mattress. A girlie magazine poked out from under the pillow, a back issue of *Paris Nights*, the cover illustrated with a laughing woman in sheer bra and panties being chased by a fez-topped monkey.

The man kneeled in front of the griddle and rolled the sausages with the palm of his hand. "Beef with pepper. Sound good?"

"Yes."

"Me, too." He pulled open a drawer underneath the wood box and took out a brown paper sack and two mason jars. Swiveling on worn heels, he put the sack on a little footstool and took out two crusty rolls, cutting them open with a penknife attached to his belt by a loop of rawhide. He speared a sausage and laid it in the yeasty cleavage of the first roll, letting the soft insides soak up the amber grease. Then he set it aside and opened the mason jars—the car filling with a pungent tang of sauerkraut and homemade mustard strong enough to keep the flies away.

He tapped each jar with his penknife and looked at Filius. "Heading west?"

"Yes."

"Stupid question, but I always ask. Like birds flying in the sky. Every car is pointed in the same direction. California?" He poured water from a canteen into a jelly jar and handed it to Filius.

"Nevada."

"Ah, the dam."

Filius nodded and took a sip. The water was warm and tasted slightly of vinegar.

"You important?"

"I'm an engineer."

"And you already have this job?"

"Yes.

"Just like me." He shuffled over and parted the curtains to the front seat, reaching over to flip the key and turn on the radio, fiddling with the knob until he picked up a polka band broadcast out of Lincoln. As the twin accordions pumped and glided, he caught Filius examining the empty sleeve pinned to his shoulder.

"This? Happened right after the war. Right after the National Security League came to Hastings. They told us we were not allowed to speak German anymore. We argued, of course, and when Carl Ringel complained they took him away. Then they burned down Ott's Bakery and Ott's house. And when Peter Samms screamed *Scheisse!*" after a bale of hay fell from his wagon outside Bob Greene's stockyard, Bob came out of the barn and shot Pete's draft horse between the eyes and beat old Pete with his pistol butt until his arm was tired. My papa lost his job at Kid Cigar Company. In school they ripped up our history books. It was a bad year. Some folks left town, thinking maybe it was better someplace else. It wasn't. My two aunts, they went to Buffalo, New York, and stuck it out. The Pragers, we stayed. Papa was firm. Hastings was our home. It was our right to be here, he said, and they couldn't make us leave. So we suffered sticks and stones and we never left. Of course, except my arm."

Joe Prager had been eleven when the four men chased him through Miller's field late one afternoon in November. It had rained that morning, and the sky was rippled with black-bottomed clouds. A translucent skin of ice covered the gravelly road leading up to Miller's farmhouse, and Prager listened to it crack beneath his shoes as he delivered a basket of goose eggs to the back door.

He stepped up to the door and looked through the window at the men sitting around the kitchen table. Kerosene lamps tainted the room with yellow light. The men were passing around a bottle of Hiram Walker and eating sliced chicken sandwiches and sour pickles out of a crock.

Mr. Miller looked up from the head of the table, his face so red the deep wrinkles in his brow seemed etched in blood. "What?"

Joe held the basket up to the window.

"I said what, boy!"

"Eggs.

"Leave the goddamn eggs, you goddamn imbecile!"

Joe heard the men laughing as he put the basket down outside the door.

"Stinkin' hiney," one of them said.

Heavy snow started to fall. Joe kept his mouth shut and walked away from the Miller farmhouse, the cold air sharp against his skin. Then he heard the kitchen door open behind him and the men's curses—"Kraut!" and "Hiney!"—carried around him in the wind. He heard Mr. Miller grunt and the bottle of Hiram Walker, still half full, somersaulted past his head and landed in a grassy clot of dirt, unbroken. Prager picked it up, watching the gold liquid slosh around inside. Then he turned to face the four men giggling drunkenly on the kitchen porch, and smashed the bottle to pieces.

He ran in earnest then, his feet already moving before the thought of escape entered his mind. The men charged after him, in sweaters and flannels and shirtsleeves, and one of them fell and skinned his naked forearm. His scream carried through the whipping snow, and Prager ran faster, sliding on the ice, allowing momentum to carry him down the hill, away from the bellowed "shit"s and "sonofabitch"s. He ran as fast as he could but his pursuers didn't fall back. He could hear the crunch of their heavy shoes and the harshness of their breath, and knew they would catch him. It was only the running that counted now, the getting away. And in the moment he took to glance over his shoulder, he hit the sagging strands of barbed wire that pulled him down. Stunned, barely aware of the fine drops of blood that bubbled out of his wirepricked skin, he felt only the snow on his face and the coldness in the air. Prager tipped his head back and, seeing the men coming, tried to wrestle free, his heart beating in his ears, but his arm was caught. His jacket was ruined, and he knew his mother would be mad because it was a gift from the two aunts. He pulled harder and kicked violently at the barbed wire, and it ensnared his legs and his other arm, coiling around him until he was hanging off the ground, trussed and floating, between two fence posts. In the moonlight he saw the ripped sleeve and the shredded arm, black and moist, and in his flesh the studded barbs glittered like jewelry. Mr. Miller and his cousins circled him, the snow bleaching their shoulders and hair. Prager held still while they stared at him, and the blood that rose in his mouth tasted rusty. He was too scared to scream, but he heard a scream anyway, and smelled vomit and whiskey before he passed out and woke up in the hospital three days later.

"One hundred and fifty stitches to hold me together. Of course, they couldn't save the arm." He flicked the empty sleeve with his finger, and a black kitten climbed out from under the front seat and jumped in his lap.

"What happened to the men?"

Joe Prager held the kitten to his chest and let it lick his greasy fingers. He grinned and looked up, and for the first time Filius saw the long thin scar that ran down his neck and under his shirt.

"The men. The men carried me to the hospital and saved my life. They are heroes, yes?"

Just after dark Filius stopped at a closed gas station west of Willow Island and knocked on the door of the little house out back. A young woman cloaked in a man's bathrobe answered the door, her brown hair tangled, and grumpily shuffled over to the single pump in unlaced boots, filling the tank and charging an extra nickel for the inconvenience. He took the bridge crossing at Maxwell and followed the Platte River south toward Colorado. The water was the only thing moving in this featureless terrain, and the heat, oppressive in its stillness, lingered until the gray hours of dawn. Outside of Paxton he stopped to stretch his legs and fill up the canvas water bag strapped over his radiator, then wandered in the clear moonlight through a prairie dog village that ran alongside the highway. Back at the car he took his binoculars from the satchel on the front seat and scanned the northern horizon, a black-on-black flatness of sky and land. Continuing west, Filius passed a few derelict vehicles on the side of the road, humped on flat tires, windshields cracked and doors hanging open. He saw signs for Ogallala and Brule, towns named for Sioux tribes that had burned the wagons of the Mormons and Swedes, ranchers and freight haulers who had followed rutted roads from the Missouri River and claimed this territory as their own. Battles raged from Julesburg to Ash Hollow, ruthless skirmishes that led to random violence and redemptive slaughter, a bloody two-handed scythe wielded back and forth until the Indians were forced into reservations, remembered mostly in the names of the cow towns and river hamlets hammered together from milled wood floated on barges down the South Fork of the Platte, paid for by capitalist profiteers and visionaries who sat up late at night, wet with whiskey and whores, in the Stockyard Hotel in Omaha.

Near the Colorado border, the sky began to pale around the edges. When the sun came up he saw the Pawnee Buttes rising over the shortgrass prairie to the north. Half an hour later, at the intersection of Highway 71, he pulled into the horseshoe parking lot of the Little Black Bear Motor Court, twelve bungalows shaded by a stand of blackjack pine along a dry streambed. An old man in a frayed white shirt pushed himself off his rocking chair on the porch of bungalow 1 and led him across a bed of crackly pine needles to number 8.

"Hotter'n matchsticks, ain't it?"

"Yes, it's hot."

"Hotter'n red sauce, surely."

They passed two girls tossing a stick just out of reach of a yelping Doberman mutt short-chained to the bumper of a Plymouth flatbed. When the old man cussed them the children scattered, and the dog lay down next to the tire, panting horribly, its muzzle stringy with spit.

Filius opened the door to the damp bungalow. The slash of sunlight that followed him inside was stormy with dust, and the paneled room smelled of cherry tobacco. He pulled the curtains shut and sat on the edge of the bed, overcome by sudden fatigue. It was eight o'clock in the morning and he had been driving for almost twenty-four hours. He undressed in the dark and stepped into the shower stall. The tepid spray, smelling of sulfur, washed the dust into brown swirls around his feet.

He dried himself with a thin towel and pulled the cotton spread off the bed. Naked, he collapsed on the muslin sheets that covered the horsehair mattress. He turned his face to the wall and fell asleep, oblivious to the sound of cars pulling in and out of the parking lot and the malicious glee of the three children as they resumed tormenting the growling Doberman mutt just outside his window.

In his dream he remembered the water. It was August of last year, and they were on Lake Michigan, thirty miles southwest of the Manitou Islands, heading back to Whitefish Bay in another summer squall, a stiff wind behind their thirty-foot sloop. The last two days had been the same—warm and breezy, with rain and sun fighting for dominance throughout the day—and Filius didn't worry much about the hard line of black clouds to the north. His navigational christening had come in this kind of weather, crewing on Tom Petersmith's gaff-headed schooner in the Chicago–Mackinac race five summers in a row, from 1922 to 1926. In seventy-mile-an-hour winds and blinding rains, half the boats turned back at Charlevoix, but never Petersmith and Poe; they won only twice but always finished. And on this trip, he thought, what they'd remember is wind and rain, all three of them, and by tomorrow evening, their vacation over, they'd be back in Chicago, sunburned and sore.

Filius was at the tiller and Addie sat next to him, wearing a pair of his white gabardine pants rolled up above her ankles, busy sewing a new grommet into the canvas tarp stretched along the wooden seat. She had designed the tarp herself, and when they anchored at the end of the day she would rig it over the boom to protect the cabin from the sun. She leaned against his raised knees as the boat dipped into a gentle trough, careful with the long metal needle she held in her hand, and Filius loved the pressure and weight of her body against his. He turned to check on his son, Ray, eight years old and sitting shirtless at the stern, trolling for lake trout. He fed line through the ferrules of the tall rod secure in its brass seat over the transom, listening to the clicks on the reel to gauge the depth, fishing a wobbly spoon at seventy feet like Sedge Wells had told him that morning at Baker's Landing on South Manitou. Sedge had helped him land a ten-pound coho salmon the day before, and they'd cooked the steaks over a wood fire that night and saved the rest for breakfast. Filius studied the boy's skinny back, brown with freckles after two weeks of sailing, and settled on the red mark just below the ribs. A week before, Filius had held Ray in his arms as Sedge extracted a fishhook with a pair of forceps he kept in his tackle box. While Sedge calmly probed his bleeding skin for the barb, Filius felt his son's muscles tense and was acutely aware of the squirming, fragile skeleton underneath, and in those shuddering moments it was as if Ray was a baby again and he himself was brimming once more with wonderment and concern. He held him tighter than necessary because he knew this was the first of many such ordeals, innocent and inevitable, and that the pain would be shared between father and son for the rest of their lives.

The wind gusted and the tiller hardened beneath his hand. He prodded the boat to the wind, sailing a little higher, and signaled Addie to tighten the jib. She put down her needle and tarp to kneel beside him, giving the sheet a strong pull before cleating it, and they moved through the water without losing speed.

Settling back on the seat, she pointed to the raggedy mass of clouds accumulating overhead. "It's going to rain again."

Filius glanced windward and saw dark splotches on the water. They were about four hours out of Sturgeon Bay, and he knew they would never beat the storm. "We've got good speed."

"I know. You always sail like you're in a race."

She was beautiful, full of sun and good humor, and he loved her best when she was this happy.

"We may want to reef the main."

"Now?"

"Only if the wind picks up."

"Good. I'm tired." She leaned against Filius and shut her eyes.

He put his arm around her, his other hand steady on the tiller, and studied the mainsail and the telltales stretched taut in the wind. The rain started slowly, moving over the bow and cabin. He looked down and saw it popping off the deck boards and the back of his hand holding the tiller. A shadow moved over him and the drops of rain became mixed with blood that fell thickly on his wrist, scarlet drops turning pink with skydriven water.

Rain and blood.

And the storm was upon them.

He willed himself awake and lay there naked, eyes wide open, outlined on the sheets by the sweat that poured off his body. He would take another shower and get back on the road, having slept for less than an hour.

*L*ew Beck stood on the small balcony and looked over the knot of streets below him, the narrow roadways partially obscured by the blasted tops of palm trees and bent-back eucalyptus. Beyond the Moorish rooftops and Turkish minarets of the cramped apartment houses on these staggered slopes above Franklin Avenue, he could hear the traffic on Hollywood Boulevard.

Eight years before, when he was twenty, Speed Owens had gotten him a construction job on a new house just east of Laurel Canyon. In those days the Hollywood Hills were all scrub brush and dirt, with only a few dozen monstrous and ornate houses built on the blighted landscape, most of them mansions for the movie stars who reigned silently in dark theaters across the country, these beautiful men and women with black eyes and black lips, flamboyant and glamorous as the houses they built in styles chosen with reckless petulance—Spanish next to Tudor next to French Normandy. And the house that Lew worked on was the strangest of all. Commissioned by a Los Angeles dentist, with an exterior of ornamental concrete blocks, the house looked to Lew like a mausoleum or a power plant, and he and Speed laughed as they hauled concrete blocks up the hill in the summer heat, their backs and arms as brown as Egyptian slaves. None of this, however, was humorous to the dentist, Dr. Storer, increasingly anxious about construction delays and the fitful attention of the architect's son, who was distracted by the various half-completed projects his father had abandoned to his care. But Lew was being paid by the day and didn't care how long it took. He helped patch the roof when the rains came, and stayed on the job until it was completed in 1924. Still, he felt sorry for the dentist, not because his budget was shot and his roof would always leak, but because he would actually have to live in it once it was finished.

That year was the last time Lew saw his parents. It was March, and he'd begged off, feigning sickness, when Speed and two other buddies pulled up at an unmarked Negro whorehouse on the corner of Adams. Speed believed him since he knew Lew had a favorite at the house, a dark girl named Teeny who shaved her body from head to toe every Wednesday and liked to straddle Lew and stroke his penis with her curved tongue while he explored the prickliness of her hinterparts.

After dropping them off, Lew borrowed Speed's Chevy coupe, but instead of returning to the apartment they shared in Echo Park, he headed downtown and crossed the Seventh Street Bridge into Boyle Heights, slowly touring the old neighborhood, from Brooklyn Avenue to Clarence Street and the block where his parents lived in a Victorian unchanged since his childhood. He parked out front and stared up at the familiar windows. His mother and father were sitting in the front parlor with Mr. and Mrs. Kipl, drinking coffee from small china cups that had traveled across the ocean in a wooden box packed with straw, every crack a precious story stained with sixty years of bitter tea. The Beckmans and the Kipls sat around the mahogany table and picked at the honey sponge cake or poppy seed cake or *mandelbrot*, talking and eating at the same time, listening to Al Jolson or the *RCA Musical Hour* on the radio as they did every Friday night at eight o'clock. His mother's back was to him, rocking in the chair closest to the window. He heard Mrs. Kipl laugh, her mouth full of cake, as her husband no doubt wiped at the splatter of coffee he'd spilled on his white shirt, and his father, fastidious as ever with a napkin stuck in his starched collar, hid his own smiling mouth with an open hand. They filled their stomachs and enjoyed themselves while their forgotten son and godson witnessed how cheerfully life went on without him. He sat there for a half hour, long enough for a policeman walking his beat to pause at the corner, light a cigarette and take note of the Chevy with suspicion. When his mother rose and the silver-plated coffeepot was passed around again, Lew pulled away from the curb and followed the same streets he'd ridden by bicycle years ago as his father's delivery boy. When he turned onto Soto, he reached under the seat where he and Speed stashed the tools they'd pilfered from the construction site. His fingers traced a wrench and wire cutters before he found the wooden-handled hammer he knew was there. Driving by Beckman's Kosher Meats without slowing down, he threw the hammer with all his might.

One of the front windows exploded and the brightly painted Star of David turned to gold dust before his eyes, the sound of shattered glass ringing in his ears as he sped away.

Mary Carsey stepped onto the balcony carrying a copper tray and two cold bottles of beer. "Thirsty, Lew?" She smiled, and he saw the smudges of fresh lipstick on her two front teeth.

Lew liked that she fixed herself up in an attempt to please him, a stranger, but then he turned away to look back out at the city, drinking the bitter beer right out of the bottle, and after a moment or two, Mary drifted back inside.

When he'd come back to California three years later, he found work in Santa Barbara as a driver for Nancy Campbell, widow of a wealthy Englishman, a retired colonel who'd died the year before. Mrs. Colonel Campbell, as she was called by the people in her employ, had completed the dream house they'd envisioned over the lagoon on the Goleta Slough, and from these large, airy rooms with uninterrupted views of the Pacific, she entertained with the brilliance the colonel had so admired when he met her in Chicago the year America entered the Great War.

It was Lew's job to pick up weekend guests at the airport or the rail station downtown in the Jordan Blue Boy convertible that had been shipped from Cleveland to Santa Barbara only two days before he was hired. It was an extravagant, ostentatious car, perfect for the tycoons with their mistresses and golf clubs that he transported along the ocean road to the adobe estate above the Goleta lagoon. Lew even enjoyed wearing the burgundy cap and gloves Mrs. Colonel Campbell insisted he wear when collecting the various Rockefellers or Carnegies from their private railway cars, those putty-faced New Yorkers who traveled with at least three valets. And he especially liked ferrying around the Hollywood dignitaries who traveled in pairs—Garbo and Lubitsch, Barrymore and Swanson—but always split up later in the evening, engaging Lew as a coconspirator as he drove them to some after-hours rendezvous in a Montecito cabana or Miramar bungalow—or if nothing else was available, in the backseat of the Jordon Blue Boy, while the driver treated himself to a walk and a cigarette on a beachfront cul-de-sac. His favorite passenger, though, was Jacqueline Logan, the young actress who had just played Mary Magdalene in Cecil B. De Mille's *King of Kings*. On the way to the Campbell estate one night, she demanded that Lew pull over at the lagoon so she could see the famous white swans that swam among the giant lily pads. And then Miss Logan, wearing a thin-strapped white dress that slipped off her shoulders and stayed there, chased the swans like a child, her breasts cherry-tipped and firm. Certain now that her audience was wholly captivated, she stripped down to her underwear, a thin Chinese watered silk ensemble, and swam with the frightened birds as if Lew were a eunuch in turban and loincloth and she were queen of the Nile.

It was a good job but Lew grew bored. After dropping Sinclair Lewis at the train station on a Monday afternoon—the man just as tight-lipped and sullen as he'd been when Lew picked him up the night before—he drove back to the estate and gave Mrs. Colonel Campbell notice. He left Santa Barbara with a suitcase and a pocketful of cash, and the moment he stepped outside the Campbell gates and put his thumb out, a big Dodge pulled over and gave him a ride all the way to Los Angeles.

It was just getting dark when Lew got out on Pico Boulevard and entered a small café, where he ordered the special, baked noodles with ham and cheese, and a cup of coffee. He left a cigarette burning in the ashtray before dialing the never-forgotten number on Clarence Street from a phone booth in the back of the room.

"Hello," his mother said.

It was the voice she used with customers, her American voice, filtered through years of practice but still straining at the basics, being especially careful not to bite down too hard when a word began with *ch*. Like everyone else from her generation, she still sprinkled her conversations with the odds and ends of the old language, and whenever the neighborhood women gathered in Hollenbeck Park or around the big kitchen table at the synagogue on Whittier Boulevard, they found comfort in this coded shorthand of shrugs and Yiddish that sounded offensive, even sinister, to those who didn't understand it.

"Hello," she said again.

Lew could see her on the phone in the parlor, alone, Isadore still wrapping chicken parts for Sam Glickman and Irving Stoll, the tailor and haberdasher whose shops were down the street and never closed until their last customers were satisfied. Isadore didn't mind this special service, not when he could talk politics and sip a glass of plum brandy with the two old bachelors, knowing his own dinner was being kept warm on the stove and that his wife would wait patiently at home for as long as he needed her to.

"Hello?"

This time it was a question, not a greeting. Lew could hear the tentativeness in her voice, that Old World fear of the unknown—and now *he* was the unknown, this vanished son, this wandering Jew. Hearing himself breathing, he wondered if she could tell it was he from the palpitations of his lungs even as she stood alone in her parlor, frightened, with the smell of roast chicken heavy in the air.

He hung up.

At the small table inlaid with blue and orange tiles, Mary drank her beer out of a highball glass in small sips, and every time she refilled her glass the foamy head would run over her fingers and darken the paper napkin she used as a coaster. They were sitting in the recessed nook off the kitchen, where in the late afternoon sun spiked shadows of palm fronds bent around the walls. Lew could see the makeup drying in the creases on her face in this harsh light. He was right about her age—thirty-one, thirty-two—but he didn't care. He drank another beer and listened to her talk about visiting her sister in Ventura.

"Sherry's a good kid—younger than me but she doesn't look it. Not after two kids, both of them brats. Harry says he likes her packin' on the extra pounds, but I think that's just so she can't say nothin' about the fat hangin' over his own belt."

When she raised her glass Lew saw the veins running up the underside of her wrist, dark and blue with Spanish blood. Her arms were soft as a girl's, which Lew took as a good sign. Mary kept on talking and drinking, and he kept her glass full, nodding when appropriate, refusing to interrupt her account of recent events, offering to fetch the next bottle from the icebox in the kitchen, where four bottles were left, more than enough. He drank the cold beer from the bottle and she continued to sip from the glass until her eyes grew wet and her voice more exaggerated.

"Harry works for Sunkist, loadin' lemons and oranges onto freight cars at the packin' house down by the water. Tons of the stuff trucked in from the big orchards in Ojai and Fillmore. Course Harry doesn't actually load them cars himself, he's a supervisor. Other guys do the back bendin', just glad to have a job no matter how hard, stacking them crates high as a house, one after the other, each one weighing about forty pounds. Some of the fruit still has part of the branch attached, all thorny and sharp—bad cuts by lazy Japs and Chinamen, Harry says—and guys get scratched deep, and when some of that lemon juice gets in, it hurts like the dickens, but they hold their tongues 'cause Harry could give their job to the guys hangin' around the fence just waitin' for a chance. People always fightin' for work down at the train yard. Fistfights every five minutes, Harry says, practically set your watch by 'em. That's why they made him supervisor, 'cause he's big and strong and can take care of himself. Fights for his job, too. Comin' home with bruised knuckles or a bloody lip. Once a woman came to the door of Sherry's house on Kalorama Street when we was eatin' dinner—fried chicken and corn—and she's banging' on the door cussin' 'cause Harry broke her husband's wrist or arm or somethin' and now he can't work and they got four kids to feed, usin' language that would burn the hair off the back of your hand. But Harry just sat there and finished his corn on the cob while the two brats giggled and Sherry just stared at the Maxwell House wall calendar over my head. When Harry was done with the last of his iced tea he got up and called the police, who come in about two minutes and took that gal with 'em and we could still hear her screamin' until they turned off Main Street about three blocks away."

Mary drank some more beer and Lew filled her glass to within an inch of the top. "Doesn't sound like much of a vacation."

"Had its moments. Me and Sherry took the kids to the pier a few times, had sodas and roast beef sandwiches and sat on the sand even though it was too cold to swim, least for me. The two boys went in, of course, takin' turns tryin' to drown each other. They're eight and nine now, and if either one of 'em makes it to ten it'll be a miracle. If they ain't chasin' themselves with two-by-fours or throwin' rocks at each other's head, they're throwin' frogs against the side of the brick schoolhouse, seein' who could make the most stick. A couple of bad Indians, them two. But me and Sherry got caught up over those four or five days, baked pies, gossiped about her neighbors, girl stuff, while Buddy, my husband, went to the rocks at Point Mugu and fished all day in the ocean. Harry dropped him off at six on his way to Sunkist and picked him up at five, fishin' together that last hour, coming back to Sherry's with buckets of calico bass and halibut and mackerel. I never liked mackerel myself, too oily, until Sherry cooked it up like this old Japanese woman across the street showed her how, covered in salt and fried till it was crispy as pork rinds. It's good eatin', Lew, if you like mackerel."

"Where's Buddy now?"

"Still in Oxnard, fishing. He's got an extra day of vacation time, so he'll drive home first thing in the morning and maybe start work at noon. Me, I've got to be at work at eight a.m. My vacation is over."

"What do you do?"

"I work the counter at the Dutch Chocolate Shop downtown. Know it?"

"Yeah. What does Buddy do?"

"He's a salesman for the Fuller Paint Company. Same job for twelve years—and it's a good one, especially these days. Sees clients from San Bernardino to Bakersfield, on the road four days a week, but they give him a car and he gets two weeks off a year, while me, I only get one."

"So what do you do when Buddy's on the road?"

"Oh, I behave myself." She looked Lew right in the eye.

The beer had gone to her head and Lew couldn't be sure if she was telling the truth.

"You want some chocolate, Lew? I always got chocolate around."

"No thanks."

"Buddy says I eat too much chocolate, but I tell him it's part of my job and I like what I do. You sure?"

"Yeah. How about we split another beer?"

"No more for me, but I'll get you one."

"Thanks." He watched Mary walk into the kitchen, admiring the stockiness of her, the soft curves he could imagine under the clothes. When she stood in front of the open icebox and yawned, stretching her arms dramatically, Lew could see her breasts rise and fall under the whiteness of her blouse, and his eyes rested on the extra pounds over the waistband of her skirt.

"Bus rides make me sleepy," she said, coming back to the table with a bottle of beer and a church key she handed to Lew. "You're a little bit of a man, ain't you, Lew?"

He flipped the cap off the beer and it spun across the table until he slammed it dead with the palm of his hand.

"My Buddy's big—softer than he was when we got married, but big. Too many hours behind the wheel of a car, I guess, plus he's always got a big bag of salted cashews at his side, like me and chocolate. And Harry, forget about it. You could fit in Harry's pocket."

Lew gripped the bottle cap until the metal teeth bit into the rounded flesh beneath his thumb.

Mary sat down. "I know boys little as me, but you're the first man I ever met who's built like he stopped growin'. Nothin' wrong with being on the short side, mind you. My favorite cowboy star, Rex Bell, he come in the chocolate shop one afternoon without his hat and boots, and if he was any taller than you, you could measure it with a hair."

She put her hand on Lew's arm and he relaxed at her touch. The bottle cap rolled out of his hand, but the circular pink impression remained. "What about Buddy?"

"Buddy?"

"What's he going to say when he finds out I was here?"

"He's not going to. Besides, you're not going to be here that long."

Lew didn't want to be there. He didn't want to fuck Mary anymore. He wasn't sure what he wanted, but would stay until he figured it out. Mary kept her hand on his arm. He poured a little beer into her glass, then gulped thirstily from the bottle, and wasn't surprised when she lifted her glass and drank with him. Looking at her, he said, "Do you like watches?"

"I already got a watch."

Lew reached into the pocket of his jacket and pulled out a ladies' Benrus, small and elegant; four miniature diamonds studded the face of the gold dial, and the leather band was thin as a pencil stroke. Mary leaned closer while he turned it slowly in his hand, the diamond chips flashing in the slanted sunlight. "Do you have one like this?"

"It's pretty."

"That's not what I asked you."

She reached for the watch as Lew closed his fist around it, then settled back in her chair, eyes on the watch strap that dangled from his fist like a rat's tail.

"Do you have one like this?"

"No."

"Would you like it?"

"Yes, but Buddy'd ask too many questions."

"Don't show him."

"I'd have to wear it. Can't have a watch like that and not wear it."

"Tell him you found it."

"He'd never believe me. Like that time two years ago when he caught our neighbor peekin' through the bathroom window while I was doin' my business, and thinkin' I invited Mr. Lyons over instead of him just swingin' over the railing on his own free will. Buddy had a conniption. Made me go with him everywhere, travel in his paint-stinkin' car to those nothin' little towns like Buttonwillow and Perris, and I'd have to sit in that car while he sold paint to men who'd scratch their heads over off-white or cream white like they was solvin' the riddle of the Sphinx, and Buddy'd come back with his sales book all filled out and wouldn't say a word to me all day. Went on nearly a week and I almost lost my job, callin' in sick from wherever, sneezin' like I had a cold you had to pray over. No, he'd never believe me."

"Depends on how good you tell him." Lew opened his fist and displayed the gold face of the watch in the palm of his hand. "Depends on how smart he is."

Mary thought about it. She stared at the pretty watch and Lew could see her disassembling the puzzle pieces of Buddy's reactions and then putting them back together again. When she leaned forward on her elbow and opened her hand, he let the watch slip off his fingers. He had her now.

Until that morning, he'd been working in San Diego, driving an ice truck for the Goode Brothers out of National City. He worked the night shift, dropping off ice to the dozen or so speakeasies that operated behind darkened storefronts and apartment buildings up and down Broadway and Third. Moe Goode, the older brother, gave Lew two hundred dollars in ten-dollar bills to take care of the cops that would be waiting in bricked alleys or patrolling Broadway in slow-cruising Cadillacs, looking to be paid their share of shut-up money. Moe had warned him that they liked to strong-arm new drivers, but a ten-dollar bill pressed into a fat palm was all it took.

"It's my money and ten's the rate, understand? I don't care if it's the chief of police asking for more. You fold, and I'll fold you back the other way." Moe's voice was burred by the three packs of Murads he smoked a day, and his windowless office reeked of Turkish tobacco. He was built like a draft horse; his nose was soft from fists faster than his, but he hadn't lost a fight since his amateur days, when he was a sparring partner for Tommy Loughran, before Tommy turned pro in '25. His hairy arms were livid with tattoos, and his deceptively soft fingers were strong enough to snatch a hundred-pound block of ice into the back of his truck without slipping. His office went doorless after he'd punched or butted six or seven doors off their hinges in fits of anger.

On his first night out, Lew was pulled over on Highland just three miles from the icehouse. He stayed in the cab as he'd been told to, and watched in the side-view mirror as the cop approached. The towheaded cop wasn't much older than Lew, and his blonde mustache looked more like a milk stain. Whistling "Button Up Your Overcoat" and tapping a duet with the loose change in his pocket, he came over to the window and held his hand out.

"New guy?"

"That's right." Lew kept the truck running and pushed a clean bill through the open window.

"Where's the rest of it?"

"That's it."

"My eye. I got a partner needs seeing to."

"Then send him next time." Lew never looked at the cop directly, but could hear his breathing change.

"You putting the blink on me, Peanut?"

Lew kept his eyes on the bugs that danced and fluttered in his headlights. "Just doing what I'm told."

"Then do it."

"I am doing it. Like the man who pays my wages told me to. You ought to try the same." Lew was still holding the creased ten-dollar bill out the window, his eyes on the road.

The cop yanked the money out of his hand, then kicked the fender and spit on the windshield. "Move it, shitbird."

Lew was waved over eight more times that night. In the alley behind JoJo's on El Prado, a detective went through the motions of shaking him down, but his heart wasn't in it and before long he was doing an Eddie Cantor routine he'd heard on the radio the night before. Lew's last stop was a basement joint called the Circus Club, which shared an entrance with the Christian Science church on Ash Street, both establishments servicing the working-class neighborhood south of Balboa Park. The bartender, a gaunt man named Wiley, helped Lew haul the ice out of the truck and invited him inside for a pint at half price. It was three o'clock in the morning and Moe didn't expect the truck back until five, so Lew bought a bottle of Four Aces to take back to his rented room in Point Loma, and sat at the bar and rolled hard-boiled eggs on the wooden plank until the shells peeled off. Wiley tapped a fresh keg and poured him a glass of beer, scraping off the foam with a flat knife. It was a slow night, and Wiley said he was tired of serving sullen hardasses who drank with their hats on and sailors who got drunk in ten minutes and then slept it off until closing time. He leaned against the back bar, stamping blank cards with the Circus Club phone number.

"On weekends we get a combo and the place is okay, guys on dates, more women stinking up the place, but on nights like this it's like the circus left town, know what I mean?"

Lew watched the two girls who were paid to prowl the room for the easy drunks or free spenders who'd make their time worthwhile. He liked the looks of the platinum-haired girl who worked the tables in the back. She wore a sleeveless dress sashed at the middle with a gold satin band, and her fingers played with the long strand of pearls that hung down between her breasts all the way to the outline of her navel. She stopped at a table full of collapsed sailors and cocked her hip and whispered something to the only one who could still cross his eyes and pretend to see, and the sailor's knees jerked appreciatively before his head snapped back and he started snoring in her face. The girl palmed a few crumpled dollar bills from the middle of the table and moved on, raising one hand to knead the back of her neck and, with the other hand, slipping the money past her palely shadowed armpit into the cup of her bra. Lew knew that he would come back Friday when the band was playing, his pockets glutted with enough cash to keep her busy for as long as he wanted.

Wiley lugged a case of mason jars from the back room and poured himself a beer. "You like working for Moe Goode?"

"Just started."

"Looking to make a few extra bucks?"

"Maybe."

The next night at ten o'clock, two hours before his shift on the ice truck, Lew arrived at a warehouse at the end of Market Street. A thick sea fog rolled off the bay, and by the time the headlights of Oskar Kaprow's panel truck appeared ten minutes later, nine more men had floated like ghouls out of the oily haze to climb alongside him into the back, followed by Oskar himself. A tall, fleshy man with a belly that ended at his knees, he needed a boost, then he banged on the roof of the cab and the driver lurched toward the harbor through a cobblestone maze of side streets.

Oskar Kaprow owned a fish market in the Mission district, and the bed of the truck was slick with the scales and slime of the yellowtail, halibut and tuna he picked up from the boats each dawn. The men cursed as they slipped on the stinking planks of the truck, but Kaprow stood fast, his weight bound up in a tight blue uniform, his big feet planted firmly in the knee-high rubber boots he wore like a Russian prince. Besides his success as a San Diego merchant and city councilman, he was also treasurer of the local American Legion post, and it was in this role that he handed each man in the truck a five-dollar bill, a creased blue cap like his own and a baseball bat as they bounced across Kettner Boulevard to the tramp camps down by the tracks.

The driver stopped next to a broken fence on a ridge overlooking the rail yard, and through the fog Lew could make out the flickering lights of cooking fires in the arroyo below. A tugboat horn blowing off Coronado sounded like it came from the street behind them, and Kaplow's harsh wheeze sounded miles away when he pointed to the gutted path that led to the tracks.

"Ten minutes. When you hear my whistle, you come back. If they're still here tomorrow, we'll come and do it again. Now go."

The men tripped and fumbled down the dark hill, leaning on their bats for balance, the fog hovering over them like a patchy blanket. Through the wispy, smoke-fed mist Lew saw a ramshackle village near the tracks. Scrapwood hovels teetered in the muddy field next to canvas tents and hammocks strung between cars. Laundry hung everywhere, fluttering partitions between the squalid claims in this treeless depression beneath the cliffs. Families moved quietly in front of dying fires, cleaning heirloom dishes that had survived the roads of Kansas and the Texas Panhandle, putting their cranky children to bed on pallets of winter clothing, the husbands and wives then sitting by the mute flames drinking bitter coffee, overwhelmed by fatigue.

The men with bats kept moving forward, Lew among them. He liked the feel of the bat in his hand and started swinging it from his knee to his shoulder as they labored down the ravine, steadying the arc as he picked up the pace, timing the motion to the rhythm of his feet. Cold and solid in the wet air, propelled by the simple mechanics of Lew's arm, the bat carried significant weight. Lew was happy.

No one expected them; no one heard them coming. When the light of a train pulling out of the Santa Fe yard illuminated the sooty encampment, the men attacked.

Lew heard a woman scream, and the first man he hit was reaching for a knife. He caught him on the upswing and broke his jaw, his cries gurgled by the blood in his throat, and the man cringed in the dirt as Lew swung again and crushed the fingers that held the knife. The enormous beam on the locomotive was bright as the sun, and Lew squinted at the frightened men racing from the circular rim of light into the darkness, away from the bats. Lew hit a man in the kneecap who was running toward him, and crushed the shoulder blade of another who was running away. Fleeing women and children banged into him, all arms and legs and streaming hair, and he let them pass. Shacks were smashed and tents trampled. Lew saw two young boys and a dog hiding under the chassis of a truck. A parakeet squawked in a tipped-over birdcage. A woman sat on a fender and held her baby while a man swung his bat over their heads, turning the passenger window into jeweled rain that settled in their hair. The train was rolling past now, and the lights of the windows flickered yellow. A man holding a Bible above his head was hit square in the face. Mongrel dogs ran right through the fires. This destruction took on the sprocketed jerkiness of the silent pictures Lew had worshiped as a boy, those brilliant epics of war and adventure that looked as glorious and otherworldly as the carnage that now unspooled before his eyes. When he again raised his bat over his head, he saw its knob was tipped in blood.

A man jumped on him, digging his ragged fingernails deep into Lew's neck. Swinging wildly, Lew hit him in the back of the head and, when the man raised his hands in pain, smashed him in the kidneys. He broke a windshield and belted a tin water can hanging from an open window. He butted a man in the small of the back and, in the same motion, broke someone's wrist. He felt electric and his arm never stopped.

Lew saw a man in a blue hat drop his bat and chase a young girl into a tent. He followed, and through the flaps saw the man rip the thin dress from the girl's shoulder. When she tried to scramble away he peeled off her underwear and flipped her on her back, slapping her as she cried out. In the dismal light, the girl tried to cover her adolescent nakedness, kicking until the man grabbed her ankles in his big hand and pushed her knees back to her shoulders, revealing her pink, hairless youth. When he yanked down his own pants, Lew pushed through the tent flap and whacked him on top of the head. The girl's hand shot over her mouth as blood splashed her belly, and Lew hit him again so he wouldn't crash down on top of her when he fell. The girl snatched up her dress and scuttled to the corner of the tent, watching Lew as he beat the man into the muddy ground, using a steady stroke that broke his ribs and pierced a lung, stopping only when he heard Oskar Kaprow's whistle blow. He bent down and picked the blue cap out of the mud, then turned to face the girl. "You got a daddy?" As the girl nodded, the man groaned through flayed lips, arm twitching convulsively. Lew pointed the bat at the man's head, hair matted with brown ooze and blood, and said, "Then he can have the rest of this one."

Lew left the tent and walked quickly toward the path, the bat dangling at his side. Children cried and women called out for husbands lost in the darkness. The train whistle blew as it disappeared around the bend, a long, sustained note that hung in the air as the men with bats retreated silently up the hill.

Oskar Kaprow stood in the truck bed counting heads as they climbed aboard.

"We're short," he said.

Lew pulled the blue cap out of his pocket and handed it over.

"I found this."

"What happened?"

Lew shrugged.

"No bat?"

"Didn't see his bat."

Oskar tucked the cap into his American Legion uniform and signaled for the driver to pull out. "Well, I hope they didn't catch the poor bastard."

The men laughed, Lew along with them.

Moe let him start his run earlier than usual that Friday night. "I like you, Lew. You're a good kid so far." He peeled off two hundred dollars' worth of tens from the roll he kept in his pocket and handed it over. "Just don't shit in my hat."

Lew made his run, paid off the cops who stopped him with upturned hands and then parked the truck behind the Circus Club. He hid the hundred and forty left of Moe's money in the ripped upholstery on the passenger door and waited for Wiley to help lug the last block of ice inside, then he stripped to his waist and washed up at the utility sink in the storage room, listening to the music seep through the walls around him. Sagging cartons of booze were stacked to the ceiling. Wiley, perched on a ladder juggling bottles of High and Dry gin in his arms, nodded at the deep scratches on Lew's neck.

"Ouch, Lew. That hurt?"

"No."

He changed into the suit Wiley had let him hang on the back door the night before. Five minutes later he walked into the alley, his hair slicked back with water, and as he straightened his tie, looked up at the bold sweep of stars in the sky. He creased the brim of his hat, a mouse gray, high-crowned Hobnob Special made by Dobbs and Son that he'd picked up in a pawnshop in Palmdale, and walked around to Ash Street, stepping through the side door of the Circus Club like any other paying customer, and scanning the floor for the girl with the platinum hair.

It was only one o'clock and the place was still crowded, the band backing two girl singers trying to harmonize like three on "My Future Just Passed," the Boswell Sisters' hit. He spotted her leading a sailor up the back stairs, a lanky boy who followed her too closely, trying to disguise the erection that blossomed in his tight pants.

Lew took a seat at the bar and kept an eye on the staircase. Wiley worked his way toward him, lining the counter with bottles and making change from his own pocket. When he poured Lew an Old Crow and soda, a man sat down on the next stool and ordered a quart of Dunbar scotch.

Wiley paused, his face flushed, and studied the man, who wore a beige suit flecked with red and gold, a white shirt and a gold tie. "That stuff's twenty years old, mister."

"I know."

"It's six bucks."

The man pulled a ten-dollar bill out of a silver money clip and laid it on the counter. His hands were long and thin, and his finger-nails were trimmed and buffed.

Wiley raised an eyebrow in Lew's direction, slipped the ten across the counter and replaced it with four singles. "We keep it locked up. Be right back."

The man nodded, took a pack of Chesterfields out of his jacket pocket and offered one to Lew. His skin was dark, the color of bruised oranges, and his mustache was neatly clipped a quarter inch below his nostrils. When he flicked his lighter under Lew's ciga-rette, he smiled and said, "Name's Gideon Hayes."

"Lew Beck."

"You got the time, Lew?"

"It's about—"

"Don't you have a watch, Lew?"

"Don't need one."

"That's not what I asked you." Gideon blew smoke through his nose. Wiley came back, presented the bottle of scotch and pulled the cork. "Dunbar, mister. You want something with it?"

Gideon poured the scotch into a tumbler and shook his head. He balanced his cigarette in the ashtray and sniffed the liquor before pouring it into his mouth, then swallowed with his eyes closed and rolled his tongue over his upper lip. Lew couldn't take his eyes off his orange-colored skin.

"Do you like scotch, Lew?"

"Bourbon."

Gideon looked wounded. He pursed out his lips and retracted them. "Let me show you something, Lew." He put his elbow on the counter and let his cuff fall, revealing the gold watch on his hairless wrist, turning his arm so Lew could get a good look at it. "It's a Bulova, Lew. The case is real gold, the strap is pigskin and all the gears, Lew, all the coils and screws and wires, are Swiss made."

Lew looked at the watch and finished his drink, shifting his body to see past Gideon's burnished ear, eye on the empty staircase.

"What do you think of this watch, Lew?"

"It's good looking."

"It's a real timepiece, Lew, and it's my business to know that. And why's that?" Gideon waited for Lew to look at him. "It's my job. It's what I do for a living."

Gideon flicked his wrist like he was shaking a tambourine, and the watch disappeared back under his cuff. "Do you know Los Angeles, Lew?"

"Yeah."

"Do you know Roth Jewelers in Beverly Hills? My account. San Francisco? Jensen Jewelers on Market Street? My account. I sell the best watches to the best jewelry stores in California, Arizona and most of Texas. Bulova, Longines, Gruen. Quality merchandise, Lew, that's how I make my reputation." He filled his tumbler and poured scotch over the ice in Lew's glass. "Watches, Lew, I'm in the watch trade. And it's been good to me. It allows me to be generous. Like right now."

Gideon moved closer, lowering his head to Lew's, face-to-face. Peat and a peppery smell rose off him like mist off a lake. "A guy like you? You need a watch. I sell watches. I think we can do something here that will make us both happy."

"How much?"

"My cost. This Bulova on my wrist? You go down to Noonan's in old town, first-rate operation, been in business since nineteen ten, they've got this watch in the window for forty-five dollars. You can buy it from me for twenty-seven. I've got fifty, sixty watches in a sample case in my car. Some more, some less. All number-one goods. Take a look, Lew. You won't be disappointed."

He drained his scotch and rubbed his tongue along his upper lip. "I'm a salesman, Lew, and you know who I sell to? Customers. You know what customers are? People. It's that simple, Lew, and it gets even simpler. A good salesman knows what people want. I'm a good salesman. I know what people want. I know what you want, Lew."

He poured them each some more scotch. Lew didn't turn it down. The piano player was running his fingers through "Kitten on the Keys," and Wiley was busy filling orders at the other end of the bar. The landing at the top of the staircase was dark and empty.

Gideon tapped Lew's naked wrist with two fingers and smiled. "Come on, Lew. Let's go outside."

. . .

His Buick was parked in the alley across from Lew's ice truck. The bottle of Dunbar and two glasses were anchored in the folds of the lowered convertible top, and Gideon was leaning into the open trunk to sort through his sample case. Lew picked up a glass and drank the sharp, smoky scotch. The moon cast gray shadows on the closed-in walls as a couple stumbled by the end of the alley, the man whistling tunelessly. A calico cat sat on a high windowsill, casing the loose-lidded garbage cans below.

"Try this on, Lew." Gideon knelt down on one knee and handed him a watch. It was stainless steel, with a black face and curved lens. "That band is genuine alligator, Lew, last you a lifetime. And the watch? Wittnauer. They don't make them any better than that. Wear it anywhere, day or night, it's that kind of watch, Lew. The hand-it-down-to-your-kids kind of watch." His voice was almost a whisper.

Lew wound the watch and strapped it on. "What time is it?"

"One forty-three, Lew. See? I told you, didn't I? You need a watch, Lew. Everybody needs a watch."

He liked the weight of it, the newness of the steel on his wrist. He brought it up to his ear and listened to the soft click of the second hand. He drank some more scotch and felt Gideon's hand run down the front of his pants and rest there.

"Hold it up to the light, Lew. Go on."

Lew raised his arm above his head and turned it until the moonlight planed across the bubbled dome. He heard his zipper open and admired the brightness of the alligator band, blacker than the darkest corners of the sky. Gideon's hand fumbled through the opening of his fly, and Lew drank off the last of the scotch in his glass as his penis flopped into the night air, cool and warm at the same time.

"What do you think, Lew?"

Lew felt fingers and lips and the warm scotch in his belly.

"What do you think?"

Lew thought of Gideon on his knees, those orangy fingers and that whispery mouth, and reached for the bottle of Dunbar scotch behind him. He lifted the bottle and brought it down on the top of Gideon's head, feeling something crack even though the bottle remained solid in his hand. Lew took a deep breath and held it. The sudden silence sucked the air out of the alley. Only when the cat jumped onto a garbage can and sent the lid spinning to the ground did he exhale and quiet the lid with his foot.

Gideon Hayes's body was jackknifed into the open trunk. Lew pushed his shoulders off the sample case, shut the latches and lifted it to the ground. Then, using both hands, he grabbed him by the belt loops and swung the rest of him into the trunk. Gideon was curled into a ball, his long arms draped around his ankles. Lew thought he saw his eyelids twitch before he gently shut and locked the trunk, but that was impossible.

Lew walked across the alley to the ice truck, fished Moe Goode's money out of the ripped upholstery on the passenger door and tossed the keys over the church wall. He picked up the sample case of watches and walked onto Ash Street, heading for the station to catch the first train for Los Angeles.

It was just growing dark when he stepped naked from Mary Carsey's bed. Lew turned on the lamp on a small table by the bathroom door and took his cigarettes from the pants he'd draped over the chair an hour ago. Mary sat up on top of the covers and watched him. Her knees were casually spread, her soft belly heaving easily over a thick wedge of pubic hair. "Jesus, Lew, look at those scratches on your neck."

Lew lit his cigarette and offered her one.

Mary shook her head. "Lots of girlfriends, I bet. Jealous types, too."

He stood in front of the small open window and smoked. The breeze blowing down from the hills above Franklin felt good on his belly. In the window of the apartment building across the street, through a swaying row of cypress trees, Lew saw a little girl sitting on her rocking horse and staring at him. He didn't move.

"You look good, Lew," Mary said. "You know that? I bet you do. You're small but strong. No belly. Hips slim as a girl's. I wish I still had my figure. Hell, I wish I had your figure." She laughed.

Lew and the little girl stared at each other through the flickering leaves, and he felt his penis stiffening. The little girl started rocking slowly; her golden hair fell forward and she smiled at him. Lew stubbed his cigarette out in the ashtray and turned to Mary, who looked at his erection.

"Hold on, Lew. Buddy'll be home in a few hours. You better save that for the next girl."

She smiled, and Lew let her. She didn't know yet that he wasn't going anywhere.

A man was following her through a city she'd never seen before. Although she was grown, she was wearing the same pale-green dress she'd loved as a child. It buttoned down the front but the two bottom buttons were missing and she could see her legs flashing beneath her, strong and womanly, as she walked faster, conscious of the man behind her. The sidewalks were crowded, yet no one looked at her. However scared she was, her face remained calm, poised. A child bouncing a ball on the corner ignored her, as did everyone ignore her except the man, who crossed the street whenever she did and followed her around every corner. Her heart was pounding but she walked lightly, her arms swinging at her side, purse bouncing on her hip. She wanted to lose him in the dense crowd, then felt compelled to stop in front of a store window and stare at naked mannequins, their fleshy pink plaster chipped and smudged. The man came up and stood right behind her. Feeling him over her shoulder, his height, his nearness, his presence, she made herself look up at his reflection in the glass. All she saw was a smile, pink and chipped and smudged, and she thought of Frank and opened her eyes.

The morning was hot and Lena lay on top of the bed, pinned to the sheets by the lazy weight of her dream. Outside she could hear Burr and Sarah Chivers, their vibrating voices caught in the still air like pistol shots. She blinked, trying to wake up, and her eyes stung with her own sweat. When she sat up and swung her feet on the floor, the dream was almost forgotten. Her nightgown was soaked, stuck at every crease and sleep-rolled wrinkle. She stood up and peeled the wet fabric from her body, freeing pockets of air that cooled her skin. She stretched her neck and looked down at the sodden print she'd left on the bed.

They'd taken the family trip two years ago, leaving Hugo early on a Monday morning at the start of Frank's workweek, and were deep inside Arkansas by the end of the day. Burr slept through the still, dark stretch of Oklahoma, but made his mother promise to wake him when they crossed the border east of Eagletown at dawn. Lena stayed awake to keep Frank company and to see the changes in towns and terrain as the light grayed. For the first few hours they drove through the cotton-covered flatlands that stretched to the horizon, lined by diversion ditches tapped from the Little River and West Fork Creek. She kept the window open and caught the distant smell of cows on the whispered air.

Lena was twenty-six, and this was her first time out of Oklahoma. Burr, only six, was already sleeping through parts of the country she'd never seen before, curled up on the backseat crowded with boxes of Bibles and their suitcases. They were traveling northeast, on what Frank called his Ozark route, along the hill country that stretched from Alabama to the Virginias. It was their first trip as a family, and Lena and Burr would visit with some of Frank's family on their shanty boat while he made his annual loop through the God-stricken hamlets of the Appalachian Mountains.

Lena had seen only photographs of Frank's family—no Mullenses had attended the small wedding in Hugo. Before their marriage they'd leafed through the moldy old album he carried around with him, the pages as yellow as the glue that couldn't stop the old pictures from curling. There was Uncle Henry Joe, who had a face so lean and ruined it looked knife-slashed, and cousin Jacob, sixty years old and simple as a child, who smiled and waved in every photograph, showing off the four teeth in his mouth and the six fingers on each hand. There was Frank's mother, Violet, a fat-legged woman with a face as scrunched as dried fruit, and his younger sister, Irene, her big arms gobbing out of the dotted dress she wore on special occasions, looking almost as old as her mother. Other relations stood in prickly fields of cut tobacco stalks, surrounded by wiry dogs and blurred children, or on a rickety dock next to a gutted five-foot catfish. Frank and Lena joked about it, and even he admitted that going home was like Saturday night at a carnival sideshow. Looking at the pictures, Lena was almost convinced it was true. But they were her family now, as much as Frank was, and she felt a gush of tenderness and pity each time she opened the album. In the winter of 1930, after Burr turned six, she'd suggested that they accompany Frank on his next trip, and they headed off that last week in July.

The first few days they'd stopped in little towns like Tokio and Caddo Gap, small communities where the same families had been filling churches and cemeteries for over two hundred years, families named Smith and Hawes, Farmann and Lynne, descendants of English traders and lapsed Utopians who'd fought Indians and one another, people whose sons and daughters married and propagated and had a power and presence in the southern part of the state that politicians could only pretend to command. These people distrusted most anyone from west of Sevier County, but they looked forward to Frank Mullens's arrival every summer. He, too, was a Methodist, and he was good-natured and well traveled; he brought the men new jokes and the women his easy charm, and in turn they fed and coddled him and bought his books through a special fund they set up for just that purpose. They accepted Lena and Burr with a stiff but genuine courtesy, affording the Mullenses hospitality wherever they went.

After five days they drove north from Little Rock to Cabot and Beebe, a new territory for Frank. He stopped at every church he could find and introduced himself and left behind samples in preparation for his next visit. Ingratiating and sure of himself, he repeated his name six times in his ten-minute sales pitch, spinning Bible stories like a moral zealot and finishing off with a joke that could easily be repeated in mixed company, making sure the ministers and Sunday-school teachers wouldn't forget him. Lena and Burr waited in the car, and sometimes barefoot, dusty children would bring them iced tea or milk and watch them drink every drop. In the late afternoon they would pull over someplace nice, where Lena would help Frank record his sales and estimate future prospects while Burr chased grasshoppers through the wild grape and goldenrod. Days went by like this, lazy and uncountable, and as the stack of boxes gradually disappeared, Burr was able to stretch out and prop his feet amidst the suitcases.

Lena dozed, too, falling into a half sleep with her eyes open and mind elsewhere, up ahead in the imagined riverrun hollow of Frank's family, standing in their tea-stained midst, she alone smiling and looking straight ahead. Then she would go back to Hugo, to the house where she was born and now lived with her husband and son. She let her eyes close tighter and she tarried there, in the companionable hum of familiar surroundings. Although Lena was grateful for the simple connections that made her life ordinary and good, it was a life not without change and circumstance. When her parents died together in a tragic embrace of limbs and metal, her heart had been squeezed and chipped, forever altered, and she learned through the years to accept the loss of good dogs and devilish cats and boyfriends who begged for her kisses and later disappeared. But she'd adjusted and persevered, and her life soared high like fireworks when she married Frank Mullens, and blossomed into showering sparks when she gave birth to Burr. Although her world sometimes tumbled and spun, it always righted itself and remained straightforward. She loved her husband. Even if he was gone more than half the year, when he came home their time apart was easily recaptured, like love rewound, and those memories would stay with her long after he left again, coiled within her and kept safe. When they were together Frank was funny and kind, letting her hold on to him as much as she needed, or sitting patiently on the porch in the early evening, stroking her head as it rested in his lap. On the hottest days they drove to Lake Hugo and spread a blanket on the blistered grass close to the water, where they ate jam sandwiches in the shade provided by the car's open door. When the heat became unbearable they changed into swimsuits, Lena letting Frank ease her breasts into the scratchy pockets of cotton that adhered like a second skin to her hardened nipples. Then they'd run together into the wind-slapped water, jumping in and out to let the weak breeze cool their wet skin. Sometimes they drove to the livestock auctions in Durant, where Lena liked to show off Frank to her father's friends, polite farmers who smoked pipes and watched the bidding in silence, men familiar with harvesters and brood mares and the pretty daughter of Oren McCardell. Frank would lean with these men on the wooden rail and trade comments about the polled short-horns with the dwarf calves that caught a fair price, or the big Angus with too much white on his legs that didn't, and Lena was proud to watch these men accept her husband, knowing that her father would've accepted him too. They held each other on those humid nights in Hugo, stretched naked on top of the bed her parents had once slept in, and she stroked his penis until it awoke beneath her fingers and he bent over her with a knowing hand, causing her to stretch out like a cat, clenching and relaxing as she rolled over and over, loving where he touched her and never asking how he knew how to please her. That's what Lena kept with her in those empty months when he was away—the depth of his touch and the recol-lected sensations that went deeper than skin or thought.

Lena blinked as the sun flared above her in the sky, Frank whistling "Camptown Ladies" at her side, changing octaves every time he inhaled. Then he stopped and said, "Who's hungry?"

Lena smiled. Married eight years, she was still amazed by his appetite. He ate six meals a day when he was on the road, and he was on the road half the year. Early in their marriage, when Frank came home from selling cheap editions of favorite hymns on his Gulf route, from New Orleans to Saint Petersburg, Florida, she made him stay up half the night confessing his many meals as if they were sins: prawns and pralines and corn bread and squirrel stew, boiled mustard greens and smothered pork with pepper gravy, cream pies and butter beans and sugary lemonade. Lena shook her head but he grinned and went on: ear after ear of fresh sweet corn at the kitchen tables of grateful parishioners along Lake Pontchartrain, the home-made potato salad and okra and crowder peas dished out by mothers and wives of every preacher on Apalachee Bay, two identical meals of pan-fried redfish and buttermilk pie on a twenty-mile stretch between Otter Creek and Lebanon. But it was part of his job not to give offense, and he did his job well.

By now it was after midnight and they were sitting on the end of the bed. Lena reached for his hand, and he reached for her breasts, loose and irresistible under her nightgown. Pulling her toward him, he said, "In Mobile I had fried chicken three times in one day," and she laughed until her ribs hurt, and Frank removed her nightgown and pulled the covers back. By the time he left the next Tuesday, Lena was pregnant with Burr.

"I've got ham," she said.

"You got tomatoes, too?"

"I've got tomatoes."

"That sounds like a sandwich."

Frank peeked over the backseat. "How about you, Burr? You want a sandwich?"

"Ham and tomato, please."

Frank's short laugh shook the car. "Travelin' makes you hungry, don't it, son?"

"Yes sir."

"Ain't nothing wrong with the road, is there?"

"No sir."

"Just like his daddy."

Frank pulled off a dirt road near the Hatchie River and drove through the spongy bottomland of west Tennessee, the sky soon closed in by cypress trees that grew warped and dense in this liquid soil.

They ate sandwiches that quickly became limp in the August heat, and Frank told Burr stories about the Cherokees who'd hunted bear and whitetails and wild turkey in these swampy woods over a hundred years ago, and how the white man had killed off most of the game for skin and sport, but that the deer were finally showing themselves again, their flattened nests visible among the cattails. When it came time to leave, Lena picked up the blanket and tossed their bread scraps into the brush while Frank hoisted Burr onto a cypress knee to look for black bass in the burbly ooze of the slough.

They crossed the Tennessee River at the Perryville Bridge and turned down the first dirt road, following the gutted track that ran straight along the water, dodging rocks and the yellow bones and hide of a dead dog that someone had thrown off the bridge weeks before. Lena saw the houseboat first, moored a hundred yards south of the bridge, almost hidden from view in a small cove overgrown with willows. The boat was squat and about twenty feet square, with a cabin in the center.

Frank pulled up by the hand-painted sign that read, CATS — I CENT PER POUND, as two merle collies ran down the planked ramp from the boat and lunged barking through the wet grass. Their long fur was wild with knots and burrs, and Burr watched them hang suspended in the air before flipping in the dirt ten feet in front of him, yanked backward by the ropes tied around their necks. While the dogs lay in the grass staring at the car with moist, dumb eyes, a gnomish face appeared from behind the boat's cabin under a long-billed cap.

Frank grinned. "That's George Whelks."

The little man wore old duck cloth pants slit up the sides to accommodate his rubber boots. "You folks want some cats? I still got a couple nickel boys left that'll fry up real nice."

Frank led Lena out of the car and said, "Mr. Whelks? I'm Frank Mullens, Oswell's boy."

The man pushed back his cap, and his red face relaxed into a pulpy mass of veins and creases. "Frank Mullens, sure you are."

"I'm looking for my family. Thought they'd be docked near the bridge this time of year."

"They were." He laughed into his hand.

One of the collies strained forward and put her face on Lena's hip. She petted the dog and saw that her right eye was pink and blind.

"It was back in June when your father got into it with Normie Powers. Oswell was fishing the west shore not far from Decaturville. There was a storm brewing that day and Oswell come out in the littler of his two push boats to move his nets closer to the bank. Normie was already there musselin' in what he pretended was open water. Your daddy saw him getting ready to drag where he likes to set his trots and told Normie to move upriver. Normie said, 'Sure, Oswell, didn't see you,' even though the barrels on Oswell's drift nets was floating high in the current, and Normie pulled on his motor and turned north without a bit of disrespect. Got home that night and thought about it, and Normie not being much of a thinker, he took up against the way your daddy was cuttin' up the river. Oswell thought about it, too, over a couple glasses of whiskey, and decided he didn't like the way Normie said his name. So Normie comes back to the same spot the next morning to start draggin' the bottom and Oswell's waiting for him around the bend. He stood in the bow and took a shot at Normie with that old Maynard rifle he uses on snapping turtles. Gun must be a hundred years old and blew a shot over Normie's head. Even Normie said so, but Sheriff Rice didn't worry about that and told Oswell to pull up and get out, so your folks is moored up in Humphreys County, below Waverly at Duck Creek."

"I hear you."

"And you know your daddy when he's been drinkin' too much."

Lena knew that, too, because Frank had told her stories about his father's intemperate life.

Oswell had married Violet Rutherford when he tied up at Paducah in a cedar houseboat he'd built himself, and they had a child every summer, three summers in a row, conceived in winter when the fishing slowed down. He never hit his wife and kids, beyond the necessary swat and slap, and he went to church on alternate Sundays. He took care of his johnboats and mended his own nets with shuttles he carved from beech wood. He ruled the creeks like a freshwater Ahab, searching for the whiskered beasts that shadowed the muddy bottoms. But he drank when a hook accidentally imbedded in his finger, and he drank when it didn't. He had a drink with his coffee in the morning and a drink with his coffee at night. He drank when the fish were plentiful, and during the spring floods when they weren't. He drank all day, and it never interfered until he drank too much. Then he became mallet-headed and abusive, and he knew it, disappearing for days on end to save himself from the horrors of shame and introspection. He fed and clothed his children but remained as alien to them as the great-uncles who stared out from behind beards in the stained, oval photographs over their mother's dresser. People on the river thought Oswell drank because he didn't care much for anybody or anything, and his brother, Carl, said he drank "to cut the fool." But Violet knew that his family made Oswell Mullens drink—not because he didn't love them, but because he didn't know how.

Frank had sworn at an early age that he would never be like his father. He was four years old when they first went fishing together, and he couldn't bear the silence the older man demanded. For interminable hours they drifted on the river, checking hoop nets for buffalo and carp and the strong sag lines for the big catfish Oswell was known for. They sat across from each other in the narrow confines of the damp boat and ate the egg sandwiches Violet had wrapped that morning in brown paper, not saying a word to each other, communicating only in grunts and scratches. As the day dragged on, Frank talked in his head to keep himself company, and he sat there, in word-deprived stupefaction, as his father pulled the heavy twine out of the river and the deck piled up with the slimy, river ripe fish. He stared past the broad shoulders yoked in sweat and gazed instead at the watery horizon, waiting for the dimness of dusk that would send them home.

Lena recognized the Mullenses' houseboat once they pulled into the meadow on Duck Creek, as it hadn't changed much in the five years since Frank took those curling pictures that bloated the family album. The old boat sat low in the water of a wide cove, shaded by giant elms and a sheet of grim clouds that hung above the river. A string of laundry billowed and snapped from a line that stretched from the cabin top to a lightning-struck sycamore tree, the deadwood blanched white and surrounded by marigolds.

Burr sat up and watched children emerge from the woods like Indians—children with dirty knees and pie pan faces, carrying long sticks in sweaty hands, narrow chests heaving and nostrils bellowing as if in suspicion. One boy raised his hand to shade his eyes, and in this simple gesture he conjured up a pack of dogs that broke through the thorny brush and raced back and forth across the worn patch of shoreline. Beyond these feral relations Burr saw a dozen chickens roosting in a pyramid of overturned barrels, squawking at the dogs as they flattened themselves in their straw nests, flicking their comb-bright heads in different directions. Three goats were tethered to a stand of mulberry bushes, their back legs bowed around aching udders as they bent their necks to chew at the rotten muskmelons scattered in the dirt. Tangled tomato plants grew wild in an overgrown garden, and a long double row of corn stood as tall and straight as any frontier stockade.

Lena recognized the two women who sat on the stern of the boat, shaded by the wooden overhang that extended off the cabin, their faces frozen in photographs and unchanged over the years. Frank's older sister, called Aunt Polly for reasons everyone in the family had long forgotten, sat there rocking on the deck, looking older than her forty-five years, her face pinched and her teeth crooked; perched on the back of her chair was her crow, wing-damaged by a blast from a child's .22 and devoted to the sour woman who kept it tied there, feeding it crumbled biscuits from her own plate. Sitting next to her was younger sister Irene, soft and white as a puffball. Oswell and Aunt Polly's husband, Jimmy, joined the women when they heard the car pull up, Oswell's back curled with arthritis and Jimmy leaning on a crutch. When the children gathered in front of the boat, the immediate family stood there on display in the wavering heat. Except for Frank, alone in his beauty, the Mullenses were the ugliest family Lena had ever seen.

It was the first time Frank had been home in four years, since his mother died. Jimmy hobbled down the plank to greet his brother-in-law, and they shook hands in the yard. It took Irene three attempts to get out of her chair, but she came bowlegged down the plank to smother her brother with a hug. Oswell stood on the boat deck next to Aunt Polly, bracing himself with a hand on her chair; when the crow cawed and flapped its useless wings and pecked at his knuckles, Oswell cuffed him.

Lena and Burr stood by the side of the car, waiting, and she knew this was only the beginning. Frank would be leaving first thing in the morning to sell his Bibles in southern Kentucky, and for the next five days these were the people she would be left with. She forced a smile as her nieces and nephews approached, surrounding her like a band of pygmies from some South Sea island, and she kept glancing at Frank, hoping he'd motion her over, and when he did she ran to him. She took his hand and held on to him until he left at dawn. Although she didn't know this yet, it would be the last time she would truly miss her husband.

· · ·

On the morning of the second day, Lena worked on the bow with Aunt Polly and Irene. The women darned nets and patched old clothes, brewed iced tea and kneaded bread, pounded nails into boards that had warped in the heat, swept hornets' nests from the corners of the roof and then made lunch; no time wasted, hands always busy, and always a line in the water. At the end of the day they took to their chairs and faced the river and made room for Lena, the three of them sitting in a row under the eave, hands flitting like mosquitoes in the dusk, shelling peas or plucking chickens, watching the distant shoreline for Oswell's and Jimmy's boats. They sat in silence, mostly, never once asking Lena about her life before or after Frank; they just handed her things, making sure she had something to do. And the crow fussed and cawed on the post of the rocking chair, and Aunt Polly fed it dried twists of bacon she carried in her apron pocket, and muttered to it while she worked, "That's Polly's good boy. That's Polly's special one."

The long, hot hours of summer daylight blended and disappeared into one another, as if time were moving slowly backward, without escape. She followed her sisters-in-law around, thankful when they handed her a bar of lye soap to help them wash their clothes in a big tub at the edge of the river. She saw little of Burr, who'd gone native in the woods with his cousins, his face grease-smeared from whatever meal he'd just gobbled down.

Evenings were the worst. Oswell and Jimmy would sit outside and drink their homemade whiskey while the women cooked catfish or frog legs in bubbling lard or bacon grease, boiling greens until they were limp and tasteless and baking the toughest biscuits Lena had ever chewed. When Aunt Polly whistled, everyone would crowd around the big kitchen table as smoke curled through the rafters, and the room filled with the musky presence of unwashed men who refilled their jars and continued to drink through supper. The children giggled and pinched one another until Aunt Polly or Irene slapped wrists or cuffed ears, but no one talked. Only the crow complained, tethered outside and waiting for the pieces of broken biscuit that Aunt Polly tossed through the open window.

In the morning it would all start again. Oswell would leave for his fishing waters before dawn, and Jimmy, hungover and cranky, would rise later with the kids, cursing the damn crow for shitting in his boots again. Aunt Polly laughed and followed her husband to his boat, handing him down two bags of lunch and a jar of tea.

"Shitty old crow," Jimmy complained.

"Take your boots inside next time," Aunt Polly answered.

"I ought to shoot that damn bird."

"I'll shoot you first." She pushed the bow of Jimmy's boat out into the cove while the crow perched on her rocking chair, the back of it caked with the white and black shit that ran thick as candle wax down the slats.

Burr liked this part of the day, sitting on the boat with Edgar, their bony legs dangling side by side, dipping the tips of their home-made fishing poles into the water to splash each other with a spray that felt cool as crushed mint leaves on their sunburned skin.

"You ever eat a orange in Oklahoma, Burr?"

"Sure, lots of times."

Edgar jiggled his line and looked down at his reflection in the water. He pressed out a fat string of spit and let it fall right between his reflected eyes.

"You ever eat a orange, Edgar?"

"No, but I ate orange juice once in a café in Sugar Tree."

"That counts for something."

"You bet."

Out of all his cousins, Burr liked Edgar the best, and he wished sometimes that he could take him along when they left, at least for a while. Both boys leaned over and spit at their wavering images, and when Burr stopped to wipe his chin, the tip of his fishing pole started to twitch and he grabbed the handle.

"I think I got one, Edgar." He felt a jolt in the rod and held it tighter, but the pole kept bending, forcing itself down toward the water like a divining rod. "I think it's a big one."

The line suddenly went slack, and he looked at Edgar and eased the muscles in his back, but then it started moving again, away from the boat, toward shore. Burr doubled his grip and fixed his eyes on the brown water. Whatever he'd hooked was strong enough to pull him to his feet and march him along the deck. He leaned back at an impossible angle, putting his weight behind the pole and digging in his heels, yet even this wasn't enough to slow the thing.

Edgar reeled in his own line and caught up to him. "I'll get Clemmie."

"Just hurry."

Edgar ran off and when Burr reached the end of the deck he stepped overboard without thinking, his hands tight on the rod. Underwater, he felt the brown thickness of it rushing against his eyes; he couldn't see a thing as he went deeper, his hands choking the pole but his body limp and streamlined, fishlike himself as he was pulled through the river grass.

Standing over the washtub on the shore, Lena heard the splash and looked at the houseboat. Although Edgar was screaming, the splash had seemed louder, and she started running without knowing why. She saw Clemmie jump to his feet on the roof of the cabin and stare at the water where Edgar was screaming and pointing, at the rings that radiated gracefully off the stern. Clemmie swung down from the roof with one hand, dropping through the open window and emerging from the cabin door with Oswell's twelve-gauge Winchester field gun, feeding it shells as he took long strides along the deck, his eyes never leaving the ever-widening ripples on the water. Lena stopped at the river's edge as Clemmie raised the shotgun to his shoulder, aiming low, and fired again and again in a deafening roar, the buckshot walloping the water in an even row of exploding fountains.

Burr heard the explosions above him, and the amphibious power dragging him through the depths slowly weakened. Then he was floating freely through the caramel depths, no longer sinking, almost tumbling, overcome by weariness but feeling only the pressure in his ears. And suddenly he was hooked himself, hoisted under his arms, and he let go of the fishing pole and broke the surface of the river, clinging to his mother and spitting up water he didn't even know he'd swallowed. Over her shoulder he saw Clemmie dive off the back of the houseboat and disappear underwater, and his two aunts standing by the big tub, their arms soapy up to the elbows, staring at him. And then he saw Edgar waiting on the gangplank, his mouth hanging open as always, and everything was all right.

Lena hugged Burr to her chest and felt flushed with relief as the warm spume spilled out of his mouth and ran down her arm. She pushed through the water, her dress wet and heavy between her legs, and she lost one of her shoes in the muck. When she sat Burr down on the gangplank, he was smiling.

Clemmie surfaced with the fishing pole and trudged ashore through the water and the reeds. He laid the pole down in the grass and started retrieving the line, hand over hand, the muscles in his back straining as the water parted around the great, mossy back of a snapping turtle. He dropped the line, which disappeared into the horned beak, and dragged the creature onto the bank. Blood streaked the turtle's leathery neck, and its front claws, sharp as plow tines, scored the mud. Dripping wet and bouncing on his toes, Clemmie crouched down and poked the turtle between its small beady eyes as Aunty Polly stepped up behind him, carrying a small hatchet.

"He dead, Clemmie?"

"He's all gone."

"Big boy."

"Fifty pounds, easy."

Aunt Polly raised the hatchet and brought it down swiftly, severing the turtle's neck just behind the head, and Edgar jumped up and down on its massive, slippery shell, jigging to keep his balance.

Aunt Polly put her hand on Clemmie's shoulder and slowly got to her feet, grinning at Burr. "You hung on, didn't you, boy?"

"Yes, ma'am."

She laughed, "You woulda rode old mossback clear down to China."

Burr laughed with her, even though he didn't know where China was.

"You're a Mullens all right!"

Lena sat there on the gangplank and shuddered, damp and itchy from the river water, and drew her son, the Mullens, back to her.

His hair combed flat to his head, Burr sat on the deck wearing a clean striped shirt and a pair of Edgar's shorts, studying his catch where it hung by its tail from a hickory pole. The enormous shell was two feet wide, and as it dried it changed colors, graying in the heat; its twelve even plates took on the dullness of stone decorated with strands of bright moss and jeweled with tiny snails. It looked like a shield, strong enough to withstand a rain of arrows, and if Burr leaned just right, it was big enough to block out the entire sun.

Clemmie perched on the roof again, cleaning the old shotgun he'd used to kill the turtle, while Edgar, perfectly naked, peed off the side of the boat.

It was the end of the day, and Lena sat next to Aunt Polly and Irene, facing the river and waiting for Oswell and Jimmy to return. She paged through an old copy of *Reader's Digest* so faded and brown it looked as if it had been lying around the houseboat for twenty years.

Aunt Polly rocked back and forth in her chair, writing figures in the columned ledger in her lap. She nibbled at a carrot with the wilted greens still hanging from the end, and the crow swayed back and forth watching it. Aunt Polly scratched at her figures and shook her head. "Irene, did Sam Rockwell pay us yet for the twenty pounds of catfish we dropped off in Linden?"

Irene looked up past the apples she was peeling. "I never seen his money."

"He pay Oswell direct like last time?"

"Maybe."

"Then it's drunk up and good-bye." Aunt Polly rocked back and attacked her last notation with an eraser. She held the carrot in the same hand as she held the pencil, and the crow snapped at the greens and missed, catching her in the soft wad of skin between thumb and forefinger. She let out a yelp, shook the blood off her hand and grabbed her crow by his tethered leg. The bird fought and screamed but Aunt Polly was deaf to the racket. She bent over the arm of the chair with the crow in her hand and held it under the rocker until her own weight broke its neck.

Lena checked over the side of the houseboat for Burr and Edgar, but they were running with the dogs onshore and squealing with pleasure, involved in games that had no rules. She looked back in time to see Aunt Polly snap the string from the back of her chair and swing her dead crow overboard.

"I see Jimmy," Irene said, pointing over the water with the small, wood-handled knife she was peeling apples with.

"That's him." Aunt Polly grinned, like nothing had happened.

Instead of looking over the river, Lena turned toward the road that had brought them to this place, knowing that Frank was coming for them in the morning and that by this time tomorrow they would be heading home.

Rough clouds gathered between the peaks of the San Franciscos, the air cooling slowly as the sun set behind them. The high meadows of the Chivers farm looked frozen in the bluish light, but the flowering bugbane was deeply yellow, and Burr and Sarah were shoeless and shirtless as they wheeled through the front yard with the dogs.

Lena and Charlie sat on the front porch watching the children. Her suitcase was packed and standing by the steps. Charlie honed his penknife, impervious to the noise coming from the barn. Bill had come home from Joseph City an hour ago and went right to work on his tractor. He'd bent the rear axle the week before, when the brakes gave out and the old Ford rolled into a ditch, and now was trying to bang it straight with a sledgehammer. Betty was alone in the house, peeking past the drawn curtains as she moved from room to room.

Charlie closed the knife blade and slipped the stone back in his pocket, watching the children as they ran from the swing in the side yard. "You've been good to me, Lena. I appreciate it."

"That was easy."

"I don't know if my wife would agree."

"I think she would."

Burr and Sarah darted up on the porch, and Charlie hoisted his granddaughter onto his lap.

Lena rubbed the goose bumps on her son's skinny shoulders, then told him, "Go inside and get dressed. We'll be leaving before long."

Sarah squirmed off Charlie's lap as Burr started inside.

"Hold it, Burr," Charlie said. "I got something here." He held out his big hand, opened it, and the abalone-inlaid penknife was resting in the center of his palm. "You remember how to keep it sharp?"

"Tip the blade at an angle no bigger than your thumb and run it along the stone in one direction."

"That's right."

"You want me to sharpen it, Charlie?"

"I want you to have it."

Burr stared at the penknife's pearly luster as Charlie flipped the knife in his hand and held it out to him. "Come on," he said. "Take it."

Burr held the knife and looked at it, still shiny in the fading light.

Charlie reached into his pocket and handed the boy his honing stone. "Take good care of it."

"I will, Charlie. Thanks, Charlie." He closed his fingers around the knife, then Sarah pulled him away, the screen door rattling behind them.

Lena looked over at Charlie, his face as luminous as a new moon. They sat quietly for a moment, until Bill again raised his hammer and the clanging of metal chimed across the meadow. "Are you going to be okay here, Charlie?"

"Sure." He looked back at her. "I'm okay wherever I am."

He turned toward the road leading up to the Chivers farm. "Car coming," he said.

*T*he pair of young coyotes cut across the road and disappeared into the piney arroyo along Rawhide Creek. Filius had been watching them for a few miles now, first spotting them as daylight spread over the wind-flattened and dusty grasslands. They surfaced again on an old wagon trace that led to a distant farm; he could make out a big red cow barn and the roof of the ranch house below the sandstone cliffs that jutted out from the Wyoming plains. A large herd of shorthorns grazed along the road, but the coyotes ignored them as they zigzagged back and forth across the rutted trail, their lean, bony bodies more gray than tan, then turned south to lope alongside the sagging barbed wire, playing catch-up with the car. One of them had the foreleg of a calf in his mouth, the meat stripped off long ago, the hoof still tufted with hide. Without reason, they shifted direction and surged forward, leaping back in front of the car before darting into a deep ravine on the other side of the road, gone for good.

An hour later, he turned west on Route 26 and followed the North Platte River. The drought-stricken banks were chalk white and exposed on both sides, cradling a slim channel of barely moving water. Filius could remember when these rangelands were fuzzy with wheat grass and the small towns between the Nebraska border and Casper jumped with commerce and social activity. Every restaurant was a red-velvet steak house where cowboys and cattlemen mingled with prosperous sugar beet farmers, the new pioneer gentry. Now all he could see was graying homesteads, and the wide streets of towns like Fort Laramie were nearly deserted, the boards that covered the storefront windows as shrunken and withered as the prairie was forlorn.

He drove into Guernsey and stopped at Leonard's Café. An old man in a white apron sat in a chair in the open doorway, rocking a baby boy in the cradle at his feet. He held a birch stick from which a feather dangled on a string, and he bobbed it up and down between his legs, always just out of the baby's chubby grip. The baby screamed and swatted, his puffed and teary face as red as his tormentor's, his image in miniature. The old man winked at Filius. "Feisty little bastard, ain't it?" Then he pointed at the Chrysler.

"Illinois plates, huh?"

Filius inhaled deeply, looking at his dust-speckled car.

"Son," the man said, "you a long way from home."

Addie called her husband a "dam bum."

After the Don Pedro Dam was completed in 1923, they lived like nomads, touring the country with their infant son and setting down temporary roots wherever the Reclamation Services sent them. They camped in the Crazy Mountains on their way to build the Hubbard Dam in Montana, and returning to California they looked for fossils in the badlands where wild horses still roamed outside of Melville. During a break on the Mormon Flats Project at the Salt River in Arizona, they hiked the southern rim of the Grand Canyon, taking turns holding the baby on the easy cutbacks of Bright Angel Trail, and celebrated Addie's twenty-fourth birthday at the El Tovar Hotel, where a sudden midnight lightning storm opened like a black iris to illuminate the abyss of the canyon. When Filius finished his work on the Bullards Bar Dam on the Yuba River, they took mules into the High Sierras and fished for golden trout in the clear, fathomless Cottonwood Lakes below Mount Whitney. In two years they put a decade's worth of miles on their Essex sedan and saved boxes full of photographs and postcards so they could recount the trip to Ray when he grew up, telling him of the wonders of the western states he'd slept and cried through as a child passed back and forth between mother and father.

After another government job in Oregon, Filius signed on with the Utah Construction Company in 1925, hired by the great dam builder himself, Frank Crowe. They'd first met the year before in Denver, when Crowe was still acting superintendent of the western region for the newly titled Bureau of Reclamation. Before that he'd been a field engineer, used to scraped knuckles and a sunburnt scalp, and he took this job with the bureau because he thought overseeing dam construction in the nineteen western states would be a challenge, and because he now had a family to think about. But most of the challenges he faced here were administrative and petty, and he missed smelling the clay and diesel that hovered over a dam site and walking the canyons and tunnels carved from the earth.

A turbulent soul, he was unable to sit still, especially behind a desk, and since his chair rarely saw the seat of his pants, he did most of his business while pacing back and forth on an antique Bessarabian donated by the estate of an Aspen silver tycoon. Once inside his office, Filius found all the windows wide open, allowing a flurry of a late spring snow to blow inside, and noted that Crowe was wearing a crisp white shirt, with no jacket or sweater, despite the fact that his words formed puffs of steam in the cold air. He was a tall man, bigger and broader than Filius, but quickly slipped across the room, grabbing his suit jacket off the coatrack and his gray Stetson off his desk. Then he threw an arm around his visitor and swung him toward the door. "Mr. Poe?"

"Sir?"

"Let's get out of here."

They'd headed down Colfax to Broadway on the slushy sidewalk, climbed into Crowe's big Packard and driven west with the windows down, Filius all the while fielding questions about his engineering experience and the detailed history of the dams he'd worked on. They passed through cottonwood forests and followed the road higher into the mountains, where the trees began to thin, and Crowe listened attentively, envious of the younger man's wanderings. He missed the foul language and the hard work of actual construction, the day-to-day problems of such a huge endeavor and the spur-of-the-moment decisions that saved time and lives. He missed living where men worked for years to achieve something so grand they couldn't recognize its beauty until it was completed. He listened to Filius as they drove through Empire and climbed higher into the Fraser River valley, and only when the mountains closed around them did he complain about the Bureau of Reclamation and the weak-chinned politicians who held it together.

"I feel stuck, Mr. Poe. Nothing gets done. I voice an opinion to men too goddamn afraid to react or respond, then they water it down and send it along proper channels, and by the time it reaches Washington there's nothing left. And that bothers the hell out of me."

"What about the dam in Oregon, Mr. Crowe?"

"What about it?"

"Build it."

Crowe threw his head back and laughed. "If only I could!"

The clouds broke over the Continental Divide, and the sun threw bright lances from a sudden expanse of deep blue sky.

"I'll rumble around Denver and take my medicine. Hell, I wanted the title and now I'm paying for it. But you go to Oregon, Mr. Poe. You build the dam."

"I will, Mr. Crowe."

"I have no doubt."

They had driven through the Corona Pass, fifty miles outside of Denver, and climbed into the Front Range. The spruce stood tall and straight in the frozen ground of the northern slopes, their upper boughs crusted with snow. Here it was cold enough for even Crowe to roll up the windows. When they came around a bend, there was a huge explosion. A plume of gray smoke and dirt rose like a storm cloud in front of them, and as it collapsed and settled, Filius was able to make out the grand excavation site at the base of James Peak.

Crowe had smiled, turning onto the dirt road that led to the east portal of the Moffat Tunnel, and parked amidst the trucks a quarter mile from the entrance, the air buzzing with the sound of a thousand drills. Filius buttoned his jacket and followed him to the mouth of the tunnel. Every man they passed tipped his hat or greeted Crowe with a handshake, and he had a name and a smile for each of them, stopping to talk to a thin man in khakis and a plaid woolen coat who was unloading dynamite crates from a flatbed into a battered jeep.

"When's the next blast, Sam?"

"Twenty minutes on the nose, Frank."

They all climbed into his jeep, and Filius perched over a box of fresh drill bits as they entered the tunnel. Once his eyes adjusted to the bright flashes of lanterns attached to the walls, he admired the timberwork holding back the muddy shale that seeped and dried on the tightly framed planks. After two miles, the sound of drilling became a high-pitched scream. A hundred yards ahead, Filius saw men working under incandescent lights on the granite walls of the exposed mountain. The jeep lurched to a stop and twenty hands reached into the back to remove the dynamite and drill bits, the crew working in synchronized haste to set the dynamite in the blasting holes that pocked the granite, and in this rush of activity the drilling never ceased.

Crowe put his lips to Filius's ear. "Six miles of railroad right through the heart of a mountain range! Think of it, Mr. Poe! What audacity!"

Filius shut his eyes, succumbing to the sharp whir around him and the wet force of Crowe's words.

"To hell with the money it costs or the time it takes. We can afford it. It's the earth herself, Mr. Poe! We will beat her with our hammers and scorch her with our fires. We will mold her and tame her, and in turn she will reward us all."

The drilling stopped, and for a brief moment Filius felt an utter stillness under the twenty-foot ceiling of jagged rock. Then the lights went out, casting the tunnel into a divine darkness. This lasted only long enough for him to catch his breath, and then the generators and engines thundered and the lanterns and headlights came on and the air was filled with the sour smell of diesel. Filius and Crowe climbed into the jeep as all around them men scrambled onto open-backed trucks that would speed through the tunnel and deliver them to daylight.

After they parked in the muddy lot, Filius walked up the slippery bank to admire the thick bands of gray and black clouds above the timberline. In a light snow he stared at James Peak and awaited the dynamite, bracing himself for the moment the land would tremble and swell beneath him. Then he heard the detonation, dull and distant in the core of the mountain, and saw snow shimmer and fall from the tallest pines—the earth itself shaking as if it were being re-created, only to settle again into something familiar and perfect, except for the smoke and dust that billowed out of the tunnel's mouth like a great snort of contentment.

Crowe climbed the bank and stood next to him, both listening to the rumbling of the mountain. And as the echoes from within softened and relaxed, he put his hand on Filius's shoulder. "Will you have dinner with us tonight, Mr. Poe?"

A blue dusk had already shadowed west of Denver when he drove Addie and their sleeping son to the Crowes' modest stucco house on the edge of Capitol Hill. Linnie met them at the door and ushered them into a warmth fragrant with roasted lamb. When Ray woke up and started crying, she twirled him in her arms until his tears dried and he was laughing in dizzy glee, then led them to where Patricia, her little girl, was playing with blocks and balls on a hooked rug in front of the living room fireplace. Frank made the women martinis, using good English gin from a Boise contractor who was trying to lure him away from the bureau, and for Filius and himself poured tall glasses of bonded scotch obtained from the same source.

While Addie and Linnie sat on the couch and kept an eye on the children, the men moved onto the back porch, fortified against the cold by the aged and smoky whiskey.

"Why did you join the bureau, Mr. Poe?"

"To build dams, sir. Same as you, I expect."

They drank and talked about the dams Crowe had built, from the Arrowrock on the Boise River, as tall as a New York skyscraper, to the Tieton Dam in Washington State, which he'd completed just before moving behind a desk in Denver, still grieving over the loss of his young son to cholera. But he had survived the helplessness and pain, he said, because he loved his wife and daughter. And he still loved building dams, and the places where they needed to be built. The men drank their whiskey slowly, in the warm light that pulsed through the window behind them, beyond which their wives and children were softened by the yellow flickering of the fireplace.

"I'll build dams again," Frank Crowe said, then drained his glass. "At least one dam."

Which one, Filius knew without thinking. "Boulder?"

The older man—forty-two to his twenty-four—looked at him and nodded.

Then Linnie tapped on the window. Filius finished his whiskey, and they rose together, smiling, their noses tipped with cold, and went inside for dinner.

Filius and Addie had started across the Mojave in the middle of the night, and at dawn they watched the sun rise over the pink-and-yellow valley that bowled around them, the same colors as the pale streaks that lightened the sky. Outside of Barstow they passed wooden shacks abandoned on the smooth dolomite hills, and caught sight of jackrabbits racing through the saltbrush and creosote that fought through the cracked earth. They drove over ancient dry lake beds where alkali drifted in low, white sheets and watched the sharp, twisted peaks in the distance change from black to purple to blue. They stopped at a filling station in Baker, topped up their radiator water bags and washed down hamburgers with two Coca-Colas each in the shade of the café porch as noonday heat waves rose like shimmer from a fire and blurred the desert all around them.

It was the early summer of 1922, and they were traveling to the Colorado River to see the proposed site of the Boulder Dam. The sun was dry and unforgiving, and Addie's feet swelled so badly that she stayed barefoot until they hit the Nevada line. A few hours later, they came into Las Vegas. They bought fresh eggs from a little girl selling chickens out of the back of her father's pickup truck on Fremont Street, and stopped at a market on Third for a loaf of bread and thick steaks for dinner, filling paper sacks with all the apples and tomatoes that weren't bruised or wormy. They left town and continued southeast on unmarked dirt roads through the small farm community of Saint Thomas, where goats ran wild as dogs through unfenced yards, and saw trucks returning from the silver mines in the Eldorado Range, appearing like ghost ships on the dusty road. At dusk, Filius found the black wooden marker he was looking for and turned down a gravel road that followed a dry wash the last twelve miles to the Colorado. They saw the cottonwoods before they saw the river, which they followed to the big bend where they had been told the campground would be. While Filius pitched the tent and laid out their bedrolls, Addie sat at the crescent beach and dipped her aching feet into the water, as warm and thick as milky tea, lying back on the soft sand with her hands beneath her head and watching the first star appear like a pinhole in the rich blue sky. By now Filius had uncovered the old fire pit and started some dried mesquite with unread pages from the *Las Vegas Review-Journal*, rubbed the steaks with butter, cracked pepper and salt and then, when the fire blazed, placed the meat directly in the flames to sear it quickly and blacken in the seasoned crust. He sliced tomatoes and bread, and when he flipped the steaks, Addie sat down beside him.

"It's beautiful here, Filius."

"Yes, it is."

"They'll build the dam someday and it will change, won't it?"

"Someday. But not today."

As they ate their steaks, a cat's-eye moon rose above Black Canyon to the north, and the row of cottonwoods along the river threw long, bent stripes across the desert floor. The sky maintained an eerie nocturnal brightness through which bats flitted from nearby peaks. While Filius cleaned the dinner plates in a pail of water, Addie took off her clothes and crouched in the shallows to bathe. He observed the curve and cleft of her nakedness, her back shining like polished wood in the blue light, and when she stood and stretched her arms, he came up behind her and cupped her breasts and let his hands run down her smooth belly and rest on the flange of her hipbones. They stood there, resting against each other, and listened to the gurgle and brush of the river as it flowed south, its surface smooth and bright as chrome.

They slept well that night, tangled and tired, and at dawn Filius woke when he heard the bottom of a boat scrape against their sandy beach. He pulled on his pants and crawled out of the tent, and when he stood up a dozen kangaroo rats bounced up from their feast of fat drippings around the fire pit and hopped away on ruddering tails, disappearing into the brushy ocotillo. Shielding his eyes and turning toward the water, Filius saw a thin man in a long-billed hat pulling his wooden boat onto the shore. He turned and smiled, rubbing his hands on faded dungarees.

His name was Bobby Corn and he had a little farm in Overton, but to make ends meet he trapped beaver in the winter and ferried bootleg whiskey across the Virgin River to Chevrolets waiting on the Arizona side. He did what he had to do, and he did it good-naturedly and without complaint because he enjoyed the desert and the freedom it allowed.

"My wife's still getting used to it, but that's okay. Sue's only been out here a year from Reno, and she's just seventeen. Me, I'm an old man of nineteen."

He grinned, his sunburned face the color of slapped skin, and reached out to shake Filius's hand. "You with the bureau, mister?"

"That's right."

"Want me to run you up to Black Canyon?"

They drifted a few hundred yards before Bobby got his motor started and pointed the boat upstream. The boat was very long and narrow, and Bobby steered with a long tiller that extended from the stern. Addie sat in front of him with her wide hat tied down with a scarf, and Filius sat in the bow. He didn't mind the splash of brown water that cooled his skin, and no matter how far he turned down the brim of his felt Stetson, it didn't keep the tip of his nose from getting burned. They chugged slowly into the middle of the channel, and when they turned the wide bend into Black Canyon, he saw the walls gradually rising like bruised knuckles on a closed fist. As the canyon deepened, the sun threw black shadows on the eastern side and he felt as if they were entering a geographic standstill where nothing had changed since this molten landscape had stretched and rolled and sent these rock cliffs soaring up out of the water. Looking ahead to where the river narrowed and bent in the cool clutch of the canyon, he knew exactly where the dam would be built. It didn't matter that the angry water roiled and eddied and smacked the red walls, the strong current forming dangerous sand banks under its rippling surface. He could see it. A dam could be built and the river could be mastered and the whole desert transformed. Bobby Corn's farm and town would be lost under the green depths, one of many communities swallowed by the surge, their meager histories to be read in the rusted bicycles and broken crockery and bloated books washed up on new shorelines, picked over by old-timers who would look past half-submerged peaks and visit sunken cemeteries in memory only. All because a great wedge of concrete would someday fill the gorge.

When Bobby steered his boat into the center of the canyon, Filius stared up at the crusty volcanic cliffs that flared, pink and orange, above the dark shade lines, and reached back to take his wife's hand. "Here, Addie, here!"

All she could see was brown, swirling water, jagged rocks and sun. "How?"

And he just squeezed.

They turned back to the campsite, Bobby letting his boat motor quietly in the current. Filius and Addie sat side by side as he told them about his plans.

"When they get around to building this dam, I'm gonna open a ferry service and run people up and down the river so they can see what's going on themselves. Get some tourists, make a little extra money between beavering. I know the water well enough, and I already toted a senator and a congressman come across from Arizona. Maybe when business is good I'll build a canopy to keep the sun off and advertise in the Los Angeles newspapers and get some movie people to come see. Have my picture made with Ken Maynard. Wouldn't that be something?"

He beached the boat up at the campsite and they sat in the shade of a tarp while Addie made tomato sandwiches. Bobby ate and then napped for an hour before climbing back into his boat and pushing off the sandbar with a long oar, waving good-bye as he drifted into the gray shadows that fell down down the rocks.

In the heat of the afternoon Addie went down to the beach with a book, while Filius sat in the tent over his portfolio and sketched the canyon and features of the dam. The project had been talked about for years, but only today as they traveled down the river was he certain that it would happen. At dusk he found Addie asleep under a tarp, the open book next to her. He crouched down and ruffled her honey-colored hair. "Feel like taking a swim?"

She smiled, sitting up, and Filius undressed her on the sandy beach before slipping out of his own clothes. They walked into the shallows, their bodies warmed by the setting sun, and stopped where the water came to Addie's shoulders. Turning, she pulled Filius toward her, and he shut his eyes and kissed her neck, smelling the warm dampness of her skin, and after a moment he put his hands on her rib cage and lifted her smoothly out of the water. Addie arched her back and slid onto him, the only sound the lapping of the current as they gently moved and held each other.

Months later, back in Chicago, Addie was showing, and they were convinced it was on this night, under the shadow of Black Canyon, that Ray was conceived.

Driving into the hills above Guernsey, Filius recognized the flattened crest of tableland where the reservoir had been built, and remembered the day he'd received the letter from the Utah Construction Company asking him to leave the bureau and build this dam in Wyoming. Frank Crowe had signed the letter, and under the formal request were the handwritten words "Let's go to work."

In September 1925, Filius and Addie gave up their rented bungalow next to a lemon grove in Glendale, California, and drove with young Ray across Utah and Idaho, arriving in Guernsey less than a week after he'd accepted the job. Frank and Linnie Crowe were there to meet them, and helped them get set up in a small wooden house picketed by enormous sunflowers that stood as high as the front porch. Filius went to work the next morning, supervising two hundred men who were moving earth and clay out of the narrow canyon that would support the dam. Although the dam would be small, especially compared to the one being built on the Baker River outside Seattle, it was Filius's first job as supervising engineer. He listened to Frank Crowe and worked alongside the men, learning to register their complaints about work and wives, girlfriends and children, and to understand their needs for security and safety, and in turn they learned to trust him. Filius wore a white shirt and tie every day, but the knees of his khakis were stained and often ripped, and the leather of his boots cracked in the dry Wyoming heat, and his knuckles bled when he forgot to wear gloves. He taught himself how to operate a steam shovel and unload the skips on the dam's growing embankment, and he was the first man on the site in the morning and the last to leave. At first the men called him Mr. Poe, and joked behind his back about his New York nose and Rockefeller manners, but when he helped pull a man from a rock slide on the downstream portal, they relaxed and called him Filius. Some invited him and Addie to their modest homes for supper, where their shy wives served boiled meat and potatoes around a kitchen table crowded with restless children, and the hospitality was always reciprocated, and Addie was the perfect hostess. At the beginning and end of each season Filius threw a barbecue in the field behind his house, where he and Frank Crowe cooked slabs of ribs and steaks over a wood fire while the women sat in clusters drinking sugary iced tea and the men bet on horseshoes and drank homemade beer. If the night was warm and clear the party would go on long after dark, the exhausted and overfed children falling asleep right there in the tall grass, surrounded by gnawed bones and panting dogs.

Over the two years it took to build the Guernsey Dam, Addie noticed the changes that were taking hold of her husband. He was still not gregarious or talkative, but he was forthright and open with an opinion when asked, and if he wasn't the most approachable boss, he was clearly respected. Because she knew easy companionship wasn't natural for him, she was proud that he'd accomplished it outside the small orbital reach of herself and their son.

In the evenings when he returned home, Filius kissed her before soaking his long, dusty body in the cramped little tub, then came out in a clean white shirt and khakis to sit in the small, dimly lit parlor with Ray while she prepared their supper. He told her about his day while cradling his son, and if Ray fell asleep, he carried him to the table and held him when dinner was served. Filius couldn't get enough of looking at the boy, honey-colored like his mother, with the same long fingers and small chin. And in Guernsey Ray finally developed a bridge on his nose, and his nostrils now flared, willful and defiant. Addie loved the nose, and although Filius kept quiet, he did, too. During that first summer, Ray often woke in the middle of the night, crying from a nightmare, and Filius would carry him out onto the front porch, rocking on the glider until the boy fell back asleep, and Addie would find them like that in the morning, Filius wide awake, Ray's fingers curled around the tip of his nose.

The first winter in Guernsey, after construction had shut down, snowdrifts covered the porch in February and blacked out the downstairs windows. Neighbors helped dig them out, and on the first sunny, bitter day after the blizzard, Filius and Addie bundled Ray in a papoose of blankets and snowshoed across the pure, dizzying whiteness that stretched outside their own back door. When spring came and the crews went back to work, the family would go hiking every Saturday morning in the hills near the dam site, and one afternoon, above Cold Springs, they crouched in a cedar grove and watched an old wolverine tear apart a baby fox snared in a hunter's trap. On the long nights of summer they swam at a wide bend in the Platte River near Fairbanks, and on weekends they explored the ruins of the old fort by the Laramie Bridge, poking around the brush and elder trees for horse and ox shoes and bayonets, the detritus of settlers traveling west on the Oregon Trail. In October, they went with other families from Guernsey to the worker colonies that bordered the sugar beet fields outside of Lingle, where Mexican field hands served tortillas with barbecued goat and red chiles that grew fiery under the Wyoming sun.

Those were good years, and Filius remembered them now as he stood above the nearly empty reservoir behind the Guernsey Darn. The drought ravaging the plains had exposed the steep banks of the manmade lake, and the water, achingly low, had the yellowish tint of something poisoned. He turned into the hot wind, holding his hat tight to his head as he looked over the boiled landscape. The cottonwood break along the road leading to the dam stood dead and brittle. In the distance the North Platte River was barely visible, its stream thin as catgut. The once gray fields were devoid of cattle and bitten down to naked soil, but the fences still stood, and each post was crowned with gopher pelts, and the posts ran on for miles.

The air was scratchy with dust, and Filius coughed and ducked his chin as it swirled and moaned like a banshee over the northern ridge. He looked again over the gentle contours of the earthen dam below him and thought of the years he'd spent building it. But his memories, exact and wistful as they were, didn't always suffice, because there was something doubtful and needy in their retelling, like a story known secondhand.

They moved back to Chicago in the late fall of 1930, when Ray was seven and ready to start school. They found an apartment with a big window overlooking Lincoln Park, where the maple trees that lined the street were bare, and the park itself was a sward of green wilderness in the middle of the city.

Filius would have only five weeks before driving back to California. He was going alone this time, to supervise construction on the San Gabriel Dam as a favor to Sam Ross, a fellow engineer he'd met on the Don Pedro site who was finally checking into a Los Angeles hospital after complaining for years about a bad stomach ruined by whiskey and little food. Filius would be separated from Addie for the first time in eight years, but for seven months he would work hard and put Sam ahead of schedule before returning to Chicago for the summer, where he would wait for Frank Crowe's call about Boulder Dam. President Hoover had authorized the project the summer before, and Frank was swamped with bids and details, eager to start blasting, though seasoned enough to realize that day was still far off.

Filius walked Ray down Lincoln Park West to school every weekday morning that September and October. At the corner of Ogden Street they turned right, and only then would he allow his son to drop his hand and run into the playground to join his friends and, when the first bell rang, race up the limestone steps and into the school building. Then Filius would walk home and have breakfast with Addie, and in the afternoon they would pick Ray up together.

On the first Tuesday night in November, while his wife and son slept, he packed his suitcase, and after midnight, when the wind turned from the north and blew cold across the park, he went into Ray's room and shut the window the boy liked to keep open. Content in the quiet darkness, he sat and watched his son stretch and settle under the blankets piled on the bed. At dawn he woke Addie and they had breakfast together, coffee and an apple pie her mother had made the night before, then he kissed her good-bye at the front door and drove out of Chicago as the first snow of the season blew in from Lake Michigan.

He arrived in Azusa, California, six days later and went directly to the site in the San Gabriel Mountains. The dam was being constructed under the auspices of the Los Angeles County Flood Control District, and Sam Ross had things well under control before turning the project over to Filius. It was a beautiful site and a well-designed dam, and Filius enjoyed his time there. He shared a bungalow in Azusa with three other men, ate most of his meals out of cans or at the roadside hamburger stand in Duarte, but he offset these bad habits by snacking throughout the day on the oranges he'd picked from the trees in front of the rental house. On weekends he drove into the San Bernardino Mountains to the north and fished for trout in the streams that fed Lake Arrowhead. And every evening he collected his mail and sat alone on the porch to read the letters that Addie sent almost daily.

Dear Filius,

It is snowing now, and has been for three days. Yesterday we had eight inches on the ground and the sun came out for a few hours so my father and I took Ray for his first ski lesson on that little hill above Duck Pond. Of course, it loomed like the Alps to Ray, but Daniel was a tower of patience and strapped my old wooden skis on him, and together they tramped up the slope and Ray came flying down alongside Daniel, his legs splayed like a baby crow's, and after falling at my feet he lifted his head out of the snow, red-faced and laughing, and couldn't wait to do it again. This went on for two hours, up and down this little pimple of a hill, the two of them, my father and your son, until their noses were about frostbitten. Ray was soaking wet and bottom sore, and we only left when it started to snow again, and by that time he had stopped falling and was almost able to turn and glide to a stop. And small as he is, darling, he was so full of himself, acting as if he had been born to ski. My father and I struggled to keep a straight face, but we did, and it was a moment to cherish, and I wish you had been here to cherish it with me.

Dear Filius,

Ray's class is visiting the Field Museum this afternoon, so I'm sitting in the Mundelein College library working on an article for the Tribune about our two years in Wyoming, and of course they wanted a womanly approach, with recipes and gossip and folktales, but I insisted the womanly approach was more about dealing with a baby in a small town while your husband worked ten hours a day and you were surrounded by strangers in an isolated community without culture or libraries, where suspicion preceded acceptance and acceptance took time. The editor agreed, as long as I included at least one recipe, so here I am in the library, working by the window as a heavy rain falls, watching the Sisters of Charity of the Blessed Virgin Mary scurry about the courtyard below, unruffled by the downpour as students splash and race around them, almost smug in their pious detachment. So as I write about Wyoming and the dam and the people we met, I think about you. How I miss you. Which vexes me, because when I was a little girl the idea of marriage was repulsive, so I went through school and dated the boys I was attracted to, but never enough to consider seeing them more than three consecutive Saturday nights. I was content with this and accepted my looming spinsterhood, ready to become the odd duck in the family, brilliant (of course!) and alone. And then I met you and I fell in love, and now I miss you and it's still raining.

Dear Filius,

I woke up Saturday morning and the sky was blue and clear, and when I opened the window I realized that spring had arrived. I hadn't noticed before that the trees in Lincoln Park had started to leaf out, or that if you breathed in deeply you could smell the water lapping the shoreline at Diversey Beach. So I borrowed my father's car and picked up Ray at school and we arrived in Madison just after dark. We're here now—it's Sunday night—and Ray is asleep downstairs and I'm sitting on the bed in your old room on Livingston Street with the window open, listening to a chained and lovesick dog in a neighbor's *backyard. Yesterday I took Ray to the university to show him where we'd gone to school, and he wanted to see where you studied to be an engineer and where I wrote my articles for the* Daily Cardinal, *and of course wants to come here when he's old enough, but I think it's mostly because we went swimming at the indoor pool at Lathrop Hall, and your father took us to a Badger basketball game at the Armory (we beat Purdue, again). Ray made me take him back to the pool this morning, and you'd be proud of his long strokes and his ability to stay underwater, and when we took a break and floated around the pool on our backs, he asked questions incessantly—"How did they build a pool inside?" and "How come I don't sink?"—and I thought this is how you must've been as a boy, inquisitive and never shutting up, but then I realized you probably didn't ask many questions, and when I asked your father if you did, he just laughed. And I know why. My father always says he has a gift for understanding people, but he doesn't understand you or why I love you, and I imagine it's a puzzle he ponders nightly, scratching that bald spot that is getting larger all the time. And you're not like your own parents, although they're wonderful people and you're lucky to have them. What you are sets you apart from everybody but me and Ray, and I hope our son inherits something more than your nose. I mean your sense of awe and the excitement of knowing what makes things work. I hope he will someday grow up to become part of something important and, like you, still be able to stand alone.*

He saved all the letters and kept them tightly bundled in a box, the weight of them tangible and precious to him. He worked long hours, the weather was good and the job on schedule when, on March 1, Sam Ross came out of the hospital and started working a few hours a day, drinking milk from a bottle and eating the chicken salad sandwiches his wife made for him, making sure her husband stayed strong and sober and healthy.

Two days later Filius received a telegram from Frank Crowe; the newly formed construction giant Six Companies had won the bid on Boulder Dam, and he was expected in Nevada that fall. Two weeks later he left for Chicago, where he'd spend the spring and summer with his family, celebrating Ray's eighth birthday in August with a surprise sailing trip to the Manitou Islands.

He drove through the night and crossed the Utah border an hour before dawn. The sky was shot through with stars, and in the crisp gray light he saw deer nosing through the buckbrush along the north bank of the Green River. He took an old dirt road that climbed through a cedar forest and followed the river through a ruddy gorge. After a few miles he stopped and walked to the canyon rim with a bag full of overripe peaches he'd bought the day before. He stared at the river five hundred feet below him, wide and fast and rushing madly through higher gorges to the west as the rising sun speckled its surface. He ate around the bad spots and studied the landscape as the peach juice ran down his chin, concluding that someday this would be a good place for a dam.

About thirty miles south of Vernal, he saw a humped figure sitting at the end of an oiled road that led to the small reservation town of Randlett. The Indian's face was wide and heavy under his black Stetson, and a dark pinstriped suit was buttoned up and stretched tight across his belly, one sleeve ripped at the elbow. He was leaning against a handsomely tooled saddle, squinting at the car, just waking up.

Filius stopped. It wasn't conversation that he craved, just a voice to listen to, an excuse not to think.

"You need a ride?" he called through the open window.

When the Indian smiled, the blood that had dried at the corner of his lip now cracked, and he wiped away the fresh drops with the back of his hand and stood up, stocky and strong, his suit trousers bunching around his cowboy boots like pantaloons. He picked up the saddle and put it on the front seat. Filius smelled evaporated sweat and alcohol as the Indian opened the back door and climbed in, then stretched out and pulled a paper bag out of his suit pocket, the knuckles on both hands bruised and soiled.

"Where are you headed?" Filius asked him.

"Gandy."

"Where's that?"

"West."

"How far?"

"How far you goin'?"

"Nevada."

"Not that far."

Filius pulled back onto the empty highway. The Indian shook a handful of pine nuts out of the bag and popped them into his mouth, crushing the shells with his teeth and sucking out the meat; he spit the shells out the open window, and in five minutes was fast asleep.

His snoring presence, Filius decided, was not enough, nor was the heat blistering off the alkali flats. All the obstacles and discomfort he threw in front of himself could not keep him focused on the present, on this dull leisurely stretch of U.S. 40, instead of the frayed weave of his past.

He saw sheep grazing on the distant hills and counted them as he drove. The Indian hacked and coughed on the backseat, filling the car with the scent of stale whiskey that rose with every contented snore.

The road went on, straight and forever.

Oh, Addie. Oh, Ray.

The storm had seemed to come out of nowhere, but of course Filius knew better than that. Weather changes. Clouds turn black and bully together when you least expect it. Temperatures drop suddenly and the wind comes up just as fast, especially on the open water.

Around noon, the wind picked up from the east and the temperature started to drop. Filius saw the clouds massing in the sky behind them. Ray kept trolling for lake trout off the stern, letting out line even though he knew it would never go deep enough. As the sun blurred in the haze, Addie gave him a sweater and sat next to Filius on the bench, leaning against him and closing her eyes. The insides of her bare calves, he noticed, were sunburned.

Even then there had been nothing to worry about. A summer squall, typical in August. He had sailed harsher weather in smaller boats, and while the wind was blowing steady at twenty knots, the boat rode smoothly over the gray chop.

An hour later, the rain started and the boat was dipping in the troughs between sets of waves. Addie had Ray pull in his fishing line and come off the stern. Down below she helped him into a dry sweatshirt and oilskin jacket so he could sit by his father at the tiller. She leaned on the transom and watched Filius survey the quickly changing sky.

"I think it's time to bring in the sail," he said when the clouds began to tower, their bottoms rolling out. They wouldn't be able to outride the storm, he realized; it would catch them and shake them and drench them when it went over.

By the time they had finished bringing down the sail, they were both soaked. "It's going to be bad, isn't it?"

"We'll get wet. But it'll blow over quickly, and the sun will come out long before we get to Whitefish Bay."

They huddled together with Ray between them. The rain came down faster now, and the boat rocked in the crested waves. Filius fought with the tiller as sheets of water rose over the bow. The clouds continued rolling in from the west, and then they heard the roar of distant thunder and saw the first lightning strike, a forked talon of brightness thrown down ahead of them from the darkest part of the sky. The severity of it dazzled them.

Addie gripped his arm. "Can we turn back?"

"The storm's moving too fast."

The clouds rose higher and their tops flattened in the sky. The downdrafts of strong winds blew out their bottoms and a thick veil of rain approached with blistering speed.

"Jesus, Filius."

"It'll be all right." Filius looked down at his son, who was staring wide-eyed at the storm and flinched only when another crack of lightning tore through the sky. "Get below, Ray."

"I want to stay with you!" He grabbed his father's leg and held tight.

The sailboat rocked into another deep trough, and rain danced violently over the planks. Addie knelt behind Ray, took his shoulders and spoke firmly, inches from his ear. "Go below, right now. I'll be down in a few minutes."

Filius felt the fingers loosen on his thigh and looked down at the water streaming off his son's scalp. Ray glanced up at his father with his lips held tight, blinking in the rain, before unlatching the door and heading below.

Addie stumbled as the boat rose and fell, grabbing on to the mast halyards. The wind blew directly into them now. The bow nosed down again, hard enough to shoot up a spray of white water higher than the spreaders. The wind shifts became extreme, roaring like runaway freight trains from all directions. The curling waves swelled into giant hammerheads that crashed onto the boat and rushed over the sides. And the wall of rain came down.

Addie braced herself against the boom. Filius let go of the tiller and lunged toward her just as a steep wave broke over the windward side, the boat heeling at an acute angle. He slipped on the wet plank and fell forward, hitting his forehead on the turnbuckle. The pain shot all the way to his fingertips, and for a moment everything went black. He felt blood on his face, and it rolled off his oilskin jacket like grease. He rose to his knees and let the fierce and biting rain clear his head. The wind-kicked waves were coming closer together now, and he made his way to Addie.

She clung to the mast as the next wave washed over the deck. Hearing dishes shattering below, she thought of Ray's frightened face, but blinked it away, closing her eyes as the wind screamed around her. It's only the wind, she told herself, but the wind howled in her ear like an animal near death. Suddenly, she felt something around her waist, and realized Filius was holding her. The boat yawed as it careened down the next trough. She leaned into her husband's chest, and for a moment she felt them rising like angels, but then they were smashed down hard against the churning lake and were drenched again.

"Get below!" he shouted.

She saw the ugly gash on Filius's forehead, and as she raised up her hand, drops of his blood mixed with rain washed down her arm.

"Get below now!" he yelled into the wind. Seeing a new set of waves rearing up in front of the boat, he pushed Addie onto the deck and fell on top of her as they crashed over the side. Filius heard the mast snap, and the wood cracking around the cabin roof. The boat, following the flow of the wave, heeled high on the water. He held on to Addie as they were thrown against the planking, and the pressure of the water on his back and kidneys made him gasp.

Addie was smothered under her husband's weight, but squirmed enough to raise her head in time to see the door of the crushed cabin torn off by the wind. Filius's chin jabbed into her shoulder and they both watched in horror as Ray was washed up onto the deck in a great surge of water, his eyes blank with panic and his arms straining to reach his parents as the sailboat went over.

Filius didn't know how long he had been under when Addie was swept from his arms. He was spinning in the pounding waves, aware of the boat rolling next to him, its broken lines slicing through the water. He curled around himself and spun until the water released him and shot him upward into the wet, deafening air, and in the gray heart of the storm he saw the overturned sailboat with Addie clinging to its floating mast, screaming and pointing wildly behind him. He turned, and in the gulling waves, Ray's back quickly disappeared into the froth.

Filius kicked forward and dove into the silence below. In those first moments he thought he saw his son being tossed and battered in the angry swells, close enough that he was sure he could reach him. He dove deeper, boring into the water that pushed against him. He didn't know how deep he swam, but he kept his eye on what he thought was his son and didn't stop diving until a rope tangled around his left ankle with a sudden, shocking pain. Desperate, he grabbed at the rope, but the more he pulled the tighter it became, wrapped and knotted, and he knew then the ankle was broken. He held his breath and floated there, staring down at what looked like the impression of a boy spinning gently in the gray depths, his arms and legs spread, drifting and fading away. Filius felt a crushing pressure in his ears and knew that he was screaming. He kicked until the pain in his body seared the raging wound in his brain, and he stayed underwater until his lungs burned empty and he floated back to the churning surface more dead than alive. He came up on the other side of the stern and couldn't see Addie. It was still raining, but not as hard. He pulled himself along the rudder and finally saw her draped over the splintered mast, looking at the spot in front of her where Ray had gone down. He called to her so softly that he didn't hear himself. Addie didn't turn around, didn't face him, just stared into the water and began to howl.

Within five minutes the winds died down. Within ten the sun came out and warmed the air. It was August 25 and they were sixty miles from Whitefish Bay, drifting in their wreckage and torment, unable to look at each other in the six hours they waited for rescue.

The Indian tapped him on the shoulder.

"Gandy, mister."

Filius wiped a hand across his eyes.

"This is where I get out."

Filius pulled over by a stand of poplars. He had driven all day, stopping only for gasoline in Provo and Delta, while his passenger slept and snored behind him. Somewhere west of the Confusion Mountains he had begun to cry, silently and without knowing it.

The Indian opened the front door and didn't even look at him as he dragged his handsome saddle across the seat. He lifted it to his shoulder and walked thirty feet to the gravel ranch road, dropped it and sat down, pulled off his tall boots and rubbed his feet, then rested his head on the saddle seat and dipped his hat over his eyes, going back to sleep, the same humped figure Filius picked up almost three hundred miles ago.

Filius drove on. When he crossed the Nevada border six miles later, he pulled over again and gave into long, wrenching sobs that carried over the empty landscape. He cried for his son, drifting still through inland waves, and he cried for Addie and himself, drifting forever. He cried because he was haunted, and he cried until there was nothing left but the dull ache inside him.

It was five o'clock, the sun bright in the clear sky. Mounds of wild peas grew by the roadside, and the low flat-topped hills to the south were banded in bronze and red stone. He wiped his eyes, suddenly hungry and tired, and thought about driving into Ely and having dinner in a comfortable hotel, steak and dessert and a tall glass of whiskey from the bottle he carried with him, hoping that maybe then he'd be able to sleep without incident or despair, and wake up rested and grateful enough to drive the last miles to Boulder Dam.

*N*aked, he stepped into Mary's small, dark bathroom and turned on the light before sitting at the glass-topped vanity next to the sink. He pushed aside an open tube of ointment, wiping his finger through a white smear of cold cream that smelled of lilacs, and angled the standing mirror so he could study his face.

Lew's eyes were puffy, and when the small round lights above the vanity bounced off the aqua wallpaper printed with sea horses and starfish and ocean weeds, his complexion turned blue. The only thing familiar and likable was his nose, broken and set many times over, a much-handled curiosity molded from his own flesh and bone. Sitting there pondering his reflection, he thought he looked old, closer to thirty than twenty, and for a brief moment when he narrowed his eyes and turned to the right he glimpsed his father, but when he faced front again Isadore was gone for good. Still, he was startled and upset by the fleeting resemblance and assured himself he looked nothing like his crookbacked and broken-fingered father, or his mother with her timid eyes always downcast in modest dread, or for that matter the shtetl dwellers—the rabbis and *muttis* and chicken farmers—who had sired them both. He knew all too well these strange inhabitants of the washed-out cities and muddy hills called Plock and Plonsk. Their photographs had lined the living room mantel in the house on Clarence Street, and as a little boy he used to climb up on a chair and gaze fearfully at the faded images of men and women standing glumly inside the gates of their shitty farms or on tenement stoops, always formally dressed in long dark clothes, the men hatted, bearded and gaunt, the women stocky and short.

Even back then he had understood that he didn't look like any of them—that he wasn't like any of them. A son of America, tough and slangy, he was as unremarkable as everybody else, and he liked that.

He ran the back of his fingers along his chin and cheek—he needed a shave as well as a bath—and stood up to look in the mirror at his penis, cupping his testicles in his right hand. At times like these, alone and unobserved, he could almost relax and enjoy the feel of himself.

Back in the bedroom, he stood in front of the window. The moon was bright, and in the apartment building across the way, he found the rocking horse in the window, but the little girl was nowhere in sight.

Mary groaned in the bed behind him, and as his eyes adjusted to the light he could see her twitching fitfully in her sleep, her head stuffed up and her breath sputtering. When she turned onto her back and relaxed, he saw where he'd socked her; the skin was pulpy around the closed eye, the purple bruise spilling over to her cheekbone a paisley swirl. An hour ago she had begged him to leave before Buddy came home, and when he lay on the bed smoking and drinking the last of her warm beer, ignoring her, she tried to run out of the room. He tackled her in the narrow hallway, the bare wood of the floor burning their elbows and knees, but she kicked him in the chest and scrambled away. Lew grabbed her ankle and twisted until she cried out, then he pulled her naked across the floor and climbed over her, awkward and angry, suddenly repulsed by the touch of her skin, and hit her in the face, a short chop, quick and stunning. Mary's head banged against the floor and she lay still, staring at the ceiling, her foot wrapped around a thin-legged table that they'd knocked over. A single crushed gardenia sat in a puddle next to a broken vase, and a picture frame lay facedown on shards of broken glass. He carefully slid out the photograph, a tinted picture of Mary and a tall, husky, broad-shouldered man in a brimmed hat and dark suit pants, standing in front of Lake Malibu under a huge banner: FULLER PAINT COMPANY ANNUAL PICNIC, 1929. Mary was laughing with her mouth open, her print dress bunched around her thighs making her look fat. And Buddy, surrounded by friends and coworkers, waved at the camera with a goofy grin, exposing a deep sweat stain that ran to the belt loops of his high-waisted pants.

Lew picked up the table and replaced both the picture and frame, but left the broken glass on the floor. Mary didn't so much as look at him as he lifted her in his arms. His fingers caressed the base of her breast and he watched her nipples turn hard, but when he glanced at her face she turned away. Her cheek was already pink when he carried her back into the bedroom and laid her down across the damp sheets, and when he touched the inside of her thigh she pulled the blanket up to her neck and cried herself to sleep.

He now stood over her again, reaching down to touch her shoulder.

"Don't."

Her skin felt cold as stone.

"Please don't."

Lew didn't do anything; he didn't have to. He went back into the bathroom, leaving the door open, and took Buddy's shaving soap and razor from the cabinet next to the sink. There was a small window over the bathtub, and he pushed apart the thin curtains and opened it to let in the fresh, night-scented air. He lathered up while the tub filled, and shaved close with Buddy's razor, then took a long bath in Buddy's tub and rubbed himself with Buddy's soap while watching Buddy's wife, a dark lump in the bed, in the mirror over the sink.

He stayed in the tub until the water turned tepid. Headlights threw rectangles that moved abstractly across the wall, and he listened to the drunken laughter of the neighbors in the apartment next door. When he finally stood up and reached for a towel, he heard the car door slam on the street below.

Looking out the window, he saw a big man stepping around a black Dodge parked in front of the apartment building, and he knew it was Buddy by the canvas fishing cap and the slope of his shoulders.

Lew looked into the bedroom, where Mary was on her side, watching him with one eye. He strode toward the bed, his penis half erect, and whipped the sheets away, pinning her arms next to the pillow and prying her legs apart with his knees. He rested his belly against hers for a moment, to let her know that this was for both of them, and entered her slowly. He kissed the tears away from the corners of her eyes, and when she shook her head he pressed his cheek to hers to keep her still. Then, hearing Buddy's key jingle in the front door, he pulled himself out and flipped her over onto her stomach, holding her facedown on the pillow with one hand while lifting her hips with the other. She clawed at the sheets until he applied more pressure to the back of her head, and when she finally settled down he let her breathe as he positioned himself behind her. He heard Buddy murmur, "Jesus!" when he saw the mess on the hallway floor, and he entered Mary again, slowly and tenderly, because he remembered she liked it this way. The door opened and a parallelogram of light fell across the bed. Waiting for Buddy to appreciate the sight before him, he felt Mary shudder beneath him and truly hoped she was satisfied. In the silence he could smell the stink of fish, and imagine the slack look on Buddy's dumb face as he arched deeper into Mary and allowed Buddy's brain to plod along and catch up with his eyes.

When it did, Buddy yelled, "Jesus Christ!" and dug his clammy hand into Lew's shoulder.

Trembling, on the verge of coming, Lew sprang out of the bed and saw Buddy's big, stupid, ugly face. He hit him hard in the throat, watched him collapse and never gave him a chance to fight back, kicking him in the ribs four times before he rolled onto his back, then straddling him and punching him in the nose until it cracked and shattered and grew soft under his knuckles. When Buddy began to whimper Lew broke his jaw.

Mary jumped on his back and clamped her teeth into his ear, but Lew yanked her off by the hair and smashed her head on his knee. She and Buddy were both quiet now, so he walked to the open window and stood in the citrus breeze that felt so good against his damp skin. He stared out at the dark street until he was breathing easily, and then he went into the bathroom and washed himself off. He dressed in the bedroom to the sound of Buddy's gurgling, and watched Mary crawl weeping across the floor to lay her arm across her husband's big chest.

He didn't need the money in Buddy's wallet but took it anyway,

leaving the thin-strapped little gold watch on the dresser for Mary
to explain. It was close to midnight, and he should walk down to
Hollywood Boulevard and take a taxi downtown. Leave Los Angeles
for a while, maybe even the state. He had Speed Owens's phone
number in his duffel bag at the train station. He'd call him in
Nevada and see if Speed could get him a job on the dam.

LAS VEGAS, NEVADA

*J*oe Kenny refused to let Lena sleep. He'd picked them up at the Chivers ranch at nine o'clock that evening, and four hours later he was still talking, filling the air with whatever thought breezed through his skull.

"Selma had a special order to fill out, a nice little thing for a wedding night, had to be French silk they ordered themselves from Saint Louis, and it come this morning last minute, so I sat on the porch from ten to four with the car packed and ready and every half hour or so I poked my head in the window to ask if she was done yet, and she'd say 'No,' simple as that, and I'd go back to counting the hairs on my knuckles until thirty minutes was up, and ask again, 'You done yet?' That was my afternoon."

Lena wasn't asked to respond, and she didn't.

"Sat on that porch and thought, sure wish I was on my way to Las Vegas instead of Saint George. By now I'd be done with supper and probably playing gin rummy with some fellas I know. Jim Hammond, he's got a shop on Fremont Street sells ladies' things, widower now, and his nephew, another Jim, little Jim we call him, married just a year, and Frank Seamon, sells insurance and raises Chihuahuas but a heck of a rummy player. That's our foursome. And if this special order didn't happen I'd be playing now, not driving up to Utah in the middle of the night."

Lena's eyes ached, and she prayed he'd shut up.

"Dumb as a sack of hammers, little Jim. Married a small woman, not so much in size but in mind. Rosie has a bad thought about Jim every time he gets out of her sight, accusing him of this and that no matter if he's fast asleep in the other room or delivering the mail on the north end of Bridger Street. Sometimes she even walks his route, peeking in windows and knocking on doors to find out if Jim is tending to business with a housewife other than his own. Not that Jim's anything to look at. Got a good head of hair but no backside to speak of, flat as a board. Course it don't help that he always looks guilty; got those sad kind of eyes that don't quite focus."

They were somewhere outside Marble Canyon in northern Arizona, on their way to the Utah border. Lena closed her eyes and leaned her head toward the open window; the air off the Kaibab Plateau was hot, thick and dreamy, and Lena hoped it would carry her away.

Burr was curled up on the backseat, his body wedged between the door and the purple gift boxes that were stacked to the roof and smelled of lavender and mothballs. The constant hum of the man's voice floated in the air, and he drifted in and out of sleep, sun-tired from playing with Sarah Chivers.

He didn't like Joe Kenny. When he'd picked them up, Joe held his mother's hands in both of his, and his spindly arms were covered with monkey fur. The thin black strands of hair shellacked to his scalp couldn't hide his bald head, and his smile was crammed with teeth that looked like bad corn. His tie was yellow and green and hung there like a sour tongue. The only thing interesting about him was the black patch over his left eye. When he caught Burr staring, he grinned and squatted before the boy.

"Know how it happened? I'll tell you. Five years ago I was out back of my house chopping firewood and put up an old gray piece of oak that'd been sitting in the shed for years. I sighted the log and lifted my axe and just as I brought it down I saw a big chunk of granite the wood had grown over, but it was too late to stop, and *whack!* A chip of that rock flew up and took out my eye clean as a bullet." Kenny wobbled forward until his eye patch was as big as a movie screen and Burr could smell cheese on his breath. "Wanna look?"

When Joe Kenny started to lift the edge of his eye patch, Burr jumped backward and looked away.

Now, hours later, startled awake, confused about where he was, the sight of his mother's head over the front seat was all the comfort he needed, and he knew that by tomorrow morning they would be somewhere in the Nevada desert.

Lena kept her face to the window and her eyes closed. They'd just stopped for gasoline outside of Fredonia, and Kenny was whistling a piercing trill that drilled her ears and popped her eyes open.

"I picked up a guy bummin' through here last April. It was cold and I felt bad about anybody being on the road even though I usually don't. Happened just before daylight after raining all night and I almost didn't see him standing there hugging his chest. I heard enough stories about these guys catchin' rides, hard-luckers who'd rather stick a knife in your ribs than do a day's work, then walk off with your last nickel that isn't even worth but three cents. But this guy was soaking wet and harmless looking, so I stopped anyway and when he shuts the door the first thing I smell is garbage. Rotten garbage. 'What the hell!' I said and he opened his dripping jacket, and a little turkey head's poking out of a gunnysack tied to his waist. Alive! And on his other side he's got another sack full of old lettuce and apple cores and melon rinds—the garbage I was smelling. His name was Oliver and he was headed back to his wife and kids in Pocatello after building outdoor toilets in west Texas for the WPA. Told me he was gonna fatten up his little turkey no matter what it took, even if he stunk to high heaven, because for the first time in three years there'd be a bird on his table for Thanksgiving dinner!"

Joe Kenny laughed, and Lena glanced up and caught his good eye staring at her legs, then twisted in her seat and straightened her dress.

"You know, my wife makes nighties and lingerie that are cut just right for a figure like yours. I got a lot of things piled on the backseat that would fit you right out of the box. No pins or alterations, just go over your shoulders or up your legs like it was custom-made. Me and my wife have our own label, Kenny Originals. Pretty things for pretty girls, that's how we sell them."

Lena looked out the window. The moonlight had turned the landscape a deep gray, and the air smelled of sagebrush and dust.

Joe Kenny shifted his weight and gave her a good look.

"That dam's been good for Las Vegas. You got people coming in, money being spent, more opportunities to get something back. A good-looking woman like you is bound to attract attention. Men spend money on good-looking women, and that's nice. You wear Kenny Originals and it's nicer."

"No, but thanks." This was the first thing she'd said since they'd crossed the Painted Desert. He didn't hear it.

"You get a whole lingerie wardrobe for free. That's the deal. And get to keep it even if we don't sell a thing."

"No, thank you."

"I know a place up ahead where the boy can sleep while we have a little fashion show behind the trees, just you and me. And if this underwear don't fit better than anything you ever tried on before, I'll just pack it back up and we'll keep on driving." He stared at Lena with his finger dancing slowly in her face.

Lena stared back until Joe Kenny raised his eyebrows in defeat and turned his attention to the road. For the next forty-five minutes he didn't say a word, but Lena was too angry to sleep.

Burr woke up and looked through the windshield at the warm hump of city lights that rose before them. "Is this it?"

Lena turned around, smiling, and ran a hand through his hair, tucking the long parts behind his ears. "Not yet."

Saint George was still a few miles off, but she could already see the vaulted arches of the great Mormon Temple, white as a snowy peak under exterior lights that shined day and night, illuminating its sacred grandeur for the inhabitants of the valley below, the grandchildren of the farmers and Indian fighters and millennialists who had settled this wilderness kingdom.

It was three o'clock in the morning when they entered town, the streets quiet and dark, the occasional dog ducking between the sumac trees that grew tight against the adobe cottages lining West Street. Joe Kenny parked in front of a flat-roofed house like all the others, except for the portico that extended into a green, well-watered yard. Foot-tall lilies bloomed orchidlike along the stone path, and pink hollyhocks climbed all the way to the tiled roof. A shiny Dodge Victory Six sat in the driveway.

Joe put on his suit jacket and tightened his tie before opening the car's back door to select eight of the purple boxes. Balancing them across his outstretched arms, he slammed the car door shut with the bone of his hip. In the house a dog barked, and a light came on in the front room. He looked at his watch and smiled. "I'll have you and the boy in Las Vegas by breakfast time."

Burr watched him walk up the path. The front door opened and a white-haired man in a bathrobe stood to the side as a blonde woman half his age ran past in her pajamas and eagerly took the top box out of Kenny's arms, dancing around in childish delight while a clipped poodle yapped and jumped at the ribbon. The older man kissed his girl, waving her inside, then shook Kenny's hand and led him into the house.

Suddenly hungry, Burr turned to ask his mother for one of the hard-boiled eggs Betty Chivers had packed for them, but she was dead asleep.

Only four days ago, Lena had been sitting on the floor of the front room of her house in Hugo. Frank had been home for three weeks, and had another one off before heading out again with his boxes of Bibles. He was cutting the cattails that were taking over the back-yard pond, choking out the crappies that he liked to catch for their dinner, and Burr was riding bikes with Eddie Gomer, the neighbor's nephew, who was visiting from Norman.

Lena was cleaning the delicate ivorine figures she'd inherited from her mother, twelve perfect little dogs that her father had purchased at a small shop on Mockingbird Lane every time he'd gone to Dallas on a business trip. Clare had loved these exact French miniatures, displaying the greyhounds, setters and Labrador retrievers on a mahogany stand next to the piano. Every year, as her mother had, Lena took them down, spread them on a clean towel and renewed them to their milky shine, even using the same cleaning solution from *Smileys' New and Complete Guide for House-keepers*, a well-used book thick as a dictionary, stuffed with her mother's handwritten recipes for chutney and grape catsup, marked throughout with colored ribbons and scraps of papers. Lena remembered her mother's chutney as delicious with a leg of lamb, and the grape catsup not good with anything, but Oren never once made a disparaging remark or a sour face, convinced that a cook who wasn't open to experimentation might just as well keep a pot of water boiling on the stove for ham or chicken or whatever else could be tossed inside to be overcooked and served over a mound of mashed potatoes. Lena smiled on that humid morning, as content within this house as her parents had been, and with her own family now. This evening they would go next door for a chicken barbecue at the Gomers', and Burr would spend the night with Eddie, giving Frank and Lena rare time alone. The thought of his hand on her body in their warm bed made Lena shiver, and she forced her attention back to the book open across her knees. She finally found the proper cleaning method for the ivorine, and had started for the kitchen for the turpentine and soapwort root when she heard the mailman outside and the letters cascading through the brass slot.

Once she discarded the bills and church pamphlets, only a single piece of mail was left, addressed to her in a bold, blocky handwriting she didn't recognize. There was no return address. Inside the envelope was a single photograph. Frank was standing in a square wooden boat holding a fishing rod and wearing the green plaid shirt she'd given him for Christmas, which made her smile, though she puzzled over the mossy cypress behind him and the young woman with curly black hair at his side, a baby girl cradled in her arms. Lena was still smiling when she turned the photograph over and read, in the same blocky letters: FRANK AND GINA MULLENS AND BABY KAYLEEN, BAYOU TECHE, LOUISIANA, 1931.

She walked out the kitchen door and across the back lawn that sloped down to the pond, where Frank stood in the water up to his knees, raking plant debris into a pile on the bank.

Covered in sweat and mud, he leaned on his rake and grinned when he saw his wife walking toward him. "I was just hoping for an iced tea."

The smell of the putrid muck made Lena sick to her stomach, but she swallowed it back and walked to the pond's edge, holding the photograph out to him. Frank craned his neck to see it, and Lena waited as his skin drained of color and his eyes grew blank. She watched, letting him suffer the consequences of his pleasures and deceits. "Who is she?"

He swayed on his rake, the pond water roiling at his knees.

"Who is she, Frank?"

"A woman I know in New Orleans."

Lena flipped the photograph around to show him the writing on the back.

"She's my wife." The water steamed and hissed. "My other wife." The water turned to flames around him.

Lena stepped back and let him wither in the blaze. Alone at the edge of the foul and stagnant pond, she knew he was gone before he'd even said a word. She strode past her own house to the Gomers' back door, entered without knocking and sat crying at Cissy's kitchen table for an hour before she was able to tell her what was wrong. At noon she called R. T. Miller, the attorney who'd helped settle her parents' affairs ten years ago, and got the advice she needed. At one o'clock she called Fanny Kruger in Boulder City, Nevada, and cried again when Fanny insisted she and Burr get on the next bus and come stay with her at the dam.

Lena hung up when she saw Burr and Eddie come pedaling up the dusty road. She dashed into the bathroom and washed her face while Cissy cut the boys slices of the cherry cobbler she'd baked that morning. At the end of the afternoon, Lena walked home as Burr rode lazy circles around her on his bicycle, describing how three older boys had launched a homemade raft into the lake and swum back to shore when it sank twenty feet out. At the house, Burr went out to the pond to continue his daily frogging, and Lena walked into the front room, where she knew Frank would be waiting for her. She stood at the window without looking at him, and he sat calmly in his chair. Watching her son play along the muddy pond, Lena pretended to be talking to a living, breathing human being as she told Frank she was leaving with Burr that night, and that R. T. Miller suggested he turn himself in to the authorities in the morning and call any lawyer but him.

Frank began to speak and Lena knew she would never hear

the truth from him again. She stayed in the room for exactly five seconds, which was as long as she could stand being alone with the ghost of her husband, and went upstairs to pack.

She could smell the alcohol as soon as Kenny opened the car door and slid onto the seat. He fumbled with the key and let the car idle at the curb as he took off his suit jacket, with every grunt and wheeze oozing the stale odor of whiskey and sweat. But he kept his mouth shut and started driving west, so Lena relaxed and thought of Fanny Kruger waiting for them in Nevada. She hadn't seen Fanny in over a year, since she'd left Hugo and the family pig farm to find a job out west. She wrote Lena often, and she'd sit on the back porch and read the letters as the fields turned to dust, deciphering the crinkled handwriting and misspelled words to slowly piece together her friend's desert adventures. Fanny sent a photograph of herself with a new boyfriend every few weeks, always looking as if she'd gained another five pounds, but she wore it well and the men of Nevada flocked to her as avidly as the boys of Oklahoma had. Fanny liked to say she'd dated everyone of age within forty miles of Hugo, sometimes stringing suitors along for weeks but always setting them free. She soon grew tired of the jilted faces of the farm boys, frozen in their fields like mopey scarecrows, and of the tear-stained poems and gold bracelets that brokenhearted town men sent in an attempt to win her back. But Fanny didn't believe in second chances, and at twenty-eight she was restless and ready to move on.

Lena missed her and had loved her wild ways since childhood. Two independent women—one by choice, the other by calamity— they would soon be together again.

Dry air rushed through the open window and down the front of her dress. It felt good on her body, and she shifted her weight and moved her knees to allow the coolness to spread up the inside of her leg, until she opened her eyes and saw that her dress and slip had been pushed up to her thighs and that Joe Kenny's fingers were slowly working their way toward her underwear. He was breathing hard with his mouth open, and Lena hit him right in his good eye. He grabbed his face with one hand, wrenching the steering wheel with the other as he slammed on the brakes. Feeling the car go into a horizontal skid, Lena swiveled in the seat and saw the boxes spilling over on Burr, his eyes wide open as the car bounced down a steep embankment at an angle that seemed impossible to sustain. She held her left hand in front of her face and Kenny cursed loudly when he hit the boulder that tipped the car up on two wheels for shrieking, endless seconds, and then onto its side and spinning sideways into a dry riverbed, shedding its doors before slamming against a sandstone wall.

Lena remembered clutching Burr's hand until the last moment of dizzying impact, and felt Joe Kenny's full weight across her chest, pinning her like a lover. She struggled out from under him and frantically looked behind her. The backseat was empty. She stopped breathing and knew she would never breathe again unless she scrambled out of the car and concentrated on the immediate seconds. Begging for God's help, she grabbed the running board and dragged herself up onto the side panel. When she saw Burr running toward her, she fell to the ground. They clung to each other in the shadow of the overturned car, unbroken and alert. Lena ran her hands along her son's small bones, and tears ran down her own face as the back tire spun slowly in the desert calm.

"Are you okay?" Burr asked. Lena saw him looking at the blood on her ankle and the scrapes on her bare foot. She touched her scalp where it was throbbing. The skin was tender but wasn't bleeding. "I'm fine."

"Me, too."

She brushed at the red dust on Burr's face. "You look like an Indian."

"So do you." He squinted at the overturned car behind them. "What about him?"

The Chrysler's front end was crumpled all the way to the windshield, and a black puddle formed under the sprung radiator. The trunk had popped open, and their suitcase sat on the ground in a tangle of Kenny Originals.

Looking back up the canyon, Lena could trace the wide skid mark for about a hundred yards. A car door was propped up against a boulder fifty feet away, and the canyon floor was strewn with purple gift boxes.

She took Burr's hand and walked around the car to where Joe Kenny was slumped in the front seat, visible only through the blown-out windshield. Burr crouched and stared. The eye patch was still in place, and Joe was breathing heavily.

Lena reached her hand inside and fished her left shoe from under Kenny's elbow, poking him in the ribs with the heel. He groaned and rolled around as she fitted the shoe back on her foot. "He's okay," she said, then climbed up where she could reach the metal water can still strapped on the trunk. She washed Burr's face as best she could and brushed his clothes. She cleaned the cut on her ankle, kneeling down to press her hem against it until the bleeding stopped. When she glanced at her watch, it was almost six o'clock.

Burr stood there beside her. "Where are we?"

"I don't know."

"Are we close?"

"We better be."

"Are we going to leave him?"

She looked back to where the windshield had been, and could see only a small cut on Kenny's chin and drops of blood that spotted his fancy tie.

"Yes, we are." She kissed Burr on top of the head. "Now wait here while I see where we are."

He crouched there and stared at Joe Kenny's patch. He would've given anything to know what was behind it, but wasn't about to look.

He drove into Ely and parked in front of the old Collins Hotel downtown. He asked for a room with a view of the street and sat with his feet on the windowsill, drinking a glass of whiskey and watching the men in their good beaver hats, the women in the most stylish fashions from Denver, all walking toward the Hotel Nevada for a night of champagne and oysters in the opulent new dining room, where these titans of the West, flush with railroad and copper money, could keep an eye on one another and carry on business in an atmosphere of sophistication new to the frontier. Even when mines were closing throughout the West, Ely was still a boomtown, and Las Vegas would soon become one, too, making Filius wonder if Nevada wasn't the most financially secure state in the nation. He finished his whiskey and went to the restaurant downstairs, quiet now due to the flashier competition down the street, and ordered a T-bone steak and fried potatoes and two orders of the chilled lettuce salad, because it was still rare to see fresh vegetables this side of the Missouri River. He skipped dessert but had another small glass of whiskey in front of the window in his room, then read the local paper in the bath, and when he went to bed at ten o'clock he knew he'd never be able to sleep, so close to his destination now, and too anxious. An hour later he'd checked out and was heading south on Route 93.

It was pitch black when he drove through the shallow dish of Lake Valley, and the juniper grew so thick and close to the road he felt crowded and confined. This changed on the floodplain below the Highland Range, where he crossed meadows of creosote and the road's gradual elevations and sudden dips revealed the histories of spring torrents that continued to contour the landscape. Filius loved this part of the country, its endlessness and harsh beauty, and tonight he loved the darkness arching over him like a shroud. He'd planned on driving straight through to the site on the Colorado after stopping for gasoline in Caliente, but the café in Alamo was open at two o'clock in the morning and he was suddenly hungry again. A good sign, he thought, hoping that the closer he got to the dam, the healthier he'd become.

Two men were playing cards inside the café, old cowboys hunched from years of lazy riding, wide through the shoulders and backsides, their noses blown out from decades of fierce sun and bad liquor.

One of them stood up, wearing an apron, and slid his cards into his back pocket.

"I ain't gonna cheat," his partner snorted.

"I ain't gonna tempt you," the cook replied, as he stepped around the counter. When Filius ordered coffee and scrambled eggs, he said, "I got some chopped steak and onions."

Filius nodded. He was thinking of the letters Frank Crowe had sent him over the past year, prodding but not insisting, telling him about progress at the dam during his absence. He'd written to Filius of blasting out railroad beds and access roads from Las Vegas to the dam site, when for months on end the air was chalky with dust and sweet with diesel fumes, and about the squatters' camps that grew along the Hemenway Wash, cardboard towns and shanties the men had set up after driving with their families from all over the country in hopes of finding work. But mostly he wrote about the process itself, about sculpting Black Canyon with dynamite to prepare for the march of equipment and "the miners and muckers and drillers and tunnel men" who would finish this job over the next five years. During his year of mourning, it had been Frank's words that Filius most looked forward to, this poetry of endeavor that slowly drew him away from the sadness of death. A month ago he'd decided to come out, though he wasn't wholly convinced that he was ready.

Filius ate his breakfast and the old cowboys went back to their cards. Over the next few hours he had the old highway to himself, driving south toward the Sheep Range through poplar forests and the farmland of the Pahranagat Valley, where wild horses watered along Maynard Lake. Sunrise turned the desert into a whole other country. The tops of mesas shone, and the warped peaks above Arrow Canyon were striped pink and red.

Filius was less than twenty miles from Las Vegas when he saw them walking along the side of the highway. At first he thought it was just heat dancing, or wandering coyotes, but as he got closer the shapes transformed into a woman and child and he had already started to slow down. The woman put down the suitcase she was carrying to wave, and when he pulled up alongside them, she was tentative. Filius let her study him through the open window. He tried to smile, but his face was numbed by the dry wind, and he wasn't sure if he succeeded. The woman was pretty but looked tired, as if she'd been on the road a long time. Filius couldn't bear to look at the boy.

The woman stepped closer to the car. "We're going to the dam."

Her voice was clear and precise, and Filius imagined it traveling over great distances.

"So am I," he said.

. . .

It was early in the morning when the bus pulled into the Union Pacific Depot on Fremont Street, and Lew Beck was determined to be the first one off. Most of the passengers were still asleep, and he jumped from his seat when the bus first started slowing, and stepped over feet and nudged aside the dangling arms and elbows in the aisle. He had been awake for two hours and felt queasy in the sticky air. The couple who shared the seat next to him slept with their mouths open, and must've split a bag of raw onions for dinner. The little girl two rows back had a shitty diaper again, and although she didn't wake up wailing this time, her parents feigned sleep and left her unattended. When the bus pulled up in front of the station, Lew stepped onto the pavement and walked half a block before he took his first deep breath of fresh air in ten hours.

He stopped on the corner of Second Street, pulled a cigarette out of his pocket and looked around at Las Vegas. The almost treeless streets were as wide as any he'd ever seen in a frontier town, and the buildings up and down Fremont had the freshly painted look of good times. Every other business seemed to be a saloon, and even though the front doors were locked at the Barrelhouse and the Black Cat and Texas Acres, lights still shone beyond the dingy glass, and the whiskey-sick men emerging from the alleys tried hard not to stagger as they made their way home to angry wives and bosses. Speed Owens had told him that Las Vegas was full of bootleggers and gamblers and prostitutes, the police department tending to be open-minded about cash payments from the business community. The dam project was stimulating a growing commerce, both legitimate and not, where civic-minded establishments like the Overland Hotel and Penney's co-existed with saloons run by the Strella brothers and Sammy Stearns, backdoor funhouses open twenty-four hours a day. At six in the morning Lew saw cowboys ride into town and hitch their horses to the rails along Fremont Street, then walk down North Third, where Speed told him there were cribs for underage girls on Block 16. He saw Mormons driving their trucks in from the neighboring ranches to turn market day into a Bible lesson, casting stern judgment while their multiple wives and many children sold eggs and vegetables to the faithless. He saw the sad-eyed men waiting for the Six Companies employment office to open and call out day jobs on the dam, the line already stretched around the corner of Fourth Street. He stopped in front of the Union Drug Store and studied the faces that passed, the men corrupt or corruptible, the women resigned to living with them. He knew he'd like it here.

"Hey, Shorty, do a guy a favor."

Lew looked down at the legless man who skittered back and forth in front of him on a roller board. He wore a bowler hat and a pearl-snapped green shirt and black suit pants bunched up around his stumps. His face was ugly and sunburned, and his neck banded by a rosy eruption of prickly heat that boiled in the dip of his collarbone. The big, dirty hand he held out to Lew was callused as a dog's paw.

"Come on, Shorty, help a guy out." He smiled with his yellow lips.

Lew smiled back. "Sure, buddy," he said, making a show of reaching deep into his pocket, pulling out two silver dollars and jiggling them in his hand. He waited for the legless man to cock his head and calculate the value of the sound, then he extended his hand and let the coins roll off his palm, watching them spin together on the sidewalk in front of the roller board. When the man reached down to pick them up, Lew placed the heel of his boot on top of his knuckles. As people moved around them on the sidewalk, he shifted his weight forward, grinding his fingers into the pavement.

The pain shot up the man's arm and through his heart and ended in the deadened stumps of his half self. His blinking became more rapid when he heard his knuckle pop, but he knew the coins were his as long as he didn't protest, so he bit his lip and said, "Thanks, mister."

And Lew released him.

Without a backward glance, he walked down Fremont Street. He realized he was irritable and very hungry, and that hunger affected his mood, and the last thing he'd had to eat was a bad ham salad sandwich at the bus station in Los Angeles. He'd get something to eat and then call Speed, and they could figure out what Lew could do until it was safe to go back to California.

The Apache Café across the street looked good, and he stepped off the sidewalk without looking. He heard the horn before he saw the car swerve around him, stumbling backward but keeping his balance, and he stared at the Chrysler as it swung back into its lane as if nothing had happened. He glimpsed a man with a long Jew nose and a pretty woman behind him, and saw the boy sit up to stare at him out the rear window. Lew hated being stared at. He brushed off the knees of his pants even though he hadn't fallen, and ignored the passersby, who thought he was just another stumblebum with the blind staggers, and he knew he would remember that car.

Burr knew he shouldn't be staring, but he couldn't help it. Lew Beck was the smallest man he had ever seen.

BOULDER
DAM

*T*he lights went out, and Filius found himself in supreme darkness. Three quarters of a mile into the tunnel at the base of Black Canyon, he filled his lungs with the acrid stink of gelatin blasts and damp andesite. In the blackness, over the constant whirr of compressors, more than a hundred men grunted and cursed around him, and he listened to the small crew of electricians scuttle like rats as they scraped their equipment across the rocky floor to check the lines. He heard men tap their drills against the steel rail of their platforms and whistle, perched like bats in a cave. The men waited stiff and impatient in air already thick with diesel fumes and sweat. Then, an answering whistle came from two hundred yards away, and the lights spit and sputtered and the tunnel shone white and blue again, and the men came to life and resumed their drilling from the multilevel jumbo backed up to the left wall of tunnel, where the nippers and water boys waited for commands, crouching like dogs on point, and foremen inspected the bench heading, and paced and scowled, and over the sound of jackhammers and drills yelled whatever nonsense came to mind. Under this grand attack of men and machinery, the earth shuddered, and Filius felt at home.

Driving through Las Vegas with the woman and boy that morning, he'd felt fine and unhurried. He followed the railroad through the desert, the tracks gleaming like inlaid silver, and still found it hard to believe that twenty miles away, behind the distant surge of crusted peaks that ringed this vast and lonely moonscape, the great dream was under way.

Although punchy with exhaustion, Lena could not sleep. She sat in the back of Filius's Chrysler, leaning her head against the open window and staring at the desert that stretched around them, mesmerized by its overwhelming incompleteness, as if it were an impulse of creation begun and then abandoned. She had traveled the desolate heights of Utah and the endless Texas plains, but nothing had prepared her for the dull richness of this carmine palette, with its rugged skin and dismal reach.

Looking out the window across from his mother, Burr spotted a dead jackrabbit stretched along the side of the road; it was the size of a small dog, long-legged and bony. He looked into the pinkish blur of the desert, scanning the piles of rocks and scrub for bursts of furry life. The desert seemed monumental, a place to be respected and feared, like church. He stuck his face out the window to feel the heat roll over him, liking the way it made his lips tighten and his vision sharpen. He couldn't get enough of this Nevada.

About ten miles beyond Las Vegas, where the road started climbing and the railroad tracks veered off to the north, they passed a roadhouse cobbled together from used bricks and discarded wood, with mismatched windows on either side of the open door. The building looked at once permanent and temporary, a place of mischief erected during the night. A hand-painted sign washed out by sunlight read COME ON IN. Four cars were parked out front with all their doors open, and men lay across the front and back seats with their feet sticking out, some shod, others barefoot. Two women in identical flimsy pink bathrobes, the feathery necklines lying flat in the heat, were sitting on barrels by the front door. One drank coffee from a porcelain cup, her elbows propped on white knees and her bare toes dipped in a metal trough of sudsy water. The other had her blonde hair piled high and her bathrobe drawn down from her naked shoulders. She raised an arm as they drove past, and began to shave her armpit with a razor she'd pulled from the same sudsy trough. Only Burr seemed to notice, and the woman smiled at the staring boy as she stroked upward and flicked away the creamy lather.

Filius glanced at Lena in the rearview mirror. A pretty woman, she reminded him of Addie. Her hair was longer and darker, but her skin held the same warm tone. He knew that her name was Lena McCardell, and that she was traveling west from Oklahoma with her son to see a friend in Boulder City who'd promised her a job.

"McCardell. Are you Welsh?"

Lena was surprised by the question, and she turned from the window to the man in the front seat. She looked at the back of his head, at his neatly trimmed hair, more golden than brown, at his clean-shaven cheek and the long, prominent nose. "Why not Irish, Mr. Poe? Most people think I'm Irish."

"I don't."

"Why not?"

"Because my wife's Irish."

She shifted her weight and saw the ring on his finger. "Scottish," she said. "My parents were both Scottish." She watched him drive, both hands on the steering wheel, his white shirtsleeves rolled above the elbows. When she looked in the mirror he glanced back at her, and then looked away.

"Where are you from, Mr. Poe?"

"I was born in Wisconsin but I haven't lived there in a while. I travel a lot."

"Are you a salesman?"

He smiled. "I'm an engineer."

The boy shot forward, a blur of brown hair and striped shirt. "Are you going to build the dam?"

The boy. Filius felt the pressure of small hands on the seat cushion near his shoulder and heard him breathing at the back of his neck, waiting for an answer. The boy was innocent of everything but youth and inquiry, but those were the very things Filius missed the most. He took a breath and tried not to blame him. "I'm going to help."

"Did you build other dams?"

"Yes."

"As big as this one?"

"Big dams, yes, but this is the biggest."

Lena noticed how Filius tensed up when Burr gripped the back of the seat. Some people, she knew, were intimidated by children's energy, especially childless men, like Mr. Poe, perhaps, who weren't used to their endearing selfishness and sudden bursts of interrogation. "Burr . . ."

The boy shrugged her off and stared at Filius. "Can you take me to the dam sometime?"

"We'll see." He kept his eyes on the distant, broken peaks.

"Can we see tomorrow?"

"Burr. Please don't bother Mr. Poe."

"It's no bother."

Burr felt the squeeze of his mother's hand and, though he didn't think he was bothering Mr. Poe, settled back beside her. Over a year ago, when the Oklahoma newspapers ran drawings of the proposed dam, his father had explained to him how big a job it was going to be, almost "like building the pyramids in Egypt." That very afternoon he'd taken a book of his father's Bible stories out onto the back porch and devoured the pictures of Egyptian slaves pulling huge blocks to half-completed monuments in the desert, and if Boulder Dam was going to be anything like that, he couldn't wait to see it. For the next two miles he watched the back of Mr. Poe's head and tried unsuccessfully to catch his eye in the mirror.

Then the road started to level off and they came to a small, white-washed gatehouse with stop signs posted on both sides of the road. A government ranger was perched on a two-rail fence in the shadow of another sign mounted on a wooden post: ENTERING BOULDER CANYON PROJECT FEDERAL RESERVATION. STOP!

The ranger put up his hand and eased himself off the fence. He was wearing a dark blue uniform and a wide-brimmed hat, and his pants were tucked into high cordovan boots laced tight to just below his knees. A black holster was slung low on his hip, the polished leather bulging with the weight of his handgun. He was young and muscular, and Burr thought he looked like the actor who played Flash Haliway in *The Fighting Sheriff*, the last cowboy movie he'd seen at the State Theater in Hugo.

The ranger walked around the car, looking into every window with his face expressionless, and even Burr sensed a lazy cockiness that came with the job. Then he leaned on Filius's door. "State your business, sir."

When the morning light caught the lower half of the ranger's face, Burr saw a bloom of fresh acne under the stubble on his chin.

After Filius gave his name and title, the ranger checked the book inside the gatehouse and waved them through. Burr swung around in the seat and watched him resume his position in the patch of shade along the fence rail.

When they came over the last rise, Filius saw Boulder City stretched out on the plateau above the Hemenway Wash. He remembered scouting this area with Addie years ago, and neither one of them could imagine sustained life on this remote frontier. But now here it was, fanned out in front of him in the shape of a butterfly wing: municipal buildings and arid parks and simple two-room bungalows laid out in five neat avenues, an outpost above the sandy flats. The railroad tracks from Las Vegas ran to a small depot on the edge of town, and electric and telephone lines crisscrossed the desert for miles. Rye grass was already growing around the administrative buildings overlooking the town, and patches of green lawns were beginning to sprout in the tiny yards where the workers and their families lived; and it seemed that every house had a cactus garden and a Chevrolet parked out front. Young, spindly trees were staked between the corner streetlamps, and the fast-growing Tecate cypresses planted along Colorado Street were healthy and tall, their crowns spreading gracefully above the wide paths that curved through the freshly mowed park. Beyond the small city, though, Filius could see trailing plumes of dust rising from the trucks heading to the dam.

He parked across the plaza from Fanny's Café, inching between the Fords and Oldsmobiles and other cars that were lined up in front of Boulder Theater, where Mervyn Le Roy's *I Am a Fugitive from a Chain Gang* was playing four times a day. When Lena stepped out of the car, the front door of the café burst open and a plump blonde in a tight, light blue uniform shrieked and covered her face in her hands. Filius kept his car running and watched the woman hug Lena in her strong, sunburned arms. When Burr came up, she hoisted him high and kissed him full on the lips, laughing and pressing the squirming boy to her bosom. People in the café peered through the window at them, their faces flashing white between the red words stenciled in the glass, FRIED CHICKEN SERVED ALL DAY scrawled across one side of the entrance, and FINE CUISINE on the other.

Filius set their suitcase on the sidewalk. When he climbed into his car and backed it into the street, the boy saw him and broke free from the women.

"Mr. Poe! Mr. Poe!"

He stepped on the brakes.

The boy stopped and waved his arm. "Good-bye, Mr. Poe! Don't forget me!"

Filius waved back and turned onto Arizona Street. It wasn't until he got on the Nevada Highway that he realized he didn't even remember the boy's name.

Filius pulled into the parking area at the Bureau of Reclamation headquarters, and Frank Crowe was there to greet him.

"You're a week early, Mr. Poe." Crowe's tie was tight to his neck, and the collar of his white shirt already stained with desert grime. It was eight o'clock in the morning and the ninety-degree heat rose and shimmered from the pavement.

"I'm a year late, Mr. Crowe."

He smiled, and the two of them shook hands.

"I'd like to go to work, Frank."

"Filius, I knew you would."

They drove east toward the distant cliffs that rose above the Colorado River. Frank Crowe sped his Buick sedan around the bumps and jags on the seven miles of hard road with incautious delight. All around them were the rusted shells of wrecked cars and trucks, now the junked habitat of kangaroo rats and tarantulas. Even going downhill, Frank steered with one hand and kept his foot heavier on the accelerator than the brake. He'd cut this road and knew it well, gliding around potholes deep enough to snap an axle and weaving in and out of the transport caravans hauling men and equipment to and from Black Canyon. He swung wide to avoid a man on foot, dopey with heat, and when three huge dump trucks lumbered up the hill he held his speed and let his tires grip the edge of the narrow roadway, firing pebbles and dust into the valley below.

Filius kept his eyes trained on the cliffs ahead, waiting for his first glimpse of the site. Frank sped around a two-ton International, and when he screeched to a stop on a narrow pull-off at the lip of the canyon, Filius looked over the edge, blinking in the flurry of dust, and was amazed. Even though he'd seen Black Canyon years ago and drawn rough sketches of what was taking place below him, the sight and sound of it, the hundreds of vehicles and thousands of men, made it look more like a battlefield than a construction site. Barges floated heavy equipment and portable compressors to landing areas on either side of the river, and Caterpillars and electric shovels moved in and out of the diversion tunnels that were being completed just above the river's flow. There were gravel pits and screening plants where the concrete could be made, and a train trestle six miles upstream so locomotives could run between the two. Cableways were being rigged on the walls of the canyon to move men and machinery across, but for now workers still crossed by foot to the Arizona side on suspension bridges that swayed low over the river. The water was browner than Filius remembered it, stained by the dirt and mud churned into the current as the tunnels were mucked and cleared. From this spot, the Colorado River seemed less daunting, already tamed of its wildness, almost trapped by the men sculpting the canyon around it, but Filius knew the strength of running water.

Frank checked his watch, leaned close and pointed to the tunnel on the Nevada side. "We're about to fire a shot now."

Filius looked down and saw men running out of the entrance, others clinging to the running boards and gates of the trucks that followed. Then the commotion abruptly stopped on both sides of the river. For a moment no one moved, caught in the sharp desert light, and though the compressors and engines were still running, Filius felt as if he was looking at a photograph.

At the instant of detonation he could feel the earth jump beneath his feet. A second later the canyon rolled as the interior walls cracked and fell, and a great storm of gray smoke blew out of the portal and across the river below, spraying dirt and rocks that rattled down on metal sheds and truck hoods and crouching men, dappling the water that rushed by unfettered.

Five minutes later, Frank deposited him at the river camp outside tunnel number 1, where the explosion had just occurred. It was the last tunnel to be holed out. Filius got out of the car and took a deep breath, sucking in air tangy with gas fumes and blasting powder. He stepped around the electric shovels and dump trucks idling at the mouth of the tunnel and looked through the unsettled haze. Far off he could hear the scalers already at work with crowbars and jack-hammers, prying away loose rock that had survived the explosion. When the safety miner gave the signal, he followed a squad of electricians inside, staying close behind as they trotted the half-mile tunnel wall, backs stooped as they checked the cables, feeling for cracks in the rubber hosing that kept them dry and unfrayed. When the lights came on, Filius looked up at the bare bulbs high above him, their wattage dulled a noxious blue by tunnel haze. Behind him the electric shovel rumbled down the deep shaft again, the front bucket bent and hanging inches below the jagged ceiling. Filius backed against the wall and watched it rock past on its thick treads, slow and ponderous, its engine torqued and whining like something gutshot. When the shovel stopped and began to pick up debris from the blast, the first dump truck raced in backward, the driver leaning out of the doorless cab with one hand on the wheel and the other on the frame, looking over his shoulder as he steered blindly, denting the truck's fenders as he scraped the walls and kept on coming. When the shovel finished loading that first dump truck, another lurched into its place, its headlights booming crazily against the tunnel walls. It was always the same: trucks coming and going with the abandon of bumper cars at a carnival ride, until all the rock was hauled away and the drilling jumbo could be rolled back and locked into place. The noise never ceased—abated sometimes, but always purred underfoot, caught in the ground and held like heat.

Filius sat just inside the entrance, his back against a smooth pocket of the blasted wall. It was noon and the men had stopped for lunch, and he sat with them and ate the ham sandwich that Perlie Trimble had given him. Perlie's lunch box was crammed with sandwiches from the mess hall, always more than he could eat but handy enough if some other driller came up short. Perlie had just turned thirty and was almost toothless, and these flattened, pulpy sandwiches suited him fine, and no one complained when he produced another one from his lunch box like a rabbit out of a hat.

Filius also ate the sandwich and apple Frank had tossed him before he left, washing it down with coffee from the ten-gallon milk can nearby, enjoying these fifteen minutes of quiet. His khakis were stiff as cardboard from the moisture and muck inside the tunnel, and his tie hung limp and twisted against his dirty shirt. For three hours he'd stayed underground with the tunnel crew, knuckle-skinned Irishmen with names like McDingle, Murray and Ryan. His ears still rang with the machine roar that had carried through the morning, and with the flow of blue language he hadn't heard in years, this dizzying vernacular of raw life and hangovers, rough words strung together in an impious hymn as the miners attacked the tunnel walls, spurred on by their boss, Floyd Huntington, who cursed magnificently in a loud, cunning streak that made his men proud. When Filius entered the tunnel that morning, they watched him as they ranted and worked to gauge his reaction, but either he didn't have one or didn't mind.

"Mr. Poe. You still hungry?" Perlie was holding out another oval of sandwich.

"No thanks."

"Got three more."

Filius smiled and shook his head. "Pass them around, Perlie. I'm full as a tick."

Sucking his gums, Perlie put the extra sandwiches on a rock by the coffee urn and started back into the tunnel as another crew came out to eat.

Floyd Huntington emerged with them, sweat streaming out from beneath the dented Ballard that sat cockeyed on his big head. He perched on a rock next to Filius and stretched his legs, ignoring the ripped scab on his forearm and the strings of dried blood that ran down to his wrist. He took off his metal hard hat and scratched at his bald spot, bronzed as a Roman coin; the rest of his hair was cut high above his ears, shaved so close to the skin that it was colorless. He was dark all over, reedy but strong, and the lines on his face were so deep that he might have been wearing a mask. Ten years older than Filius, Huntington had worked on the Olive Bridge Dam in the

Catskills and on the Gibraltar, high in the Los Padres Forest above Santa Barbara. Then he'd taken a government job on the Muscle Shoals Dam that stole power from the Tennessee River near Florence, Alabama, and in 1921 he drove cross-country to work for Frank Crowe on the Tieton Dam. "All he cares about," Frank had told Filius, "is when he goes to work." Now Frank was moving him across the river to oversee the pouring of concrete in tunnel number 3, and giving Filius his job.

Huntington lit a cigarette and didn't try to hide his disappointment. Before turning to Filius, he coughed violently. "Air stinks."

He spat out a wad of phlegm the color of bilgewater and wiped his nose on his forearm. The scab started bleeding again. "'Filius'—what the hell kind of name is that?"

"My grandfather's name."

"He wear a fez? Some kind of Hebrew?"

"No."

"He come from Turkey?"

"Wisconsin."

Huntington sucked on his cigarette and coughed again. The tendons on his neck stood up like ridges that melted back beneath his skin when the coughing stopped.

"I don't care where you're from, Poe. You could be a three-legged Chinaman and shit peanuts for all I care, long as you do the job Frank Crowe says you can." He put the cigarette in the corner of his mouth and left it there as he talked. "You got good men here. Bad ones don't last, and lazy I got no use for. When they work for me they work steady as rats, and what they do when they ain't on the job is nobody's business. Arguments they take outside. Problems with each other they figure out on somebody else's time. Tunnel work is all I want."

Filius saw the color rise to his face and stain his cheeks. The cigarette in his mouth had burned down to his lips, and he pinched it out between yellow fingers.

"They're tough bastards, every one of 'em. Be fair and push hard. There's no room in this tunnel for foolishness or lip. I see even a cross-eyed look and they get their cut-loose papers. They know it. They seen it happen. That's the way I do it. You do what you want."

"I'll be fine."

Filius took out his pack of Viceroys, and saw Huntington smirk at the silver lighter.

"You got a couple thousand men working three different shifts a day and they don't stop except to piss. On a good day it's a hundred degrees down here, and on a bad day the inside of your head feels like a bowl of soup. Every day somebody gets hurt, somebody passes out and somebody doesn't come back. A man makes a mistake, he's fired, he complains, he's fired, and every one of them gets down to this dam site here on a brakeless, piece-of-shit transport that feels like a runaway train, so they're praying and feeling lucky to be alive even before they go to work. After eight hours the good ones go home and kiss their babies and screw their wives and forget about it, and the bad ones get drunk and beat their wives and they can't forget about it, it stays inside them like a broken bone, till they crawl under their houses and fall asleep like dogs because it's too hot to sleep inside. Then they get up and do it again, the good and the bad ones, every single one of these bastards . . . Yeah, you'll be fine."

"I've done this before, Huntington."

"Not here you haven't. Not here, goddammit." He pushed himself to his feet. The rock where he'd been sitting was pooled with sweat. He put his Ballard back on, lifted his chin and looked into the mouth of the tunnel. "It's a good hole. We're ahead of schedule. Don't fuck it up." Then he whistled for the driver of a Caterpillar 60 to stop, jumped onto the cow-dozer and hoisted himself under the tin canopy. He tapped the driver's hard hat and the Caterpillar lurched toward the trestle bridge and the other side of the river.

Filius noticed three young men drinking coffee by the tunnel entrance. They'd come out with Huntington and loitered there in the shade twenty feet away.

The one in the middle wore dungarees that were faded almost white, and a denim shirt rolled up above his biceps. Strong and rangy, he grinned at Filius, tossed the last of his coffee in the dirt and brushed his hand through his long black hair. "You the new tunnel boss?"

Filius nodded.

The young man stuck out his hand. "Speed Owens."

. . .

An hour later the tunnel rocked with the second blast of the day. The air was still thick with dirt when Filius put on his Ballard and entered with the high-powered lantern that Perlie Trimble handed him. Far down the tunnel where the blast had occurred, chunks of rock were still falling from the walls. He kept to the middle of the tunnel and took shallow breaths that didn't sear his lungs, walking quickly and swinging the lantern in the fouled air, occasionally banging at loose rock with the crowbar he carried in his right hand. The farther he went, the cooler it became, the freshly exposed rock letting out the chill captured underground. It was here, at the site of the blast, that the sound of the outside world was dulled. Filius stood in this newly hollowed cavity in the solid earth, the first man to see it, and turned off the lantern to linger in the utter blackness, thrilled at the power it still had over him.

When he gave the signal, the electricians ran forward to reconnect the lights, and Speed Owens came in with the scalers, loaded down with ropes and ladders and crowbars to finish the work of prying loose rock. By the time Filius got outside, the dump trucks were backed up and ready to move in.

Filius took immediate control. He introduced himself to the shifters and foremen that Huntington appointed, and told them they still had jobs. The only change he made was safety miner, relieving Eddie Gwynn—a veteran miner who hated being the first one in the tunnel after a blast—and taking the job himself. Eddie grinned like a cat and gladly went back to work on the top level of the jumbo without any change in pay. For the rest of the day, Filius worked alongside the men with a quiet authority. He brought the drillers new steel when they needed it and he managed the double jack when it was time to block the jumbo into place. He kept the men working at the fierce pace Huntington had established, and when the second shift arrived at four o'clock, he stayed on the job. At midnight, Filius greeted the last shift of the day, and a half hour later Frank came into the tunnel to take him home.

At the entrance Filius stumbled, wobbly and overwhelmed by the spectacle around him, but caught himself and looked at the huge lights that glared from high on the canyon walls where men were working on the cableways, and from the top of tall steel posts suspended over each end of the trestle bridge. He looked at the headlight beams of the trucks bouncing eerily from the high road above, and he looked at the bare bulbs that were strung anywhere cables could reach, a brilliant patchwork swaying brightly as the ground rolled and chattered, giving the construction site a deceptive levity that lasted only moments. The tunnel entrances on both sides of the river shone like black eyes, dilated by the lights of the bulldozers and mucking trucks that passed inside and out. He could hear the hum of the drum mixers at the concrete plant upstream, and the distant chug of locomotives that ran endlessly from the Arizona gravel pits, where Negroes worked in isolation. In front of him men screamed over the noise of whirring generators, their faces pinched into hideous welts of flesh. The night air rang with a language of indistinguishable violence, spoken loud and unclear. And all around the bright lights reflected the brutal landscape in metallic sheets, and the artificiality was stunning.

It was eighty-five degrees at the bottom of the canyon, where thousands of men were hard at work. Filius looked up at the galaxy of stars squeezed between the canyon walls and felt at ease.

Frank drove him back to Boulder City, to a small brick house in the middle of Denver Street, where someone had parked Filius's car in the driveway and left a lamp shining in the front window. When he stepped out of the Buick, the heat rolled over him, at least fifteen degrees hotter than by the river, and for the first time that day he felt tired.

Frank Crowe leaned across the front seat of his car. "It's good to have you here."

"Thanks, Frank."

"Hell, thank me in three years when we're finished."

When he pulled away, Filius turned to his house, squarely built and stout with a Midwest classicism that sat comfortably behind a small garden of cacti and hollyhocks. The front door was unlocked and Filius stepped into the parlor. Even with all the windows open, the air inside was stifling, and the scent of fresh plaster was still sharp. The few pieces of furniture he'd sent ahead were already in place: the wooden-slat settle his father had given him years ago from their house in Wisconsin, a tall oak cabinet he'd bought at auction in Chicago, and his desk. On the desk was a bottle of I. W. Harper whiskey, the brand Frank Crowe was never without, and even though Filius knew it was illegal to have alcohol on this government reservation, he also knew exceptions would be made. Above the stone fireplace was the large photograph of Black Canyon that Addie had framed for him years ago.

He walked down a short hallway and into the bedroom. His suitcase was open on a chair and his clothes neatly piled on the bed. A mirror was hung above the dresser, on which sat a silver-framed photograph that Filius had taken of Ray rowing Addie across the Garfield Park lagoon. They were both dressed in white and smiling at the camera, and Filius had snapped the picture just as Ray lifted the oars out of the water and leaned way back, his head in Addie's lap. It was his favorite photograph of his wife and son, and he had forgotten that he'd packed it, and in this strange room its sudden presence startled him. He caught his reflection in the mirror and stepped away.

In the kitchen he took out a tumbler from the glass-fronted cabinet next to a four-burner O'Keefe & Merritt stove he knew wouldn't see much use. He opened the refrigerator and saw a carton of milk and a dozen eggs, a loaf of bread and a block of yellow cheese, a head of lettuce already wilting around the edges, eight bottles of Coca-Cola. In the cupboard next to the refrigerator he found coffee, saltines and tins of various meats and fish and fruit. In the middle of a table surrounded by four chairs was a freshly baked peach pie, yet another housewarming present from Linnie Crowe. He opened the freezer compartment and filled his glass with ice cubes. Back in the parlor, he broke the seal on the whiskey bottle and covered his ice to the brim.

Filius found his cigarettes and some paper in the middle drawer of his desk, and took them out to the small screened porch on the east side of the house. It wasn't any cooler here, but the lights of Boulder City below gave him something to focus on, a stability that for the moment felt slightly out of his grasp. He sat at the table and sipped his whiskey and smoked, listening to the fragile drone of the motorized world around him. Finally, he turned on the lamp, found his pen and started to write.

> *Dear Addie,*
>
> *It's as beautiful here as it was when we first came years ago, and the river still runs wild but not for long. Do you remember when we drove through the desert that summer and the heat was so intense it made us sick, almost giddy, with the weight of it? It's the same again today, and it's after midnight now and still over a hundred degrees—the temperature hasn't fluctuated much since I arrived this morning. Now I'm sitting outside on a small porch and looking up at a Nevada sky full of uncountable stars. I'm drinking from a bottle of whiskey Frank left for me, good friend that he is, and I'm still wearing the same shirt that I've had on all day. I'm tired, almost sleepy, but I have to write to you now and tell you everything first, as I always have, as I always will. I went to the dam site the moment I arrived this morning, drawn immediately to the river I hadn't seen in nine years. Do you remember its brown surge? The ragged beauty of the dark canyon walls? That enormous silence broken by rushing water? Its very different now, Addie. The construction is overwhelming. There are enough men working on the dam to form an army and take over the state of California. The sound of all the machines drums through your skin and stays with you all day, and stays with you long after you've left the river, droning in your ears like a forgotten hymn. And it will go on twenty-four hours a day, seven days a week, until the work is complete. It's more than I imagined, and I'm lucky to be a part of it. And I wish you were here with me now. I wish you could see it with me. I wish*

Filius stopped writing. His cigarette had burned down unsmoked, and the bright ash shone just above his knuckles. He carefully folded the letter into thirds and sat there holding it.

. . .

Cece was standing in the window when she saw the little man cross the street and come to the house. At first she thought it was the boy coming to pick up last night's receipts for Mr. Jimmy, or maybe just a boy coming to pick up his drunken daddy. It was too early to think too much of anything, and she watched because it was hot and she was standing in front of the window, and he was the only thing moving on Third Street. Probably in all Las Vegas. She yawned and ran her fingers through her short kinky hair, straightened a few days before and oiled into a shiny cap, with spit curls over the ears. Then she rubbed her breasts beneath her robe, both of them still sore from the big nigger last night who mauled them like he was slapping dough. He showed up from the dam after midnight, stinking like the last bath he had was some long-ago Friday, not caring that when he came through the door his big dick was already pointing through his pants to where she stood against the wall with the other girls. And she knew she was in trouble when she saw his big fingers moving in some private craziness while he watched her with his dumb eyes and shiny face. He followed her up the hall, poking at her with that prideful thing and wheezing out some quiet laughter. When she shut the door to her room he pushed her down on the bed and unzipped himself without bothering to drop his pants. He pulled the muslin shift over her head and stared at her naked, but she was used to that and leaned back on her elbows and raised a leg to expose the thing he came for, waiting for his callused hands to grip and pinch and assert their will, because he owned her flesh now for just this half hour, and the brevity of this arrangement made all the half hours that filled her long days sufferable. The big man reached out and cupped her breasts, never gentle, not even then, and pulled her head toward him, holding the back of her neck. She closed her eyes and took his wholeself in her mouth, closer to him now than she wished to be, trying not to breathe in the odor of his bad habits, but to swim through the idle thoughts that filled her head, counting the canned jars of snap peas and white corn and red peppers stacked in the small pantry next to Shirley's room, jars they filled themselves from the little garden Miss Williams let them tend out back. Before she could finish he let go of her head and pushed her back on the bed, forcing apart her legs like she was some kind of wishbone. He didn't even bother to drop his pants lower than his knees before he smothered her with himself, and she knew by his actions his business wouldn't take long, so she closed her eyes again and forgot the pain and the old smell of his clothes and body and drifted back to the pantry and the neatly stacked jars of vegetables she'd picked herself. When he was done he rolled off and sprawled across her bed, and she lay still and waited for him to fall asleep. She knew Miss Williams would soon knock on the door and rouse him, and although he paid for the time, what was left of it was hers. She watched headlights chase one another across the walls and ceiling. She listened to the other girls laughing in the big parlor down the hall, heard Daisy's voice and the heavy footfalls of the man who followed her past her door. She lay quietly and let the sweat dry on her body, his and hers, and when she touched her nipples they weren't as tender as she had feared. The second Miss Williams knocked she jumped up and shrugged into her white shift, and when the light came on the big man moaned, his thick dick soft and sideways on his fat leg, and she was already scooting under Miss Williams's arm and running barefoot to the bathroom down the hall. She turned on the water in the little porcelain tub and squatted there, cleaning herself quickly and efficiently like Miss Williams had taught her. In the back of her mind she could hear Miss Williams's scolding voice ("Time is money and the day's too short and men too cheap to flitter it away") and didn't want to be caught flittering and feel the back of her knuckly hand. In a few minutes she had on a clean shift and was sitting at a table in the big parlor, playing gin rummy with Shirley as dark men smoked and laughed at the side of the room, eyes roaming over poker hands as they drank bootleg punch from Railroad Pass. These men lingered half the night, gambling and drinking the bad liquor that Mr. Jimmy supplied, spending their wages on girls and cards, sometimes the same girl twice if they got lucky with aces. Married or not, they commiserated about work and homesickness and amused one another with tales of woman woes. They flirted and drank and ran up debts, high-toned and frivolous in the only house in town where they were welcome. And this was the part of the night she loved the best, when the men joked musically on the sidelines and she could play gin rummy with Shirley or Celia or Fayette, whoever wasn't entertaining at the time. Throughout the long night they would rotate seats when one or more got busy, playing one another's hands and totaling up the points they shared.

Her mind was drifting from last night's cards to her achy flesh when Miss Williams knocked on her door and let the little man inside. She was wary at first because he was white and she'd never had anything to do with a white man before, and she remembered Fayette saying to watch out if it ever happened, because there's meanness behind every white man's smile, even if he's stark naked and rolling around on top of you. The little man stood across from her at the foot of the bed. He didn't say anything and neither did she. He was a few inches shorter, small as her little brother back home, ungrown and grown at the same time, with a child's heft and a man's swagger—all hips and shoulder, like he knew where he was going. A completely strange package, she thought, until she looked into his eyes. It was his eyes that told the whole story.

The heat was already bad this morning and she could feel the lines of sweat running down her belly and itching along her back. The little man put his hands on her hips and she raised her arms up high so he could lift the clean shift over her head. Naked now, she felt a cramp in her side and put her weight on her left foot before reaching beyond the buttons on his trousers and into his pants. They stood like that, almost together, and when he touched her for the first time she could feel the heat rising off him. His hands followed the contours of her body and she moved against his fingers like she thought he wanted, and when he put his hands flat on her shoulders and pushed her onto the bed she leaned there on her elbows and watched him undress. She could tell he didn't mind, her toy man, ass proud like the rest of them, wagging at her with his stiff little finger. Then she remembered Fayette's warning and looked away. When he came toward her she inched back on the bed and bent and spread her knees. He ducked down and slid in low, hooking his arms around her thighs and pulling her closer, her backside burning across the sheet, holding her still while he ran his tongue deep between her legs. She squirmed and he gripped her tighter and did it again. Her body tensed and she held it that way and waited.

Cece would be eighteen next month. She thought about that and about the cake Miss Williams would bake for the occasion, and she let the little man do whatever he wanted because that's what he paid for.

Lew stepped into the shade of the front porch where Cece and a big girl were sprawled on a metal glider, the white paint chipped and showing starbursts of bright rust. Fanning themselves with pieces of cardboard, they wore matching white shifts, the material tight against their dark skin and almost luminous as it rode over hips and breasts and the prominence of soft bellies.

The big girl smiled at him. "Mornin', Mr. Man." She put a hand behind her head, and Lew saw a plump breast outlined against her shift. "You gonna visit us again?"

"I might."

"You might ask for Shirley then."

Shirley laughed and showed her nice white teeth, and Cece blushed and pushed her, both of them snickering.

Lew leaned against the railing and looked up at the bleached sky. Although it was hot, he felt calm as a snake on a rock, drowsy and safe. He looked down the street and could see cars moving on Fremont, then caught the scent of fresh biscuits that lingered in the overheated air.

A tall, skinny white man came up the walkway carrying his suit jacket over his shoulder, his yellow shirt flattened damp against his skin. The tie he wore matched his suspenders, and his wide straw hat was pushed way back, showing a lock of dark hair.

He came up the steps, breathing through his mouth, and the top of Lew's head came just below the breast pocket of his shirt. "You making a delivery, pal?"

"No."

"Then what do you want?"

Shirley pushed on her bare foot and rocked the glider. "He already got what he wanted, Mr. Jimmy."

Cece giggled into a closed fist as Mr. Jimmy hovered over Lew and smiled. "You blind, or just peculiar?"

Lew could see the tiny hairs poking out of the pores on Mr. Jimmy's nose and he could smell onions and peppers on his breath.

"You stumble up here in the dark and get too flustered to stumble away?"

Lew lit a cigarette and pushed off the railing.

Mr. Jimmy moved with him. "We got a house full of white girls just down the street. Blondes, brunettes, young, old. You could fuck 'em till Tuesday and not see the same face twice. And they all take your money. Nigger girls here may take a little less, but you get what you pay for—right, girls?"

"We give good, Mr. Jimmy." Shirley pouted.

"Sure you do. Niggers and cheapskates never complain. You ain't complaining, are you, Sonny?"

When Lew moved toward the steps, Mr. Jimmy put a hand on his shoulder and stopped him. Lew expected it; he wanted it. He smoked his cigarette, relaxed now, and the tall man looked over his shoulder at the girls. "Sonny didn't complain any, did he, girls?"

"He only talked to Cece."

"He give you any notion of displeasure, Miss Cece?"

"No sir."

"You fuck him good like you'd fuck any nigger?"

She looked at Lew and shut her mouth tight.

Mr. Jimmy turned back to Lew with his stink and smile and dug his bony fingers into his neck. "Sure you did. That's what Sonny was looking for. That's what—"

Lew spun and hit him hard in the Adam's apple, and when Mr. Jimmy gagged and reached for his throat, leaving his body exposed, he punched him twice in the belly. Mr. Jimmy jumped with each blow and his hat popped off his head, and as his body slid past Lew, Lew hit him again, first in the right eye and then in the temple, before the tall man landed facefirst on the porch, his knees bent beneath him and his backside in the air. He didn't get up.

It happened quickly. In the fluid moment between the first and last blow, Lew could hear girls laughing in the front parlor behind him, and the soft ping of tentative fingers on an out-of-tune piano. Lew rubbed his knuckles, the bones still humming beneath his skin, and looked at the girls. Cece was staring at him. Shirley stretched her leg and pushed her bare toe into Mr. Jimmy's cheek, blood dribbling to the porch boards as he moaned.

Lew saw a wad of money bulging out of his back pocket and

counted out an even six hundred dollars. He turned to Cece. "Whose money is it?"

"Frank Strella. Or maybe his brother, Joe."

"Strella brothers is all business, Mr. Man. They'll shoot you."

"Where are they?"

"They got the Mexico Club out on the Boulder Highway."

Lew took a twenty-dollar bill from the roll before folding the rest into his pocket. "See you later, girls," he said, handing the money to Cece, winking at Shirley. He stepped over Mr. Jimmy and headed down the walk.

Shirley scooted across the glider and yelled over the railing as Cece giggled and swatted her.

"I'll be here, Mr. Man! I'll be here till my teeth fall out! If I'm dead you come lookin' for me underground 'cause I'll still be waitin'!"

Cece and Shirley fell together on the glider, laughing in each other's arms, and Lew could still hear them half a block away when he turned onto Fremont Street.

The Mexico Club stood like a carnival palace on the eastern edge of town, but even from a distance Lew could tell it was all façade, a magic act of chicken wire and plywood, its turrets and crenellated roofline held together with brushed stucco. He walked through the large parking lot that had been cleared of desert weeds and rubble. A long row of sickly cottonwoods led up to the entrance. Lew walked under their feeble shade and stopped in front of a fat man sitting on top of a ladder.

He had a box balanced on his knees and was replacing burnt lightbulbs in the sign above the front door. He was shirtless, and the swirls of dark hair across his neck and shoulder blades reminded Lew of moth wings.

The man looked at him, his face fuchsia and shiny. "What you want?"

"I'm looking for the Strella brothers."

"Which one?"

"I don't care."

"We're closed."

"No you're not."

Lew pushed open wooden doors with a cutout cactus motif and stepped into a small front lobby, its floor tiled in burnished Saltillos, then went through the huge maroon velvet curtains and climbed the wide, three-step staircase into the club itself. There were two large rooms, divided by an elaborately tiered fountain: to the left was the casino; to the right, the dining room tables and banquettes were set with white linen tablecloths and carnations, under wagon-wheel chandeliers and a magnificent bison head mounted over the private dining room in the rear. Along the back wall, a bar ran the length of the club and serviced both rooms. Behind the bar was a life-size painting of the Strella brothers, sitting on horseback outside the club, in short *chaleco* jackets and wide sombreros. They were handsome men with thin mustaches and full faces, stiff as cattle barons in their saddles.

In the casino, a dozen men were hunched over small tables by the bar, playing nickel cards and drinking beer. They didn't look up when Lew walked past, but when the bartender stepped through a side door with a box of whiskey bottles, he moved quickly and planted himself right in front of him. "Where you going?"

"Back there."

"Who says?"

"Mr. Jimmy." Lew held up the roll of money and walked around the bartender. Off a narrow hallway behind the bar he found Frank Strella hunched over a desk facing the open door in a large office, two oversized fans blasting air on either side of him. He wore a tailored black suit with a pale blue shirt and a dark blue silk tie. Lew could see the pointed toes of his high-heeled cowboy boots sticking out from under the desk, and his knees were knocking as he held a pencil over the crossword puzzle on the back page of the newspaper. When Lew strolled into the room, he glanced up.

"What is it?"

Lew pulled the money roll out of his pocket and tossed it across the room. It landed on the newspaper and bounced off Strella's chest.

"Goddammit!" Strella jumped up behind the desk. He'd put on weight since that portrait over the bar was painted. Lew figured twenty pounds easy, enough to make him fleshy but not really fat, just sedentary meat. Strella picked up the cash with his left hand, dangling his right hand into the open desk drawer. "What the fuck is this?"

"I took it off Mr. Jimmy," Lew said, idly wondering what sort of gun this dago kept in his desk. A ladies' gun, probably. A show-off gun.

"You took it off him?"

Lew didn't answer.

"How much?"

"Six hundred."

"Where?"

"A nigger house on Third Street."

Strella eased his hand away from the gun in the drawer and sat back down. "And Mr. Jimmy just let you take his money?"

"It's not his money, is it?"

Strella smiled and relaxed in his chair. "You want to tell me what happened?"

Lew was admiring the fancy tooling on Strella's cowboy boots. "He's got a big mouth. He'll tell you."

The fans oscillated gently, flipping the hair off Strella's forehead, and Lew walked out the door.

"What's your name?" Strella called.

"Beck." Lew didn't even bother to turn around. "Lew Beck."

He had a late lunch of breaded pork chops and shoestring potatoes at the White Spot Café, sitting at a window table for over an hour, drinking iced tea and watching women go in and out of Ronzone's Department Store.

At two-thirty he walked over to the Ambassador Apartments on East Fremont, and talked the landlady into unlocking Speed Owens's room on the fourth floor. At five-thirty, Speed came home from the dam and found Lew fast asleep in his bed, the covers pulled to his chin and his thumb in his mouth, sweet as any baby.

. . .

A week after arriving in Boulder City, Burr and Lena were sitting on the back steps of Fanny's house on Avenue K, watching the orange sky buckle and settle over the brokeback ridge on the horizon. It was eight o'clock at night, as hot as most summer afternoons in Oklahoma, but not nearly as humid.

Burr had been shirtless and barefoot when she left for work that morning and still was, his brown shoulders flexing as he flipped the abalone-handled knife Charlie had given him, trying to make it stick in the hard ground. She could only imagine how he spent his days, picturing him running wild through backyards with the neighborhood boys, a pack of desert rascals.

Wearily, Lena kicked off her own shoes, having just gotten off a twelve-hour shift that began over the giant KitchenAid mixer in back of the café, beating up batch after batch of dough for Hi Carter, Fanny's treasured cook, who was preparing the fillings for his famous pies: apple, pear, coconut cream, blackberry and chocolate. A Negro, Hi slept on a cot in a small room behind the kitchen, where he listened to the radio and drew pictures of desert life for his wife and two little daughters back in Stockton, California. Lena liked café work and she felt like a girl again, spending the days with Fanny, watching her flirt and sass with customers instead of boys, irresistible to anyone she encountered. Lena hadn't realized how badly she'd missed Fanny, and now felt that she and Burr had a new home, a thousand miles from the one that had evaporated into her past.

She was tired, but already had the chicken and potatoes roasting in the oven. The kitchen was stifling, even with the windows open, and she found it more pleasant to sit with Burr on the back step.

He kept up his efforts until the knife blade finally stuck, quivering there in the hard ground. "Is Dad coming soon?"

She'd expected the question before now, and told him the truth. "He's not coming."

He knew this but had to ask, had to hear the telling of it out loud, then he could stop wondering and hoping and just remember. He pulled the knife out of the dirt, wiped off the blade on his pant leg, then folded it and put it in his pocket.

They sat there listening to the chicken sizzle in the oven, to the rumble of distant trucks and to people talking in the little house next to Fanny's. The early evening was filled with quiet sounds, the after-thoughts and punctuations of a long day. Lulled by it, Burr almost fell asleep as the last rusty wisps of sunlight receded over the faraway hills.

Fanny rented her three-room stuccoed box from Harvey Perle, a shovel operator who'd gone back to Des Moines because the dry air made his nose bleed, and his nosebleeds drove his wife crazy. The morning she set Harvey to packing up, Fanny was waiting outside Sims Ely's office, trailing a Max Factor lilac scent that overpowered the smell of the fresh-baked doughnuts she carried in a paper sack.

Ely, the city manager, governed Boulder City like a feudal prince. In his late sixties, he looked ten years older, with thick, flat hair cut high above the ears, and a nose forged of iron. Tall as Goliath and thin as a corpse, he was particularly fond of tweed suits and was never seen without a tie. He was easily the most feared and hated man in town, and even roughnecks were known to cross the street when he approached, or spit in the dusty wake of his shoes. Fanny called him "the God Almighty of Boulder City," determined to rid the community of profanity and susceptibility, the hallmarks of the common man. Alcohol and gambling were forbidden and any violence meant immediate banishment. He set the laws and stood by each one, personally mediating domestic disputes with all the tolerance of Pilate. Vain and loveless, he possessed only one flaw: a weakness for the ladies. He was polite and forgiving even to the prostitutes he had roughly escorted out of the Boulder gate, and he could be unnerved and bedridden by the sheer whiff of an erotic dream. When the secretaries in the administration building played softball during their lunch break, Sims was their biggest fan, drinking his iced coffee and watching from a bench on the sidelines, his eyebrows rising with every lift of a skirt.

Fanny used this to her advantage. On the day she'd applied for a café license, Sims' inherent gruffness was mitigated when she sat across from his desk and crossed her legs, allowing a dimpled knee to peek discreetly from below the hem of her dress. Sims approved her application that very afternoon. Three months later, she invited him to the opening and ceremonially served him the first breakfast. He still stopped by three or four times a week, sitting by himself at a window table, smiling contentedly as Fanny brought him his coffee and doughnuts and watching her walk away before he even took a bite. When she sat across from him two months later and asked to rent the Perles' house, Sims inhaled the fresh doughnut and lilac scent again, and agreed to let her have it, but since those houses were reserved for married dam workers, there was one condition: she was to marry a Boulder City man within the year. It wasn't the deal Fanny had expected, but it fit Sims's narrow character to dole out favors like an Irish priest, and she accepted. A year was a lifetime and she was sick and tired of driving in from Las Vegas every morning before dawn.

Fanny had covered the pine floors with linoleum and the bare bulbs with shades, laid down throw rugs she bought at Penney's by the handful and put up curtains she made herself. In the evenings, after she closed the café, she'd built herself kitchen cupboards and a big closet with wood scavenged from the dam site by Tom Moore, a carpenter who walked her home every time he got the chance. As a final indulgence, she bought a used Westinghouse electric refrigerator and an RCA Radiola from Rockwell's. The radio sat on the chiffonier under the front window, and after Lena and Burr moved in, the three of them would sit on the couch and listen to Richard Gordon play Sherlock Holmes. During commercial breaks, Lena liked to tease her.

"So when are you getting married?"

"I got till March."

"Who's the lucky guy?"

"Haven't picked him yet."

"Got anybody in mind?"

"My mind's full of them."

"Anyone special?"

"They're all special."

"How do you know?"

"'Cause they tell me so."

They'd banter back and forth until the program came back on and Burr nudged them or turned up the volume.

When Fanny first arrived in Las Vegas, she'd worked seven days a week in the Overland Hotel, starting in the kitchen and making her way to the front of the main dining room. Whenever her shift was over, she lingered to see how the kitchen and restaurant were run, and later, when the manager, Mr. McNulty, trusted her enough, he let her stay after midnight and help him count receipts. On the days she worked the breakfast shift, she came in before dawn to inventory the meat and vegetables that had just arrived; on her nights off, she came in anyway and learned how to prepare the daily menu. On Monday mornings she drove the hotel's pickup truck to the McWilliams Ranch and collected fresh eggs and milk, and on Sundays she worked in the kitchen alongside Hi Carter, who had all the responsibility and none of the respect, and whom she stole away the minute her own café was approved by Sims Ely five months later.

She had worked long hours for low pay, stoic as the Mormon girls who came into town from Caliente to waitress and glower at the drunks and sinners they served. The only night Fanny took off was Friday night, and she used all twelve hours of it to dance and flirt, coming directly from the Red Rooster on the highway or the Sal Sagev on Fremont Street to work the Saturday morning shift, her hair smelling of cigarette smoke and her cheeks red as strawberries. She dated muckers and miners and a rodeo cowboy on his way to Reno, a bootlegger who had a hideout at Railroad Pass and the choir director at the Methodist church on Bridger Street. She dated a teller from the First State Bank and a top aide to Senator Tasker Oddie. She dated malcontents and civic leaders and none of them stuck, they never did, until she met a young police sergeant in Boulder City.

Archie Swerling had worked in Cut Bank, Montana, as an agent for the Bureau of Indian Affairs on the Blackfeet Reservation. He liked the job, but after frostbite took the tip of his right pinkie, he left the cold North to join the police force in Boulder City. He was a tall man, lean through the belly and strong as a ranch hand, but he had a soft face, pale and unlined, and no matter how trim his mustache and tall his boot heel, some thought he was just playing dress-up in his uniform. But he proved them wrong his first week, when he took the rifle Joe Muggs was pointing at him then cracked his skull with it, and single-handedly tore apart the still he was operating in the hills behind the Four Mile Saloon. Two days later he strode into a Ragtown brawl, his fists up and his head down, and knocked out three men before a hard jaw broke his index finger and he was forced to draw his pistol left-handed and hold the other combatants at bay until help arrived. Swerling took his knocks and paraded his bruises and black eyes around town like a sporting boy on a Sunday stroll, tipping his cream Bailey hat to the ladies and walking straight despite his fractured ribs. The day he collected his first paycheck, Chief of Police Bud Bodell made him sergeant.

Fanny liked Swerling's straw-colored hair and good manners, and flirted with him the first morning he came into the café. He'd come back for dinner that same night and stayed long after he'd finished his second slice of pie. He drove Fanny home, all of three blocks, in his police car, and was waiting at the curb the next morning to drive her to work. He hadn't asked, he was just there. Fanny saw the car but took her time, sitting in the living room and brushing her hair and drinking her coffee, and only after the local radio station announced the weather for the second time in fifteen minutes did she get up. A few moments later she stepped onto the porch and the morning sunlight made her sneeze. When she looked up, she blinked and caught a glimpse of the world at a momentary standstill, blurred at the edges but crisp as an old photograph. There was Archie Swerling, leaning against his patrol car with the passenger door open, his blue uniform pressed and his Sam Browne belt polished and snug on his hips. She knew other women were watching from behind curtains and half-closed doors up and down the block, eyeing him with an ache she hadn't suspected before, and she saw the dam workers, walking to the buses on top of the hill, waving at Archie or else pretending not to notice him until they could glance over their shoulders without being seen.

And Fanny liked all of it.

Lena was introduced to him her first morning at the café when he came in at ten o'clock for his usual ice-cold glass of Coca-Cola, cowboy hat in hand. She had to smile when she saw the sergeant's lanky body towering over Fanny's stocky healthiness, both of them pink and happy, although Fanny wasn't ready to admit it just yet.

The café was crowded from five in the morning until eight

o'clock at night. Fanny keep her daily menu simple and reserved more exotic specials—like Hawaiian curry with ham and pineapples, or Chinese ravioli stuffed with ginger and pork—for the weekends. And if they didn't sell, she'd offer a Sunday-night jungle stew, with all the leftovers tossed together with enough onions and tomatoes to confound any taste bud. Wednesday night was family night, and for two dollars a table of four got a whole roasted chicken and all the fixings. Once a month she offered two-for-one steak dinners that packed the café until closing time, and she made her profit by doubling the number of chairs at every table and moving the crowd along.

When Fanny went to Ely about the Perle house, he'd asked why she'd come to Boulder City in the first place. She weighed the purse on her lap, bulging with cash she was taking to the bank, and smiled. "Because it's the only city in America where everybody has a job."

The days at the café were full of talk and went by quickly, and when it got busy and Fanny was needed out front, Lena liked to help Hi back in the kitchen, flipping hamburgers or stirring the great vats of whipped potatoes and red beans that were always simmering on the stove. She preferred his easy company to the raucousness out front, where Fanny was always trying to introduce her to the single men who came in for food and attention. Lena was polite and cheerful, and when some of the men asked her out she demurred so smoothly that they didn't even realize they'd been rejected until they were halfway out the door.

One evening in August, when midnight rolled around and it was still too hot to sleep, the two friends sat on the screened porch in their nightgowns and drank iced tea. Their feet were bare and muddy, their knees smudged with dirt from the small flower garden by the front steps. For the past few nights they'd been planting poppy and columbine seeds and miniature rosebushes, trying to find something other than cactus that could withstand the desert burn. They'd filled the bed with good soil and left the hose running until it stayed a rich brown.

"You left him because you had to. If you found out earlier, you would've left him earlier—but it's not your fault you didn't find out, it's his."

"I know."

"I'm sorry Frank was such a rotten sonofabitch, and if I could send Archie to wherever the rotten sonofabitch is and teach him a lesson he'd feel in his bones until the day he died, I'd do it."

Lena smiled and let the tears roll down her cheeks.

"You're single again and you're pretty and most men aren't as stupid as they appear to be. I don't expect you to start acting like me and torment every father and son who thinks he's the dream you haven't even dreamed yet, but there's too much life left for you to go blind and dumb every time a man looks your way."

In the distance they heard another tunnel explosion at the dam. A dog barked on the next block, a frightened yap that ended with the last echo of the blast.

"You did a brave thing."

"Maybe."

"But you can't let it turn you into stone."

"I won't."

"I won't either."

Under a gray moon, the two women planted the last of the rosebushes and then went inside to bed.

Burr and his new friend Stanley Chubb ran wild through the reservation, barefoot in overalls, rampaging across the grid of streets with the Colleen twins and Gus Varner, the five of them a gang that took no prisoners and knew no boundaries, as lawless as the overheated days of summer allowed. They hid behind mounds of dirt by the empty lot on Arizona Street, spying on the men from Utah who'd come in I. M. Bay construction trucks to build the new brick schoolhouse. They began staying away when the second story went up, changing their loop through town to avoid the sight of it, knowing they'd be ensnared there soon enough. Most of all they liked to race through the park and run up the slope to the government dormitories, where trucks and buses shuttled men to the dam. Sometimes they'd meet Tony Colleen, May and Lilly's father, a shovel operator who always smelled of garlic, raw or cooked, depending on the weather. He carried his daughters home no matter how tired he was, and Burr couldn't stand to watch; he'd break away with the other boys and take shortcuts through the housing district, jumping backyard fences on Avenue C and zigzagging around barrel cactus and sleeping dogs on Avenue D, running with surefooted, arrogant abandon, all of them collapsing loudly on Stanley's front stoop and waking Ethel Chubb from her long nap.

Of all the kids he'd met in Boulder City, Burr liked Stanley the best. The Chubbs came from DeQueen, Arkansas, so the boys shared a common geography, and each had made boat trips on the same Little River that ran through their neighboring states. Stanley was skinny and bucktoothed, and he always had a scratch that was bleeding somewhere, a red line that trickled through the dust on his face or hands. Burr let him flip the knife that Charlie had given him, and showed him how to sharpen it with his little stone. Stanley gave him one of the five flattened pennies he'd gotten from his father, a rodman on the lower portal railroad in Black Canyon. The boys loved to build miniature dams, to mimic the great one being built nearby, needing only sand from under the house and a few buckets of water. During one of these sessions, Stanley asked Burr where his father was.

"In Oklahoma."

"How come he ain't working on the dam?"

"He's already got a job."

And that was it.

On Friday afternoons, Earl Brothers would open his Boulder Theater to all the kids in town. Once everyone was settled and quiet, he'd show all twelve chapters of *The Lone Defender* with Rin Tin Tin and Buzz Barton, or four hours of *Devil Horse* with the outlaw Noah Beery. If there was time after the serials he'd preview the movie that would open the next night, and that's how Burr and his friends got to see parts of *King Kong* twice. One Friday in August, during a preview of some boring Joan Blondell comedy, Burr and Stanley crawled on their hands and knees past where Earl dozed on the aisle seat in the last row, then burst through the theater's side exit, laughing at their cleverness. Burr blinked in the sudden glare of sunlight, thought about the ice-cold lemonade at the café, and darted for the plaza—forgetting about the high curb and tripping into the street. He fell with his hands out, heard the sound of a honking horn, and then only a hum in the road.

Burr blinked. He blinked again.

A woman screamed and he sat up, shadows picketing his body. His elbow was scraped and when he touched it his fingertips felt sticky. He saw his mother and Fanny burst from the café, but as he tried to stand, two hands reached beneath his armpits and lifted him into the air. They spun him around and Burr came face-to-face with a man only slightly taller than himself, dressed in dirty khakis held up by suspenders, and a white undershirt streaked with dirt. Something was familiar about him, but Burr couldn't place it. He could tell by his getup that he worked at the dam, and he smiled.

The man dangled him and smiled back. "You okay?"

"I hurt my arm."

The man twisted him sideways in the air and looked at the dripping elbow. "You'll live."

Burr stared at his strong arms, at the dark hair on his head and arms and unshaven cheeks. It was as if a boy had fallen asleep for a couple of years and got older but hadn't grown. Like he was too big to be in his skin, but it fit him anyway.

"You work at the dam, mister?"

Lena pulled the boy out of his arms. She held him close and examined the blood on his elbow and the scrape on his cheek. "Are you hurt?"

"I'll live."

Burr kept his eyes on the man, who'd leaned back against the fender of the Dodge convertible that had stopped only two feet from where he'd fallen in the street. Another man came around the driver's side of the car and stood next to the little one. A small crowd started to gather, mostly from the café, and Burr caught sight of Stanley Chubb skulking behind them.

Fanny glowered at the taller man. "You ought to be more careful, Speed."

"Come on, Fanny. I never hit anything in my entire life. Not even a dog."

"Not for lack of trying."

He liked it when Fanny Kruger talked to him, even when she scolded. "He come out of nowhere, Fanny."

"Slow down and look where you're going."

"I am looking."

Fanny was too angry to blush or parry. Speed was one of those men who orbited her at a distance, close enough to register only as a blur, an infrequent nuisance. "Next time I'll call the police."

Speed knew what that meant, and let his grin settle over his rotting teeth.

Lena put her hand on Burr's shoulder and led him toward the café. The two men were still leaning against the convertible, its engine sputtering and the empty seats getting hotter under the blazing sun.

Burr turned around and took a few steps backward, looking at the one who'd picked him up. "What's your name, mister?"

"Lew. Lew Beck."

The boy smiled and waved, but Lew was looking past him. He was looking at his mother.

He planted his feet and pushed off as hard as he could, swinging away from the canyon wall in an ever-widening arc, his head tilted way back so he could track the sky as it swam above him, and for a moment he was in flight.

He'd gotten the job through Speed Owens, who accelerated the hiring process by calling off a debt owed him by a clerk in the government employment office in Las Vegas. Lew was able to avoid the sidewalk crowds and the sorry out-of-state men hustling for work on the courthouse lawn, spending two lazy days at the Golden Camel or the Sal Sagev, playing penny slots and drinking cold beer while waiting for his work pass. On his third day in the state, he found himself high on the Nevada side of the river working alongside a line of high scalers, chipping away at rock scales and debris that clung loosely to the sheer face of the canyon walls.

The thought of dangling off a cliff with only a rope and a small plank seat gave pause to the bravest of men, even at the promise of five dollars a day, but Lew took to it with a bravado that irritated the seasoned aerialists who still prayed to God to get them through their shift. He already knew his hitches and knots the morning he arrived, and after only three hours of rope work on the lower slopes of Lookout Point, he was ready to go to the top. The foreman, B. A.

Peters, was used to braggarts and wise guys who ended up with brown stains in their drawers. Looking Lew over and figuring he was probably good for half a day, he assigned him to Wally Scofield's crew on the steepest wall. Lew strapped on a pair of water bags and endured the snickering of the other men as they rode the open truck to the top. Listening to their needling remarks on his size and swagger, he smiled at their jokes and singled out one or two who might need a lesson in the days to come.

Scofield put Lew next to Bud Allers, a big man, broad across the shoulders and upper arms but soft in the belly and thighs. Lew always looked for the soft places and remembered them. While Bud was still clowning around with Mike Conklin, tossing an orange back and forth near the canyon rim, Lew loaded his belt with wrenches and a pair of crowbars. He double-checked the knots on his bosun chair and casually pushed himself off the edge of the cliff, rappelling down the canyon wall like a monkey on a vine.

A hundred feet below the rim, he swung into position across the tangle of air hoses and cables that spidered from above, and signaled for his jackhammer, over forty pounds of steel that banged the wall and showered his Ballard hat with a plinking of stones. He braced himself, grabbed the jackhammer out of the air and hooked it up. Leaning way back on his seat, he steadied his feet and attacked the canyon wall, feeling the response of the drill all the way to the back of his neck. He took great pleasure in watching the first plate of rock he unhinged slide six hundred feet down the steep incline, smashing in a plume of gray dust at the water's edge.

He kept up a rough pace even after his hands went numb. It was 120 degrees on the canyon wall, and he stopped only to suck on the spout of his water bag or change drill bits. Bud Allers kept an eye on him, but Lew never got the shakes or froze when he looked down, so Bud just concentrated on his own patch of rock and left him alone. An hour later, the high-scaling crew got the flag for the first tunnel blast of the day; they stopped working and squared themselves on the cliff. Even though Lew was ready for the explosion that came a moment later, the force of it surprised him as it surged up the canyon and through the soles of his boots. Most of the men looked forward to the blasts because they could slump in their seats and rest, but Lew wanted the pure sensation of it, leaning into the hot wall to feel it in his cheek and hear it coming, an echo like waves of blood coursing through the rock.

When they broke for lunch, Wally Scofield sat down next to him. "Peters thought for sure you'd shit your goddamn diapers and we'd end up hand-hauling you back up the canyon, you screaming like a baby all the way."

Lew remembered Moe Goode, and said, "I'd shit in his hat first."

Scofield chuckled and drank some water. "You do this kind of work before, Beck?"

Lew saw that his hands were cracked and bleeding from the sun. "I've worked construction."

"Heights?"

"Some."

"You want the job?"

"I want it."

Scofield stood up. "I need to know which dormitory you're in, so I can get you on the time book."

"I live in town."

Scofield stopped. The back of his shirt was stippled with sweat, and he didn't bother to turn around. "Town rules. You come in drunk, you're through. You come in late, you're through. You do anything I don't like, you're through. We clear?"

"Clear."

"Then go to work."

During that first week, Lew watched the other high scalers swing out from the canyon wall when Peters and Scofield weren't looking, floating for long moments at the end of their ropes, arms and legs akimbo, poised as kids on a swing. From the ground it looked like an aerial ballet, making even the biggest and clumsiest of the men seem angelic in their flights through blue space. On the fifth day, Lew took his turn. He'd waited this long only because he'd already picked out a spot on the canyon where it dipped below a crusty ledge and gave him more room to fly.

When Scofield walked away from the rim, Lew double-checked the tender's knot and pushed off with all his might. Bud knew he was in the air when he saw his shadow pass over him, and he looked over his shoulder as Lew sailed by and lifted the Ballard right off his head and just kept going, his arms and legs spread until he came in for a landing right next to Mike Conklin, sixty feet from where he'd lifted off. Mike held on to his own rope as Lew kicked up a spray of pebbles at his side, and before he could say anything Lew took his Ballard hat and replaced it with Bud's much larger one, then sprung away with his feet, once again airbound and arcing far from the canyon wall, the other scalers tilting their heads back to witness this feat. Lew streamlined his body and gathered speed, traveling through the air at a thirty-degree angle, watching the taut, buzzing rope above him, and when he hit the apex he lifted himself out of the seat, suspended for an instant between gravity and momentum, high above the Colorado River, the world below frozen in time and fixed entirely on him. Only then did he pull on his rope and bring himself in, his knees already bent, hitting the exact spot he'd chosen. He turned to Bud and set Conklin's much smaller hat on his head, tiny and foolish as a lid on a teapot. The men around them started laughing, and from the summit and base of the canyon Lew heard whistling and applause. The shape of the canyon sustained this roar until Wally Scofield leaned over the rim and angrily put his crew back to work.

Smaller and lighter than any one else on the crew, Lew swung farther and faster than they could. He flew without friction or resistance. He flew on impulse, for the joy of performance. He was fearless and audacious. His actions astonished. No one could touch him.

Lew Beck walked on air.

Filius spent hours watching the high scalers cling to the scarred canyon. He envied their physical connection to the towering wall, their ability to navigate its welts and fissures and feel its curves with their callused hands. The engineers looking up from below, equipped with their transits and blueprints and notebooks, were safely on the ground and forever making calculations, their soft fingers stained with blue ink as they shouted out directions. No matter how much time Filius spent underground or how much rock he moved with his own hands, he couldn't change that. He gave orders. He made decisions. He was an engineer.

Filius often spent as many as twelve straight hours in the tunnel during his first month, rotating his time so he could learn how each crew operated and which men he could rely on. During the first week, he'd run into trouble with the Andereggs, brothers who worked side by side on the bottom level of the drilling jumbo. An hour after their shift came on, Filius saw Lesley Anderegg smack the ear of Perlie Trimble, his nipper, for giving him the wrong drill bit. Perlie, long conditioned to such abuse, went slack with the blow and quickly ducked back under the big wheel of the jumbo, rubbing the side of his head.

Filius waited until Anderegg had finished drilling before he approached him. "Keep your hands to yourself, Anderegg," he said.

"He gave me the wrong steel."

"Don't hit him again."

Willy, the older Anderegg, jumped to his brother's defense. "The little bastard's slow as a girl."

"Runt cost me—"

"Don't hit him again."

Finally, the Andereggs picked up their drills and went back to their positions, but over the roar of machinery, Filius saw them leaning close to each other and could imagine the ragged malediction. Ten minutes later Willy clubbed Perlie on the other ear, and Filius called both brothers off the jumbo and motioned for them to follow him. They silently walked almost a mile back through the tunnel, hugging the walls to avoid the mucking trucks that raced by. When Filius stepped outside, he waited for the brothers to catch up. Then he looked across the river and said, "Keep walking."

The Andereggs' faces were pale and lightly freckled, vague except for the blotchy irritation that ran scarlet around their eyes and noses.

"What the fuck for?" Willy demanded.

"Because you're not working in this tunnel anymore."

Angry, the Andereggs stood so close that he could smell the dumb indignation that rose as heatstink from their cropped skulls.

"'Cause we slapped Perlie?" Lesley asked.

"Because I told you not to."

"Everybody takes a poke at Perlie."

"Not in my tunnel."

The brothers flanked him, dancing on the balls of their feet.

"I seen Boss Floyd kick Perlie's ass shoulder high."

"Boss Floyd didn't give a shit long as we're diggin' dirt."

"Then go work for him."

The brothers shivered, wild thoughts of retribution pricking their simple minds. Filius knew this and stared them down as he would rabid dogs. Lesley blinked, and Willy eased back on his heels, losing his train of thought. And suddenly the danger had passed.

"What about our things?" Willy whined. "We got tools in there."

"Somebody will bring out your tools."

"When? How long are we—"

Speed Owens came out of the tunnel carrying a canvas duffel over his shoulder. He stood next to Filius and dropped the bag at the brothers' feet. A rusted wrench spun out and did a little jig across the dirt until Lesley stopped it with the toe of his boot.

"Now start walking." Filius turned back to the tunnel. Later that night, he heard that when the Andereggs appeared before Huntington and asked for jobs, Floyd laughed in their faces.

Speed fell in at Filius's side. "I got Otis and Hayes on the jumbo. They'll be okay for now."

"Good."

"Andereggs give you any trouble?"

"Why?"

"Just wondering."

"Were you coming out to help, or to watch?"

He caught a glimpse of Speed's uneven grin just before they crossed under the dark eclipse of the tunnel entrance.

"Just doing my job, boss."

. . .

Filius let each of his three crews race one another, and less than two weeks after he took over the job they broke out the other end of the tunnel. It was late in the afternoon, and the spray of light that came through the scattershot holes in the far wall brought cheers from the eighty men inside. Anxious to start the concrete lining, Filius sprawled open sheets of blueprints on the field table outside the entrance and calculated the job that still needed to be done. He worked long hours and left the tunnel only after Frank Crowe or Walker Young had come underground to find him gesturing his orders because his voice had given out.

By then Filius knew he should go back to his little brick house and get some sleep, but he wasn't tired. He was never tired. Instead, he walked around the site or drove around Boulder City, trying to deplete himself entirely so when he finally laid his head down and closed his eyes, his dreams would unspool without blame or detail.

If it was still daylight, Filius liked to drive over to the boat launch upriver, where Bobby Corn had a dock and a small store he ran with his wife at the shantytown in the Hemenway Wash. He wouldn't have recognized Bobby in the ten years since he was here with Addie; Bobby was close to thirty years old now and thirty pounds heavier.

"Wife says the extra weight makes me look successful." Bobby laughed. He had given up the Overton farm and the bootlegging business the day he heard construction was to begin, and had his ferry business set up before the first workers arrived. "Course, I ain't had Roy Rogers yet, but I did give Loretta Young and Preston Foster a ride when they was passin' through."

Bobby still had the same easy manner, and they'd sit on the end of his dock drinking orange soda and watching the brown water rush toward Black Canyon.

"Business has been good, Mr. Poe. They come down from Las Vegas, half a dozen at a time, in their best suits and cashmere overcoats and fancy beaver hats. Not much to say, any of them, at least not to me. There was this one fella I took out by himself one day, said he was the deputy attorney general from California, talkin' my ear off the whole ride up, tellin' me about the schooner he kept in the San Francisco Bay and the runs he made to Point Reyes and

Monterrey. He's not looking at anythin', not payin' the least attention to why we're out here, so when we get to Black Canyon, where
the river always misbehaves, I ask if he wants to take the wheel. He
sort of makes these sounds in his throat, but I steer out into the
channel anyway and hand it over to him before he can step away.
Now he don't know which way to turn and we end up cuttin' 'cross a
chop, and I sit flat down in the middle of the boat holdin' on like
God Almighty while he's bangin' around like a cowboy can't keep
his ass in the saddle. I know my boat and know how much she can
take, and we're thumpin' pretty hard, goin' sideways in a current
that's splashin' over the sides and soakin' us both, but I wait till he
starts screamin', 'We're tipping over!' before I take the wheel again
and bring us into calmer water closer to shore. And then this deputy
attorney general from California, this sailor of the San Francisco
Bay, gets sick all over the deck, hangin' over the side and moanin'
into his armpit all the way back to the dock, where he crawls off to
his car without so much as good-bye. I'll tell you, Mr. Poe, it was
worth the ten cents I paid that boy from Rioville to swamp out my
boat."

In the late afternoon they'd take the boat onto the river and
motor in the slow summer current. When they passed the break of
cottonwoods by the old bureau campground, Filius sat forward in
the bow and looked at the sandy beach where he had stayed with
Addie all those years ago. He allowed himself to remember her
strong arms plowing through the brown current, the way her back
rode high and her feet kicked. He remembered how she always fell
asleep on the beach with a book in her hands, waking up like nothing had happened, ready to read again. He dangled his fingers in the
water, thinking about the happy nights they'd spent here. Then he
leaned back, closed his eyes and let the sun beat down on his face.

He fell asleep in the bathtub and dreamed he was seven years old
and it was the day before Hanukkah. He was in the back of his
father's butcher shop on Soto Street. Out front the shop was busy,
filled with men and women yelling out orders in English and Russian and Yiddish for poultry and brisket. But on this day Louis

ignored the noise, and the sour smell of wet wool that steamed off the overcoats of the customers who came in from the winter rains, and the sweet smell of lemon cookies and poppy seed piroshki his mother had pulled out of the oven just that morning. Louis was in the storeroom, concerned only with the wooden crate in the middle of the floor. Inside was the big goose Isadore would butcher and braise in olive oil and wine, the centerpiece of their Hanukkah dinner. It was a special order his father had placed eight weeks ago with Morris Shenkman, the poultry man, who delivered it that morning with the usual ducks and chickens the other families would be eating tomorrow. But not the Beckmans. Isadore told Louis that this goose was special, it was as big as six chickens and mean as a rooster, and would feed them for as many days as the Maccabees had light. Louis listened with his mouth open because he could not imagine such a bird. He'd never even seen a real goose before. When he nudged the crate with his toe, his father told him to leave the bird alone. Then he smiled and patted his son's cheek. "You will see him soon enough."

But Louis couldn't wait. When the bell over the door chimed and his father went to the front, Louis cupped his hands around his eyes and peered between the tight wooden slats. All he could see was a dark shape moving in and out of the faint light that fell through the warped boards, and all he could hear was the scraping of webbed feet. So he grabbed the long wooden spoon off his mother's baking table, sat back on his heels and poked. The crate jumped, and the fat goose made hacking sounds as it panicked and thumped and beat its wings against the sides. Louis laughed, smelling the plops of liquid shit that flowed through the bottom and oozed onto the floor. When the crate stopped moving, he poked it again and the bird raged inside, shaking the box with its anger and fear. Louis did it again and again, laughing each time as the crate rose and shuddered and moved in crazy inches across the floor. But when Louis poked a sixth time, nothing happened. He hit the top of the crate with his fists. Nothing. He shoved it with both hands. Nothing. He kicked it. Still nothing. Now he panicked and leaned forward on his knees to yank apart the double strand of rope that held the crate shut. When he lifted the top half an inch to peek inside, the crate burst open and the goose emerged like a phoenix rising, its massive wings as broad as thunderclouds. Louis fell backward as the bird flapped straight up in the air screaming like a siren, its beady eyes on Louis. He scrambled across the floor as the huge bird swooped over him, smacking the top of his head with its giant wing before alighting on the table and knocking over a bag of flour, which burst open on the floor. The goose honked and dove again but missed and tipped over a pot of grease on the stove that was to be thrown out at the end of the day. Louis hid under the baking table while the goose watched him, then the shop door flew open and his father entered and chased the goose and slid in the grease and tracked the flour all over as the dinner bird flew over his head and thought only of the boy. Isadore swatted at the bird with a broom as Louis scuttled to the door on his hands and knees. When he turned the knob he looked back; the big goose roared and bit his father's hand and shat a stream of shit across the cutting board as it flew toward him. As Louis ran outside and into the alley, he heard his father yell, "Shut the door!" but he was too scared and ran blindly through the December rain, and when he reached Soto Street, he looked over his shoulder and the goose was two feet off the ground and cutting through the rain, honking bloody murder, eager to stab holes in the back of his head. Stumbling on the curb, Louis splashed down in front of the big swayback Morgan that pulled the milk wagon, but Mr. Gleason saw him and pulled hard on the reins and the old horse's shovel-sized hooves slid across the wet cobblestones inches from Louis's face. Mr. Gleason yelled at his horse and Isadore yelled at Louis and the great goose hissed in villainous glee as it landed in triumph and raised its smothering wings over Louis's head. He protected his eyes but looked up as the old Morgan whinnied and reared. When the huge goose turned to face the animal in its stupid pride, the hooves came down and smashed its wings into the pavement. Isadore yanked Louis by his shirt collar and pulled him to safety as the bird shrieked and the horse went up again and again, coming down on its chest and head. By the time Mr. Gleason controlled his horse, all that was left of the goose was feathers and blood and guts, a mess as unrecognizable as any other rubbish in the gutter. Neighbors pointed at Louis and his father and the dead goose, laughing, and he stood there, drenched to the bone, and felt his father's fingers digging slowly into his shoulder, pushing him back up the alley.

. . .

Still in the bathtub, he woke up to the sound of running water.

Shirley was relieving herself on the toilet next to him, her night-gown pushed up over her thighs and her hands on her knees. "We only got one bathroom here, and I couldn't wait no more."

Lew didn't know how long he'd been asleep, but he woke up thinking about the woman and boy at the café. The bathwater was cold, gray with the dirt he carried from the dam.

"Want me to get in there with you?" She wiped herself and pulled the chain, then stood up and let her nightgown shimmy back over her thick, dark thighs.

"No thanks, Shirley."

She walked over to the bathtub and scooped up the bar of soap that bobbed by Lew's knees. As she washed her hands, she cocked her hip and looked at him. "You sure?"

"I'm sure."

"You think I'm too big?"

"You are too big."

Shirley laughed. She swished her hands in the water between Lew's legs, dried them on his towel, and shut the bathroom door behind her. Lew could still hear her chuckling as she walked down the hallway.

After his bath, he usually went to Cece's room. If she wasn't there, he'd shut the curtains to block out the bright afternoon sun and climb between the sheets she changed after each visitor. He would shut his eyes and wait for her to come to him with a sandwich and a cold soda from Miss Williams's big kitchen. Or he'd wait for Shirley, who was bolder than Cece and would sneak into the room to suck his penis while the man paying her was next door getting undressed. Later the girls would giggle about this, slapping each other's wrists and knees, playful as sisters. There was no jealousy between them, no demands other than payment and gratification, and they knew that Lew was good for both. If Cece and Shirley were busy and Lew was hungry, he'd go to the kitchen himself and make a sandwich from one of the hams in the icebox, leaving a dime on the table. If it was cool enough, he'd take his plate to the front porch and find a place in the shade with the Negro men who gathered there, those who contemplated business inside and those who'd finished. These men, wary of Lew, grew quiet when he approached. They knew he worked at the dam, and some were righteously bitter that their color shut them out of such jobs and forced them to find work as porters at the train station or towel boys at the Mermaid Pool. A few of the Negroes did find employment in the gravel pits or the mixing plants, grateful even for these low wages and a chance to support the families waiting for them in squalid shacks on the western edge of town. Lew ignored the sidelong glances and hostile murmurs as he put his feet up and ate his sandwich. He knew they didn't want him here, and he didn't care.

Most evenings, Speed would pick him up in his old Dodge and they'd drive to the Nevada Hotel and have the big porterhouse steak special in the dining room, or eat pot pies and mashed potatoes at the Oasis Luncheonette. After dinner they went to the bars on Fremont Street or Railroad Pass, together with other dam workers escaping the strict confines of Boulder City. By the end of most nights, Speed was too drunk to drive, and Lew would drive his convertible to the small stucco house on Ogden Street where Speed's girlfriend, Nancy Thayer, an office girl at Western Air Express, stood unsmiling in the front window. Lew would walk back to the house on Third Street, where Miss Williams would sometimes charge him a dollar to spend the night, sometimes not. If Cece joined him after her shift, she'd snuggle up to his back and let him sleep. If Shirley got there first, she'd pull the sheets to the floor, turn him over with one of her big legs and smother him in her darkness.

One morning, when Lew was leaving for work, he ran into Mr. Jimmy on the porch. It had been weeks since Lew punched him in the eye, but it was still sore and watery, dripping pinkish tears, and Jimmy wiped at it with a handkerchief as he stepped aside.

"Mr. Strella's been asking about you."

Lew walked off the porch.

"I said Mr. Strella wants to see you!"

Lew kept walking. He'd known this would happen. But he had a good job and didn't need another, didn't need Strella or the Mexico Club, didn't need the trouble.

. . .

Burr sat at the counter and twirled his straw in a glass of water. He dipped the wet tip in the puddles of ketchup and mustard left on the rim of his plate and drew a picture of the Nevada mountains on the paper place mat next to him. But his heart wasn't really in it, and the soggy place mat ripped when he squiggled the Colorado River in across the bottom, so he swatted it back and forth until Fanny took it away from him.

Stanley was visiting cousins in Salt Lake City with his mother, the Colleen twins were home with colds and Burr was spending the day with his mother and Fanny. It hadn't been so bad when the café was filled with people, especially the dam workers, who'd come in with their wives and pushed tables together to make it like a breakfast party. Sitting at the counter, Burr was fascinated by the way these men ate; they grabbed at food with their fingers without being scolded and gobbled hash browns so quickly they'd have to pound their chests with closed fists just to belch.

And the early morning had been fun, when Hi let him help assemble the hundred sandwiches he'd made for men who kept a tab running at the café. Burr's job was to spread mayonnaise and mustard on the long double row of white bread that took up all the counter space, while Hi came behind him flipping slices of turkey or roast beef like playing cards, going down the row until each sandwich was filled and ready to be wrapped in waxed paper. By six-thirty, Burr was standing on a chair by the back window, handing each man a bag; by seven all the bags were gone and Burr had collected thirty-seven cents in penny tips.

Now he was playing with his straw and waiting for the rest of the day to drag by. Out the window, the almost finished school building loomed over the plaza like a cat ready to pounce. The movement of the clock over the door banged in his ear, every tick a second wasted.

Hi moved down the counter, wiping it with a wet rag. "You want another hot dog?"

"Okay."

Burr could hear Fanny in the kitchen, ripping apart big heads of iceberg lettuce. He watched his mother come around the counter to bring sixty cents change to the women at the front table.

He reached for a new straw and lifted his dull eyes to the window. "Mr. Poe! Mr. Poe!"

Filius was walking home from the post office when he heard the boy call out. He was startled at first but kept going, thinking he misheard the name.

"Mr. Poe!"

This time he stopped and looked around. In the window of the café he saw the boy waving to him as he ran to the front door and out onto the street.

"Mr. Poe!"

And then he saw the familiar woman run to open the door behind him. "Burr!"

That was his name. Burr. Filius thought of this as the boy came toward him down the sidewalk, smiling and out of breath, little legs pumping, arms swinging. He knew he should look away, but he didn't.

The boy stood in front of him, the hair on top of his head sticking up like he was still in motion, his upper lip tipped with dried mustard. "Mr. Poe. Remember me?"

"I hear the tunnel's almost a mile long."

"Almost."

They were riding on the top of the double-decker bus as it sped down the winding road to the dam, Burr sticking his head out the window into the wind, Filius holding on to his belt.

"And they got enough electricity down there to light up a skyscraper."

"I wouldn't be surprised."

"It's going to be a big dam, isn't it?"

"The biggest ever."

Ray used to ask him questions, too, and Filius loved answering them. He remembered sitting at their kitchen table in Chicago, trying to describe to Ray the dam he was going to work on in California. His son was seven years old and very inquisitive, but he still had a child's way of reaching for solutions: How many men would it take to build the dam? How big was the dam going to be? How wide was the San Gabriel River, and how fast did the water flow?

Burr leaned inside the bus again when it came around the last bend. "Can we go to the tunnel first?"

Filius nodded.

He kept his hand on the boy's shoulder as they walked inside the diversion tunnel. The bottom was already poured with concrete, and they stayed close to the track that supported the huge side form already in place a hundred feet inside the tunnel entrance. Up ahead, Burr saw trucks moving backward and cranes rising like great birds, and through the soles of his shoes he could fee the rumble of machinery he couldn't see. Bulbs were strung every ten feet, and they shone white against the glossy walls of concrete already poured. As they walked deeper into the tunnel, the light turned grayer. When Burr pushed back the metal hat that was too big on his head, he looked into the shadows above him and in front of him, and his lungs went empty and he bumped into Mr. Poe.

For the first time since they'd left the café, the boy was quiet. Filius watched him try to reckon with the underground sights and rhythms. It was an appreciative silence that fell between them; and as they walked farther into the tunnel, Filius felt the pressure of the boy against his side.

The lights grew brighter, and they stopped to watch as two big concrete buckets were hoisted to the top of the jumbo and swung into position over the chutes. A man in a Ballard hat came over to Filius and pointed to the gates on top. Burr couldn't hear what they were saying, but he saw Filius point to one of the concrete buckets and nod his head. The other man nodded, too, and signaled to a man in a wire cage on top of the jumbo, and then the bucket swiveled on the crane and tripped the gate, and the concrete poured down behind the form, where men were standing by to puddle it with their shovels and shape it against the ragged tunnel walls. Burr saw how the men reacted to Filius, how they seemed to pick up the pace in his presence and defer to him. Some of them smiled at Burr, and he smiled back, aware of the privilege he'd been given.

An hour later they sped out of the tunnel on a flatbed truck loaded with two empty concrete buckets, driving backward into daylight so bright it made Burr's eyes tear. They hitched a ride on a Boreman dump truck to the top of the canyon, and got off next to a shack on the edge. Burr saw the sagging system of cables and pulleys that stretched five hundred feet above the river, and without hesitation, followed Filius onto the skip along with four other men carrying toolboxes. They swung out over the canyon, dangling motionless until the operator checked the sway and then sent them off. It was a slow ride, and Burr held on to the side panels while Filius pointed out the diversion tunnels, two on each side of the river, and the mixing plant and the miles of railroad track that disappeared around the bend. He explained how they would build two temporary cofferdams on either side of the tunnel entrances to hold back the river and give them a place to work. He showed him exactly where the wedge of the dam would go, and the lake that would grow behind it. Burr listened and tried to take in everything around him. He leaned over as much as he dared and saw the hundreds of men scrambling down below, the trucks no bigger than toys and the river no wider than a creek. He got used to the sway of the skip and imagined he was on the back of a soaring hawk, floating high on desert vapors over a maze of roads etched into the hardpack like ancient glyphs. When they reached the Arizona landing platform, the four other workers got off and ten men boarded. Just after they started back across the river, one of them shouted. Startled out of his reverie, Burr looked to where he was pointing on the far cliffs.

Lew heard the warning screamed from above. He looked up and saw the wrench falling toward them, bright as a silver baton in the afternoon sun, with enough force to crush a man's skull. Mike Conklin put his hands over his head and Lew flattened out as best he could, but it was Bud Allers who was in trouble. Lew glanced down and saw him—frozen, staring upward with his mouth wide open—and yelled "Bud!" just as the wrench tore off half Bud's ear and broke his shoulder. Lew had already pushed off the wall with both feet when Bud howled and slumped sideways and backward on his bosun's seat. Lew eased on his own rope as he quickly dropped, slicing his arm on the sharp rocks. He bounced over Mike Conklin and stepped on Johnny Perrots's hand before he braced himself and reached between his legs to grip Bud as he fell, throwing an arm around his chest and pulling him into his lap. They twisted madly as the rope that held them adjusted to the tension and added weight, Bud screaming and Lew telling him to shut the fuck up. The rope slowly unwound, four hundred feet from the top and three hundred feet from the bottom, and Lew imagined that from either perspective they looked like graceful dancers twirling in the air. In the last dizzying revolution, Bud vomited down the front of his overalls and passed out, his head falling back on Lew's shoulder.

He felt the sticky blood from the mangled ear wipe across his cheek, and his own blood running warm as jam between his fingers.

He could hear Wally Scofield screaming on the cliff top, "Pull them up, goddammit, now!" and felt a sudden, jerky rush of air as he was hauled upward, the streaks of blood cooling on his skin. It was a pleasant sensation, and Lew shut his eye and smiled, every nerve vibrating like a plucked string.

The workers on the skip clapped and whistled. Burr stood next to Filius at the rail, staring just over the top as the two men were pulled onto the lip of the canyon.

The man next to Burr shook his head. "Look at that Beck—a fucking spider."

"A fucking lunatic," his friend corrected.

Filius cut them a look and they fell quiet, but Burr had seen and heard it all.

. . .

Lew recognized Frank Crowe immediately as he charged down the hall of the Boulder City Hospital in his buff-colored Stetson, his tie trailing behind him. He was limber for a man his size and moved with deliberate precision, marching right up to Lew and taking his hand. "You're a good man, Beck."

From the day he'd arrived, Crowe had been an everyday presence, always lurking in the corner of your eye, hanging over the shoulders of supervisors and foremen to make sure quotas were being met or bested, keeping his bosses in San Francisco and Washington, D.C., happy. He roamed the desert like a politician with bruised knuckles, and Lew, like everybody else, learned to stay out of his way.

Now the man wouldn't stop grinning or let go of Lew's hand. "Wally Scofield said it was the damnedest thing he ever saw. Said you flew through the air like a goddamn squirrel."

Six hours after the accident, he was still flying. From the moment they pried Bud out of his arms, he felt as if he were levitating on the physical hum of each of his five senses, and as the crew shook his hand and patted him on the back, every touch seemed to prolong the sensation, like the brushing of a cymbal. He felt like pure energy.

In the ambulance, medics gave Bud a shot of morphine and held him down as they sped along the bumpy road. The top of his ear was gone, and what was left reminded Lew of a broken teacup. At the hospital, word about the accident at the dam had already spread. Strangers came up to congratulate Lew; others looked and pointed, whispering his name, but the only thing he heard clearly was the singing in his head, and he didn't tell the doctor about this.

The cut on Lew's arm took sixteen stitches. The young nurse who bandaged it was very pretty but he hardly noticed. Bud Allers, she told him, was already on his way to a hospital in Los Angeles. "You're a very brave man, and he's very lucky."

Lew nodded, light-headed. Every breath he took felt vital.

The young nurse let her hand rest on his. "You must feel good."

He shook his head. It wasn't that at all.

His body was still humming when Speed picked him up at six o'clock. The ragged peaks beyond the river were tipped in gray light, and for the first time since he'd arrived there was a hint of coolness in the air.

Speed was looking at him with the same dumb grin he'd seen on everybody else. "So, buddy, how do you feel?"

Lew knew, but he couldn't voice it. He felt like an angel.

Every table at the café was occupied, but in a rare lull between orders, Lena had taken Burr's chair when he went into the kitchen to pick out dessert.

"He remembers everything you tell him. Weights. Distances. Jokes. Promises. Especially promises."

Her hair was tied back, but a few wisps had fallen across her face, and the kitchen heat had flushed cheeks already tanned by the inescapable sun. She looked healthy and pleased, and Filius was glad of her company as he finished his roast beef dinner.

"Thanks for taking him to the dam today."

"I'm glad I could do it."

"It'll keep him happy for weeks."

Archie Swerling sat at the counter, still in uniform, and his Bailey hat occupied the next stool. He counted to five as he poured sugar into his coffee cup, and propped his feet on the bottom rail as he stirred it, his long legs sticking out like a cricket's on a blade of grass. Fanny flirted with Archie every chance she got, brushing his hip with hers as she passed with bowls of mashed potatoes or beef stew, or standing across from him while pretending to wipe the counter as she played with the nub of his pinkie.

Filius watched Lena check the tables around them. Satisfied that everyone was content, she relaxed and let her gaze meet his. "We've been here all summer and I think this is the first time I've seen you in the café."

"It is."

"Don't you eat?"

"I usually take things down to the dam."

"What sort of things?"

"Coffee. Fruit. Sandwiches."

"And what about breakfast?"

"Coffee. Fruit."

"Dinner?"

"Coffee. Sandwiches."

She smiled. "Do you eat every meal at the dam?"

"Just about."

Burr walked carefully to the table, carrying two orders of chocolate cake, sliding one in front of Filius and the other in front of the empty chair next to his mother.

"When can we go back to the dam?"

"Soon. I promise."

Speed Owens held open the door for Lew Beck, who stopped just inside and scanned the room, listening to the diners murmur over their plates, imagining they were all chattering about his bold exploits. It was a soothing background to the singing in his own head.

Fanny glanced at Speed as she walked by, counting the spray of bills in her hand, then she stopped and looked at the other man, who had a bandage on his arm. "This him?"

"Yep. Lew Beck . . . the one and only."

"Dinner's on the house tonight." Fanny looked down and finished counting her money. "We should have a table free in a minute or two."

Lew saw the woman sitting at a table in the corner. She was with the boy and a tall man he thought he recognized, but couldn't place. The boy was staring at him over a wedge of chocolate cake, chewing furiously as Lew walked up to them, standing to the left of the woman's chair and waiting for the boy to swallow.

"Lew Beck. I saw you!" Burr looked at his mother and pointed. "That's the man."

When she turned, Lew was already smiling at her. He saw the surprise in her face, her eyes taking in the size of him, the dam sweat on his clothes, the bandage on his arm. Her face, he thought, was beautiful and not judgmental, and he allowed her this first inspection because she deserved to know who he was. "I'd like to buy you dinner."

"I'm sorry, I can't. I'm busy." She smiled and averted her eyes.

It was all right if she was shy. And maybe she didn't know yet, exactly, what he'd done. When she got up to clear the empty plate, he didn't move. He stood very close to her, and when her arm brushed his it was like a match passing over his skin. "All I want to do is buy you a steak."

"No, thank you."

"What's your name?"

She didn't answer and moved to walk around him.

Blocking her way, Lew leaned forward and breathed in the kitchen smells that rose off her uniform, and underneath that, the clean scent of her. "I just want to know—"

"That's enough."

The tall man was standing now. Lew looked at the long taper of his nose, at his clean white shirt and tie, and he kept his smile, but it wasn't easy. The man was a dam boss, Lew was sure of that, but there was something else, too, playing on the fringes of his memory. A hand fell on his shoulder, and he turned to see the sergeant standing there. Solemn and sure of himself, he was about Lew's age, lanky and muscular as a cowboy.

Things happened quickly. Lew saw the woman put her arm around the boy and lead him over to the counter where Fanny stood. He saw Speed looking nervous, his eyes moving everywhere before landing on the dam boss, and it made him angry to see his friend bow his head and shuffle his feet like a Chinaman. But he concentrated on the cop standing over him, his badge at eye level.

"I want you to leave," he said.

"This isn't your business."

"Oh, it is. Most certainly is."

"Come on, Lew."

He could feel Speed fidgeting behind him on his goosey legs, but he refused to move. People in the café went silent and stared over their water glasses and forks.

"I'm not bothering anybody." He chewed the words, unable to control the flutter of rage in his own voice.

"You're bothering me," the cop said.

"Jesus Christ, Lew," Speed hissed in his ear. His breath smelled dead and familiar.

Suddenly his arm felt warm, and when he looked down he saw fresh blood on the bandage. The only sound he heard was the lilting buzz in his own head, but he could sense the contempt in the room, eyes burning him like steel pellets from a rifle. He didn't dare look around for the woman.

Everything that had been right was suddenly wrong.

Lew turned away from the sergeant and pushed Speed out of the way as he strode toward the door.

Filius stepped onto his screened porch with a glass and the almost empty bottle of bourbon. It was after midnight, the black sky shot with stars. Over the craggy range in the distance, the lights of the dam site formed a delicate nimbus. He poured himself a drink and lit a cigarette, rolled up the blueprints on the table and slipped them in the metal tube leaning against his chair, then pulled out his notepad and sat down.

> *Dear Addie,*
>
> *Work goes well and it's hard to believe that summer is almost over. We are lining the tunnel now, and every day I'm amazed at the progress we make. I'm fortunate to have good crews on all my shifts so we're ahead of schedule and I plan to keep it that way.*
>
> *Last week I had dinner with Frank and Linnie Crowe. I put it off as long as I could, but they've always been good to me, and there's a limit to even my lack of social graces. There were ten of us for cocktails and steaks grilled outdoors, all engineers and engineers' wives. You remember Walker Young, he was there, and Tom Loomis, who as usual drank too much, and Gus Adams, who didn't drink a drop. Patricia was there, all grown up now and a young lady in a dress and patent leather shoes, serving canapés and fresh drinks under Linnie's watchful eye. She took me in her room and showed me a picture of her and Ray playing in the shallow water of the Platte River when Frank and I were working on the Guernsey Dam. That was a good summer, and Patty remembered it as well as I did. She*

wanted me to have the photograph, but I couldn't take it, and I thanked her very much and we went back to the party together.

It's the children that make it difficult for me, and I forget sometimes how easy they are to be around. Today I took a boy on his first trip to the dam. He's about Ray's age, inquisitive and clever and ready to dip his toe into any new experience. It is probably the best time I've spent here since the day I arrived. His name is Burr McCardell, and he came here with his mother from Oklahoma. She works at a café in town, and I had dinner there tonight. I think you'd like her.

Filius stopped for a moment, lit another cigarette, finished his drink and went on.

I think you'd like them both.

Lew and Speed ended up at Texas Acres, a rough place on the Las Vegas side of the pass that was favored by Irish workers who drank cheap liquor and fought one another without skill, banging away with fists like hammers, assailing friends or cousins, it mattered little, all of them drunk and numb, chopping away at one another until they littered the parking lot like blown-down timber. They had girls there, too, in a row of sheds out back, rumored to be so ugly that men refused to visit them by daylight. The owners of Texas Acres were tolerant men, blind to the violent ambitions of their clientele as long as business wasn't hurt. They were desert scavengers who knew their stewardship was temporary, that the authorities would someday chase them out as surely as the rats and foxes they'd run off when they came out here to string their lights and post their sign.

Tonight, Lew had come for the darkness and anonymity, away from the eyes that appraised him and tried to take him apart. He stood at the bar with Speed and quickly drank two beers, but the alcohol couldn't quiet the noise in his head, and every inch of his flesh still trembled and ached. He wanted it to stop, and was ordering another beer when he heard the laughter and glanced behind him. The Anderegg brothers were sitting together at a small table nearby, grinning wildly, their faces shiny with whiskey, and he knew what their laughter was directed at. Lesley mumbled incoherently, and Lew heard Willy shout out, "Fucking idiot," to the men around them, who weren't listening and didn't care. Willy went on anyway, staring at him, and in his rambling spew of drunken nonsense, Lew could make out a few words: *"lunatic"* and *"monkey"* and *"Little Jew."* When Lew picked up his beer from the counter and walked past the Andereggs, the laughter started again and boomed off his back as he left the bar. When Speed came outside, he was sitting on a crate with his back against the wall, taking slow sips of his beer. Speed suggested they head home, but when Lew didn't answer, he knew what was coming, so he climbed into his car and fell asleep in the front seat. Lew sat in front of the Texas Acres, thinking about the good and the bad things that had happened to him during the day, as he nursed his beer. An hour later the Anderegg brothers came outside. They didn't see Lew sitting in the shadows as they stumbled to their car. Lew followed them to the parking lot next to the railroad tracks, and swiftly brought his beer bottle down on Lesley's head to put him out early, because it was the older brother he wanted. He jumped over Lesley and grabbed Willy's head, ramming it down on the fender of the coupe next to them. Willy fell into a prayerful position, and Lew got a handful of his hair and slammed his head against the fender until the moonlight picked up a sparkle of loose teeth on the running board and his loud mouth was nothing but a crimson mush. Willy groaned and gurgled in the parking lot dirt, trying to pull away on his elbows and knees, but Lew wasn't finished. He kicked and punched and stomped him until there was only silence, true silence.

For the first time in hours Lew no longer heard the roar in his head, and he knew that everything was going to be fine.

*O*ne morning in September, Lena told Fanny she was going to leave work early that night. They were standing together in the kitchen cutting up the two bushels of golden apples that had arrived at dawn from the Guthrie Ranch in Paradise Valley. Fanny just nodded and continued quartering the apples, some for Hi's pies and others for Lena's applesauce, to accompany the pork chops Fanny would serve for that night's dinner special.

The breakfast hours were typically busy, and Lena did mostly kitchen work while Fanny played hostess to Sims Ely, who reveled in the change of weather and lingered at his corner table a half hour longer than usual. The two women didn't find themselves together again until noon, waiting at the counter for Hi to finish frying the half dozen hamburgers that sizzled and smoked on the grill.

Fanny kept busy chopping tomatoes and onions to garnish them. "So why are you leaving early today?"

"I want to bring Mr. Poe some food."

Fanny nodded, then picked up the coffeepot and checked on refills, by which time the hamburgers were ready.

At one o'clock Archie came in, and Fanny sat down with him over glasses of root beer. Lena took care of the late lunch customers, mostly women in groups of three or five who drank endless cups of sweet tea and ordered the dainty sandwiches Fanny always made especially for them. It was the easiest time of day, and Lena was used to the airy habits of Mrs. Gray, who needed to have the crust cut away, and Mrs. Popowski, who wanted her sandwich constructed just so, with mayonnaise on the bottom slice of bread and never any mustard, and Mrs. Moskowitz, their matriarch, who drank her tea the Russian way, with a tablespoon of blackberry jelly.

At two o'clock, when Archie finally left to make his rounds, Fanny helped Lena clear the tables. "And why are you bringing food to Mr. Poe?"

"Because he was good to Burr."

Fanny's mouth pursed but she didn't say anything before moving off to finish the front tables, while Lena went to wash the dishes that had piled up since the lunch rush. She liked this hour over the deep sink, her hands searching the hot, soapy water for the next plate or glass while Hi worked beside her. Today he was peeling potatoes and tossing them into a huge pot on the stove, talking all the while about his wife and two little girls, his voice deep and handsome.

"My Dorrie's working two jobs now, glad to have them, but she hate for the children to have to stay with their aunt Jo all day. Jo's my sister and her husband's dead of pneumonia, but kids ain't what she's good at. She takes in laundry, and my girls got nothing to do 'cause their cousins, four boys born lazy, spend all day sleeping on the banks of the deepwater channel or throwing rocks at the fishing boats till the police chase 'em away. Dorrie picks up the girls each night around six, dead beat after eight hours at the mineral baths handing out towels and swimsuits to old folks come each day for a dip in the marsh-gas water. Girls help out best they can. Sue's a good cook like her daddy, boiling chickens for corn bread pie like she was born to it, and Eugenia rubs her poor mother's feet until she about to cry. Then on Monday to Thursday Dorrie eats fast as she can to do her night work, sweeping and mopping up the Forty-Nine Drugstore after hours, gets home round midnight to sleep and she does that hard, too, long gone till daybreak. They coming out next summer for good, and I'm glad of that since I miss 'em like front teeth."

Lena stayed in the kitchen, happy to listen to Hi as she made the applesauce the way her mother taught her, simmering the apples in salted water until the quarters turned gently by themselves and the skin started to shrink back from the fruit. After the apples were allowed to cool, she strained half of them through the food mill and cut the others by hand so the sauce would be chunky and firm. Instead of cinnamon she added lemon juice and a taste of vanilla, and when the mixture started to bubble again in the two-handled pot, she turned off the heat and stirred in big dollops of homemade horseradish that would allow the applesauce to stand up to Hi's seasoned pork chops.

Fanny leaned in the doorway, where she could keep one eye on the café, and rubbed her broad, achy hip. "Archie knows a lot of single men."

"I bet he does."

"Men ready whenever you're ready. Men just waiting for Archie to say it's okay."

Lena dipped a wooden spoon into the applesauce and handed it to Fanny. "I want to thank you and Archie for taking such an interest in my business."

"You're welcome." She tasted the applesauce. The heat from the horseradish brought tears to her eyes, but she finished what was on the spoon before handing it back. "It's good."

"Thank you."

"Mr. Poe wears a wedding ring."

"I know."

"You're wasting your time."

"It's not about that." Lena turned back to the stove, and could feel Fanny scowling behind her, huffing and rustling the sleeves of her blouse, making more of a fuss than her grandmother. She also knew that if she looked at her friend, she'd start laughing.

When Lena finally turned onto Denver Street, it was after nine, and bands of sheer clouds floated in the black sky, passing over the sliver of moon like a celadon glaze. She'd found his address in the directory at the Bureau of Reclamation office the day before, and didn't really expect him to be there, but that wasn't the point. She was being gracious to someone who had helped them without question or qualms, a man she should have thanked then, a man who was kind to her son. She walked around the car and opened the passenger door to slide out the cardboard box containing pantry staples like eggs and bread and oranges and cheese, and a few cuts of beef and chicken breasts wrapped in ice so they would keep overnight on the front porch if necessary, and keep longer in one of the refrigerators that was rumored to be in each of these brick houses built especially for bureau supervisors and engineers.

Balancing the box in her arms, she started up the walk and was almost relieved that the house was dark. This makes it easier, she thought. Less complicated for both of them.

"Hello."

She was so startled she almost dropped the box. The voice came from the side of the house, but there was no one there. Lena was about to turn away when her eye caught the red glow of a cigarette on the screen porch, and when it moved upward and burned hotter, she saw the silhouette of a man behind it.

"Wait," he called, disappearing for a moment and then coming across the front yard. He was still wearing a white shirt and tie, but this time the tie was different, maroon and blue, and she was surprised to have noticed—until recalling her father and his collection of seven ties, one for each day of the week, and how for each Christmas and birthday her mother would buy him a new one, and they'd make a joke of it by letting Lena pick which of the old ties to retire. She always went for the brightest and gaudiest one left, which she'd take back to her room and cut up into hair ribbons for Fanny and herself.

"I didn't mean to frighten you."

"I didn't expect to find someone sitting in the dark."

"Let me take that." He lifted the box from her arms, smiling, and she saw his curiosity as he tried to look past the open flaps. She didn't remember him smiling before.

When he turned on the lights it was like walking onto an empty stage: the house appeared unlived in, furnished but somehow incomplete. There were rugs on the floors and pictures on the walls, and an appropriate number of chairs and tables in the living room. In the room down the hall she could see a perfectly made bed reflected in the mirror over the dresser. Except for the smell of cigarettes and the whiskey bottle on the sideboard, the house reminded her of an exhibit she saw years ago, when Frank took her to the state fair in Tulsa. One of the most popular attractions was "Modern

Life," where fair-goers entered huge wooden cubicles converted into the model living spaces of tomorrow. Most of all Lena remembered the kitchen and living room at the exhibit, where you stood behind a rope and watched the most up-to-date appliances whirr and bake quietly while the newest in radio consoles played "Bye Bye Blackbird" over and over.

Lena sat in the living room and listened to him put the groceries up while he waited for the kettle to boil for coffee. When she shifted her legs and tried to get comfortable, the sweet and greasy scent of Hi's cooking rose from her body, and she wished she'd gone home first for a bath. She stood up quickly, embarrassed by her own vanity, and noticed the single photograph in a silver frame on the mantel opposite her. Walking closer, she stared at the picture of the woman and child in the boat on a lake, and knew immediately who they were. She wanted to reach out and touch it, trace their smiling faces with her forefinger, but she didn't dare.

"My family."

She heard him come in behind her, but she didn't turn around. "They're beautiful."

"Yes."

"Where was it taken?"

"Garfield Park. In Chicago."

Lena could hear the water begin to roll in the kettle. "Your son?"

"Ray."

"How old is he?"

"He was seven that summer."

"Where are they now?"

They stood and looked at the photograph until the kettle began to whistle. "They're not with me anymore."

The whistle grew louder, a high lonesome sound that seemed to her intolerable.

The sun was shining as they drifted in the wreckage of the sailboat; the storm clouds that surprised them earlier were delivering no more than light showers and a rumble of thunder over Charlevoix and Northpoint and the inlets of Traverse Bay. He still held on to the rudder, letting his legs float just under the surface of the water to keep pressure off the broken ankle. He'd improvised a splint as best he could from a shattered piece of coaming and a length of rope, but in the last hour a maroon cuff of bruised flesh had begun to show around the bone. Addie was still clinging to the end of the broken mast, her back to him, bobbing lightly in the water. She was quiet now, and he was relieved. When he first went to her she was looking toward the bow and didn't hear him as he slipped his body over the exposed keel and pulled himself along the frame. When he touched her shoulder she raised her head and screamed as if he'd run a knife through her ribs. She spun in the water and tried to bite his hand, and all he saw was red—of her eyes, of her mouth and of her skin, raw and blotchy and flayed with tears, her beautiful face now a mask of heartache. He moved away and called her name, and she only screamed louder and beat the water with her fists and shook her head, her eyes everywhere and nowhere. "Addie, no!" he called, and she wailed until her lungs were empty and her throat was raw.

Filius treaded water. Addie looked at him, and he reached out his hand. She shut her eyes and raised her arms over her head and let herself go, sinking fast through the rings of her own torment. Filius dove and found her underwater and took her around the waist. She struggled, clawing at his arms and kicking at his legs, wrapping herself around him, squeezing to hurt him, but he held her and fought his way to the surface, the pain in his ankle excruciating. He gripped the mast with one arm and his wife with the other as she attacked him again, scratching his nose and biting his arm. But he pulled her to his chest and wouldn't let go, clinching her until she no longer resisted and he felt her muscles go soft against him. Addie rested her head on his shoulder, and her breath came like shivers across his neck as she whispered in his ear, "Go away." He whispered back, "No." "Go away" she said, pushing him softly and grabbing on to the broken mast, again turning her back to him. Filius found the halyard floating on the water and coiled it until he had the end. He looped it twice around Addie's waist and she didn't struggle when he knotted it and tethered her to the end of the mast. She didn't look at him as he swam to the other side of the boat, where he held on to the rudder and watched her. Sometimes he heard her crying, but it never lasted long. Sometimes he cried himself.

. . .

Cece knew better than to say anything. She'd already seen Shirley make the mistake of coming in there laughing, just being her old naked self, shaking her big behind in his face and stretching her fingers between the buttons on his pants until he spun her around and slapped her in a way that wasn't playful. Cece didn't want any of that and kept her own mouth shut. He'd been in her bed for three days now, and she still walked around him like you would a colicky baby.

When he came in that first night his hands were all scraped and swollen, but she didn't ask him anything about it, only tended to his hurt. She brought him food when he was hungry, thick slices of pork and biscuits and coffee, and changed the dressing on his arm every day. Most of the time he kept the door shut, and the girls who entertained nearby knew to do their business quietly. If Miss Williams minded any of this, she didn't say. Cece never saw her ask him for any money or make a fuss. She let him stay without a single complaint, and on the seventh day, when he wanted the stitches out before the doctor would do it, she took the small scissors from her sewing kit and cut them out of his arm herself.

He didn't touch Cece once that whole week. She slept with Shirley, never soundly, with one eye open.

One afternoon Lew woke from a nap to see Mr. Jimmy staring at him from the doorway of Cece's room. He leaned there on the rounded hump of his shoulders, arms crossed and grinning like a fool.

"What do you want?" Lew asked him.

"I hear you roughed up some big boys out on the pass."

"Bigger than you." Lew stretched his arms and squeezed his eyes shut. When he opened them, Mr. Jimmy was gone.

The doctor in Boulder City had told him to stay away from work for at least a week, and he lay in Cece's bed brain-tired and muscle-sore, a victim of unease since that afternoon when he and Bud Allers swung in unison off the wall of Black Canyon. On the tenth night, Speed came by at three in the morning and tapped on Cece's window, flailing his arms like his pants were on fire. Lew got up and the two men sat on the porch together, drinking beer from Miss Williams's kitchen. Speed was already drunk, and rocked there with his boots scraping the wooden rail, blithering away about the fight he had that night with Nancy at the Cactus Garden.

"I took her out three times this week and I'm broke by Tuesday. I tell her this, I'm broke by Tuesday, and she don't listen, don't hear, only looking at the menu like it don't matter a thing I say. So she orders a rib eye and I tell the waiter to make it a hamburger, two of them, and her eyes get beady and she calls me cheap so I grab the waiter again and tell him to cancel one hamburger, hers. Now she's squirming around like she's sitting on a frying pan, so mad I can smell it over the stinkin' perfume she's using, and she's not saying a word and I—"

"Go home, Speed," Lew said. The sound of Speed's voice was making him sick. The meandering nonsense of it. "Go on home."

Speed took a quick gulp of his beer and leaned way back on his chair. "So Nancy just sits there staring at me with those eyes that could drop the dick off the devil, as if I could give a shit, and the waiter comes over and sets down that big Cactus Garden hamburger right in front of me and says, 'Anything for the lady?' Nancy crosses her arms and she hardly opens her mouth when she says, 'Rib eye steak.' So I shrug and tell the waiter, 'Then you better pick her up and turn her upside down and see what kind a change falls out 'cause I ain't paying.' And Nancy yelps like a poodle and throws her whiskey right in my—"

"Beat it, Speed." Lew stood up, his body tight and his hands clenched at his side.

Speed peered at him, trying to see straight. "Lew?"

"Go home."

"You okay, Lew?"

"Now."

Speed rolled his skinny shoulders and stood up. Without saying another word, he finished his beer, left the empty on the railing, walked down the steps and cut across the lawn.

And Lew was glad, because he liked Speed, but if he'd opened his mouth just one more time, he would've broken his goddamn jaw.

She knocked on her own bedroom door, and when he didn't answer, quietly pushed it open. It was ten o'clock at night, and he was lying under the covers in the dark, facing the open window. He didn't even look up when she sat down next to him holding a tray with a dish of warm water and fresh bandages. Cece carefully lifted his arm, laid it across her bare knees and began to unwind the gauze. Since his stitches had come out too soon, his arm bled where the skin pulled apart and left marks like tiny butterflies. She got the old dressing off and cleaned the wound with a sponge. It was getting better, almost healed. She let her fingers run over the ridged skin, long and curved like a sliver of the moon. Cece dabbed at the small bloody punctures where the stitches had been, and cleaned the arm with peroxide before wrapping it up again. When she got up to leave, he reached out and took her hand—startling her—and then tossed back the covers. Cece saw that he was naked and looking at her for the first time since he got hurt. She looked back, unable to get enough of his perfect smallness, then raised the loose white shift over her head and climbed into bed with him. He pulled her closer and wrapped her in his arms, contorting her body until she fit comfortably around the jut of his knees and the angle of his hips. He held her tight, and Cece felt him breathing deeply and warmly behind her. She stayed with him all night and eventually relaxed, but she was wary still and waited until he was asleep before she shut her own eyes, both of them this time.

Lew slept a dreamless sleep and woke up feeling restless and confined. He stood naked at the window, watching three strays trot down the center of the street on jaunty paws, their tails straight and faces alert as they scoured hedges for squirrels and cats. Lew decided he was hungry himself and craved runny eggs and sausage. He wanted a chance to sit in the front window of a restaurant and read the newspaper while traffic passed and voices flew around him, picking up bits and pieces of everyday noise that he suddenly missed.

Leaving Cece asleep in bed, he got dressed and headed down Third Street, past the whorehouses where white girls sat on porch swings and banisters, smoking cigarettes and taking advantage of these slow hours. No one said a word to him. No one looked twice. When he crossed Ogden Street, a new Cadillac turned the corner and stopped, idling at the far curb. Lew saw Frank Strella behind the wheel, dressed in a light blue suit and wearing sunglasses. Mr. Jimmy sat beside him, whispering in his ear. Strella followed Lew in the mirror, nodding his head and smiling as Mr. Jimmy waved his hands to make some point.

When Lew came abreast of the car, Strella leaned on the window like a comrade, like someone with a joke to share. "Beck. I hear you've been holing up at Miss Williams's house. I hear you've taken over."

"What of it?"

"I ought to charge you rent."

"How much?"

Strella paused a moment and laughed. He laughed loud and hard, as if this was the funniest thing he ever heard, and then drove off, shaking his head.

Lew watched the Cadillac turn onto Fremont Street, and knew it was time to go back to work.

It was the first Sunday in October, warm and breezy, and Filius had borrowed Bobby Corn's boat to take Lena, Burr and some of his friends to the cove on the Colorado River where he'd camped ten years before. They pulled onto shore at about ten in the morning, and the boys waded into the murky shallows to skip stones and splash one another while the Colleen twins picked bouquets of Spanish needles and stems of bright orange globemallow to take back to their mother. Filius stood on the deck and saw a pack of wild burros grazing on the open rangeland, their black snouts mowing through the last blooms of sage. He called the children over, hoisting Burr onto his shoulders.

"Look at them all! Can we get closer?" Burr asked.

"You can try," Filius replied.

"We can sneak up on them."

"That's what I would do."

"How would you do it?"

Lena smiled. She was sitting on the bow tying up the girls' flowers with string she'd found in Bobby's toolbox. She watched Filius as he pointed out the way, and saw her son shade his eyes and scan the landscape.

"I'd go around the cottonwoods and follow that line of creosote," Filius told him. "Take my time and stay low. Then I'd make a run for that big gully over there. See it?"

"I see it."

Burr squirmed and Filius put him down. The boy jumped over the side of the boat into water that came just below his knees and the other children followed. They sat on the shore and put dry socks over their wet feet and quickly tied their shoes.

Lena put down the flowers and leaned over the gunwale. "We're having lunch soon."

"Okay!" Burr called, then sprinted through the spiny saltbrush that grew in clumps by the river. Stanley Chubb was right behind him, followed by the Colleen girls and Gus, who had trouble tying his laces.

From the bow, Filius and Lena watched the bare backs of the boys and the whip of the girls' sundresses as they raced for the cottonwoods. They lost sight of them in the ravine until they rose like a pack of shrieking demons to chase the burros that brayed and bolted and before long had disappeared over the far ridge.

Lena looked at the stems of Spanish needles that lay across her lap and poked over the side of the boat. The pink flowers at the tip were fragile and spare, and every time she moved they shook from the slender branches and spiraled like exotic beetles to the water below. She put the flowers down carefully and reached for the woven hamper she'd packed that morning at Fanny's Café, pulling out containers of fried chicken, coleslaw and potato salad. While she unfolded the blue tablecloth and prepared the deck for lunch, Filius picked up the knife and loaf of bread and began to slice it without being asked.

Lena didn't know what to make of this quiet man at her side. When he'd come into the café earlier that week to ask her about this boat ride, she said yes, even though she could tell Fanny was making faces behind her back. When he came in for lunch the next day and she asked if they could bring some of Burr's friends along, he'd agreed instantly. Later that afternoon, Fanny said that he was conniving and that favors would be expected in return, but Lena knew it was something else. Filius Poe had jumped to his feet when that little man had bothered her, she explained, and he'd kept his promise to Burr. Those were the important things—actions, not motives—but Fanny just pooched out her bottom lip and shook her head. "He has a reason, all right. They always have a reason."

Lena unrolled the silverware from the napkins she'd packed, and broke the silence. She wanted to tell Filius about her husband.

"At first I couldn't believe it and then I was mad, madder than I can ever remember being, and then I felt ashamed—all this as I stood there with this Christmas photograph in my hand. I knew it was true, even though it seemed so impossible. The Mullens family. The *other* Mullens family. How could he do that to me? And his son? His own son? We loved him, Burr and I; we loved him without question. That was all we needed to know. And in the short time I looked at that photograph in my hand, at the smiling faces of that man and that woman, I didn't recognize him anymore. I walked down to the pond where he was working, still carrying that picture, and saw him standing in the water with his rake, and right then and there he became a stranger I wouldn't look at twice, ever again."

The voices of the children carried on the river breeze, and Filius heard bits of their chatter, the odd word clear and distinct before fading away. He looked up to see them walking by the grove of cottonwoods, jostling one another. Lena sat on the deck, her back to him and her long legs stretched out as she organized places for lunch. She was barefoot, and the yellow dress she wore was pleated down the front.

"Where is he now?"

"He's in jail still, but they're sending him to the Oklahoma State Penitentiary in McAlester before the first of the year. We saw the prison once, on our way up to Tulsa. Burr was five then, and was sitting between us on the front seat when he asked his father what that big white building was. Frank told him it was a place where bad people go. And Burr was very serious and said, 'Like hell?' because of course he knew Frank's book of Bible stories by heart. Frank burst out laughing and nodded his head and said, 'Pretty much.'"

Lena turned in profile and Filius saw the sad lines that played out from her eyes and mouth.

"The divorce papers came three weeks ago. September fifteenth. There was a nice note from Mr. Miller, my attorney in Hugo, explaining what was happening with the case, and the details of Frank's predicament, but I didn't read it. I just signed the papers where he told me and sent them back."

"Does Burr know any of this?"

"He doesn't understand and there's no reason he should. Not yet. When he asks, I'll tell him." Lena turned to face him. She was smiling, but there was no joy in it. "I hope he waits awhile."

Filius wanted to touch her face or hand, to say something comforting and kind, but the children were running along the beach, already splashing in the shallow water in front of the boat, and he kept the words to himself.

As soon as Mr. Poe parked in front of the café, Burr jumped out so he could be the first inside to tell Fanny and Hi about the wild burros. He banged through the door but slowed down immediately, as Fanny and his mother had so often reminded him to, so he wouldn't disturb the customers. He ignored the people waiting to be served their early Sunday dinner, and started for the kitchen, where he knew Hi would be, but he saw Fanny first, leaning over a family at a table in the back. He recognized the boy at the table, Teddy Boyce, because they were in the same class, but school had started just a few weeks before and they weren't friends yet. Teddy was a skinny kid who wore wide baggy pants and long-sleeved shirts with embroidered emblems on the pockets, like small swords and knight's armor, and he talked funny because he came from Boston, and he talked a lot just to drive their teacher, Miss Morrison, to distraction.

Burr waited for Fanny to move away from the Boyce table before he caught up with her in front of the kitchen door. "Guess what I saw?"

She smiled and tousled his hair.

"Guess what *I* saw?" she said, pointing to the far end of the counter. Burr glanced over impatiently, because Fanny wanted him to, but when he saw the old man on the last stool, smiling at him over a bowl of steaming soup, it took him a full second to react.

"Charlie!"

He ran to the counter, and Charlie Chivers stood up to grab the boy and swing him high in his strong arms.

Filius stood outside the portal to diversion tunnel number 4 with Frank Crowe and Walker Young, the head construction engineer. The tunnel was finished, but trucks still roared over the temporary pile bridge just downstream, dumping loads of rock and muck that two big electric shovels pushed and shaped into a mounded coffer-dam on the dry landing below. He stepped back when a Caterpillar tractor rumbled by, the bucket loaded with canyon rock. The driver's face was filthy, and his blonde, wavy hair stuck out like Mercury's winged helmet. Two dozen crucifixes dangled from the metal canopy over his head, and on the extra gas tank chained to the side of the tractor was a drippy white sign that said, GOD DAM IT, NOT ME.

Frank led the men to the edge of the river and looked upstream. Walker Young squatted on the shoreline and ran his fingers through the shallows, scraped up some of the rocks and threw the biggest one into the center channel, where it plunked sideways as it was gulped by the brown water. The river still flowed fast, in great braids of water that rose and fell as if on the back of giant serpents, but had receded from both banks since the winter runoff from the northern mountains abated, as it did every fall, and was forced into a main current that could still suck a man into oblivion. He rose to his feet, wiped his hand on his pants and looked across the river. "Next month the rain and snows will hit the Rockies, and by February this will all turn into an ugly mess."

"Then we should do it now."

"Yes."

"The river's low enough."

Walker nodded.

Frank turned to Filius. The week before he'd put him in charge of the truck crew that would begin dumping rock and dirt on the Nevada side, where they would build a long, earthen dike to push the river toward the finished tunnels in Arizona. "How long will it take, Mr. Poe?"

"Four weeks. Maybe five."

Frank Crowe paced the shoreline. "Good. In November we turn the river." He stopped and dust rose around his legs like smoke from a stamped-out fire. He faced his engineers and smiled.

He was a year ahead of schedule.

When they drove into Boulder City that morning, Lew told Speed to go past Fanny's Café.

Speed sucked his teeth and shook his head. "Come on, Lew, you don't want any part of that."

"Just drive by."

"Jesus, Lew, that—"

"Do it."

Speed turned onto Wyoming Street and parked in front of the theater so Lew could get a good look, but he kept the car idling. The sun was still just a whisper on the horizon, and the bright light inside the café seemed vaguely green and artificial. Dam workers coming off shift or going on were elbow to elbow at the counter. Lew saw Fanny walk into the back, her plump arms loaded with plates. A Negro cook served breakfasts at the counter. But he didn't see the pretty one, Lena. He put his hand in his pocket and let his fingers find the ladies' watch he'd been carrying since going back to work. It was one of his favorites, a narrow gold Hamilton with a yellow face and roman numerals, and he wound it every day out of habit. Cece found it one morning when it slipped out of the pants he'd hung on the back of her door. She crawled off the bed and squatted naked on the floor, and when she leaned forward to pick it up, Lew admired her dark brown back and the fine arc of her spine. He'd almost given her the watch at that very moment, but when she stood and put it back in his pocket, he changed his mind.

"Hey, Lew."

He turned from the café window and saw the police car coming toward them. Archie Swerling looked right at him as he passed by, but kept going. Lew knew he'd turn around at the Nevada Highway and come right back. They always did. "Let's go," he said.

They ate quickly at the Anderson Brothers Mess Hall, a place the size of an airplane hangar, where men had to scream in order to be heard over the constant roar of voices and crossed silverware. The noise seemed to collect above the open rafters, only to be pushed back down by the constant swirl of the two dozen fans overhead. Lew stared at his plate and ignored the confusion around him, rushing through his eggs and ham and biscuits in silence, so he could escape outside. Speed gobbled away beside him, spraying crumbs as he laughed at jokes or shouted down the table, but he was ready to go when Lew stood up and shoved his chair away from the table. Before leaving they walked to the big table piled high with fruit, snacks and seven kinds of sandwiches, standing in line with other dam workers waiting to stuff their pockets and lunch boxes with all the food they could hold. Speed always carried a small tin which he'd fill with the pickled beets he craved. Sometimes the tin would leak—banged around on a double-decker bus careening down the bumpy road to the dam—but he didn't mind. While everybody cussed and moaned about the vinegary stink, Speed would pop the beets into his mouth one at a time, sucking them slowly, eyes closed in delight.

· · ·

Lew settled back on his narrow seat and reached into his pocket, unfolded the handkerchief and slipped a finger under the watch's delicate band, turning his hand until sunlight sparkled off the gold case. He couldn't hear the ticking over the noise around him, but counted along with the second hand as it moved gracefully across the dial.

"Hey, Beck. You taking a break?"

Andy Shaw, the new high scaler, banged down onto the opposite side of the long ledge. He was smiling, all nervous energy, his face dripping with sweat. He always put on a brave face, but it didn't fool anybody, and Eddie Felder told Lew the only reason Shaw worked on the cliffs was because his wife liked the extra money, and when he came home complaining, she slapped his face and told him to be a man about it.

Shaw tentatively stepped over the hoses that dangled over the ledge and yanked on his rope. He was overly cautious, slow as a crippled horse, and took half a day to do a job Lew could finish in an hour. He talked when he worked, his voice clipped and scared, and Lew knew he wouldn't last long. Either Wally would can him or he'd find the nerve to slap his wife back.

"Wally said you looked like you was sleeping down here. Said somebody oughta drop a bucket of cold water on you." Shaw laughed and checked his knots. "Wally's in a lousy mood. You notice that, Beck? Yelling at Eddie 'cause he can't find his wrench? Hell, they got bushels of wrenches up there. More fuckin' wrenches than Henry Ford. And he's yelling at Eddie at the top of his lungs? Jesus Christ."

Lew watched him finally reach for his crowbar, holding on to the rope with one hand while he pried loose rocks with the other.

"My kid's on the baseball team at school. Plays catcher. Ten years old. Wasn't paying attention, watchin' ants in the dirt or somethin'. Took a ball right in the face. Broke his damn nose. That won't happen again." He looked at Lew. "What you got there, Beck?"

Lew didn't realize he was still holding the watch. After carefully stowing it in his pocket, he reached for one of the jackhammers.

Andy Shaw poked daintily at the shelf of rock next to him.

"Yesterday I had a jackhammer with a loose bit. Shook so much it loosened a tooth in my mouth. I swear, Beck, I—"

Lew cut loose on the great bump of rock between his feet. His jackhammer was torqued high, and he guided it between the fractured layers. When the bit caught, he leaned into the handles and let the vibrations run through his arms and into his ears, where they itched and hummed, loud and efficient, a world away from the frightened, blustery whine of Andy Shaw.

Charlie drove them out to his new home in late October, the sun low over the jagged hilltops. Lena sat up front while Burr lounged in the pickup bed, cushioned between three bales of hay fitted together like a tufted throne. He leaned way back, mesmerized by the sweetness of the fresh-cut hay, and let the warm air rush around him. The ranch was eight miles north of Boulder City, marked by a faded sign posted on the road. When the double row of tall poplar trees flickered overhead, Burr rose to his knees and leaned on the roof of the cab to look around.

The Dickens Ranch was a forty-acre swath of brilliant green wedged between irrigation ditches. Fields of oat hay and alfalfa grew on either side of the road, breeze-swept and shimmering in the sunshine like landlocked ponds. Cattle stood motionless in the pinched and browned pastures closest to the Las Vegas Wash, and fat Hampshire pigs, their hulking white bodies mottled with pee-muck and grime, looked up from their wire pens and slop troughs as Charlie drove by.

He pulled up in front of a modest adobe ranch house at the end of the tree-lined driveway. It was a simple building, freshly whitewashed, with a pitched tin roof and a dark green door. All the windows were open and Burr could see straight through the house to the orchards at the rear of the property. Two barefoot Paiutes in white dresses sat on the porch steps, separating wormy apples from the dozen bushel baskets in front of them. A large woman came through the open front door and stepped between them. She wore an old gray dress and a man's suit vest. Her hair was washed out, not gray or white or brown or blonde, just short and choppy and parted on the side. She was stocky and waistless, and her shoulders were almost as wide as Archie Swerling's.

"Charlie, you brought us company."

"I sure did, Uncle Judy."

"Then I guess we'll have to feed them."

Uncle Judy Dickens had moved here twenty years ago with her brother, Evan. They'd come from the country outside Huntsville, Utah, which their grandfather had helped establish in the early 1860s. Brigham Young had sent Abbott Dickens and Hyrum Hunt and Charlie Wood and other Latter-day Saints to settle the fertile basin below the Wasatch Range, and these men brought their families and drove their cattle along the gutted road that Isaac Goodall had carved out of this wilderness the year before. They'd planted the barley and oats that took hold that first summer, and built the fences and cabins that turned into a town. It was Abbott Dickens who made peace with Little Soldier and his Shoshone tribe across the valley, trading food and goods to stop the Indians from shooting cattle dogs and stealing stock, and Huntsville became the heart of the Ogden Valley. Judy's grandfather introduced sheep to the community, and her father lost their entire flock, five hundred or more, in a single storm that had dropped quickly from the north. Thunder could be heard as far away as Ogden, and young Judy and Evan saw the forked lightning dig into the mountainside like crippled fingers. Before bedtime, they prayed with their parents in front of the fire, and in their unconsoling dreams they thought they heard a desperate bleating. The storm had weakened after midnight, but by the time Judy's father arrived at the open pasture the next morning, the sheep lay dead. They had huddled together, bewildered and dumb, as the storm raged, until lightning struck one and the electric charge shot through and killed them all.

Even now, thirty years later, as they ate their lunch in the adobe ranch house, Uncle Judy told the story with sadness and wonder. "Same storm I saw an eagle struck in flight. It landed in a heap of singed feathers on top of the hay shed. Drove the cats crazy."

Afterward, she vowed never to raise sheep, and kept half a dozen goats on the ranch to keep the horses company. "They're more companionable than sheep," she said.

Charlie winked at Burr. "She means they're not so dumb."

"Oh, they're dumb all right, they just don't look so bad being it."

Uncle Judy squatted in front of the hearth and flipped second helpings of griddle cakes and bacon in the cast-iron skillets suspended over the flames, then filled a platter and put it down in front of Burr. "Can you fit some more?"

"Yes, Uncle Judy." The first piece of bacon was so salty and good that his mouth filled with spit.

Judy Dickens was only forty, but looked closer to Charlie's age than Lena's. Two years after she and her brother, Evan, bought the ranch, a cowboy refused to pay the dollar they charged for a night's stay and shot Evan to death. When Judy heard the shot and ran outside with their old Brushmaster shotgun, Evan was flat on his back with a bullet hole in his forehead, and the stranger, who Judy never even met, was long gone. Judy Dickens was twenty-two years old, and she built the ranch up with the help of a Mormon family that came down from Huntsville after Evan was killed, and a couple of Paiutes who used to grow cabbage and pinto beans just west of here. Now she had a successful cattle operation, and grew figs for markets in the western states.

"We used to have leghorns, and they were good layers until we got a new shipment of birds from a breeder in Tucson. One of those Arizona birds was sick, and in a week they were all sneezing and wheezing like old men, and we lost half of them to bronchitis. Sold the rest for meat. But now we got Charlie—and we got chickens again."

Charlie leaned back in his chair, his pink cheeks bulging with griddle cake, and grinned.

The evening after Charlie had shown up at the café, Lena cooked him dinner at the house in Boulder. Fanny had a date with Archie that night, so she fried the steaks while the old man sat at the table with Burr and told him stories about climbing Humphreys Peak with Sarah, and how Chester and Ev chased a couple of pronghorns until they were just dots on the horizon. Later, after Burr fell asleep on the couch, Lena and Charlie sat outside on the front stairs. Lena brought them coffee, and they watched dam workers appear out of the shadowy dusk as they walked home from the transports that dropped them off on top of the hill.

"I don't blame Bill so much. He moved away when he could and has his own life now. Has a wife who has a say in what they do, and she should. I thought maybe I'd be welcome and could help out some, but they saw it different and I accept that. They didn't say it to my face, and they didn't have to. Yelled at each other instead or didn't talk at all, and poor Sarah slinking through the house like a shy kitten, not knowing what was going on but feeling bad about it anyway."

Mina Drummond came out of the house across the street and poured a bucket of water on the castor beans that grew up the side of her porch, then saw Lena and waved.

"When Bill was growing up, we didn't get along all that well. You sometimes forget that when you're apart, and I hadn't seen him in a couple of years, but the minute he pulled up in his truck it all came back, and I'm sure it came back to him, too. When he was a boy I was always pushing him, and when he resisted I pushed some more. Couldn't say anything to one another without it sounding mean. Peggy was the patient one. Tried to teach it to me, but it didn't take. Too late anyway."

"I'm sorry it didn't work out, Charlie."

"It just worked out different. Bill had an old Ford pickup truck in the barn that didn't run and I fixed it up, patched the radiator and such, paid for new tires Bill got cheap from a friend in Winslow. When I got the truck running, I got to spending time at Mickey's in Flagstaff, playing rummy to pass the day. Sarah missed me and I missed her, but Betty was holding her close anyway and I always got back to the ranch before she went to bed so we could walk along the telephone lines with the dogs. A man come into Mickey's one day and I heard him say he lived in Las Vegas and was on his way to Albuquerque to visit his sister. Don't know why, but I asked him if he knew any ranches out that way that needed help, and he said they might be hiring at the Kyle place and the Dickens Ranch. So right there I decided to drive back to Bill's and pack my bag and leave behind a hundred dollars for the truck. Bill was working but Betty didn't try to stop me. He wouldn't have, either. I gave Sarah a big kiss and headed straight for the Dickens Ranch first, no particular reason why, and Uncle Judy laid on a job and place to stay without thinking twice about it. And goddamn, I'm in the chicken business again."

Lena could smell the ranch on his clothes and skin, that sweet-and-sour odor of cow manure and dust, and it reminded her of the Saturday afternoons she spent with her father when she was little, visiting cattle dealers on their spreads along the Red River, driving with the windows open to the pungent air. She smiled now, remembering that no matter how hard her mother scrubbed her arms or how often she dunked her head in the tub, it would be the smell of cattle and muddy pastures that she would carry with her into sleep.

She covered Charlie's hand with her own, and they sat like that, hushed and close, as the evening cooled around them.

Filius stood at the rounded edge of the dike and let his heels sink into the wet, untamped earth. He watched the river flow before him, and knew that for the first time in its history, the Colorado would be turned, and that the cofferdam he stood on, once finished, could contain any threat of flood or natural mayhem that would impede the building of this dam.

The dike stretched halfway across the river, curving like a hook and forcing the water toward the Arizona side of the canyon. Tractors lumbered along the narrow roadway, dragging prong-studded rollers that compacted the mounds of dirt and rock left there by the endless caravan of dump trucks that shuttled down the hill. Filius walked to the upstream edge of the dike and looked down at the huge muddy hole below him, where electric shovels were already digging deep, scooping out buckets of muck and trying to find bedrock.

The week before, he'd stood here with Walker Young and studied the calm water collecting behind the dike, finally deciding to hook up a generator and pump out the backwater. They'd been dredging the river bottom for days, removing centuries of deposits, and Filius knew they would probably have to go down at least twenty feet more. The pace grew frantic as his crew stayed on schedule, working in an effluvial haze of dirt and exhaust whipped into the air by the procession of Caterpillar tractors and bulldozers and dump trucks that threaded past one another at pitched speeds.

Floyd Huntington watched the work and wagered Filius a bottle of whiskey that the river would start rising through the tunnels by the end of November. Filius didn't doubt it, and he didn't take the bet.

Filius and Burr lined up six pumpkins on the rail of Fanny's porch. Charlie had dropped them off the day before, picked fresh from a small patch Uncle Judy planted every year. Burr took his time as he moved down the row, sizing up each one for its curves and heft, for the brightness of its orange skin and the dramatic flair of its cut stem. He assessed every blemish and squashy pock with great seriousness, and rocked each pumpkin on its side to inspect for cracks.

Filius lit a cigarette and watched, remembering when he and Addie and Ray had visited his parents in Madison a week before Halloween. It had been a cold fall, especially north of Chicago, and there was already a crinkle of ice on the lake behind the house. Just south of McFarland, the fields were covered with hoarfrost, and when they turned down a farm road, all around them were pumpkins, thousands of them, their orange heads and tangled vines looking sugarcoated. Ray had jumped out and run into the field before his parents even had their doors open. On a table outside the barn, a scrawled sign—PUMPKINS PENNY A POUND, SUGAR BABIES NICKEL EACH—was propped up against a small, rusty scale, and an upended Massey Ferguson hubcap was filled with small change. Addie picked out a few pie pumpkins from the nearby crate while Filius watched his son romp through the patch with the farmer's springer spaniel, and they ended up standing there for almost an hour, their noses raw and dripping and their feet numb in their shoes while Ray painstakingly surveyed the pumpkins. He finally found the biggest one, a bulbous monster that came up to his waist, and because it was too heavy to carry, he rolled it to the barn himself, allowing Filius to help only when it came time to load it into the car.

Now Burr turned to him with a smile, pointing to a large, oblong pumpkin. "That one."

Filius gripped his cigarette tightly in his lips and felt like crying. "This one's mine," he said, indicating a squat thing next to the one Burr had chosen.

They carried their pumpkins to a table covered with pages of yesterday's *Review-Journal*. Filius cut off the tops and let Burr scrape out the stringy orange guts and seeds with a metal spatula from Fanny's kitchen. They rinsed the seeds in a bucket and laid them on clean dish towels to dry, and saved the slimy pulp for Charlie's chickens. Then, side by side on the stairs, they started carving. Burr used his abalone-handled penknife, and Filius the pocketknife his father had given him for his tenth birthday.

Lena stood in the open window watching them. She balanced a yellow bowl against her hip and stirred together stewed apples, bread crumbs and the diced salt pork she'd just taken off the stove. It still surprised her, this relationship between her son and the man who sat beside him—even after three months of surprises, starting with that photograph. There was a kindness in Filius Poe, a startling generosity. Every question asked or comment made was greeted with considerate attention, whether a child's request or an adult's caustic aside. In this, at least, Fanny concurred, even though she said it was only because he "treated everyone like they came from the same family of idiots." But Lena thought it was a respect for opinions and ideas, an honest reaction to the thoughts of others. Fanny shivered and shook her head. "I don't know what you're talking about, but the way those big eyes lock on you when you talk to him just gives me the creeps." Lena admitted it had taken some getting used to, this mindfulness, but she also realized it was why Burr and other children were attracted to him. Because he was mindful. He listened, and the answers he gave were not born of impatience or scorn.

Smiling at their bent backs, Lena called, "Dinner will be ready in half an hour."

They both nodded, knives moving in and out of their jack-o'-lanterns' hollow eyes and gap-toothed grins.

At six o'clock they were sitting at the kitchen table over the stuffed pork shoulder and creamed spinach that Lena had prepared. Burr ate quickly, especially the apple stuffing, then went into the bathroom to get ready for the Halloween party in the park, changing into the white pants, white shirt and white sneakers stacked on the hamper. From a bag below the sink he pulled out a stethoscope, a veterinary relic that Uncle Judy kept in her cow barn for emergencies. Burr put it around his neck and examined himself in the mirror. The stethoscope hung down below his belt, but he didn't care. The Colleen twins were wearing nurses' costumes, and he'd recently developed a crush on Lilly.

Stanley Chubb came to the front door dressed as a cowboy, most of his face hidden behind a droopy moustache made of horsehair and attached with spirit glue. His mother waited on the sidewalk and waved to Lena before she walked the boys up to the park.

It was a cool evening and the last bits of sunlight puddled in the cups of fallen leaves below the sycamores planted along the street. Filius sat on the porch and lit a cigarette as the children paraded by, ghosts and clowns, fairies and princesses. Though it pained him to watch, he did it, and he was grateful when Lena came outside carrying a small metal tray crowded with two glasses, a bowl of ice and a bottle of whiskey. "I know Sims Ely tries to keep this a dry town," she said, "but whiskey seems as easy to get as a tin of sardines."

She poured them each a drink and then stretched her legs in front of her, her calves and forearms tight and sore from working five long days in a row. She shut her eyes for a moment, listening to the hum of the telephone wires overhead, and when she opened them Filius was watching her.

"I want to tell you about my wife and son."

"It was growing dark when the rescue boat found us. We'd been in the water for more than six hours, and Addie had taken the worst of it. She couldn't stop shaking when they finally lifted her on board, her teeth chattering and her fingers cramped and shriveled, her entire body hard as rock. When we got to the hospital in Whitefish Bay, the doctors put a cast on my ankle and treated Addie for exposure. They did everything they should have, everything they could. But Addie didn't help them. She didn't try to fight the fever, or the shivering that was painful to watch and kept making the blankets slip from her shoulders. She lay in her hospital bed for a week with her eyes open, staring at the ceiling or the walls, whichever way the nurse happened to turn her. After the first day, she wouldn't speak. To me or the doctors. Her parents came up from Chicago, and mine from Madison, but it didn't make any difference. She wouldn't talk to anyone. It was shock, of course, and sorrow. I knew that. Ray was gone. We had lost our son."

He lit a cigarette and Lena was thankful for the silence. There was brittleness to his voice, a matter-of-factness that was almost unbearable. He inhaled deeply and shook his match until it went out, the sulfurous wisps hanging in the air between them. She still held her scotch, the ice already melted and the moisture trickling down the outside of the glass between her fingers. She flicked her hand, and when she looked up, Filius was watching her intently.

"We loved that lake. Both of us. Even when we were still in school, before we were married, we'd drive to Milwaukee on weekends and follow the roads north, hugging the coastline and camping at night, all the way to Gill's Rock and then around the point to Egg Harbor. After we were married, whenever we had enough time, we'd travel along the Michigan shore up to the inlets of Grand Traverse Bay, to Cat's Head Point and the Old Mission Lighthouse. We rented a cabin on Clam Lake, where we could catch walleyes and crappies from a canoe, or cast into the Grass River for trout. And then we'd drive up to the Straits of Mackinac, and all around us was deep-blue water—Lake Michigan on one side, Lake Huron on the other. It was like being on the ocean. Water was the first thing Addie and I knew we had in common, and we wanted Ray to share that.

"We took him out on Lake Michigan when he was just two, and both his grandfathers joined us that day on a twenty-four-foot sailboat we chartered out of the Chicago Harbor. It was a balmy afternoon, an easy day for sailing, and Ray was in heaven, the center of attention, handled constantly, a prince on a throne of canvas sail sacks, doted on by his grandfathers and held up to catch the northerly breeze and see the Drake Tower and the Palmolive Building and the skyline that shaded Oak Street Beach. When we were tacking just north of the Navy Pier, heading back in, Ray fell asleep in Addie's arms. He woke while we were tying up at the harbor dock, and when he realized it was over, he began to cry."

Lena could hear the distant voices of the children playing in the park. On occasion, laughter carried sharply through the dusk.

"I sat with Addie every night in her room on the second floor of that hospital. It was a corner room and I kept the windows open because I knew she liked fresh air, the colder the better, and it helped to clear out the medicinal smells, the whiff of alcohol and disinfectants that carried everywhere. And through those windows, just past the trees, you could see Lake Michigan. If the wind was right, you could smell the water. But Addie slept most of the time. She was too weak to do much else. Long after dark, when the hospital was quiet, she would cry, every night for a week. She was always startled when I woke her, swatting at me with her hands, blinking uncontrollably, and if I asked her what was wrong she'd fall quiet and ignore me, laying her head back on the pillow, her eyes half closed, like she was blind, her eyelids fluttering so you could just see the whites. It wasn't sleeping really, just a wretched state of turmoil, and she'd call for Ray. If she started to cry again I wouldn't try to stop her. I'd just lay my hand next to hers, and sometimes she took it and sometimes she didn't, but when she did I told her I loved her and I knew she loved me, and when I said those things she squeezed as hard as she could, and I squeezed back to let her know that I was there."

It was dark as Filius sipped his whiskey and stood up. Music still came quietly from the playground, and Lena thought she could hear the bumps and scratches on the phonograph record before Bing Crosby began singing. Filius walked over to the jack-o'-lanterns on the porch railing, lit the candles inside, and gazed down at the sputtering glow.

"During the second week, the base of Addie's fingernails started to turn blue. When her lips turned blue, I knew she was dying. Her parents wanted to take her back to Chicago, to the doctors there, but I refused. Her mother begged me, my mother too, the both of them crying. They knew it was too late. We all did. I waited with Addie in her room, all the windows open to the smell of the lake. She didn't tell me what she wanted, but I knew."

Filius looked at Lena, his face amber there on the porch.

"She knew where Ray was. And she was going to stay with him."

.   .   .

After the party, Burr left Stanley at the corner and walked home alone. From across the street, he stared at the pair of orange gargoyles on either end of Fanny's porch rail. Behind the pumpkins he could see his mother and Mr. Poe sitting together in the darkness. Their faces were barely visible, but he could tell from their postures that something had happened between them. Though they seemed to be looking in his direction, he knew they didn't see him. One of the candles flared in the breeze, and Burr thought he saw his mother holding Mr. Poe's hand. He decided he didn't want to interrupt them; that he liked seeing them this way.

Burr sat down on the curb, reached into his shirt and fitted the stethoscope into his ears. Then, holding the silver disc to his mouth, he began to count to a hundred.

At four o'clock in the morning, Filius sat up and let the chilly sweat dry and tighten across his skin. Through his bedroom window he could see a golden haze of construction dust on the horizon. He sat there in the darkness and smoked a cigarette. He despised sleep for its false promises of peace and consolation. He despised sleep and the tragedies that it conjured and exposed. Though he knew Addie didn't blame him for what happened that day, he blamed himself. That was the sadness he carried deep inside. And while he was glad he could tell Lena everything else, this was the one thing he could never say.

On the first Friday morning in November, Lew Beck woke up in a good mood. He lay on his back a few extra minutes to savor the moment, unable to remember the last time he'd awakened without the miserable apprehension of the coming day. For a month he'd gone to bed each night with an unaccountable despair he chose not to examine and could not escape, this ballast that pressed against his skull and felt like hot stones in his belly.

Cece's back was to him, the bony point of her exposed shoulder black against the white sheet. The short braids at the back of her head poked out like pieces of stiff rope burnt at the ends. Cece slept naked—they both did—and he carefully ran his hand under the sheet and placed it on the wide blade of her hip. Her breathing was steady and quiet and unchanging, a rhythmic fakery she'd learned from Miss Williams to fool the strange men she slept with. Lew wasn't fooled. He moved his fingers slowly and waited for her twitch, and when it came he smiled. He knew how to tickle her. He knew she liked it. When Lew drew his fingers backward, below her belly button, the sensation was too much and Cece burst out laughing and flipped over and curled around Lew's hand and buried her face against his chest. They held each other and breathed together as a cool breeze pushed through the window.

Lew walked over to Carson Street that morning, dressed in a dark blue shirt Cece had ironed while he sat alone at the big table in the kitchen and watched Miss Williams fry his eggs and burn his toast. The day was moist and chilly, and when he left the house he wore the short leather jacket he'd bought in Los Angeles a year ago. He had on a new pair of cowboy boots, black, with a walking heel, and the front pocket of his pants was heavy with cash.

Las Vegas was already awake when Lew turned onto Fremont Street. Cars were parked along every inch of curb space, and sidewalk traffic was brisk. There were no empty storefronts along Fremont, and the Chamber of Commerce was as busy as a church on Easter Sunday. Every other window had a *Grand Opening!* sign taped to the glass. There were jewelry stores and appliance stores, stores that sold records and record players, stores that sold women's fine apparel and stores that sold only men's hats. The cafés were full and the steaks were thick and every salesgirl at Ronzone's was too beautiful to behold. In this desert boomtown, money was freely changing hands and everybody wanted it. The local nabobs stood in the upstairs windows of City Hall and saw a place where young trees grew from cracks in the sidewalk, where the men looked like bankers and their women looked worldly, where high school kids drove to school in new cars. But when the stores closed and respectability faded into dusk, the saloons and casinos that stretched from downtown to the Boulder Highway stayed open all night and catered to the dam workers and locals who came in droves to the dance halls and rickety shacks for drinks and bets. Prohibition was still in effect and old-timers used the back doors out of habit, rapping out passwords and double-checking alleyways. The liquor that was poured inside was cheap and plentiful, and public displays of drunkenness were common. Police and federal agents rode the wide streets with deliberately blind eyes, stopping only to break up knife fights or investigate the increasingly popular predawn slayings. These were the consequences of prosperity, but it didn't matter. There was a Depression everywhere else, and the citizens of Las Vegas were happy to deal with the downside of their own good fortune.

At the corner of Fifth Street, red signboards leaning against the streetlamp advertised STAN'S USED CARS and GOOD DEALS and Lew followed their white arrows south to Carson Street. Twenty cars sat on a dirt lot under a string of multicolored banners. Homemade signs were posted everywhere—AUTO LOANS, PAID FOR OR NOT, CARS WANTED FOR CASH!—and every car had a price soaped in the windshield.

A skinny Mexican boy was moving down the front row of cars with towels and a bucket, washing the dust off hubcaps until they squeaked. He crouched in front of a big Buick and was scraping a butterfly out of the grill with his fingernail when Lew tapped him on the shoulder. When the boy looked up, the few strands of his wispy mustache failed to conceal the harelip that ran up to his nostril.

"Where's the boss?"

The boy nodded toward a small stucco building in the middle of the lot. Through two tall windows that faced the street, Lew could see Stan Weiser—his pants belted high over a perfectly round belly—pacing around his desk as he talked on the telephone. He was making chopping motions with his right hand, and Lew could hear the dull tones of his loud voice through the plaster and glass forty yards away. Suddenly, the Mexican boy whistled sharply, and Stan looked up—his mouth making a little O as he peered out the window into the lot. Spotting Lew, he waved and smiled broadly and hung up the phone without saying good-bye.

Lew walked past STAN'S DEAL OF THE DAY, a two-year-old Ford Roadster Special on sale for seventy dollars, and the old Studebaker Commander that his father might covet, and a 1930 Ford Model A coach with broken headlight and a 1926 Dodge Brothers Highboy that seemed to bow out over thin tires and was marked down to forty-five dollars. But he stopped in front of the 1928 Lincoln Convertible Phaeton parked, still dusty, at the end of the front row. It was a big four-door, with a wide running board and a new roof. No price was soaped on its glass.

Lew made one pass around the Lincoln before Stan came striding across the lot chuckling as he walked, and stuck out his hand when he was still ten feet away. "You look like a man who's shopping for a Roadster."

"I'm not."

Stan's chuckling grew louder, and he seized Lew's hand and gave it a great shake. The man's brown suit was so shiny that in the morning light it almost looked red. "You dam fellas don't fool around. You work out at the dam, right?"

Lew pulled his hand free.

"On or off the job, get it done. Forget the monkey business. Right to the point. No whipped cream on this pie. I like that. I like that a lot. Saves me time."

"How much for the Lincoln?"

"That's an awful lot of car, mister."

Lew noted the insinuation, the tone in the fat man's voice, but he let it slide. "How much?"

"I just got it in last night. Good shape. Like new. Driven in from Fresno, no wear and tear. Was gonna make it my special next week."

Lew waited. Stan looked at the car, his head tilted until his left cheek bubbled over his collar. "It's a real honey. I was going to ask ninety."

"I'll give you eighty."

Stan chuckled into his pudgy fist. The phone was ringing in the little stucco building, and they both stared at it until the ringing stopped.

"I don't know what kind of business you think I'm in, but I ain't selling Turkish rugs. Deals are wrote in stone before I ever post them. Best prices in Nevada, too, just check for yourself. I stand by every car, and not many can say that. I say it every day."

Lew pulled out his roll of bills. "Seventy-five."

Stan crossed his arms and watched the little man peel off a wave of tens. He didn't like him much—arrogance up to his ears—but this was business. It was the end of a slow week, not even nine o'clock in the morning, and the wife expected him to take her to the Meadows this weekend. Or the Mexico Club.

Lew held out the eight bills.

Stan Weiser took them. "Sold."

That same day, Lena got another letter from R. T. Miller in Hugo. In late October, Frank had been sentenced to twenty years in prison for bigamy, to run concurrent with the same charges handed down in Louisiana. Mr. Miller also mentioned that Frank's lawyer requested Lena's address and permission to allow Frank to write to his son, "the boy he loves and cherishes in his heart." Her first response was a quick, angry letter, the bitter words flowing so easily that the pen she'd grabbed spat out eight sheets of paper that collected at her feet like shredded confetti. The request rattled her—its boldness, its weak-kneed contrition—and kept her up at night and distracted all day. Although she dreaded to think of the questions Burr would ask about his father, she knew they would come, and Frank should be given the chance to defend himself or apologize or, in fact, grovel, and then beg his son for forgiveness. On Thursday night she wrote to Mr. Miller that he could forward Frank Mullens her Boulder City address on Burr's birthday in December, but that she reserved the right to read his letter first and decide when to deliver it. Those were the terms, nonnegotiable. If Frank agreed, that would also be his last communication with them, unless Burr wished to respond.

. . .

Lena was bent over her shopping list, planning a trip to the Company Store to buy winter clothes for Burr. Two women sat by the window drinking coffee and eating peach pie, and three dam workers across the room were eating chicken salad sandwiches and Hi's vinegary coleslaw. It was a slow day, for which Lena was grateful. Fanny had driven into Las Vegas with Archie Swerling, and Hi was alone in the kitchen cutting up fatty pork shoulders.

Another dam worker, his right arm immobilized by a dirty plaster cast, sat at the other end of the counter, chasing a greasy sausage through his plate of spaghetti. Lena looked down at him—not noticing Lew Beck climb out of his big car and stand watching her through the window—and said, "You want me to cut that up for you, John?"

"Naw, I got it." He held up the sausage, pierced on his knife tip, and ate it end to end.

Lena got up and walked over to the men's table. She started clearing their plates, and waited as Howard Gimble poked and prodded through a jumble of coins, his thick calluses scribed with dirt that dated back to the first days of construction. Finally, he sighed through his nose and pushed the money into a neat pile by his plate.

Lena smiled. "You need any change, Howard?"

"Nope. You keep it, Lena."

"Thanks."

"See you Monday."

"See you Monday, Howard."

As the men filed out, she stacked the three empty plates and glasses and sat them on the kitchen ledge, then reached for the damp cloth she kept there. Until she turned around to wipe the table off, she didn't know anyone else had even entered the café.

Lew Beck: sitting there in front of her at the counter. Lena recognized him immediately. Weeks had passed since the incident in the café, and the murmurs and high talk had long since subsided, but the impression he'd made that day was as fresh as a bruise. He was even shorter than Lena remembered, and his arm had healed, but the threat lurking behind his smile was unforgettable.

"Coffee," he said.

Lena bunched up the damp cloth in her hand and turned to get the coffeepot; she tried to get Hi's attention, but his back was to her as he braised stew meat on the stove. When she faced Lew Beck again, a gold ladies' watch was stretched across the cup in front of him. She pulled back, splattering muddy drops of coffee on the counter.

Lew continued to smile. "It's for you."

Lena didn't know what to say. She didn't want to say anything.

"Take it."

"I can't."

"Sure you can."

"I have a watch, thank you."

Lew reached out and ran a finger along her naked wrist. His touch startled her, and Lena almost dropped the coffeepot as she jerked away from him.

"Where is it?"

"What?"

"Your watch."

"Home. Broken."

"Take this one. It works."

"No. Thank you."

Lew shrugged and left the watch draped over his cup. "I've got an early shift tomorrow. Why don't I pick you up when I'm done and we go for a ride."

"I don't think so."

"We can have a late supper, drive down to Las Vegas. I know lots of places."

"No."

"Your choice."

"I have to get back to work now."

"I haven't had my coffee yet."

Lena saw the smile freeze on Lew Beck's face and felt a shadow pass behind her, a sudden breeze on the back of her neck as Archie came through the kitchen door and walked around the counter.

He took off his hat and settled comfortably on the stool next to Lew. "I'll have some of that coffee too, Lena."

Lena forgot she was still holding the pot. She poured Archie a cup, and when she stepped back again Fanny was standing at her side.

"Everything okay?"

"Fine."

"Busy while we were gone?"

"Not too bad."

"Good. Why don't you come out back and see how we're fixed for lunch."

Lew watched Fanny put an arm around Lena and draw her into the kitchen. The sergeant sitting next to him sipped his coffee, and Lew tried very hard to ignore him.

"Beck, right?"

"Right."

"You don't live in Boulder City, do you, Beck?"

"No."

"You just drive in to work."

"Yes."

"You working today?"

"Yes."

"When?"

"Soon."

"I think soon's right now." The cop stood and waited by Lew's stool.

Lew could hear him breathing, and the chafing of his cuffs as they caught on the top of his boot. He caught the gleam of his belt buckle, the nub of his pinkie and the lazy droop of his holster. He could smell leather and steel and he clenched his tongue between his teeth. The sergeant towered over Lew, like they all did—starting with his father and Danny McHugh, all of them laughing, forcing him to prove himself, and he would, gladly, grabbing them by the testicles or punching them in the kidneys until they gagged and collapsed and learned that every injury they dealt Lew Beck would be compounded and avenged.

But not here. Not now. He got up and walked to the door, looking straight ahead, seeing nothing but the blur of soft, cool light that filled the café windows.

"Hey, Beck."

He turned and saw a flash of gold and caught the watch right in front of his face, the solid clasp snapping at the corner of his eye. He took a long breath and slipped the Hamilton into his pocket.

The cop smiled. "Don't come back."

Lew walked outside, crossed the empty street and climbed behind the wheel of his Lincoln Phaeton, leaning his head back as far as he could go. The top was down, and he wanted to feel the November sun, but he was aware only of the tender skin touched by the watch clasp.

Sitting up, he started the engine and turned around in the street. Swerling was standing outside the café now, his hat pushed back on his head, his face the fleshy pink of a baby. Still watching, still smiling.

Lew would make the sergeant wait. Sometimes it was better that way.

The boys were playing softball in the dirt field behind the school. Although city officials put down new grass seed every month, it was always trampled or pecked or blown away, and the boys were glad. The field was fast, and their pounding feet would fill the air with fine dirt that they carried back inside after recess and deposited like gold dust under their desks. They liked how a hard-hit ball would spurt across the withered weeds that never died, kicking up explosions of dirt with every bounce.

Burr was playing in the outfield, and the grounders that came his way reminded him of matinee cartoons, of rabbits pinging across the desert and cannonballs gone amok. He glanced at the clock on the school. It was almost eleven, and Miss Gustin would be calling them in before long. His team was winning, three to one in the fifth inning, and Andy Corbett was up to bat. Andy never hit a ball out of the infield, so Burr relaxed and backed up to rub his shoulder against the fence, and saw the Lincoln convertible rolling down Colorado Street. The top was down, and at first it didn't look like anybody was driving, but as it got closer he saw the little man behind the wheel. Burr threw up his hand and waved as the car passed the schoolyard. Lew Beck looked right at him but didn't wave back.

.   .   .

It didn't matter to Lew Beck that Hoover showed up that morning. When the lame duck president arrived for his ceremonial tour of the dam, Lew stopped working only because everyone else did. He set aside his drill, settled back on his narrow seat and viewed the commotion from his perch high on the pocked terrace of the Arizona side of the canyon. The men he worked with, Mike Conklin and Andy Shaw among them, leaned forward and cupped their hands to their mouths, shouting, "Fuck you, you bum!" and, "Catch my wrench, you sonofabitch!" The high scalers laughed as they ranted, trying to outdo one another, embellishing their favorite Hooverisms with bestial detail. They knew their words would never be heard over the rumbling noise of construction, but screamed their guts out anyway because it felt good and necessary and within their rights, because they needed to do something more than merely vote him out of office.

Lew didn't pay much attention to Hoover or the New Deal. He'd never once voted, and arguments over fiscal policies and German elections bored him silly. He was grateful when Hoover and his entourage finally left and Wally whistled down from the rim. The high scalers picked up their jackhammers and went back to drilling the anchorage platforms for the powerhouse that would be built above them. The men around Lew were quiet now, letting their ears fill with the whirr of their machinery. Watching them, he despised their almost simian passivity as they hung from their ropes, exhausted from their catcalling, embarrassed by their inarticulate scorn, clueless to their own sudden melancholy.

Filius and Burr were part of the crowd listening to Hoover's speech outside the administration building, and he had enjoyed having the weight of the boy on his shoulders, partly because he had an almost physical recollection of being the boy himself.

This was in Milwaukee, in the fall of 1912, and Teddy Roosevelt had just come out of retirement to run against Taft and Wilson. As the Progressive candidate moved through the auditorium, shaking hands and smiling with the robust confidence of a man used to winning, a stranger with a pistol burst forward and shot him at point-blank range. The impact staggered Roosevelt, but the thick pages of his manuscript and the metal eyeglass case in his pocket slowed the bullet. Though doctors urged him to go immediately to the hospital, he insisted on giving his speech, and he stepped up to the podium with the bullet still lodged in his chest. "Friends," he said, "I shall ask you to be as quiet as possible. I don't know if you fully understand that I have just been shot; but it takes more than that to kill a Bull Moose."

As the crowd roared, his father lifted Filius to his shoulder so he could see his boyhood hero. The Rough Rider was stouter and smaller than Filius imagined, but he cheered along with the rest, and remembered that speech as vividly as he did the blood that stained and darkened the front of Roosevelt's tweed jacket.

Sixteen years later, Ray had been the boy hoisted into the air, having ridden with his father on the streetcar from Lincoln Park to the Navy Pier. It was a humid afternoon—the men sweating through their shirts, the women fanning themselves with tiny American flags—but a large crowd had gathered on the promenade, and a small brass band by the stage played the "Washington Post March" over and over again. When Hoover had arrived, waving to the thousands who greeted him with thunderous applause, Filius had lifted his son to his shoulders and felt the thrill run through his body.

Now, years later, he stood through another of Hoover's speeches, and he gave Burr's leg a squeeze, grateful for a second chance.

Lena joined Fanny in the window and watched the crowd that gathered at the curb outside the café—mostly women at this time of day, proud women who wore their best dresses for the occasion and stood with their arms crossed or carried babies or tightly held the hands of spinning children. Although they knew their lives were better now, and were truly thankful to have homes and comforts in Boulder City, they were still angry about the things they'd lost during the long years of misery when money was scarce and they fought with their husbands and slapped their children and walked the streets in shabby coats and worn-out shoes and total shame. They stood shoulder to shoulder now, looking east and waiting for the motorcade to go by, waiting patiently for a glimpse of the man who'd wrecked their dreams.

The café was empty except for Hi, who sat at the counter with his elbows in the air, eating a cheese sandwich, and writing a letter to his girls.

Lena handed Fanny a glass of Coca-Cola and stared out the window, up the street. "Did you vote for him, Fanny?"

"Yeah, once. A long time ago."

"Me too."

The big Packard suddenly appeared at the far end of Arizona Street, led by a police escort, and the motorcade showed no sign of slowing down to acknowledge the local turnout. As the Packard passed by, Lena saw blurred shadows in the backseat, thick shapes leaning forward with arms raised and hands fluttering.

The women on the sidewalk turned quietly to watch the big car turn west onto the Nevada Highway. Ethel Chubb stepped into the street to spit in the Packard's dusty tracks as the crowd quietly broke up, some heading home, others turning toward the café.

Fanny finished her soda, handing the empty glass to Lena so she could tighten the apron strings behind her back.

"Come on, Sweetie. They'll be hungry now."

Filius watched the four explosions blow simultaneously, and once the rounded heads of dirt and stone that rose high above the river's edge had collapsed back into it, he walked to the bank and looked over the remains of the demolished cofferdam in front of the Arizona tunnel. Water suddenly rose around the broken peaks of concrete that had once held it back, and Floyd Huntington leapt onto the treads of the steam shovel next to him, whistling sharply through his fingers. Eddie Gwynn waited at the base of the Boulder Road, shielding his eyes, and at Floyd's signal he turned and looked up the line of dump trucks that stretched up the steep hill behind him, each of the hundred trucks piled high with muck and rock. Eddie waved his orange flag and jumped back as the first truck lurched forward onto the trestle bridge downstream from the diversion tunnel. The driver spun his steering wheel, backed to the edge of the bridge, and dumped his load into the Colorado. He rocked the truck, hard, to clean the bed, and sped off the bridge to make way for the next truck in line. The initial traffic flow was ugly, an unruly procession that churned up a dust storm tinged blue with exhaust.

Filius had been on-site for thirty-six hours. He'd spent most of the morning with Frank, supervising the placement of explosives on the cofferdam, then had gone up on the rim with Walker Young to inspect the dozen electric shovels that would load rubble from the Hemenway Wash into the bumper-to-bumper dump trucks stretched two miles down the Boulder City road. They had ten mechanics on hand to deal with engine problems and broken belts and blown gaskets, and more than enough relief drivers on twenty-four-hour call.

This was one of the more elaborate engineering feats that Frank Crowe had choreographed in the initial phase of construction, and an hour before the blast he joined Filius and Walker on the rim, gazing from the river to the trucks strung out behind him. "Soon, gentlemen, this river will be ours."

Lew and Speed Owens sat on an abandoned Morland chassis, watching the dump trucks moving on and off the bridge while they ate their lunch. Speed's legs scissored back and forth, his fingertips dyed red from the pickled beets he stuffed into his mouth between bites of a cold bacon sandwich.

"It ain't like she's a good cook, 'cause she ain't. Talkin' all the time while I'm tryin' to drink a beer, stretched out on her couch 'cause my feet hurt, one cushion under my head and another under my ass so I'm almost floatin' there, feelin' good for the first time in ten hours. And Nancy's in the other room needin' me to open a can or get her a cigarette or give her a sip of my beer, and I ain't budgin'. I close my eyes and her voice is like air comin' out of a pinched balloon, but I fall asleep anyway till she comes out screamin' in my face like I murdered her mother or something."

Lew ate one of the hard-boiled eggs he'd brought for lunch, not bothering to comment on this lullaby gone stale. He was watching one of the water boys walk along the dusty fringe of activity, his brown overalls frayed above the ankles. There was a wooden yoke across his shoulders, with canvas water bags dangling from each end. From the green bandanna he wore cowboy-style around his neck, Lew recognized him: Gunther Crewe, the son of the signal-man on the skip Lew rode across the canyon every day. The boy was young, tall enough to pass for eighteen but probably closer to twelve, with a feathery growth of mustache at the corners of his mouth. Nobody ever made a fuss about his age, not the supervisors or dam bosses, because he did his job and never complained—a sore point with older water boys who did nothing but.

"I don't start any of it, Lew. Nope, she's the one with all the big ideas. Like me movin' in over there. Nice and cozy, just us two, right? Hell, it ain't cozy, Lew, it's a goddamn nuthouse."

Lew was peeling the shell off his last egg when he heard a brutal clang of metal on the roadway above him. He looked up and saw a truck buck forward and swerve crazily out of line about two hundred yards up the hill, sideswiping the rig in front of it, ripping off its rear bumper. Through the dust Lew could see the driver rocking back and forth, pumping at his brake pedal, his hands frozen on the big steering wheel. But the truck kept gaining speed as it careened down the hill, workmen diving out of the way as it veered wildly under the uneven weight of stone. An empty dump truck was forced off the road, flipping sideways into a ditch, and the flagmen started running.

Looking down the slope for Gunther Crewe, Lew spotted him trudging toward the bridge, propelled forward by the weight of the water bags on his shoulders, concentrating on his step and unaware of the trouble behind him. Lew looked back at the truck just as the driver leapt out of the cab and bounced to safety in bursts of dust and gravel.

"Watch out!" he screamed.

The water boy lost his step in the loose stones and almost fell.

Lew jumped to the ground and cupped his hands over his mouth. "Gunther! Run!"

The boy was being pulled off balance by the heft of the yoke.

"Drop it now! Run!"

Gunther cocked his chin and saw Lew waving at him. He smiled and waved back, pausing just long enough to glimpse the shadow of the runaway truck that ran him over.

Filius started running the moment he realized the truck had lost its brakes. He ran from the middle of the bridge and kept his eye on the boy the whole time, until the truck erased his presence. The inconceivable suddenness of it, artful as a sleight of hand, stopped his legs and his breath, and he was held there, part of the ossified moment. The only thing still moving was the vagabond truck, racing through dumbstruck life, past frozen expressions and sudden flight, to crash into a heap of gravel and slag.

And when it burst into flames that blossomed in the bright daylight, Filius was able to take a breath and look at the boy again. Gunther Crewe was facedown on the road, his neck broken by the yoke across his shoulders, his feet snapped and pointing in opposite directions.

It had all happened too quickly for Lew to do anything. When it was over, he ran to the scene, and stared not at the boy, but at the severed hand that lay a few feet from the body.

"Jesus Christ." Speed stood at his side, perching on his toes and fluting his neck to get a better look over the heads and shoulders of the men who reached the body first. Lew saw the dump trucks still chugging in line, radiating heat and exhaust as the drivers waited impatiently for the road to be cleared so they could go back to work. When he looked back at the severed hand, at the fingers curled upward, humble and innocent, he knew he'd had enough and pushed through the crowd.

"Hey, Lew," Speed called. "Where you goin'?"

Lew walked directly to the high road that would take him away from the dam, moving against the steady current of men drawn to the spectacle of fire and death.

"Hey, Lew!"

He kept walking uphill, past truck after truck, moving deeper into the oily haze of engine shimmer and dust, until he was nothing but shimmer himself, his body fractured into waves of heat.

Burr threw the knife like Charlie taught him, with a quick flick of the wrist, and hit the moving target about four inches left of where he was aiming. The blade was inside the biggest red circle on the board and he knew it was worth a point, but he was hoping for better; if not a kill worth four points, at least a body shot worth two.

Earlier that afternoon, Charlie had hung the wooden target between two spindly trees in Fanny's backyard. The image of a leaping rabbit—brightly white with brilliant orange eyes—was hand-painted on the board, with three red circles on its body, the smallest being on the neck.

Charlie pushed the target again, swinging it back and forth, and stepped to the side. Burr dug his bare toes into the line in the dirt, counted and aimed and hit the rabbit around its tail.

"Good shot."

"I was aiming for the middle."

"You'll get it."

Burr knew he was right, so he'd try to be patient, at least for a while. He walked to the target and pulled the abalone-inlaid knife out of the knotty wood, and walked back ten feet to try it again.

Charlie and Uncle Judy had driven into town with three plucked chickens and a basket of the potatoes and carrots that grew abundantly at the ranch. When Lena, Fanny and Judy went inside to prepare a stew for dinner, Charlie took Burr out back and set up the target.

"My father's uncle used to make these targets at his place outside of Elmore City. When I knew him he was already old, old as me now, and he used to sit on the road in front of his house with a stack of boards and an easel, painting the rabbits on and selling them for a nickel each to the farmers on wagons going to the cotton market in Wynnewood. Folks sometimes asked for a picture of a black bear or a moose, and he'd oblige, finishing up by the time they came back down the road."

Filius sat on the back porch, listening and watching; the boy hung on every word while Charlie paused to give the target a push.

"I remember once somebody asked for an elephant, and he said he'd do it even though he wasn't sure if there was different kinds, and promised it'd be ready that Friday. So he sent his daughter to the big library in Pauls Valley, and she brings him back a picture book of African wildlife that he studied like he was the dumbest man on earth. Up half the night looking at pictures of animals he knew he'd never see. The next day he drove to town himself and bought every African picture book there was, and ordered some others until his wife said enough. He painted that man his elephant just like he promised—and until he died, he wouldn't paint anything but jungle creatures. Target after target with pictures of rhinos and hippos and monkeys and lions and leopards, spotted and black. Well, people drove by in their buggies and wagons and kept on going. Never bought a single one. The pictures piled up so high you could use the boards for siding, and that's just what my uncle did—fixed up his old barn—and when he was done, he had himself a painted zoo. Folks came from as far away as Texas and Arkansas to look at it, and he charged them a nickel for the pleasure. And when he passed on his wife sat on his chair by the road and collected the money, but after a time the paintings faded in the sun and the traffic stopped, and then she married a stranger and moved to Wyoming, leaving that old barn to collapse into a heap of splintered wood—with no more pictures but a heck of a story to tell."

Burr held the knife loose in his fingers, his mind foggy with thoughts of Africa, imagining himself sneaking through tall grass that parted to reveal the cracked gray shoulders of a lone elephant. "Can you make me a target with an elephant on it, Charlie?"

"Sure I can."

Uncle Judy came out and sat on the porch step next to Filius. She offered him a cigarette and he accepted, and she lit them both with a match she'd snapped to flame with the yellow end of her thumbnail. She was a big woman, big enough to be Charlie's sister, the two of them solid pillars of sunburned flesh. "You're an engineer, Mr. Poe."

"Yes."

"Build many dams?"

"A few."

"I bet you've seen lots of things building dams, done a lot of traveling."

"I have."

"I've only been out west. Nevada and Utah, that's it. Half my life there, the other half here. I've been happy in both places, though, especially here. Be sad to leave."

"Why are you leaving?"

"Because I can't swim, Mr. Poe. I can't swim!" She laughed and let the smoke snort out of her nose. "When this dam you're building is done my ranch'll be underwater. Washed away with the rest of this valley. Houses and fences, roads and churches, all of it at the bottom of a great big lake." She wiped tobacco flecks from her lips. "Yeah, I'll get some government money when they kick me out, and I can buy some other land on higher ground. Nearby, maybe. I like it here."

Uncle Judy looked over the yard and watched Charlie and the boy. Filius saw her smile, and for a brief moment, she seemed elastic and calm.

"Maybe Charlie will come with me." She waved the smoke away and turned back to him. "It's not the end of the world, Mr. Poe, but it changes things. And you know the worst of it? I have to leave my brother where I buried him nineteen years ago. I could dig him up, maybe, and tote him with the rest of my belongings when I go, but Evan wouldn't want that. He'll stay where he is, and when they flood my land I'll never be able to visit him again. That's the worst of it. The hard part. I wonder if you ever think about such things when you're traveling around building your dams. If you don't, you should."

She rose to her feet, and Filius could hear her knees crack. She stubbed out her cigarette and didn't look at him again.

"We'll call you boys when supper's done."

It was just getting dark when Lew saw them leave the house. He recognized the man immediately—the beaky curve of his nose and the forward thrust of his walk, the white shirt with the sleeves rolled above the elbows. Even off the job he had a quiet authority, a supreme confidence in his own worth and promise. Lew figured these were qualities that allowed him to walk through life unfettered, his every footfall padded by the broken backs of others. He sat still behind the wheel of his car and watched this careful man lead the woman off the porch, and was overcome by a feeling of numb serenity. To see the two of them walk side by side to the big Chrysler didn't bother him, nor that they bantered lightly and the engineer offered Lena his hand as she slipped into the front seat. Their intimacy was the pantomime of strangers, and for the moment he didn't care. For the moment he felt neither envy nor anger. For the moment he felt nothing.

To pass the time while he sat in front of the house, Lew had sharpened his pocketknife; it was dull from lack of use, and a thin lip of rust had formed on the blade. Now he put it away and followed the Chrysler down Arizona Street, staying a block behind until it turned again on Park and headed down to the dam. Lew stopped at the corner with his engine running, and when the Chrysler's taillights dipped out of sight, he turned around in the empty street, driving past the administration buildings and parking in the lot across from the mess hall, where no one would notice it or think twice about his presence. Inside, he would sit at a table crowded with men he knew, and smile at jokes he could barely hear in the roar that filled the room. He would order the roast beef dinner, drink some coffee, eat some pie and wait.

She sat between Filius and Floyd Huntington in the front seat of the speeding truck, her feet firmly planted on the rusted floorboards and her leg muscles clenched tight as she tried hard not to bump into the men who flanked her. When Floyd steered the truck around the last bend on the canyon road and hit the straightaway that led to the dam site, she found herself leaning backward, weightless against Filius's shoulder as the construction site came into view, a dazzling spectacle so bright it was washed of color, the brittle landscape toned only by contours and shade. Rows of powerful arc lights lined the banks of the river, their wide beams trained on the trestle bridge and the long line of trucks that lumbered forward in the cobalt haze.

Lena watched their vast shadows slowly transmogrify into eerie abstractions and demonic contortions, then shrink into boxy clarity as the trucks came closer to the lights. Flagmen who walked into the beams were turned into colossal shadow puppets, their profiles stretched in ghoulish caricature, and below all the bright lights, the river flowed as harsh and roughskinnned as hammered steel.

Floyd dropped them off under the shed roof at a viewing area just above the bridge, where Six Companies executives stood stiff and silent as the convoy of trucks deposited ton after ton of excavation waste into the angry water. These men, who'd arrived from San Francisco and Los Angeles and Portland with money and grand ambitions, had been on-site since eleven o'clock that morning, to witness the surrender of the river.

Filius found Lena a chair next to Linnie Crowe and went off for coffee to warm their hands in the November chill, and she sat there, shocked into stillness by the immensity of the project in front of her. During all those long months in Boulder City, serving dam workers in the café, she'd been eager to see it, and had known it was going to be colossal. But until that evening it had been nothing more than a glow on the nighttime horizon, a landmark growing in the faraway dust. The size and scope of the project was something she had only followed in the local papers and heard eagerly discussed in the café. Until that evening, the only dams she'd ever seen were the earthen dams molded on the Boggy River tributaries to irrigate the cotton fields in Choctaw County.

She watched the trucks move over the bridge, and the high scalers on the canyon walls, and the skips that crisscrossed overhead. The noise everywhere around her was barbaric in its intensity, confounding and chaotic, illuminated under an umbrella of false light that made the enormity of it seem perversely intimate.

Filius crouched next to her and handed her a cup of coffee.

For the first time around him, she felt embarrassed and shy. "I didn't know."

Filius smiled, undaunted, the steam from his coffee rising in furious whiffs.

Lena liked it when he smiled at her, the joy in his face youthful and honest, and she wished he would do it more. "It's beautiful."

And she meant it.

. . .

He was sitting with his back against the wall of the Thompson bungalow when the police car pulled up in front of the house across the street. He cupped his cigarette as the sergeant walked around to open the passenger door for Fanny. He watched them stroll side by side to the little house, where the cop leaned down and whispered something and Fanny laughed, abrupt and shrill, as the door shut behind them.

A few minutes after the porch light went out, another light came on in a room at the back of the house. A dog howled somewhere down the street, a single note that held in the night air soulful as a church bell, and then it was quiet. He stretched out his legs, comfortable in the darkness, and finished his cigarette. He'd been there for about an hour, long enough to hear the Thompsons' after-dinner squabble about Thanksgiving plans. Kaye had asked most of the questions and Harry had answered in distracted oinks and dismissals, and Lew could picture the stubborn fatigue in his face, the line of his lips drawn tight and bloodless as a worm. Harry's failure to engage had only inspired Kaye, and she picked and prodded him as she would a sweating roast. The Thompsons bickered on, half-hearted and practiced as a long-running play, and he could tell they were bored with each other and the routine of their lives, the habits of their marriage dull and binding as common prayer. He sat there in the grass until the voices stopped and the table was cleared without further discussion, and after a while the house became silent except for footfalls and running water and snoring.

When the police car had finally arrived it was after midnight, and he waited another five minutes before he pushed himself up and walked across the street.

Lew sauntered up the front walk of Fanny's house as if he'd been invited, but when he got to the porch he veered to the right, into the screen of oleander bushes and around a fat patch of devil's-head cactus. Staying close to the side of the house and deep in the shadows, he moved to the first window, crouched below the sill and paused a moment, glancing through the gray moonlight at the quiet bungalow next door, not more than thirty feet away. He turned then, with his hands flat against the rough stucco of Fanny's house, and lifted himself up to look through the window into the living room, where the boy was asleep on the couch. He watched long enough to see him flip onto his stomach and then onto his back and then onto his side again, the blanket rising and falling with the rhythm of his sleep.

Lew smiled. He felt like tapping on the glass and amusing the boy with the game his father had played with him years ago: Isadore the Joker sneaking into his son's bedroom at night to duck behind the bedpost and rise like a great whiskered monkey, grunting and making faces until little Louis woke up scared and disoriented and started to cry. Isadore would grin dumbly and pick his wailing son out of bed and walk him around the room, his voice gruff with raspy coos, never knowing that Louis had been waiting for this moment all along, waiting for his father in the dark with his eyes pinched shut, waiting for him to creak open the door and tiptoe to the end of the bed, waiting in shivering patience for his father to turn into a monkey just so he could cry and scream, knowing that Isadore would lift him into his strong arms and hold him for as long as he needed. Louis had loved that more than anything, to be held by his father, crimped between his elbow and forearm, rocking with his ear pressed tight against his father's chest, trying to find the heartbeat that so often was overwhelmed by soothing laughter and Yiddish babble. And by the time Isadore finally laid him back in bed and kissed him on his cheek, Louis was happily exhausted and already falling into the deepest sleep.

The light at the back of the house went out, and Lew turned away from the boy. He slid below the sill and listened to the sounds of the neighborhood—the spinning of the dial on a faraway radio, the night call of sage sparrows—and waited for a car on the next street over to turn the corner and disappear. With the street quiet and dark again, he stepped quickly to the rear of the house.

In a room lit only by the hallway light, Fanny was sitting naked on her bed with one leg raised on the blanket, and he was thrilled by the bounty of her body, the lavishness of flesh that folded like velvet over her frame. Her skin was whiter than Lew imagined it could be, luminous against the blonde hair that fell wildly across her shoulders and showed darker between her legs. The sergeant was poised in front of her, his back to Lew, and she smiled as he took off his uniform. Lew stood where he was, still as a shadow, his eyes just above the windowsill. He watched Archie Swerling undress and took notice of the stump of his right pinkie. The cop dropped his clothes to the floor and leaned his knees on the bed, and Fanny reached between his legs. Lew listened to her soft laughter and never lowered his eyes as they moved together in a coiled strand of voice and limb, his eyes focused on the streaky shine of their skin, on the hands that glided without resistance into the dips and furrows of pressed flesh, on the pleasures they enacted in a privacy they did not know he shared. Lew stood immobile in the chilly night and pressed his fingers against his own erection.

The water continued to rise, swallowing the rocks that tumbled into it. Filius and Lena were standing closer now, leaning into each other as their bodies stretched over the wooden barricades and their faces peered into the misty air. They stood next to men in Ballard hats and stiffened canvas coats and watched the Colorado's angry fingers pull the canyon debris into the raging water beneath the trestle bridge. They didn't feel the wind that blustered and pricked like needles, or hear the high chirp of mechanical brakes, or notice that the air smelled scorched and bitter, or sense the earth humming beneath their feet as it was pummeled and smoothed by a thousand truck tires. They stood transfixed, etched in the white lights, and watched the river continue to rise and roll along the opposite bank, fighting against the loads of muck that pushed it toward the great black eye of the diversion tunnel on the other side.

Filius felt increasingly frustrated to be watching from the viewing area, shunted to the side with the wives of engineers and the monied men from western capitals, the group of them itchy with impatience as they counted heads and machinery and tried to gauge the wisdom of their investments. It was safer there, he knew, and less clamorous, but he needed to be where the river pulsed true as an artery, and he finally put out his cigarette and knelt by Lena's chair. "Would you like to go to the bridge?"

Glad when she nodded, he took her elbow and waited while she said her good-byes to Linnie Crowe, then tipped his own hat before guiding Lena over ground rough with stones and discarded tools, careful not to rush her no matter how anxious he was himself.

He stood behind her at the barricade, his hands encircling her and resting on the wooden plank on either side, using his bent frame to form a protective shield from the men and noise around them. Looking upriver, away from the glare of white lights, he let his eyes settle and refocus on the sheet of water that rushed toward them. He saw the beginnings of a pool forming along the Arizona bank; he saw the water furious and snapping as if stormdriven, eating away at the slope of the road, trying in vain to hold its course. And he knew it was only a matter of hours before the Colorado would be turned.

After her first shocked silence, Lena turned to him with a flurry of questions that he answered with a pleasure forgotten since he'd traveled west on dam jobs with Addie. For years she had listened to him extol the engineering assumptions of Stoddard and Atherley, based on the dam models they built to study tensile stress and profiles, and she was patient as he explained the mathematical advantages of a curved dam, as first investigated by the great French engineer M. Delorce; but it wasn't until she witnessed actual construction at the Don Pedro Dam in northern California that she had understood and appreciated what he was doing.

Filius's hand drifted to Lena's bare arm and he felt her shiver. Until that moment he hadn't realized how cold it was, oblivious to all but the dam and the memories that standing here with her had engendered. In two hours the sun would come up and warm the pink rocks, but for now he took off his jacket and draped it over Lena's shoulders. She pulled it tight and he let his hand rest softly by her neck. They stood together and watched the agitated river carry on, stubborn and undeterred.

Lew waited under the dark arcade in front of the Boulder City Company Store. It was three in the morning when he strolled through the shadowy white arches that lined the sidewalk, looking at the window displays. In the first he saw an artfully stepped ziggurat of Toastmasters, with the new electric coffeemaker from the Chicago Flexible Shaft Company gleaming like a silver spire on top. The next was filled with men's fashions, from felt hats by Stetson and Dobbs cocked on blank-faced mannequins to a velvet-lined case filled with silk ties from Ormond of New York. Farther down the sidewalk he found a window with a bright array of women's cosmetics, powder tins with fancy decorations of exotically plumed birds and dancing nudes and pampered ladies in lingerie, French perfumes from Molinard and Lanvin, Oriental toilet water from A. A. Vantine. He knelt close and recognized the slender pink bottles of Rose of Omar talcum powder that Cece liked to use after her bath, and he thought of coming back the next day to buy her some for Christmas. Or he might take her for a long ride in his new Lincoln—maybe all the way to Los Angeles, where they could have dinner downtown, either at the Biltmore Hotel or Casa La Golondrina on Olvera Street. On the drive back Cece could curl beside him on the front seat, her head on his lap as she slept.

Lew craved a cigarette but wasn't about to smoke just now. He remained vigilant and invisible in the cold darkness. He heard a scraping behind him and spun around to see a stray cat with a stubby tail jumping on and off the curb, licking furiously at the sticky candy wrapper that was stuck on a front paw. Then headlights cut across the front of the Company Store, and Lew saw the police car take the corner and stop in front of the recreation hall across the street. He backed slowly away from the window, pushing his back against one of the narrow pillars, his profile as narrow as the shadow that held him.

Archie Swerling got out of the car and turned on his flashlight. Lew waited while he walked along the sidewalk, checking every door and window of the recreation hall. He waited while he paused to smoke a cigarette, and when a pickup truck full of dam workers honked and waved and slowed down for a quick exchange. He waited while he went around back to rattle the three doors in the alley, and while he stopped to piss against a pile of broken bricks. He waited until Swerling crossed the street and started walking toward him, swinging his flashlight loosely at his side, the beam riding up and down in lazy loops. He waited until Swerling pulled on the front door of the Company Store and perused the same windows that Lew had admired. He could hear Swerling getting closer, and pulled the wrench out of his back pocket. When the policeman finally walked past him, he aimed for the crease in the high-crowned Bailey hat and saw it widen as the wrench came down. Swerling reeled and threw up his hands, and Lew hit him again. It was less of a reach the second time. When Swerling dropped to his knees, Lew kicked him in the back and pressed his face flat to the pavement. Swerling lay there with his cheek against the curb and his mouth open, his flashlight still on and the beam shining right in his face. There was a fine spray of blood around the back of Swerling's head, and a richer trickle running into a crack on the sidewalk. His hat had fallen off, and his blonde hair was darker where the wrench had caught him. Lew straddled Swerling and threw back his blue wool coat to unhook the ivory-handled Colt revolver from his holster, and secured it in his own belt. In the still air he could hear Swerling's shallow breath. Lying there, sprawled and outlined in his own blood, Archie Swerling looked almost pitiable. But Lew knew his wounds would heal, and the disgrace of this occasion would fade, and it wouldn't be long before the sergeant regained his arrogant strut and swagger. Swerling would never know who he'd run into this night, but Lew wanted to leave him a permanent reminder of their rendezvous. He took out his pocketknife, planted a knee on the small of Swerling's back, pulled out his left hand—the one with all five fingers—and splayed it across the sidewalk before severing the policeman's remaining pinkie at the second knuckle. As it rolled across the sidewalk, Lew looked into the shadows to see if the cat was still around.

The dawn had fooled Lena when it broke over the canyon. What she'd first thought was a stand of dwarf pines on the Nevada rim turned out to be an ever-growing crowd of spectators who had come to watch the surrender of the river. She felt Filius's hand on her shoulder and turned, following his finger to where he was pointing upriver to the sudden brightness that fell over the canyon. She had to shield her eyes and squint before she could make out the rising pool of brown water that was eating away at the last dirt embankment before the diversion tunnel. She looked at the bridge and saw that the last three trucks had stopped there without unloading, the drivers lifting themselves out of their cabs to look upstream. Machinery stopped altogether and the deafening roar that had filled the canyon now came to an abrupt halt—the only sounds the water itself and the panting of three men hastily setting up their big Mitchell Ultra Speed movie camera on a flatbed next to her to record the final rise of the Colorado River.

Everyone stood frozen, staring at the gray slickness of the concrete tunnel. She could smell a metallic excitement in the cold air, in the sweat and gasoline, in the breath of a hundred tired men who surrounded and ignored her. Floyd Huntington bullied his way to their side, and Filius gently coaxed Lena closer so she could have a better view. Upriver, she saw the water popping and crashing up against the crumbling embankment in front of the tunnel, and even she knew the river could no longer resist its forced detour. For a moment it held on the brink of its ancient flow, calm and majestic, then suddenly succumbed, a great brown bubble plunging violently into the huge tunnel and splashing up its smooth, shiny walls.

"She's taking it, boys!" Floyd Huntington whipped off his hat and sent it sailing. "Goddammit, she's taking it!"

As a thousand arms shot up into the air and the crowd cheered, Filius took Lena's hand and held on.

He pulled into the parking lot of the Mexico Club. It was early in the morning but Frank Strella's Cadillac was already there. Lew parked next to it and stepped into the new day.

He paused a moment to straighten his clothes. He had bathed and changed at Miss Williams's, but still noticed speckles of blood on the toes of his boots. In the morning light they looked as harmless as mud. Walking toward the club entrance, he saw the fat-faced man out front sweeping up broken bottles. He expected to be stopped and bothered, to be asked too many questions too early. Lew clenched his fist, digging his fingernails into the mushy part of his palm, but the fat man barely glanced up as he pushed open the front door and headed to Strella's office.

He'd been home long enough to shower and shave, and now sat on the screen porch in a clean shirt and khakis.

> *Dear Addie,*
> *We turned the river this morning, and she fought us to the bitter end. You should have seen her, Addie. She raged as if she were still as wild as the day we swam in her so many years ago, the two of us staying close to shore, careful to avoid that current strong enough to carry us to the Gulf of California. The current is still strong but it has a bend in it now, and soon we will be able to start building the dam. Although I sit here in the cold morning with a touch of remorse for interfering with such a mighty river, I know what we accomplished today was a necessary and magnificent achievement, and I'm glad to have been a part of it. It will be a great dam, the best of its kind, and I only wish you could be here with me. I wish that same thing every day. Every day. I am happy now. It won't last, it never does, but while it's here I will savor it.*

Filius put down his pen, pointed his face into the sun and shut his eyes.

*I*t was just getting dark when the first waves of freezing rain lashed the bottom of Black Canyon, and Filius turned up the collar on his slicker and raised his shoulders to let the water sheet down his back. That morning, riding down to the riverbed in an open-backed truck, he'd looked up and seen a quilted, charcoal-smudged mass collecting to the west. The clouds had stayed, low and unmoving, all day, but he was grateful the rain had held off until the shift ended.

Now the rain strafed him as he shivered on top of the dike, looking down into the muck pit below, where electric shovels were still digging out the riverbed. For days they'd been scooping out wet mounds of sand and stone, and had already gone down fifteen feet without finding solid ground. Before excavation began, Walker Young and Floyd Huntington and Filius had placed bets on how deep they'd have to go before laying the cofferdam foundation. Walker was the first to slip his ten-dollar bill into the old soup can that sat on a shelf in the construction shed, and Filius was half a foot away from giving up his. Everybody had heard the rumors that Floyd hadn't lost a bet like this since he was a kid working on the Cheesman Dam outside of Denver, when Charlie Harrison, the chief engineer, took him for a nickel, but they'd bet him anyway. Floyd tried hard not to gloat as he peeked each morning into the soup can, but the smirk on his face was hard to avoid. When Frank Crowe heard about the wager he laughed out loud and offered to pay anyone within hearing range ten-to-one if Floyd didn't come in on the money.

The cold rain fell in silvery sheets. Filius held his ground and watched the electric shovels whirr and pivot as they pawed the watery muck, the swinging buckets missing one another by inches. He loved the choreography of big machines, and he was anxious for construction to begin. He and Walker had designed this cofferdam to span the canyon, an earthen fill 480 feet long and almost a hundred feet high, made from tons of dry fill carved from the cratered terrain of Hemenway Wash. The base would be 750 feet thick and strong enough to withstand any flood the river might unleash after the winter thaw. Even though the Colorado was successfully channeled through the first of the tunnels, she was still capable of tremendous havoc, and Six Companies wanted guarantees. They wanted the principle dam site dry and protected, no matter what, so construction could continue without threat or surprise, and didn't care that this costly solution would someday be underwater.

Filius turned and looked downstream, where a necklace of huge puddles was strung along the scarred waterway. Some were as wide as duck ponds, others deep enough to submerge a bus. For centuries the river had cut an ever-widening path through this canyon of volcanic rock, carrying with it the broken rubble of the Rocky Mountains, spinning like thrown hammers in the turbulent current, gouging the canyon floor until the rubble itself disintegrated and became nothing more than silt washed out to sea.

The newly exposed landscape, from where Filius stood, was dark and gutted, as eerie as a plundered grave.

He heard a whistle, and saw Speed Owens waving at him from one of the idling shovels, his canvas coat soaked and pulling heavily on his arms. Filius waved back, giving him the go-ahead to send the men home, and watched as they abandoned their shovels and splashed off through the rain and mud to the trucks that would return them to Boulder City. The crews had been making good progress, but now were digging hour after hour through November storms and slippery riverbed, until the chipped buckets on their shovels hit solid rock and threw sparks.

Filius wiped the splatter of rain from his watch. It was four-thirty, and the deep gray swirls in the sky were quickly coalescing into overwhelming blackness. He decided to leave himself, and come back if the weather cleared later that night. But now he'd pick up Burr and take him home so they could work on the rabbit hutch the boy was building for Charlie. It was going to be a Christmas present, and Filius had promised to help him whenever he could. They'd sat around Filius's kitchen table and collaborated on the design, agreeing on a slanted roof and windows on the sides for better circulation during boiling summer days. He taught Burr how to draw out the plans, and to lay out the proper tools and materials as his father had taught him. Then they set up a shop in the unused bedroom. The first thing they built as a team were the three nesting boxes, and now they were ready to put together the hutch itself. All that Filius had left to do was order the two-by-four-inch wire mesh from the hardware store in Las Vegas.

Filius had been spending more time with Lena and the boy. Whether he saw them collectively, as mother or son, or separately, as woman and as boy, he felt easy in their presence and grateful for their friendship. In the past year and a half he'd felt separated from the world around him, wandering without solace on the blurred edges of his quiet life. In his infrequent periods of sleep, he sometimes saw himself drifting over the withered landscape like a ghost. He wanted no more of those dreams; he wanted to sleep deeply and come out the other side, and thought Lena and the boy might help. For all the pleasure he took in their company, he hoped he gave some back.

Earlier that morning, Frank had joined him on the dike that reached into the riverbed. His Stetson was still damp from the night before, but the mud on his wool pants was fresh. They stood and watched a crew of electricians drag a 2,300-volt cable through the mud, to power one of the big pumps and drain the puddles and stay ahead of the rain.

"How deep are you?" Frank asked.

"Sixteen feet this morning."

"And Floyd bet what?"

"Eighteen feet."

Crowe grinned. "Then we should be there tomorrow." The uncanny accuracy of Huntington's predictions was a respite from the pressures of schedules and the numbers, and Frank chewed it like tobacco. "Why do you bet him, Filius?"

"Because it makes you happy."

Below them, the trio of shovels swiveled and dumped buckets of streaming muck into the waiting Boreman trucks.

Frank looked up at the gray sky, dull as a tarnished knife. "I can get you all the wrenches you need. Hell, I can probably put in a requisition for enough dynamite to blow a trench to Mexico. But I can't do a thing about the goddamn weather." Out of his leather jacket he pulled a yellow notebook crammed with slips of crinkled papers, all of them overrun with names and dates and numbers. He shuffled through them and put the notebook back in his pocket. "I've got to meet Charlie Shea across the river. Some questions about the Arizona spillway."

Frank stood still, and Filius took sudden note of this uncharacteristic pose.

"Linnie mentioned she met your friend the other night."

"Yes. Lena."

"She liked her."

"So do I."

"If it's none of my business, say so."

"It's okay."

"We're friends."

"I know."

Crowe stopped nodding and Filius could tell that he was relieved. "Linnie wants you both to come to dinner between the holidays."

"We will."

"And apparently she has a little boy?"

"Yes, Burr."

"Then bring him, too."

"I will."

"Good." Frank smiled at him. "Good for you, Mr. Poe."

After Addie's death, Filius went to his father's old hunting cabin in the woods north of Military Ridge. The new road was slippery with maple leaves mashed yellow on the pavement, and ran past the Sammett place, where hunting dogs still raced and barked along the fence, and the Martin farm, now abandoned. It had been fifteen years since Filius had been to the cabin, and the new electric wires followed the road all the way from Blue Mounds. It was dusk when Filius arrived in late September, and he made a fire in the woodstove and lit the coal lamp before remembering that he only had to flick the switch by the door.

He started hiking when his ankle was stronger, finding the same rutted tracks he'd explored as a boy with Amos. The mazelike paths soon came back to him. He walked for hours on the high ridge, and looked down on deer feeding on the red berries of staghorn sumac. He carried his father's rifle and it had a comfortable weight, the strap tight on his shoulder and the steel barrel cold on his back, but he never took a shot. When he woke up to the first hard frost, he spent three days chopping firewood even though at least seven cords were stacked in the shed out back. He fished for trout and bluegill until a thin sheet of ice lay like glass on the pond in the meadow. On the first of November it snowed, and he wrapped himself in blankets and sat on the porch with a glass of whiskey to watch it come down.

Winter was short that year and by March the creeks were running clear and spring blooms beginning to show. Filius started walking again, following the lower streambeds; in the moist woods he trod on bloodroot flowers thick as carpet under his feet, and from a sunny clearing he saw the first trout lilies rising like yellow parachutes at the water's edge. When a truly warm day came midmonth, he put together the old bamboo fly rod he'd made for himself and walked to the pools his father loved the best. He sat on the bank and ate lunch, his back against a silver birch, his feet inches from the water and surrounded by jewelweed, and he remembered when he was seven and his father broke the stems of the plant and used the clear juice to deaden the itch of poison ivy that ran in pink splotches down his legs. He spent the afternoon fishing in a cold current that barely cleared his ankles, releasing all but two of the brook trout, which he gutted at streamside and took home for dinner. He kept to this routine for the rest of the spring, even when a late-season flurry swirled through the hills like Christmas and left a quarter inch of snow.

When darkness came, Filius sat on the porch and had the one glass of whiskey he allowed himself each night, because more than that made him want to drink until he hurt himself, to writhe on the ground and scream and feel guilt and pain instead of nothing at all. He'd hoped his time in the Wisconsin woods might teach him to sleep again, like everyone else; that he might've been able to close his eyes without seeing his wife and son and water; that by being alone he might grieve fully and emerge as himself or someone else.

At the end of April, in the midst of a thunderstorm that littered the roof of the old springhouse with broken pine boughs, Filius closed up the cabin and left the woods. He drove to Chicago to see Addie's parents, staying in the bed he'd shared with his wife when they were first married. He left the next morning and drove north to Madison, following Lake Michigan as far as Racine before heading west on the small roads that would take him home. He arrived late on an afternoon as brilliant and warm as a false summer, so his mother decided to serve dinner—the venison roast that Jack Sammett had sent back with Filius—on the back porch overlooking Lake Mendota. They talked about everything except what mattered the most, and his mother gripped his hand throughout the entire meal. They stayed out long enough to watch the constellations fill the sky, reflecting on the smooth water in front of them. After midnight, Filius took his glass of whiskey upstairs and lay down in the bed he'd slept in as a boy. In the morning he called Frank Crowe in Boulder City and told him he was ready to go to work.

Filius walked across the dike to hitch a ride back to Boulder City on one of the trucks. The rain came harder now, cold as pinpricks on the back of his neck, and he knew that the mud oozing below his boots would be frozen into hard ridges by morning.

It was just before sunrise and still dark when Lew and Mr. Jimmy came through the back door of Oscar Wells's house on Bridger Street. It was a nice Mission-style house, with a red-tiled roof and stuccoed walls and ornamental iron grates over the second-story windows, a block away from the new Las Vegas High School in a neighborhood of fine houses favored by successful, civic-minded businessmen.

The back door was unlocked, as Lew knew it would be, and opened to a small service porch and a generous kitchen. The kitchen was dim, and Mr. Jimmy sat down at the small round table, already covered with a linen cloth and set with sugar bowl and butter dish, as Lew turned on a small lamp and looked around. A new Barstow range stood against the far wall, its gray porcelain shining smart and bright. The cupboards above the spotless counters were glass-fronted, the good china and the glassware arranged as neatly as in a shop window. Lew walked over to the two-door Frigidaire and found a bowl of brown eggs on the bottom shelf, behind the turkey waiting to be stuffed for Thanksgiving dinner. He took two eggs and put them in a small pot already sitting on the stove, added a half inch of water from the tap, put it back on the front burner, and lit the gas with a match.

"What're you doing?" Mr. Jimmy said, watching him from the small table, dipping a wet finger into the sugar bowl and licking it clean.

Lew didn't answer and walked into the spacious dining room. A first glow of morning showed in the four elongated windows that faced the front yard, and the long, formal table was bare except for an empty silver bowl and matching candlesticks. He continued on into the living room, where thin wisps of smoke drifted off the smol-dering wood in the fireplace. He stopped in front of the spinet to look at a gallery of silver-framed photographs arranged in front of a vase whose white roses had begun to drop their petals. There was Oscar Wells, looking handsome in his pinstripe suit and mustache in front of the Red Crown Gasoline station he owned in town; and a pretty wife with a slender neck and brazen smile, standing poolside at Ladd's resort; and a boy suited up for football, virile and good-looking as his father; and a girl as blonde as her mother but sadly chubby and shy behind curly locks. Lew found the images elegant and dreamy, and he walked silently to the staircase and peeked up the balustrade to the second-floor landing, where an oil painting of trellised bougainvillea hung above a small oak chiffonier, and he lis-tened to the sounds of sleep that carried from room to room and drifted down the stairs.

Back in the kitchen, Mr. Jimmy was standing over the stove. "Water's gone, Lew."

Lew walked up and looked down at the two eggs banging and rolling around the bottom of the hot pan, and smiled. When he'd shared a room with Speed Owens and Henry Faulk on Van Buren Street in Phoenix, one morning Speed woke before the others, hungover and sick to his stomach, craving deviled eggs with lots of mustard. He stumbled around the dark kitchen in his underwear and managed to put three eggs into a pot full of water, set the heat to high and went back to bed, falling quickly asleep while the eggs boiled away on the hot plate.

Lew stared down at the dry pan on the pretty stove. The eggs hissed, as if ready to crack, rolling in shells spotted brown and black.

"Step back, Jimmy."

"What?"

"Step back."

They moved away from the stove just as the first egg popped. Before they could blink, the second egg did too, and the sudden stench was fierce.

"Jesus Christ," Mr. Jimmy muttered.

That's what Lew had said that morning in Phoenix when he and Henry gagged themselves awake and dragged Speed outside in his underwear, pelting him with the burnt pot and his rotten eggs.

Lew turned off the flame and Mr. Jimmy buried his nose in his handkerchief.

"Open a goddamn window, Lew."

"What for?"

"You're stinking up the place."

He could hear footsteps and muffled voices in the rooms above the kitchen. "Shut up and sit down."

Mr. Jimmy pulled out a chair in the breakfast nook and did what he was told, cracking the window open just enough to let in some fresh air.

Lew stood in the middle of the kitchen and listened to feet thumping down the stairs, the angry voices half asleep. He turned calmly to the doorway and saw Oscar Wells and his wife coming toward him. This early in the morning she was not so beautiful, her face puffy and creased by the pillow she'd hugged; and Oscar, his robe loose around his shoulders, was not fat yet but getting there. Lew waited until he was right in front of him; his nostrils flared at the awful smell in his private fiefdom, and before he could open his mouth Lew hit him hard on the forehead and knocked him to his knees.

Mrs. Wells filled her lungs for a scream.

Lew relaxed his fist into an open hand and held it out in front of her. "You make a sound, and when your boy comes down I'll give him the same. And then you."

She caught herself, a small hand propped up to her lips, and backed up against the laundry room door. Lew caught a hint of fear rising from her skin, and it was not an unwelcome scent. He turned his attention back to Oscar and dragged him by the lapels of his robe across the room, his leather slippers squeaking over the linoleum, and he groaned and held his head while Lew kicked out a chair and yanked him by the shoulders into a sitting position.

Wells closed his eyes, swatting blindly, trying to protect his face. "Please, no. Please."

The buttons were stripped from the front of Wells's pajamas, and Lew could see the shivering in his chest and the double roll of fat above his belly, and wanted to punch him there, but instead slapped him across the face, then put his hand on his chest and pushed until he looked up at him. The bruise on his forehead was already beginning to show, a soft mound of purple flesh over his right eyebrow.

"Go away. Please."

Lew slapped him again. "You owe Mr. Strella and the Mexico Club one thousand dollars. He asked for it twice, and you said yes both times, but you never delivered the money. He was patient. I'm not. That bump on your head will last about a week, and you can wear it to work and wear it through the holidays and explain it any way you want. Tell your friends you fell off a horse or walked into a door, or tell them the truth. But when it goes away I'll be back, and you better have the money."

Lew started for the service porch door. He didn't glance at the woman or listen to the boy's voice yelling from the hallway, "Mom? Dad? What's that smell?" He didn't wait for Mr. Jimmy because he knew he was right behind him. He stepped outside into the chilled morning air, his eyes on the pale orange line that was beginning to show at the bottom of the brightening sky, and walked quickly past the clipped lawns and nice houses to the car that was parked and waiting for them between the yellow buses in the high school parking lot.

Cece rolled over into the space that Lew usually occupied and snuggled up to the depression he left in the mattress, pretending it was warmer there, even though it was closer to the window and the cold draft that whistled through the cracked pane. She fidgeted a while before wrapping herself in the blanket, and fidgeted some more before flopping back to her side of the bed. She closed her eyes and tried to go back to sleep, but the morning light bothered her and she knew that any sleep she got now would be restless and unfulfilled.

She stood on the cold floor and stretched her arms over her head and behind her back, looking in the mirror on the door to admire herself in the pretty yellow nightgown. The week before, after he got his first paycheck from the Mexico Club, Lew had come back with half a dozen steaks for Miss Williams and the nightgown for Cece. He was in a fine mood, her little big man, and Miss Williams cooked two of the sirloins black on the outside, the way he liked them, and let them break the rules and have dinner and celebrate his good fortune in Cece's room. That same night Mr. Jimmy came by on business and Lew asked her to fetch him his car keys out of the nightstand while he took a shower. She did as she was told, and saw the gun tucked in the back of the drawer.

Cece never liked guns. When she was a little girl, her family used to drive across the state to visit her Uncle Lucius outside of Sampson, Alabama, at his half acre on the Pea River, where he'd retired after two decades of emptying shrimp boats in Mobile Bay. By then Lucius had bad legs and a bad back, and he couldn't do much of anything but swear to God and putter around like an old man. When he wasn't fishing for catfish from the little wooden skiff he kept tied to an iron stake behind his house, he'd be sitting on his front porch with an old Colt service revolver in his lap, his fingers tight around the rubber grip, ready to shoot at anything that moved on the dirt road in front of him, squirrels or crows or stray dogs; if he didn't recognize it, it was fair game. This was sport to Lucius, a rocking chair hunt, and it would go on for hours, until he got bored or ran out of ammunition. One afternoon, Cece was on the porch drinking lemonade with her cousins—two boys about her age who were almost deaf from the all the gunfire they had endured—when she saw her uncle shoot six times at a mud turtle that crawled out of the swampy ravine across the side yard. The first five shots missed, but the last bullet pinged off the turtle's shell and knocked it back down the bank.

Cece had cringed every time Uncle Lucius lifted that pistol. Her cousins laughed, but she didn't join in because they were stupid. It wasn't the loudness of the shots that bothered her; it was having her eyes closed, afraid to look but knowing she would.

Years had gone by and she was braver now, so she tied her bathrobe over the pretty yellow nightgown and opened the nightstand drawer. The gun she'd seen a week ago was gone, and she was glad.

Fanny drove Hi Carter's old pickup truck, downshifting on the hills and riding the gas pedal on the long stretch of new highway that led into Las Vegas. Lena sat up front with her, unable to enjoy the ride or the sunrise that glazed the desert pink, her mind still on the small package that had arrived from her lawyer the day before. She didn't have to open it to know what it was, and she'd made the mistake of waiting until that morning to read the letter that was attached. Now she was angry. Instead of taking advantage of Burr sleeping over at the Chubbs' house and going on a morning errand with her friend—picking up the half dozen turkeys they'd butter and roast back at the café—she was fuming over her ex-husband's brief words and the handsomely wrapped reminder of the one good thing they did together.

"Burr's his son, too."

Fanny's voice startled Lena, as if the voices in her own head didn't provide enough arguments. "That was my mistake."

"Yeah. Too bad nobody talked you out of it."

"You could have."

Fanny shrugged and slowed as they came up the hill to Railroad Pass. "Frank was a catch back then. I danced with him, too."

"I danced with him more."

"Lucky you, huh?"

Lena sighed and thought about the package that Frank had sent from the Oklahoma State Penitentiary. The letter attached was addressed to Lena, his handwriting still formal and precise from all those years of taking Bible orders:

LENA, THIS IS FOR BURR AND I HOPE YOU WILL ALLOW HIM TO HAVE IT. I AM STILL HIS FATHER. I WILL NEVER FORGET HIS BIRTHDAY. I STILL LOVE HIM. WHAT HAPPENED DOES NOT CHANGE THAT. HE'S STILL MY SON.

FRANK MULLENS

That's what bothered Lena the most: *Frank Mullens.* Signing both names as though he was important.

"What happened to him. That's all he cares about. Like it was someone else's fault that I found out. That his life, both of them, should've been all happy-go-lucky till the day he died. That's what gets me the most. That he's not sorry for me or for the other one. Or for the two kids he left behind. He's just sorry he got caught."

They came up to the top of the pass, and in the valley below Lena could see the warm lights that glowed throughout Las Vegas.

"I wish he'd just go away."

"He is away."

"Not long enough for me."

It was still early and traffic was light. The other vehicles were mostly filled with men coming back from the beer joints along the Boulder Highway in bleary stupefaction. The lights at Texas Acres were still blazing like Christmas when they drove past, and Lena looked at the patrons stumbling across the parking lot like wounded soldiers.

"You don't have to give Burr the present. You could throw it away, and Frank'll never know the difference. He can just go on pretending like he does about everything else in his life."

"I don't care about Frank."

"I don't either."

"Burr's the one who's going to get hurt by all this."

"If you let him."

Lena had hoped the divorce would be the end of it, that Frank would truly fade away, and if someone years from now asked her about her marriage, it might conjure vague memories but would say nothing consequential about her life. She had hoped that he would sit in prison and reflect on his mistakes and read the Bible stories he'd peddled, and feel some remorse. But he didn't, and she came to dread every yellow envelope she received from Mr. Miller in Hugo.

She looked at Fanny.

"Last week he asked me where his father was."

"What did you tell him?"

"That he was in prison."

"Did you tell him why?"

"He didn't ask."

But she knew that he would someday, and that it would probably come out of the blue, in the middle of an argument about homework or bedtime. She looked through the spotted windshield; shadows from the power lines fell across the road in black bars. "I'm going to let Burr have the present."

"Good."

She looked over and saw that Fanny was smiling.

It was nearly eight on Thanksgiving morning when Fanny and Lena drove into the parking lot at the Union Depot. Uncle Judy's truck was already parked in front of the ticket office and Charlie had the back gate down and a sign propped up against the front wheel: DICKENS FARM TURKEYS: TEN CENTS A POUND. A big Dodge sedan was idling there, floating on a thin cloud of exhaust, and a man in a topcoat stood at the back of the truck with his arms out. Charlie handed him a large cardboard box with the bald white hump of turkey sticking out of the top, and took the two dollar bills the man had crimped between his gloved fingers. He tipped his hat to the man's back and passed the money to Uncle Judy, who loosened the leather pouch she wore around her waist and shoved the bills inside.

Lena got out of the truck, and Charlie broke into a big grin and rubbed his hands together when he saw her.

"Nippy, ain't it?" He stomped his big feet and did a little dance before coming over to give her a hug.

She pulled him close and his cheeks were cold and bristly against her own. He smelled bracingly clean, as if his clothes had been dipped in bleach, and she didn't want to let go.

There were at least thirty boxes of turkeys stacked on the truck bed, and Uncle Judy was stepping around them, pushing six of them onto the tailgate for Fanny.

"I saved the fattest for you," she told her. "Twenty-four pounds apiece. No blemishes and no broken bones, so they'll stand up straight and come out of the oven looking like something you'd want to put up on your mantel."

While Charlie helped the women load the boxes into the bed of Hi's truck, Uncle Judy waited on a well-dressed woman who'd just pulled up.

Fanny got her purse off the front seat and counted out fourteen dollars and forty cents. "Thanks, Charlie."

"You bet, Fanny."

He put the money in his pocket, and Lena reached up to kiss him on the cheek.

"We'll see you at four. Don't be late," she said as she climbed into the cab.

"The way Uncle Judy's selling turkeys, we may be early."

They drove out of the parking lot, but at the corner of Main and Fremont Streets, Fanny jerked the truck to a stop. "Are you hungry?"

Lena had been so angry that morning that she hadn't even made coffee. "I'm starving."

.   .   .

At a window table in the Overland Hotel they were served by Alice Eaton, Fanny's first boss in Las Vegas and still the doyen of the floor staff. Sixty years old and fighting it, her hair dyed black and cut as short and perky as a Hollywood starlet, she fawned over them and sat down at the table while her regulars, most of them local merchants and bank tellers, cooled their heels and waited for Alice to take their orders. Amused, Fanny played the role of princess until her own breakfast was served, and appeased the other patrons with a rueful smile, so gracious they couldn't help but smile back.

As they finished their steak and eggs, Mr. McNulty came out of his office to pay his respects. He had long ago forgiven Fanny for stealing Hi Carter away from his kitchen when she opened her café. When the bill came, Fanny reached for her wallet, but Mr. McNulty grabbed her hand and insisted it was his treat, then begged her to taste the pumpkin pudding he'd concocted for Thanksgiving, while his eyes lingered on the starched V of her blouse.

They each had a helping of the pudding, and Fanny spooned some sugar into another cup of coffee.

"How's your engineer?"

Lena was glad Fanny no longer prodded her to see other men. Although Fanny found Filius Poe as exciting as the Methodist clergymen on her mother's side of the family, she also saw how fond he was of Lena and Burr, and had come to accept him as a benevolent presence, warm-blooded or not.

"He's fine."

Fanny scooped up the last of her pumpkin pudding. "You could've done worse."

Lena smiled. "If I was doing anything at all. How's your cop?"

"He's got a little lighter handshake, but if it doesn't bother him, it doesn't bother me."

Archie Swerling was lucky. Bud Bodell, the chief of police, had found him on the sidewalk fifteen minutes after the attack, wrapped his bloody hand in his scarf and drove him straight to the Boulder City Hospital, siren howling. Archie had lost a lot of blood, and during the three days he remained under watch, Fanny never left his side. She held his mutilated left hand while he lay in bed, unconscious. On the second night, she was able to fall asleep in the chair next to him. When the nurse came in at midnight, Fanny blinked awake and thought his bandaged hand was a big wad of cotton candy. He regained consciousness the next day, smiled at Fanny, and she rushed into the hallway to cry. When Bud came in to check on Archie, he saw Fanny weeping uncontrollably and was sure that the sergeant had died.

Archie recovered quickly. He was a little different, more of a man and less of a boy, but he still kept his sense of humor.

"Doctor's going to take his bandage off next week. Said he made sure to leave just as much of a stump as the other pinky so Archie won't have to be lopsided and look too peculiar. Archie said he just wanted the doctor to leave enough so he could give his ears a good cleaning."

When they were ready to go, Fanny ducked into the kitchen to say good-bye to Alice, and Lena struggled into her old coat as she walked toward the door, wondering if Burr was up yet and if the sniffles he had yesterday had turned into a cold. She looked down as she fastened the last button, barely hanging on by a frayed thread, and nearly stumbled into someone standing just outside the front door. At first she thought it was a child, and was startled when she raised her eyes and saw Lew Beck.

It was too late to stop the words already on her tongue. "Excuse me."

He stared up at Lena and fear gripped her like a fist around the heart; she was scared because of the things she heard, because he was still here. He was with a tall, skinny man who breathed through his mouth and had a white smudge on his upper lip. They were a mismatched pair, almost comical, but Beck's dark eyes had no humor. The skinny man flipped up the collar of his jacket. "You going to let us in, lady?"

"Shut up, Jimmy."

"I'm cold and I'm hungry."

"Shut up."

Beck's eyes held on Lena. His expression began to change, and she watched in queasy fascination as he cocked his head to the right and slowly raised the corners of his mouth. Seeing his smile, Lena wanted to run.

"You. You did it." Fanny pressed alongside Lena and faced him, her cheeks splotched with anger. "You did it, didn't you?"

Her voice was loud and people in the restaurant glanced up from their plates and conversation. Some raised themselves from their seats and hovered awkwardly with strained necks. Waitresses turned to the commotion, and Mr. McNulty peeked around his office door.

"Answer me, you little coward! You hit him from behind."

Lew Beck turned to Fanny. He wanted to slam her pretty lips against his kneecap and fill her tongue with broken teeth, but held his smile and didn't say a word.

"You weasely sonofabitch."

Lena put her hand on Fanny's arm, then someone touched her back and she turned to see Mr. McNulty angling himself in front of them. He turned from Fanny to Lew Beck, his voice warbly as a frightened boy's. "Fanny. Mr. Beck. Is there a problem?"

Fanny's eyes went wide and her back stiff. She glared at Beck as if someone had just poked a finger in her spine.

"*Mister* Beck?"

Fanny shoved past them and walked furiously up the sidewalk. Lena was right behind her, careful not to touch Beck or the skinny man as she whisked by. From the corner of her eye she saw that Beck was still smiling, cryptic as a china doll.

Filius and Ray were in the backyard of his parents' house, playing with the pregnant cat his father had discovered the week before roaming the hallway outside his office in Engineering Hall. Claude had cleaned an old ashtray and given the cat some water, and the next day she was back again, mewing incessantly until he cracked the door open and let her inside. He always kept a tin of sardines in his desk drawer for a snack, and the cat made quick work of them, stretched out in a patch of sunlight on the floor and fell asleep, whiskers still fish-damp, belly extended and teats sticking out like rubber bullets. After his last class that afternoon, he locked up his office and took her home for his grandson. The bond was uncanny and instantaneous. Ray named her Ajax and she came whenever he called.

The cat was white except for a stain of black on her mouth and one black paw. Addie thought it was the ugliest cat she'd ever seen, with her fat belly and slender flanks, and she had a queer smell, like old rose water, but Ray was smitten. It was the end of May, and the family was staying in Madison until the middle of August, when Filius had to report to work on the Gibson Dam in Montana. In those ten weeks, Ray and the cat were inseparable. They slept together and played together, and Ajax wrapped herself across Ray's shoulders while he ate. When the family went sailing on Lake Mendota, the cat would wait for them on the dock behind the house—not even Ajax could keep Ray off the water that summer. On calm days, Filius would sometimes let his son take the tiller, and began teaching him how to find the wind and read the telltales on top of the main. On rainy afternoons they'd sit on the sun porch with a length of rope and tie bowlines and sheepshanks, and Filius told stories about racing his boyhood friends all the way across Lake Michigan, from Bailey's Harbor to Cecil Bay.

Toward the end of June, Ajax's naps started getting longer and she spent most of her days in Ray's bedroom, curled up in the crease of his pillow. After dinner on the first of July, Ray went upstairs and found her shivering in a damp stain that saturated the middle of his bed. While Filius and Ray sat there and watched her lick her matted and rumbling stomach, Addie went for a clean blanket and towels. The same Addie, who until that night had ignored the cat or passed dismissive judgment on her bony rump and wizened thighs, now allowed her maternal instincts to take over, and cooed to the straining animal and stroked her ears. Ten minutes later, Ajax lifted her hindquarters and the first kitten rolled onto the blanket, a barely feline shape curled inside a gelatinous ball. Ajax licked at the newborn until the face was exposed, then she licked at the nose and the eyes and the little mouth that gasped its first breath. The first kitten was gray and white. The one that arrived twenty minutes later was as black as the mark on Ajax's face. By midnight there were seven healthy kittens, safely nestled in a flannel blanket in a wooden box at the foot of Ray's bed. Later that night, Filius held Addie under the covers as she tried to figure out how many different toms were responsible for the brood: "Imagine them all fooled by that skinny old cat, with her rear end raised high on some backyard picnic table." They laughed and turned out the light, and a few minutes later heard Ray calling them. From the light in the hall they could see Ajax on Ray's bed, making her way toward him with a kitten dangling from her mouth. She lay the kitten next to the one that was already curled in his outstretched hand, an act she repeated five more times. Wide-eyed, Ray looked up at his parents, and it was an expression Filius would never forget.

"Mr. Poe?"

Filius was sitting at the kitchen table with a cup of coffee, savoring the reverie. It had been the first good memory he'd had in a year, and he wanted to hold on to it like a prayer he could repeat to himself every day for the rest of his life.

"Mr. Poe?"

Burr stood patiently in front of him, clutching one of the door frames they were building for the rabbit hutch.

"The glue's dry, Mr. Poe."

Filius had left him alone in the workshop because he'd insisted on gluing the frames together himself. Now he was running his fingers over the four corners to show Filius that the lap joints were smooth and square.

"It looks good. Do you have the right screws?"

"Are these the ones?" He opened his other hand and held out a fistful of small brass screws.

"It looks like we're ready."

Burr nodded and put the screws into his pocket. "Can I put the screws in, Mr. Poe?"

Filius felt like picking him up and holding him close, wanting to feel the press of his bones and to revive memories he hadn't yet recovered but knew were still there, buried like treasures in the sand. "Yes, of course you can."

He put his hand on the boy's shoulder and led him to where the rabbit hutch lay waiting to be put together.

Cece and Shirley sat in front of the woodstove in Miss Williams's parlor. It was a cold morning, and they wore two pair of socks and bathrobes over the white nightgowns Miss Williams always insisted on. Shirley, leaning on the arm of the couch, sneezed like a dray horse and wiped at her nose with the back of her hand. Cece walked to the window to look out at the fine dusting of snow that hung like white velvet on the antlers of the two concrete deer that stood on either side of the walk. She liked these winter mornings in the house on Third Street, the rooms smelling of wood smoke instead of pomade and homemade beer, but the dry air played havoc with Shirley's sinuses and she woke up complaining about the dark rings under her eyes and a throat itchy from the cold.

"You want me to see if I can get Miss Williams to make you some hot chocolate?" Cece asked.

"Won't be any good if I can't taste it."

"How 'bout I beat up some egg whites for your eyes?"

"No."

"You want some rock candy and lemon?"

Shirley pressed her hands against her temples and threw her head back. The mournful whine that passed between her lips sounded only slightly female.

She glanced at Cece and caught her smiling. "It ain't funny."

"It sure is." She sat back on the couch and Shirley lay her head in her lap. Cece ran her hand over her dull hair and wished she had a brush to make it shiny.

"You lucky, Cece. You don't have to worry about looking good no more. You get to sleep at night 'cause you only got one little man sneaking into your room, treating you like you some married girl. You don't got 'em climbing over you like rats, like the one I had last night. Took off his clothes and smelled so bad I was afraid to look. Then him lying there on top of me, me with my eyes closed and my mouth open so I could still breathe, and him sticking his tongue down there trying to choke me to death."

Cece laughed.

"It's true. I was spitting up pieces of the steak he had for dinner, made me sick."

Shirley sat up and sniffed until one nostril was clear. "I got him back. Minute he roll over and shut his eyes, I snatched a dollar bill out of his dirty old pants."

"Miss Williams don't like that."

"She don't mind, long as I give her fifty cents."

"You give it to her?"

"Don't give her nothin' long as she don't know to ask." She giggled, then looked her friend square in the face. "You lucky all right, Cece. Mr. Man take good care of you."

She knew Shirley was right. She didn't have to see any man but him, and he came to her almost every night. He was good to her and he was clean, and she'd stopped minding the jealous eyes of the other girls. Even Miss Williams gave her privileges, careful to stay on the sweet side of Lew Beck's girl.

Shirley lay her head back on Cece's lap and let out another moan, untamed as a cry heard in the woods. Then she turned to her, her eyes so puffy and sore she could barely keep them open.

"You gonna get me them eggs?"

He hated the snow, hated the way it blew in his eyes and made the sidewalks feel greasy when it melted into slush, then turned gray and black and filthy, poisoned by exhaust.

He pulled into the space reserved for him near the front door of the Mexico Club, parking alongside Frank Strella's brand new boat-tailed Auburn Speedster. He thought the cars looked good together, and he'd made a deal with George Lenski, a Polish kid whose father mopped floors and worked in the club's big kitchen. George came every morning before school to kick the gravel for dropped coins or lost poker chips; Lew bought him a bucket and a couple of towels and paid him ten cents a day to wash both cars, whether they needed it or not. Strella never said a word but Lew knew he appreciated the courtesy since it was the little gestures that often made the biggest impression.

The Mexico Club never closed, and the casino was lit up like it was Saturday night, even though only a few men sat at the poker tables. Days were slow, but Frank Strella always kept a small staff on duty, and Lew knew them all by name. The dealer working today was Henry Coyne, and the bartender, Perry Stubbs. Sally Dawes, the coat-check girl who also took drink orders, was sitting alone at a table reading a back issue of *New Movie Magazine* with Joan Crawford on the cover, and the two pit bosses sitting in the narrow alcoves above the casino floor, trying to stay awake, were Carl and Ernest Mann, cousins from Kansas City. Lew nodded to each of them.

Gambling had been legalized in Nevada the year before, and Frank Strella took full advantage of it. Prohibition didn't matter, because selling alcohol was a federal—not a state—offense, and casino owners paid local authorities monthly incentives to mind their own business. Most raids were conducted outside city limits, where government agents shut down the smaller establishments that sold whiskey by the gallon and were as transitory as revival meetings. In this version of frontier justice, no one got hurt except the competition.

The Strella brothers had the reputation and swagger that came straight from the western movies Lew loved as a boy; they were the outlaws he'd always admired, who held sway with cunning and guts. He met Frank's brother, Joe, only once, early that December. He kept a suite at the Fairmont Hotel in San Francisco, from which he ran a bootlegging operation out of every hidden port from San Diego to Vancouver. Joe was heavier than Frank, with rougher features and a louder voice, and he had neither his brother's patience nor his ability to smile at men he didn't respect in order to profit from dealing with them. What he did have was an iron fist and tangible results. He also had a hot temper that he exhibited in a blink, which was one reason he was driving up and down the coast of California watching cases of whiskey being unloaded from boats that smelled of old fish instead of enjoying a better life in the Nevada desert with his brother Frank.

Lew had heard the story from Mr. Jimmy. A year ago, just after the brothers had celebrated the grand opening of the Mexico Club—their picture on the front page of the *Las Vegas Age*, grinning broadly with Phil Tobin, the Nevada legislator who'd written the bill that legalized gambling—Joe got word about an impulsive young bootlegger from Tucson who was trying to undercut his business in the small bars out on the pass. Joe found the man at the Apache Hotel, dragged him out of bed and the arms of his wife, pulled him across Fremont Street in his pajamas and pistol-whipped him right in front of the police station. It took six officers to pull him off, and six weeks and sixty stitches before the liquor salesman was strong enough to be escorted onto an outbound train. Joe left the morning after the beating, but the men who owed him money still paid Frank every penny—just in case. Joe Strella scared even the hardest men, and when he shook Lew's hand that morning in December it was as if a torch was being passed. It was Lew Beck's turn now, and he was glad to do it.

When he entered the office, Frank was standing in front of the full-length mirror behind his desk, buttoning the white shirt he'd just put on, a maroon tie patterned with little deer hanging loose around his neck. The door to his walk-in closet was open, and Lew could see dozens of suits and shelves of shirts and ties and a rack filled with cowboy boots Frank ordered from a boot maker in Mexicali. Vain and fastidious, he changed into a new suit every morning even though he spent most of the day alone in his office, and again at six o'clock, when the club started to fill and he could outshine the patrons.

Lew watched him comb his hair and pick out a pair of cuff links. Then he chose a pair of black boots with a modest white tooling on the toe and sides, and sat down at his desk to put them on.

"Perry's got a case of champagne out front. Mickey Bogg's wife had a kid, and I want you to drop it off at his house."

"Where's Jimmy?"

"Up in Reno."

Lew frowned. He wasn't the errand boy. "Can't it wait till Jimmy's back?"

"No."

"You want me to collect anything while I'm there?"

Frank shook his head. He stood up to let his pants shake down over his boots and then sat down again. "Let him have his day. The rest can wait."

"Anything else?"

"Not now, Lew. Come back tonight and we'll see."

By the time he got to the parking lot, Perry had already loaded the case of champagne into the backseat of his Lincoln and George was going over the windshield with a damp cloth. A big boy, fifteen years old and already over six feet, George wore thick glasses and the same turtleneck sweater every day, the collar stretched and the elbows worn out. He looked up from the car and grinned. "Mr. Beck—look what I found!"

George loped around the Lincoln and towered over Lew as he pulled a handkerchief out of his back pocket and unfolded it. "See?"

He held out a woman's stickpin, which Lew lifted up and turned in the light. The pin was made of white gold, with a fleur-de-lis of tiny diamonds and a single sapphire.

"I found it right by the edge of the parking lot, sticking straight up like it growed there."

"What do you plan to do with it, George?"

"Sell it, I guess."

"How much?"

He squinted at Lew through his glasses. "Jeez, I don't know. Ten bucks sound fair?"

Lew put his hand in his pocket and pulled the top bill free of his money clip. He laid it on top of George's handkerchief and closed his own hand around the pin. "Seems fair enough to me."

Lew put the diamond stickpin in his jacket and got into the car, waving at George as he pulled out of the lot and turned toward town.

It wasn't until the Lincoln was almost out of sight that George bothered to look down at the money Lew had left in his hand. It was a crisp fifty-dollar bill, and George gawked and pressed his fingers against it to keep it from floating away.

A thousand trucks a day emerged through the choking dust at the bottom of the canyon, slowed down by the weight of dry silt and gravel, lumbering forward as if part of a vast herd. Filius stood on top of the cofferdam and watched, thinking of what Scipio must have witnessed when Hannibal's army appeared before him in the valley mist, a long line of mighty Carthaginian warriors looming on the banks of the river Po.

They had started work on the upper cofferdam two weeks before, having dug down eighteen feet before reaching solid ground, just as Floyd Huntington had predicted. They had already finished the bottom level, layering it with heavier rock and boulders, and cut sleeves for the concrete reinforcements. They'd carried thousands of tons of sand and gravel from the Hemenway Wash to form the bulk of the structure. Bulldozers with long blades were spreading the fresh mixture along the top, and when they had a layer twelve inches thick it was doused with water and rolled smooth by iron-ball rollers pulled by tractors from one cliff face to the other, and then the process would start all over again. The cofferdam was already more than five stories high and almost a quarter mile wide, and the monotony of the job was relieved by the perceptible advances they made every day. The men worked through the cold weather, their faces raw from the grit and the freezing rain, their fingers dead around the sticks that maneuvered their shovel buckets. They all knew this was still preliminary, that the size of this massive coffer-dam would soon be eclipsed by the concrete monster that would fill the canyon, and after almost two years of preparation they were ready to start the job they'd come to do.

Floyd Huntington stopped and stood on the growing hump of the cofferdam, admiring the quick pace of the work. He no longer begrudged Filius his experience or his clean white shirts, and as they had a cigarette, he told Filius about an accident the day before.

"I was standing on the high road when I heard yelling, and I look over and see these two big generators swinging on a cable over the middle of the canyon, and the signalmen on either side of the cable-way were waving fists and screaming at each other, neither one hearing a goddamn thing the other's saying, they're so far apart. I know those generators must weigh fifteen tons the two of them, and that cable's sagging like a broken back. Should've sent them over one at a time, but everybody's in such a goddamn hurry around here they forget to think smart. And now the cable's stuck, and the only place those generators are going is down. Everybody knows it and stops to watch because it's gonna be one hell of a crash. Then I hear something loud as a rifle shot and that cable just pops. Generators fall like a ton of shit, and those cables are whipping through the air, making sounds like a baby crying. And I look over and see Dave Muller standing next to his Cat on the other side of the river, watching like everyone else, and one of those cables is spinning like crazy right at him. Dave doesn't know which way to jump so he just stands there

and closes his eyes and wishes he was nicer to his wife and was anywhere but here. And that cable snaps the air next to him and takes
off his ear clean as a razor, and Dave doesn't even know it, the lucky
bastard, doesn't even know he's still alive 'cause the moment before
it happened he passed out on his feet."

Floyd laughed and drew hard on his cigarette before tossing it
into the dirt. "How about you, Poe. You feel lucky?"

"Not as lucky as Muller."

"That was dumb luck, Poe. This is something else. I'll bet you
twenty bucks this cofferdam of yours is gonna to be ready for concrete by the first of the year."

Filius looked down at the handsome work boots Floyd purchased
after their last bet.

"No thanks."

"Why not?"

"Because you're right."

Burr ran outside and tossed the new kick ball Archie Swerling had
just given him high into the air. Stanley Chubb and the others gave
chase across the cold ground, but Burr caught up to the bouncing
ball first and kicked it against a tree and watched it ricochet back so
hard that Andy Corbett had to duck to keep from getting smashed
in the face.

Lena stood in the kitchen window and watched the children playing in Fanny's backyard and thought of all the times she'd stood at
her own kitchen window in Hugo and watched Burr and his friends
playing in the field behind their house, season after season, trudging
through snow bundled up like woolen dolls or running almost
naked through the summer bluestem that grew wild by the pond. A
constant blur of children, moving from yard to yard like tornadoes
that touched down briefly and danced away without doing any damage. She never thought she'd leave her kitchen window in Hugo,
that it would frame her memories of Burr's childhood as it had
framed her own. She had expected to live in her parents' house forever, with her husband and son, and Boulder City, Nevada, would
have seemed as remote to her a year ago as Timbuktu.

Fanny came in from the living room and slid another dirty ice cream bowl into a sink full of suds, and joined Lena at the window. "Want a cigarette?"

"I'd love one."

It was a Saturday afternoon, and they could lounge around in their nice dresses for a few minutes if they wanted, and clean up the party mess later. Fanny had finally broken down and hired extra help right after Thanksgiving, when it seemed that every family in town had descended on the café for turkey dinners. Fanny, Lena and Hi had closed the doors at nine o'clock, already exhausted, and spent another four hours cleaning up. By the time they turned off the lights, Lena's feet were as sore as hammered thumbs, and Fanny was so tired she had to use both hands to lock the front door. At seven o'clock the next morning she'd driven over to Avenue D and offered Emma Jellicoe the part-time job she'd been hinting at for the last six months; and when Emma realized she had the upper hand, she hedged just long enough for Fanny to offer her sister-in-law Betty Turlow the same schedule, three days a week, mostly weekends.

Before moving to Boulder City, Emma and Betty had run a sweet shop in Oil City, Pennsylvania, but when the Depression shuttered most of the businesses on their once busy street, they followed their husbands, both experienced cement finishers, to the dam project in Nevada. They still concocted sweet desserts at home for their husbands and friends—chocolate cakes and sour cream gingerbread, sand tarts and apple pot pies—but their repertoire deserved a grander stage. During the three days Lena had taken to train them, Emma and Betty had prepared confectionery treats for her to sample and took orders and cleared tables with an efficiency that needed no instruction. They made cakes to rival Hi's pies, and the best cookies that Lena had ever tasted; they worked hard and were as compatible with each other as Lena was with Fanny. After the first week, even Fanny had to admit it was nice to sleep late once in a while, and to give customers another good reason to come to her café rather than the Green Hut or Ida's or the Anderson Brothers Mess Hall at the other end of town.

The children's voices rose and fell as they followed the kick ball across the yard, and Lena wondered how much longer they could stand the December chill. Fanny poured them each a cup of coffee, and they sat at the kitchen table and stirred in cream and sugar and looked into the living room, where birthday decorations still hung over the exploded remains of presents.

The front door opened and Archie stepped in. As the women watched, he stopped at the table in the middle of the room and swiped a finger through the maple syrup glaze on the birthday cake, a gift from Emma Jellicoe, and licked it clean before grabbing a thick wedge in his bare hands.

Fanny yelled. "Everything okay, Archie?"

He already had a mouthful when he turned to her, unabashed. "Sid and Ida Clarke's at it again. Bumps and bruises, just bumps and bruises." Then, cake in hand, he walked to the living room window and watched the children playing out back.

Fanny couldn't help but grin. "I'm going to marry that man."

Lena laughed out loud and almost spilled her coffee. "What?"

"I'm going to marry him."

"When?"

"As soon as he asks me."

Fanny was still smiling, but Lena knew she was dead serious.

Archie stuck his head in the doorway, and with his mouth full of cake, it took Lena a moment to understand what he was saying.

"Filius's here."

She went quickly to the door, and saw him coming up the walk with a thin tube wrapped in green paper and capped with a bow. His pace was loose and brisk, like a man who didn't know he was being watched, and when he came up the steps and saw her, he smiled. "I'm late."

"You made it."

She held the door open with her foot and wrapped her arms around herself. As Filius stepped past her into the house, he bent his head and kissed her for the first time, lightly on the cheek. The tip of his long nose was cold against her skin, and but for that sensation, that proof of contact, she might not have known she'd been kissed at all.

He had just untied his scarf when Burr barged into the living room through the kitchen door, his face red and his ears bright.

"Mr. Poe!"

Filius turned with his jacket half off and held the wrapped tube in front of him, and Burr's eyes fixed on it as if it was a magic wand. Filius handed it to him, bow end first. "Happy Birthday."

Burr knelt on the floor to open the present, running his finger under the green paper and stripping it away in one motion. He unscrewed the cap and pulled out the two-piece bait-casting rod, then removed the Pflueger reel that Filius had taped to the end of the tube. He immediately stood up and made a casting motion, and Filius knew he'd chosen the right gift.

Burr looked up at him, beaming. "When can we go fishing?"

"When school's out, I'll take you up north. We can do some camping and fish in the morning. Do you like to camp?"

"Never done it before."

"Then we'll pack up my car with a tent and sleeping bags, and fish the Truckee River all the way from Reno to the California border."

"You and me?"

"Yes, the two of us."

Burr hugged Filius around the waist, and just as quickly broke away and dashed outside, fishing rod in hand, to show his friends.

Lena watched all this from across the room—it was a moment she wanted to appreciate without interrupting. Burr's hug didn't surprise her because he was a generous and affectionate boy. What did, though, and what she would keep with her, was Filius's reaction, how unashamedly he'd cupped his hand on her son's neck and held him close, and the fleeting look of disappointment a second later, when Burr broke free.

She sat on the couch and waited for Burr to finish brushing his teeth and come to bed. It was after eight o'clock, and she'd just finished washing all the party dishes and putting the house back in order. Fanny had helped until six o'clock, when she succumbed to curiosity and sped off with Archie to see how Emma was handling her second Saturday night in the café. No matter how many times she insisted she was "just going to poke her head in the door," Lena knew she wouldn't be able to resist putting on her apron and holding court, at least through the eight o'clock rush, and that Archie would patiently wait for her at the counter over one of Hi's lamb chop dinners.

The darkness in the living room was soft and comforting, and Lena resisted the urge to find the *California Country Hour* on the radio, and knew that if she rested her head back and shut her eyes she'd be asleep before Burr turned off the water in the bathroom. Instead, she forced herself upright and made up her son's bed on the couch. The headlights of a passing car streamed through the front window, glinting on the fishing rod leaning against the table, and she smiled.

The bathroom door opened and Burr ran across the cold floor in his bare feet. He was wearing the new maroon flannel pajamas Lena bought him for his birthday, the sharp creases in the fabric making him look stiff and fragile. He hopped under the covers, and she could feel how icy his feet were even through the blanket.

"I've got something for you." She reached beneath the couch and pulled out the present Frank had sent from Oklahoma. "It's from your father."

Burr stared down at the box propped in his lap. His father was a presence he kept tucked away in the back of his mind, to be drawn upon when needed, to remind him of the life they had before he and his mother had boarded a crowded bus and rode away from Oklahoma. Sometimes Burr thought he glimpsed his father in a store-front window or a passing car, and there was a consolation in those fuzzy sightings that came to him at different times, triggered by randomness or daydreams, by something said or seen or something longed for, something just out of reach.

"Go on. Open it."

He pulled back the wrapping paper and looked at the card taped to the plain cardboard box from Turpin's Department Store, McAlester, Oklahoma. He pulled the card out of the envelope and studied the picture of a boy on horseback that decorated the front. He opened the card slowly and saw the familiar handwriting inside—HAPPY BIRTHDAY, BOY. I'LL WRITE SOON. LOVE, DADDY—and then put the card back in the envelope. He took the top off the box and pulled out a white cowboy shirt with pearl snap buttons, just like the ones his father used to wear.

Lena watched him carefully fold the shirt back into the box and set it on the floor. He pulled the blanket to his shoulders and turned his face against the couch. Lying down behind him, Lena snuggled under the blanket as he arranged his body next to hers, pushing his backside into her stomach and folding his legs next to her own. There wasn't a lot of room on the couch, but there was enough, and they fell asleep that way, folded together, keeping each other warm.

Lew liked how the women watched him as he moved through the crowded casino, turning from their sugary cocktails and their well-dressed husbands to let their eyes glide over his face in a moment of covert dalliance. They'd sometimes hook their arms through the arms of the men they sat with, or loosely hold hands, as if to camouflage their surreptitious attraction. Lew also liked how the men stepped back as he made his rounds, as if he were some Egyptian king they were forbidden to look at but would obey without question, their voices quieting and their backs stiffening, and any of them who owed the casino money would try to disappear into the shadows rather than face Lew and his tap for payment.

That Saturday night, Oscar and Helen Wells were sitting in the dining room with two other couples. It had been nearly three weeks since Lew's morning visit, and Oscar's forehead still showed a yellow bruise. He caught Lew's eye and nodded, neither humbled nor embarrassed, having made good on his debt. But Helen Wells glared across the room at him, defiant, her pretty face rigid and flushed. Lew wanted to tell her that this expression made her right eye look smaller than her left and accentuated the deep lines over her brow, but instead he smiled and nodded politely, a courteous ambassador of the Mexico Club.

He walked to the bar, and while waiting for Perry Stubbs to draw him a beer, studied his reflection in the mirror behind the rows of bottles and straightened the broad lapels of his new suit, a gift from Frank Strella. Four weeks ago Frank had sent him on an overnight train to Los Angeles, where he'd booked him into the Knicker-bocker Hotel on Ivar Avenue and sent over his personal tailor. It was Frank's idea that Lew be properly outfitted for his various duties, wanting him to make an impression that would last beyond the imprint of his punishment, and naturally Lew obliged. The tailor, Cecil Murray, was a tall, balding man who spoke with an English accent and smelled of cigars. He took one look at Lew and knew he had a preener. Murray laid out fabric and samples, and Lew picked three double-breasted suits, all silk, in dark tones, and two single-breasted, with peaked lapels and tapered wrists, and for these Lew wanted a chocolate brown cheviot for the winter and a saxony wool Prince of Wales plaid for the spring. Within two weeks they arrived by post in Boulder City, each perfectly tailored to Lew's peculiar measurement, and tonight he was wearing his favorite. He liked the straight lines of this suit, the ventless jacket and the way it tucked at the waist, but most of all he liked the depth of the color and how it played tricks under the bright casino lights, shining black and then as vivid and iridescent a blue as a songbird's throat.

Perry pushed Lew's beer across the counter and said, "Hey, Lew. Carl wants you."

Lew's eyes swept to the platform above the casino floor, where Carl Mann raised his chin toward a table in the corner. His demeanor was indifferent, and Lew knew that nothing had happened yet, but he pulled on his cuffs and crossed the casino floor because it was his job to determine what would happen next.

One of the two men sitting at the poker table was Speed Owens. Lew didn't recognize the big man with him, but he headed toward his chair when the dealer cocked his finger in that direction. Lew could tell by the rounded bulk of his shoulders that the man was angry and defeated. Speed looked up when Lew approached the table, having already flipped his cards over. He started to smile then caught himself, and eased his chair away from the card table, assuming a slouch of such dumb timidity that you'd think he had just been rapped between the eyes. Lew surveyed the cards on the table; the dealer had a queen and an ace showing, and the big man a pair of jacks. Chips were scattered in plentiful disarray across the felt, and Speed's friend held his fingertips steady on his diminished stack as the last cards were dealt down. He slid the card toward himself and bent back the corner enough to see that he hadn't got the third jack he needed to beat the dealer's two pair, and in that instant he knew that most of the money he came with was gone, including eighty or ninety dollars riding on this hand. He knew all this without calling and slammed down a fist as huge, raw-skinned and mottled as a country ham.

Lew laid his hand firmly on his shoulder. "Game's over."

The big man twisted out of Lew's grip, rocking the table as he tried to turn.

"Goddammit." He stared at Lew over his shoulder. "Who the fuck are you?"

Lew didn't answer.

Speed leaned forward and tapped his friend on the arm. "Leave it alone, Jackie."

But the man kept staring, trying to place his face, and Lew could tell he was getting ideas, good and bad, and that his mind wasn't lively enough to calculate odds in his behavior any better than he could at cards.

"Who the—?"

"Come on, Jackie. Let's go." Speed poked him again and stood up.

Lew reached into his pocket and pulled out a handful of chips, counted out twenty dollars' worth and threw them on the table. "Pick 'em up and call it a night."

While he waited, he scanned the room. He saw Speed's girlfriend, Nancy, holding a whiskey sour, her mouth red and coarse and laughing, and other gamblers busy with their own follies, and the Wells party heading toward the front door. He saw all the other customers in the Mexico Club engaged in the lightness of the hour, paying no attention to this quiet exchange, and that was as it should be.

He turned back to the card table. "Take him out of here, Speed. Don't make me do it."

He waited long enough to see the pride and belligerence on Jackie's big face settle into contrite folds that settled over his collar, then glanced at Speed and walked away. He signaled to Carl Mann that everything was all right, and let Perry draw him another beer to replace the one that had gone flat. He enjoyed this work and the ease in which he held prominence on the casino floor. He knew his reputation was embellished by the men he worked for, gilded and

stroked into taller tales about exploits in Los Angeles and the western states, stories of violence and mayhem, not all of them true,
none of them as bad as the things that were. But Lew didn't care. He
was comfortable in this world where truth and lies were inter-
changeable, where men were judged by the severity of their actions,
where some of them understood the power of secrets and whispered
threats, without necessarily understanding themselves.

Filius stood in the front window of his small brick house, drinking
his first cup of coffee. It was Christmas morning, and there were
trees shining in the windows of the Baileys and the Youngs and the
Lowrys, small blackjack pines cut by Sammy Griggs and sold behind
Reclamation Headquarters at ten cents a foot. Now decorated with
strands of tinsel and multicolored glass balls, they sparkled in the
early morning sunlight. A crèche was set up in front of the Good-
enoughs' house, and one of the kings had fallen facedown on the
hard ground, his plaster feet broken from traveling eight hundred
miles in the back of a government truck. There was smoke coming
out of all the chimneys up and down Denver Street, and if Filius
ignored the red-tiled roofs and the arched Spanish doorways, he
could have been looking at any street in the suburban Midwest,
from Prairie Village to Oak Park.

   He turned around and checked his own fire. He'd lit one every
chance he had that winter, feeding the flames with twisted pieces of
mesquite he collected around the dam site. He loved the scent of the
wood, so different from the oak he burned in Wisconsin and Illinois, and on the rare nights he was home long enough for a meal, he
cooked steaks or veal chops in a cast-iron grill over the fire, season-
ing with just salt and pepper and the smoke of that fragrant wood.

   There were Christmas cards and a few gifts on the mantel. Frank
Crowe had sent over two bottles of Overholt rye the day before, and
Floyd Huntington had given him a bottle of Old Comet sour mash
from the case his brother-in-law shipped him from Louisville, Kentucky, in a crate marked *Tools*. Floyd had bought the bourbon with
the bets he'd collected from Filius and Walker Young, and was

generous with his holiday cheer. Filius's parents sent him a big box that included the portable Victor Victrola he'd bought ten years ago, and about two dozen of his old records; these included the Vladimir de Pachmann interpretations of Chopin études that Addie loved so much, a selection of Bert Williams's ragtime records, and a copy of the novelty song, Banjo Buddy's "Oh, Doris," that they used to play over and over again for Ray when he was a little boy. At the bottom of the box, wrapped separately in tissue and ribbons, was a small gift from his mother, and he could tell what it was the second he picked it up. When he was four, Ray had found two pine cones on a summer trip to the Wisconsin Dells, and saved them until Christmas, when he painted them red and white to look like Santa Claus, with glued-on black buttons and little hats that Addie had cut out of felt, and they'd hung these decorations every Christmas. Filius didn't have a tree this year—he couldn't face that yet—and his only other ornament was a tin star Burr had made for him in school, now hanging in his front window above a small table where he displayed Ray's Santa pine cones.

He was still standing at the window when Lena and Burr arrived in Uncle Judy's truck to pick up the rabbit hutch that was waiting on the screened porch, Burr having applied the last coat of white paint three days ago. Filius pulled a scarf around his neck and went outside to greet them. He could see through the truck windows that they were watching him and smiling, but they made no effort to get out of the cab. Burr ducked out of sight for a moment, then the door swung open and a puppy leapt to the ground on its stumpy, crooked little legs, and Filius knelt just in time for the little basset hound to jump into his arms, his tail curved and beating against his arm.

"Merry Christmas, Mr. Poe!"

Filius couldn't help but laugh. He'd seen a basset hound only once before, the summer Addie was pregnant, when a friend of theirs who trained dogs showed him the proud little male he was working with for a client in Milwaukee. It was a new breed to the States, he explained, hardy and loyal, and should be good for pheasant once he "got the French" out of it.

Filius put the puppy down on the sidewalk and scratched the folds of loose skin on the back of his neck. He looked up at Lena and couldn't stop smiling.

Burr knelt down and played with the puppy's big ears. "Do you like him, Mr. Poe?"

"He's a fine little dog."

"What are you going to call him?"

He'd known the moment he saw the dog. He would continue in the tradition started by his grandfather, a religious man who'd named all his hunting dogs after Old Testament prophets. His son followed suit, and named his pointers Jeremiah and Jonas, the latter being the father of Amos, the dog Filius had loved as a boy. This new one would be Joel, shortened to fit this truncated puppy squatting in front of him. "We'll call him Joe."

"That's a funny name for a dog," Burr said.

"He's a funny dog."

He gave away watches that Christmas. He picked out his best Benrus for Frank Strella—a gold face and tiny diamonds—and lesser ones for Mr. Jimmy and his favorites at the Mexico Club. He gave watches to Shirley and Miss Williams, and he gave them to Speed Owens and Lupa Valdez, the Mexican girl who did his laundry twice a week. When he was done, he still had twenty watches left in the duffel he kept under Cece's bed, but she didn't get one. On Christmas Eve he handed her a jewelry box holding the diamond-and-sapphire stickpin, and she was so excited that she jumped out of bed naked and ran through the crowded parlor to barge into Shirley's room, interrupting her business to show off.

Early Christmas morning, he drove to the Mexico Club and parked next to Frank's Speedster. George Lenski was shuffling through the parking lot, prospecting for baubles and change, and didn't notice Lew. He was wearing a new wool cap with earflaps, and over his turtleneck sweater, a grease-stained apron.

It was a cold morning, and Lew pulled his overcoat tight as he walked over. "What's with the apron, George?"

George crooked his neck, smiled, and raised an earflap so he could hear better. "I'm working in the kitchen now, Mr. Beck. With my dad."

"Since when?"

"From here on out. No school no more for me."

His smile grew wider, and Lew could see a fresh cut at the corner of his mouth. "We both work for the Mexico Club, huh, Mr. Beck?"

Lew nodded, pulled a narrow box from his pocket that Cece had wrapped in reindeer-covered paper and handed it to him. "Merry Christmas, George."

George ripped the paper off the box and took out a new Longines with bold numbers on its porcelain dial. He ogled it and his mouth went wide again. "Thanks, Mr. Beck. I never had a watch before."

"So, put it on."

He pushed up his sweater sleeve and carefully fastened the black leather strap. When he held up his arm and twirled his skinny wrist in the sunlight, Lew saw the kitchen door open and Victor Lenski step outside. A stocky man with a lipless scowl and thick black hair, he was dragging two garbage cans, and when he spotted George he slammed them hard on the pavement. George ducked and spun around as the cans crashed and spilled gnawed bones and oyster shells and a puddle of filth at his father's feet.

"Goddammit it, George!"

His son loped toward him with his head tucked in regret. He stood cowering and foolish, one earflap still up, as his father kicked a clump of wilted vegetables against his leg.

"What the fuck's the matter with you? Clean up this goddamn mess!"

"Okay, Dad."

He bent down to pick up the carcass of a chicken, and Victor punched him in the side of the head. George tried to catch himself, but his hand slid through the oily reek of oven waste and he fell on his hip, his legs shooting out so far and fast that his father had to jump out of the way.

"Stupid kid. Pick up this shit and get back to work."

He stormed back into the kitchen, slamming the door behind him. George set one of the garbage cans upright, rubbed the side of his throbbing head, and got down on his hands and knees to gather up the trash.

Lew stood in the parking lot and watched, transfixed by this tangled bond of hatred and love. He had experienced it himself, and knew that this need to demonstrate power and inflict pain was a misery that the innocent and the culpable would have to endure, and that now it was George's turn to suffer. Even though he wanted to take Victor Lenski's head in his hands and pound it into the pavement until his skull cracked and oozed like warm jelly through his fingers, Lew knew it wouldn't help. He was still haunted by his own father; and if Isadore was still alive, Lew knew he was haunted too.

Fanny had been avoiding Sims Ely ever since he reminded her, right before Thanksgiving, of her promise to marry a Boulder City man within the year or forfeit the lease on her house. The year, he noted, was up in March. Fanny confessed she didn't know if he was serious or just flirting, and Lena had laughed. "That's the problem, Fanny. You always flirt back."

When he'd come in for lunch the day after Christmas, Fanny asked Lena to take his order. As she poured Ely a cup of coffee, she studied his sharp jawline, and high, Puritanical cheekbones. He was a fussy man, with his belted tweed sport coats and once-a-week haircuts, but Lena couldn't help but admire the force of his virtuous determination, no matter how blunt or didactic it was. "Can I get you anything else, Mr. Ely?"

He turned from the window, eyes darting from Lena to Fanny, whose face disappeared at once from the order window.

"You can tell your friend I want to see a marriage license."

There was not the slightest trace of humor in his request.

Lena nodded and held back a smile until she stepped into the kitchen where Fanny was stirring the big pot of oxtail stew for the dinner special.

"That beaky old thing is trying to catch me. He ought to sit back and mind his own business or find someplace else to eat."

"I think he likes your cooking, Fanny."

"I saw his tight little mouth moving, Lena. What did that nosy old fool say?"

"He said that if Archie Swerling doesn't propose soon, he'll do it himself."

Fanny looked stricken, then they both burst out laughing, and still were when Sims Ely placed a dollar bill by the cash register and walked out the door.

Emma Jellicoe arrived an hour later, and Lena got ready to go home. She'd promised to take Burr to the matinee at the Boulder Theatre, Bela Lugosi in *Chandu the Magician*. She loved having these random hours off and the extra time to spend with her son, even if it meant watching a horror film. Afterward, they'd come back to the café for hamburgers and a slice of pie, and then stop by Filius's house to check on Joe.

The puppy had been Burr's idea, a notion he'd carried around since October when Filius had shown him a snapshot of himself as a boy, standing on a wide lawn by a lake with a young English pointer sitting at his side. Finding a puppy in Las Vegas wasn't easy this time of year, but Archie had a friend in Glendale, Arizona, who got the little basset to them in time. Lena had never seen such a ridiculous dog, stretched and chubby as a cartoon, but she knew it was the right one. While Burr played with the puppy that Christmas morning, she'd helped Filius load the rabbit hutch into Uncle Judy's pickup truck. She offered to drop by that evening to walk the dog, and told him that she would do it anytime he was working late at the dam site or needed her help.

She had been surprised when he handed her a key, and was still surprised when she put on her coat in the back room of the café and felt the key in her pocket. Smiling, she pushed through the kitchen door and went to pick up her son.

He made his own schedule and like most of the engineers, especially the single ones, staggered his hours so he could stay on top of his various and ever-changing crews. He quickly eliminated the idlers and rounders who caused delays or consternation, and established a rapport with the men who remained. He'd learned to do this more easily over the years, with an aloofness that came naturally and an informality that did not.

The earthen bulk of the cofferdam rose almost a hundred feet from the riverbed, the top cut and smoothed into a plateau. Filius admired the brutal mass of it, the long sweep of the downstream slope and the shorter, blunter upstream slope that would be paved and strengthened with concrete before the water level rose in the spring. Its lines were as thick and primitive as the great tank dams constructed in Ceylon four hundred years ago, and just as enduring. That was one of the things Filius most appreciated about dam building, the agelessness of design that only advancements in materials could improve on. He shivered in the late December bluster, pulling his scarf tight around his neck, and squinted in the headlights of the endless flow of trucks that drove along the top of the dam, stopping only long enough to dump their tons of crushed rock down either slope, the sound of tumbling scree loud as a driving rain.

It was two o'clock in the morning and he'd been at the dam since noon, a long, cold stretch that would end only when Sammy Hayes or Speed Owens came back from their coffee break to relieve him. He wanted to go home and check on Joe, even though he was certain the puppy was fast asleep in front of the fireplace, curled up in the bed of old blankets and pillows he'd made before he left. When Ray was growing up, they moved around too much to think about getting a dog, but the summer before last, as they sailed into their vacation on Lake Michigan, he and Addie talked about finding a puppy once the family settled in Boulder City. They'd be together there for at least five years, the longest stretch of time since Ray was born, and it had occurred to each of them, gazing over the water, that their son would be a teenager by the time the dam was finished.

Filius smiled. It would have been a good match, Ray and Joe, and the little dog would've turned Addie pink with laughter. And then he thought of Burr and the puppy romping on his lawn that Christmas morning, and the look of astonishment on Lena's face when he'd handed her his key, and his own eagerness to accept her kindness.

Turning his back to the bitter wind, he considered his new responsibilities. He had a puppy to train and a woman and boy who he wanted to see, and he would arrange his shifts so he could spend more time at home and do what was necessary to accommodate them all.

. . .

They left Las Vegas at six o'clock in the morning, under a frozen black sky spangled with stars. Lew's leather gloves were lined with squirrel fur, but his fingertips still felt numb on the steering wheel. Cece and Shirley sat beside him on the front seat, bundled up like Russian peasants, only their eyes showing above their wrapped scarves, their hands stuffed deep into the pockets of their heavy coats. Too cold to talk, they sat and watched the sun rise and the stars fade over the granite peaks of the Ivanpah Mountains as they sped across Nevada toward California.

When Lew had planned this New Year's Eve trip to Los Angeles with Cece, it was supposed to be just the two of them, but she couldn't help bragging about it to Shirley, who was so unsettled that she took to her bed and put on such a teary act of grievous abandonment that he broke down and agreed to take her along. This meant filling Miss Williams's palm with enough ten-dollar bills to satisfy the projected loss of earnings on her biggest night of the year. Frank Strella had made noises, too, until Lew suggested that he simply not tell anyone he was gone, and let those who tried to take advantage of his absence know that he'd be back.

Highway 91 was empty except for a few farm trucks and buses, and no one commented on the dusting of snow that covered the Shadow Mountains to the north. When the morning sun came up, it bathed the iron hills in shades of red and violet, and cast a broad yellow band of light across the Mojave. Groves of yucca trees were scattered across the desert, their spindly limbs raised like a miserable army in the act of surrendering. Lew didn't stop until they reached Baker at nine o'clock. The sun by now was high and bright enough to have warmed them up, and Cece and Shirley began tossing scarves and coats into the backseat. The boy who shuffled out of the garage at Milo's Texaco to fill up the Lincoln wore a long blanket wrapped Navajo-style across his shoulders, and gawked at the two Negro girls in the front seat as he wiped the dust off the windshield, spitting on a stubborn splat of road grease with more passion than was necessary. When Lew held out a dime as a tip, the boy muttered and walked away, and Lew fired the coin at the back of his neck. The boy rubbed the sting and somehow knew better than to turn around until Lew climbed back in the car and drove off.

The girls hadn't noticed a thing, too busy playing with the dial on the car radio, trying to pick up something other than static and the screech of faraway voices. Just outside of Barstow, they finally picked up some music stations, flipping back and forth between the shout-and-call of the Reverend Johnny Sampson and his Sermonettes and a San Bernardino broadcast featuring Bob Wills and his Alladin Laddies. At a family restaurant in Victorville, Lew went in by himself and brought back a sack of roast beef sandwiches, potato salad and bottles of cream soda, then they drove across the railroad tracks into the old part of town and ate their lunch in a blighted apple orchard near the Mojave River, where Cece and Shirley ran through the cold water in their bare feet. Three Superior Talking Pictures trucks were parked downstream, and one of the drivers told Lew they were filming a new Wally Wales western. The girls peeked around the trucks, trying to get a look at one of the stars, but all they saw were a couple of rangy horses and some cowboys passing around a glass flask.

Lew picked up Route 66 and drove over the Cajon Pass. The temperature dropped again, and the girls climbed into the backseat with their coats on, falling asleep with their feet tucked under each other's chins. He switched off the radio and drove in silence through the conifer-covered slopes and down into the valley where citrus groves bordered the highway from San Bernardino to Fontana. The girls didn't wake up when he stopped for gasoline in Azusa. Then he crossed the foothills of the San Gabriel Mountains and drove into Pasadena, where he pulled over at an ice cream store on El Molino Street and bought chocolate cones for Cece and Shirley, who licked hungrily as he took Figueroa south into downtown Los Angeles. Neither one of them had ever been to Los Angeles before, and they looked everywhere at once as he picked up Main Street and drove past the Hall of Records and pointed out the eagle on top of the tower of the Los Angeles Times Building, the Million Dollar Theatre on Broadway and the great Cathedral of Saint Vibiana at Second Street, where they'd craned their necks to look up at the cut-stone façade and the statues of Saint John and Saint Mark that stood in second-story grottoes, both figures black as African princes. When he turned onto Central Avenue and stopped in front of the Dunbar Hotel, they had been on the road for nine hours.

. . .

Lena would be glad when the holidays were over. It felt as if she'd been serving nothing but turkey and ham since Thanksgiving, and she began to hate the smell of roasted fowl and pork butts. It must have been worse for Hi, who lived in back of the kitchen, the walls of his room rank with the grease of his labor, but he didn't seem to mind, moving from oven to oven, pulling out one brown bird after another, juicy and crisp-skinned from their hourly baste, and the glazed hams as lustrous as if dipped in amber resin.

After getting Cece and Shirley settled in the hotel, Lew headed north on Hill Street and kept on going. Although he'd been behind the wheel since dawn and had no particular destination, it was a perfect day for a drive, the air brisk and the blue sky hanging over the bitten creases of the San Gabriel Mountains like a silk curtain. With a few hours to waste while the girls rested and changed clothes, he thought he might ramble through the Hollywood Hills where he once worked construction, or drive out on Mission to see if any of the old alligators he used to pelt with rancid meat were still alive. He got as far as the traffic light at Sunset, where he glanced in his rearview mirror and had a view of the downtown skyline almost identical to the one from his house in Boyle Heights, and it brought back memories that seemed cobbled together from another boy's life. Long gone were those days when his father hoisted him to his shoulders for the sheer pleasure it gave them, his mother hiding her eyes and laughing as they twirled about in a human storm. The days of sleeping like a cat in the window of Beckman's Kosher Meats, anesthetized by the smell of coconut macaroons and the lullaby of Yiddish folktales. The Sunday afternoons when the family traveled across the First Street Bridge, holding hands, venturing into Los Angeles for a movie or a picnic at Griffith Park. He no longer trusted those few, fleeting moments of his childhood joy, and knew that someday he'd blink and they would be gone forever, replaced by truths darker and harsher. Sitting at the light on Sunset Boulevard, he remembered his last glimpses of his parents: his mother rocking in the front room of the house on Clarence Street, the look on his father's face when his fingers snapped like candy canes. By the time the light changed, he remembered why he escaped Los Angeles in the first place.

Instead of driving into the Hollywood Hills, he took a left onto Sunset and followed it to the Pacific Coast Highway, where he turned around in the parking lot of a hot dog stand, ignored the great red ball dissolving into the ocean and drove back downtown, the time and sights lost to him. Looking straight ahead, thinking only of the bad things that had happened here, he finally snapped out of it when a cop blew his whistle and directed cars around a broken traffic light at Alameda. By now it was dark, and after the cop waved him on, he drove up Spring Street, where he found himself in a second-floor pool hall called Florian's on the fringes of Chinatown. It was a rough place, crowded with sad men who would celebrate the new year in a stupor, but he had the sergeant's pistol in his overcoat and didn't care if he had to use it. An old man brought him homemade beer that tasted like sour milk, and he drank it slowly. No one bothered him. No one even looked at him. At seven o'clock he went down to his car, slipped the pistol into the glove box and drove back to Central Avenue.

The café had been full since noon, and even with Emma and Betty on duty there never seemed to be enough hands. Betty spent most of the day baking tins of fresh biscuits, and Emma helped Hi run the kitchen as Lena and Fanny ran back and forth with fresh orders and dirty plates. By six o'clock Lena's feet felt as if they'd melted into her shoes, and she consoled herself with the knowledge that Fanny would lock the doors at eight so everybody could get ready to go to the New Year's Eve dance that Six Companies was throwing at the Recreation Hall.

The crowd began to thin out, and Lena wiped down a few tables for the last time. She even took a minute to sit with Tony and Mary Colleen, who were already dressed for the dance. They had coffee and talked about their children, all of whom had been herded over to the Chubbs' house, where Stanley's older sister was going to watch them and Burr was going to spend the night. As Hi sliced his last ham of the year, Lena could see how tired he was. He sat down in the low chair he used to peel vegetables, dropped his arms to his side, his chin to his chest, and fell fast asleep. At ten minutes to eight, the last customer finally gone, bright lights suddenly flickered in the front window, and she saw Bud Bodell's police car screech up to the curb.

Fanny was standing behind the cash register counting bills when Archie rushed inside, Bud waiting behind him in the open doorway.

Fanny looked up. "You're too late for supper, boys."

Archie leaned over the counter and kissed her on the lips. "There's a fracas over at the Eliot house. Ed Carter said he saw bric-a-brac and ladies' shoes flying out the windows, so Bud and me are going over there to settle them down. But you know how those two pitch fits. I'm going to be late, Fanny."

"Don't worry about it. I'm not even dressed yet."

"Could be ten o'clock. Could be later."

"Pick me up at home."

He kissed her again and headed for the door. Lena and Fanny walked to the window in time to see the police car speed away. The café was suddenly quiet except for the clattering of pans in the kitchen.

"You want to help me clean up, Lena?"

"Sure. The only thing I'm doing tonight is walking a dog."

Then Fanny smiled back at her, hung the CLOSED sign in the window, and the women went to work.

In the lobby of the Dunbar Hotel, he sat waiting on a plush velvet couch, smoking a cigarette, watching the elevators open and close, ignoring the hostile glances of the finely dressed Negroes who walked past, the women in backless dresses that clung to their shiny skin, the men dapper as English counts. A particularly slim man stepped out of the elevator alone and looked at him with such disdain that his left eyebrow rose and seemed to break in two; he wore a tuxedo and had a fey stripe of a mustache over his lip and brilliantine hair, and Lew took him to be a musician in the orchestra playing next door at Club Alabama. The man flounced over to the front desk and confronted the Negro clerk, pointing in Lew's direction, too highborn and proper to even look at him. He raised his voice just loud enough for Lew to hear, and kept up his indignant demands until the clerk put his palms together and left his post. The clerk was as old as Lew's father, a portly man in a black suit and bow tie, and he came toward Lew sideways and unsure of himself. He stopped about twelve feet in front of the velvet couch and made noises in his throat. When Lew looked up, he put his hands back in a prayerful position and cut his eyes toward the door. "You got someplace else you want to be, mister?"

"No. I don't."

Lew stayed where he was until Cece and Shirley stepped out of the elevator. Cece was wearing the dress he'd paid Cecil Murray to find for her—an ivory silk chiffon cut high at the neck and low at the back and fastened up the side with glass buttons. As she whirled for him the dress chased her, holding tight to the lines of her young body and showing off the flawless polish of her skin. Shirley wore a long, two-piece pink rayon dress, the top tied island-style just below her breasts. Pretty and sweet and sure of themselves, they ran to Lew like schoolgirls, each taking one of his arms. Lew wished for a moment that the slick musician was still here to see it, but instead he settled for the sorry eyes of the old clerk.

Outside, Cece and Shirley reluctantly put on their coats to walk the few blocks to Babe Rickey's. The club was loud and steamy, and they stayed long enough to have champagne and oysters at a round table near the bar, listening to a few numbers from the trio playing in back of the room. Lew watched the Negroes from Central Avenue mix with the well-dressed whites who drove downtown from Hancock Park or Brentwood. They danced together on the crowded floor in front of the stage, elbows and backsides colliding in sly contact, everyone carried away by the uncomplicated rhythm and wail of the banjo, trombone and saxophone.

It was the same at Club Congo, where they were led to a table above the dance floor that he'd reserved two weeks before. No one cared he was with two Negro women, or even looked twice. Paul Howard and his Quality Serenaders were the headliners, playing music full of heat and implications, and Lew ordered a bottle of champagne and lobster thermidor for everyone, even though Cece ate nothing but rolls and butter and Shirley picked apart their lobsters like she was at a backyard crayfish boil. It was their night, and he enjoyed their pleasure. When he refused to dance they went onto the dance floor with each other, slinking and laughing as the orchestra played "The Harlem Shuffle" and "My Baby Knows How." They danced for hours with men who'd watched them like coyotes from the sidelines, until they were certain the girls were alone and it was safe to slide between them without fear of thrown punches or worse. Cece and Shirley were flirtatious and accommodating, and the men smiled and danced close, subtle as pickpockets, letting their hands caress damp waists and their fingers trace breasts and nipples. Lew took all this in from above, waiting prideful as a lord for the girls to come back to him and drink cold champagne from the second bottle he'd ordered. At midnight the bandleader counted down the new year, and streamers sprayed from the ceiling and everyone applauded and cheered. As the lights dimmed and the band played a jazzy "Auld Lang Syne," Lew kissed Cece and put his hand where other men's weren't allowed. He even kissed Shirley before the lights came back on, and didn't turn his face when she slipped her tongue between his teeth. They ate chocolate cake with brandy sauce for dessert, then Cece and Shirley danced half drunk to the Serenaders' encore, "California Swing."

It was twelve-thirty when they went back to the hotel for the Lincoln. Shirley soon passed out in the back seat, and Cece was asleep with her head in Lew's lap, just as he'd imagined. He headed east on Route 66, settling in for the long drive back to Las Vegas.

Joe began howling even before Lena slipped the key into the lock on the front door, and when she stepped inside and turned on the light he came bounding out of the kitchen and popped up on his sturdy back legs to do the funny little jig that always ended with a squat and a pee. Lena was getting used to this odd performance and the premature discharge that was its finale. Filius told her this would stop once Joe settled down and learned the rules of the house; she knew this was true, and that she'd miss these little greetings. She got on her knees and rubbed his velvety earflaps, and when he flipped over to present his spotted little belly she rubbed that, too. Joe was easily satisfied, and when he yawned in her face she got up to clean his mess and stoke the dying fire.

She laid kindling and mesquite on the grate, fanning the fire until the flames crackled and roared up the flue. She breathed in the rich scent of the wood, feeling the heat on her legs, and saw Filius's note on the mantel, asking her to go into his office to read the papers he left on his drafting table.

There were thirty letters in a box, written in weekly intervals, and in the middle of the first one she picked up Lena saw her name sticking out like a sudden bold stroke in the otherwise orderly and comprehensive spill of words. She sat at the desk and went through them in order, starting with those written in June, and ending with one written at the end of December. The letters provided a chronicle of lives, his and Addie's, but also his and hers, and from a vantage not her own. In the last hour of the old year, she read about the impression she made and the power she held, and the complications of the relationship they both wanted. She read about her son and the feelings he stirred up, unaware that he could lay open such conflicted emotions in anyone other than herself. She read about the daily life at the dam, the mechanics of it all and the contrary natures of men she'd never met. She read about things she knew and things she was glad to find out. And she read about him. All of this in letters unsent, addressed to a woman he loved who was no longer there.

"The concrete's freezing, Mr. Poe."

Filius was sitting with Walker Young in the construction shed, going over plans for the pipe cooling system that would run through the dam, when Speed Owens came in with the news. Filius jumped in the truck with him and raced wild to the upstream face of the cofferdam, following the glare of the huge arc lights that blasted the canyon walls a stark white. Speed parked by the towering dragline on top of the ridge, and both men skittered down the rocky bank to where the first strips of concrete were being poured on the Arizona side. Sammy Hayes, the concrete boss, was kneeling in front of a form already filled with mix, running a wooden float along the top, trying to smooth it out. Filius could tell the concrete wasn't giving the way it should, even before Sammy shook his head.

"It's too damn hard, Mr. Poe."

Filius turned to Speed and the two other men standing around. "Get every barrel you can, at least a dozen of them. Fill them with scrap wood and keep them burning all night—and if you can't find enough scrap, bust apart the construction shed. Go."

Only when the men ran off did Filius realize how cold it was. There had been colder nights in the past month, but they were pouring concrete now, and if it froze they might just as well be pouring sand. He looked up the face of the cofferdam, the entire length of it ribbed with concrete forms sixteen feet wide. They had started pouring slightly ahead of Floyd Huntington's prediction, and for a fleeting moment Filius wished he'd taken the bet.

Within ten minutes, Speed and the crew had gathered twenty empty drums and lined them along the section that was being poured. Perlie Trimble and Jack Campbell were breaking boards with axes and hammers while the others stuffed the drums. Sammy poured gasoline into each drum, and when he dropped in a match the wood went up in a whoosh of flames. The crew kept the fires burning; in a half hour the frost crystals had melted from the floaters, and in an hour the concrete was warm enough for Sammy to call the finishers back to work.

Filius stood on the ridge next to the dragline and watched the long arm swing over the cofferdam and lower the next big bucket of concrete into place.

Floyd Huntington walked up next to him, looking down at the burning drums that lined the cofferdam from top to bottom, the black smoke barely wavering in the still air. "Looks like you're having a goddamn party."

"No parties on my shift, Floyd."

Floyd grinned and pulled a pint bottle from the buffalo-plaid coat he wore in winter, so old that its sheepskin lining was worn down to hide. He took a long sip and handed the sour mash to Filius. "Happy New Year, Mr. Poe."

. . .

She finished the letters and put some more wood on the fire, then walked through the dark house with the dog at her feet, and poured a glass of scotch from the bottle on the mantel. She bundled up in her coat and took Joe outside, where she smoked a cigarette and sipped the whiskey while he prowled around the side yard. Back inside, she sat at the desk to read the letters again, the dog curled up next to her on the floor, backside resting against her foot. She didn't hear Filius come in half an hour later, but after a while she sensed him standing in the doorway behind her. She didn't know how long he'd been watching her, and she didn't care. She held the letters in her hand, and when she turned around, he smiled gently.

"I could tell her everything."

It had broken his heart, the life he lived, and she knew that was something they would have to learn to share.

Most of the gas stations on the highway were closed for the holiday, and Lew stopped with half tanks in Victorville and Barstow so he wouldn't come up empty somewhere else. Only a few cars were on the road, and the darkness seemed endless, black pasted against black. He passed a traffic accident about twenty miles east of Barstow, the headlights of the police car and ambulance pinned on a Dodge sedan that had flipped onto its back, the windows shattered and the road strewn with broken glass; the car looked empty, but he was sure it wasn't. Just outside of Baker, he noticed a faint glow on the horizon. As he got closer he saw a pair of Richfield gasoline pumps in front of a small garage attached to a diner called Jilly's, the little enterprise illuminated like some seaside park by strands of naked lightbulbs suspended overhead. Lew pulled off the highway and parked in front of the pumps. A man in the window of the diner waved, and Lew waved back. Cece and Shirley were still asleep under their coats, and he left the car quietly so as not to wake them. He felt the cold as soon as he stepped outside, and he walked quickly past the garage and wobbly stack of bald tires outside the open bay.

The diner was a whitewashed building with red-and-white striped awnings over the front windows, and the acrid trace of an old grease fire greeted him as he opened the door.

The counterman, who'd waved at Lew, now smiled, showing a single dimple. "What can we do for you, mister?"

"Gas and coffee."

"Comin' up."

He turned to pour a cup, and a tall hunchback dressed in coveralls and a cardigan sweater took another sip of his own coffee before standing up.

"Want me to fill it up?"

Lew nodded and the hunchback winked, friendly as the counterman, pulling a cap out of his back pocket as he shuffled to the door. Lew took the stool next to the one he'd vacated, and could smell the fumes of whiskey drifting up from his empty cup.

The counterman slid a fresh cup and a creamer in front of him. "Want something with that?"

"I'll take a couple of buttered rolls with me." He sipped his coffee and watched the counterman slice the rolls and slather them with soft butter. The coffee tasted like burnt water, but it was hot and would keep him awake for the last hundred miles.

"Traveling long, mister?"

"From Los Angeles."

"That's long, all right. You got a girl there?"

"Sure."

"I got one too. Ex-wife. Good riddance." He flashed Lew a smile, then wrapped the rolls in waxed paper. "Holidays are slow around here, but I bet you guessed that. Without my brother to talk to, I'd go crazy as a shithouse mouse. Road's empty most of the night, except for long haulers and cops who stop sometimes. Come in. Use the phone. Drink coffee and maybe order a hamburger or plate of fried chicken, cheap bastards. Especially the cops."

He put the bag of rolls on the counter and was refilling his coffee cup when Lew heard the front door open and saw the counterman stop and his face go dark.

"Hey!" he yelled. "Where do you think you're going?"

Lew turned and saw Shirley walking toward the back of the diner. She smiled at the counterman and pointed to the rest room door, showing a little pink rayon and a ribbon of black belly under her long winter coat.

"Gonna use your bathroom, mister."

"Like hell you are. Niggers and dogs go out back."

Shirley was still smiling when he said it, and Lew couldn't bear to watch the face he knew would follow. He turned back to the counterman, grabbed a fistful of his white shirt and slammed his head down on the counter. When the man began to struggle, Lew picked up his fork and jammed it into the dimple in his check.

"Don't." He heard Shirley skittering around behind him. He put his elbow on the counterman's neck and kept pressure on the fork.

"Go on, Shirley."

"Mr. Man!"

"Go on."

The bathroom door slammed shut. The counterman was panting heavily, his face outlined in the halo of spilled cream and coffee that dripped onto the stool and floor.

Lew thought his breath smelled like blood, like he spent the night sucking pennies.

"I'll get you, you bastard," the counterman wheezed.

Lew pricked his flesh with the fork. A tear bubbled at the counterman's eye, and Lew held him down until he heard Shirley run back across the room. Only after the front door closed behind her did he move his elbow and let the counterman up, still keeping the fork pressed against his bloody cheek.

"I'll get you."

Lew pulled the fork away, stepped around the stool and backed slowly toward the door. He found the knob behind him with his free hand and dropped the fork to the floor, then calmly opened the door and stepped outside. When he turned around and raised the collar of his jacket, he knew something was wrong even before the black wing crossed over him. He saw Shirley standing by the Lincoln and thought he heard her scream. He wanted to rush to the car and tell her to be quiet and drive away from the diner as fast as he could, but all he could do was rely on instinct and lean forward to lessen the blow of the pistol butt that came down on the back of his head.

. . .

Cece dreamed she was dancing alone at Club Congo, twirling end-lessly past a swipe of hungry and envious faces, her beautiful ivory dress whirling around her knees, her body never tiring, the sound of the band like the ocean in her head, until Lew appeared on the edge of the circle and offered her his hand, his features sharp and hand-some against the blur of bystanders.

And then she heard Shirley's piercing screams. She raised her head from the front seat, still dreamhappy, her eyes sandy with sleep, and looked out the window at a place she didn't know. She saw Lew on the ground in front of a diner and a man in a white shirt was kicking him in the ribs while another one, tall and hunched over, was pointing a gun at him as he tried to protect himself and crawl away. Shirley was standing beside the car with her hands on her face, screaming as loud as she could, and Cece wanted the dream to come back as she tried to make sense of what she was seeing. Her head still cloudy and unfocused, she opened the glove compartment and pulled out the gun that she knew was stuffed inside. It was heavy and cold in her hand, shiny as silver, bigger than Uncle Lucius's, and she held it loosely as she kicked the car door open. Cece sat there with her feet on the ground and Lew's gun in her lap, and when no one looked at her she lifted it in the air and yelled his name. Everyone stopped, just like that, still as blurry as the people watching her dance. She shivered in the startling cold. Lew's name echoed in the absolute quiet. For an instant she thought everything was going to be all right, and then she woke up. The man with the funny back raised his pistol. Lew squirmed on the ground until he faced her and shouted something she couldn't hear over the roar of the gunshot. Then there was a burst of brilliant light and Lew's face was the last thing she saw, just like in her dream. Thinking of that and nothing else, Cece closed her eyes in the silence that followed and never felt the bullet that killed her.

. . .

Lew rolled in the dirt and clipped the hunchback's legs with his own. The man fell on his crooked back, helpless as a beetle, and Lew scrambled for the gun that popped out of his hand. His ears were still ringing from the shot just fired, but he got to his knees and grabbed the pistol in both his hands and shot him twice in the face where he lay in the dirt three feet away. The counterman was already scrambling back to the diner, his arm spinning, and Lew shot him once in the head and twice in the back, the blown-out mess of his upper body crashing through the window of the front door. Lew sat there on his knees, put the gun to his own temple and kept firing, the trigger clicking, clicking, clicking, the bullets used up.

In the pitch dark, Lew spotted an old prospectors' road and followed it for three miles, then turned into the foothills of the Shadow Mountains, driving slowly over the rough terrain, the undercarriage of his Lincoln scraping on the broken rocks that poked through the ground like knife blades. He drove through the layered hills until he found a deep ravine, a black slash in the darkness around him, and backed into it so he wouldn't have to turn around later. He looked over at Cece, slumped where she'd fallen in the front seat, a neat bullet hole near her left eye. There was very little blood on the wound, and in the darkness it didn't look any worse than a birthmark, but he didn't dare touch or examine the back of her head. Shirley was whimpering behind him and staring out the window. She hadn't said a word since he dragged the two men into the garage and switched off the lights at the diner, and he was glad of that—not knowing what he would've done if she opened her mouth again. He stepped around and lifted Cece from the car, the weight of her almost nothing as he carried her into the deep ravine and rested her on the cold ground. After stripping her naked, he kissed her on the lips. When he stood he heard coyotes in the hills, and the ground around him moved with living things. In a matter of days her body would be spread across the desert, returned to the earth. Vanished. Gone.

Lew rolled up the ivory dress and underthings, carried them back to the car and stuffed them under the seat. Pink light shimmered on top of the mountains, and Lew could make out a smattering of dying stars and long streams of clouds unfolding like fingers in the sky, and he drove back to the dirt road and the highway that would take them home.

She woke as the sun came up, a total whiteness in the small window that faced the hills where the dam was being built, and watched him sleep. They used only one blanket that night, and through the thin material she could see the curve of his penis, the jut of one knee, the outline of an arm folded across his narrow chest. He slept facing sideways on his back, and she studied his profile and remembered tracing the long line of his nose with her finger in the darkness. The room was very cold and she dressed quickly. Holding her shoes in her hand, she stepped carefully over Joe, where he'd stretched out on the floor by the end of the bed, his plump belly heaving. She stopped at the bedroom door and looked again at Filius, and he was watching her now, awake, unmoving.

"Will you come back?"

Lena knew she had to pick Burr up at the Chubbs' house and go home and take a shower before opening the café. She knew she had things she wanted to tell him, things she hadn't thought of until that moment, things about herself and her son that he might have missed or not considered, and she knew, too, that there would be time for that, and she would be back again and wait in the dark for him to come home so she could begin.

She smiled. "Yes."

Speed Owens and Perlie Trimble were panning for gold in one of the large puddles in the exposed riverbed when the cable snapped on the dragline above them. The bucket swung into the gorge, its iron teeth gathering Perlie up as surely as the whale had swallowed Jonah. They found him unhurt, curled up around himself where the steel maw had ploughed to a stop, clutching the pie pan he had stolen from the mess hall and used to sift for gold. Speed rolled out of the way just in time, tearing his cheek open on a rock. When they pulled him out of the hole his entire body was mud-covered from the splash of the bucket, and at first he didn't even realize he was bleeding. The gash was deep enough that Filius sent him to the hospital in Boulder City, and he was tempted to give both men their layoff slips for wasting time when they should've been shoveling the muck his electric shovels couldn't reach. But if he let them go they'd be replaced by two greenhorns who, having already heard the rumors of gold nuggets found at the bottom of the river, would be just as eager to break the rules and look for riches in a geological stratum containing only volcanic waste and shattered cobble. So he sent Speed back to town and Perlie back to work, and within an hour they'd pulled the dragline bucket out of the notch and were back on schedule.

There was almost a mile of exposed riverbed between the upper and lower cofferdam, where they continued to dig out the loosened guts of Black Canyon, removing truckloads of broken rock deposited there when the earth was young and the river itself was still forging its course. They were now well below the waterline, that demarcation a ghostly stain high on the canyon wall, and concentrating on the exact spot where the dam would have its footing, carving a long, wide gorge where they could blast into the bedrock and key the structure firmly into place. High scalers still flew along the cliffs directly above them, smoothing out the surface for footholds and anchorage, the small rocks they pried out sometimes spinning off as mysteriously as shooting stars, briefly caught in the glow of the 1,500-watt lights before raining down on the men below, a constant hazard.

The dangers were compounded at night, and Filius and Walker Young devised a strategy to safely choreograph the movement between men and machines as much as possible. Their blueprints of roads and work stations allowed them to utilize all six Marion 490 shovels, and the dragline that was essential to the excavation, without putting the hundreds of men who worked this section at undue risk, their senses already addled by diesel fumes and smoke, with only tar-covered pith helmets for protection. The biggest challenge was the trucks—two hundred at a time—that coasted back and forth from the dumping grounds to the east. The fleet, already suffering after two years of abuse, was allowed to stop for gas and belt changes, but otherwise kept running, their engines cooked and bearings shot, the brakes worn down to metal sighs, the roofs fortified with dented sheets of scavenged tin, the doors hacked off so drivers could ride with one foot on the runner, windshields busted out early for fear of broken glass. These trucks were the sad workhorses of the dam business, customized by itinerant drivers and destined for the scrap heap. Floyd Huntington said he'd once seen a truck parked by the roadside suddenly burst into flames. "Nobody near it. Tired sonofabitch went up all by itself." As he told Filius the story, he shook his head and watched their trucks crawling up the narrow roads cut into the canyon banks. "There's not a one of them bastards I wouldn't toss a match under myself just to put it out of its misery."

At daybreak he climbed into his car at the top of the canyon road and drove home. The sun was already pushing through the overcast sky, caught there like a bright button knitted into the clouds. The snow was still deep in the Spring Mountains, and Filius thought about the previous Sunday, which he'd spent on Griffith Peak with Lena and Burr. On a brisk morning they drove through Las Vegas and headed northwest, past the winter-brown meadows and switchback canyons at the base of the range, and up into the dense groves of ponderosa pine where the snowline began. He kept going until the drifts made the road impassable, then parked in a stand of fir trees where grass still showed under the boughs. For two hours they sledded down the small hills on oil-drum lids borrowed from the dam site, spinning through the powdery snow with Joe nipping and barking after them. The day turned warm enough for them to strip off a layer of sweaters and their knit hats, and they laid a blanket on a grassy patch by the trees, drinking hot chocolate from a thermos and eating the ham and butter sandwiches Lena had packed at the café. Before they'd left the mountains that afternoon, Filius spotted a trio of turkey vultures circling near the top of the peak. He got his binoculars from the car and scanned the edge of the forest until he found a shallow, wobbly track through the snow and followed it to a coyote dragging the carcass of a young deer toward the sheltering trees. Filius could see the tremor in its back legs as it dug in and tugged at a burden two or three times its own weight. The coyote paused only once, panting hard as it raised its head to scout the terrain. As the animal looked directly at him, the blood visible on its teeth, Filius lowered the binoculars.

She liked to linger at his small brick house on Denver Street when she was off duty at the café and Burr was in school, indulging herself in time spent alone. The air always smelled of wood smoke and tobacco, and each room was free of clutter. She liked his office the best, his wide oak desk covered with the binary slide rules and the small field books and six drafting compasses, with their needle-thin points. On the largest wall was a big map of the Colorado River, from Arizona to the Gulf of California, surrounded by elevation drawings and cross-section renderings of the dam. There was always a dusting of graphite around the metal sharpener on the corner of the desk, and a gray thumbprint next to the light switch by the door. The box of letters still sat on the floor by the chair, but she never looked at them again.

The weather was beginning to change for the better, the days bright and cool, and she liked to take a book into the living room and read as close to the fire as she could bear, Joe asleep at her side. If she got restless she'd put on her coat and take him on longer and more frequent walks through the neighborhood reserved for engineers and their families. At first the wives would peer at her from behind their curtains, but Lena made a point of waving to them and even greeting their husbands as they drove back and forth from the dam. Eventually the peering stopped, and after two weeks, Cynthia Dunbar—pretending to check on the winter-wilted oleander by her porch—invited Lena in for coffee. The following week she brought Freda Goodenough to the café for lunch, and afterward Lena sat with them and heard all about Hank and Becky Leiter's teenage daughter, who'd suddenly been sent to relatives in Philadelphia for reasons unspoken. Lena added nothing to their speculation other than an infrequent roll of her eyes, glad enough that they had finished concocting scenarios for her own comings and goings.

Fanny started teasing her about her new big shot friends and the social engagements that were bound to follow.

"Pretty soon you'll hand me back your apron."

"No I won't."

"Yup. And then you'll be having tea with Sims Ely, and he'll drop his sugar spoon just for the opportunity to look up your dress."

But Fanny never said anything bad about Filius, and the closest she came to commenting on their arrangement was when Lena came home on New Year's Day and told her where she'd been.

"He better not hurt you."

"He won't."

"Then good for you."

When he got home, Lena was asleep. He walked into the bedroom and, leaving Joe sitting in the hallway, quietly shut the door behind him. He undressed in the gray light and climbed under the covers, trying hard not to wake her. But the mattress rose as he settled on his side of the bed and she exhaled softly and gravitated toward him, her breasts against his back and one hand thrown over his hip. Filius shifted his weight lower and waited for her knees to click behind his, knowing this movement would cause her hand to drop and her fingers to graze his stomach. He could tell by her breath on his neck that she was awake now, and her fingers began to tighten against his skin and spread below his belly button. When he turned to face her, she was smiling. Over her shoulder, Filius saw their shadows blurred against the wall, and with his fingers he traced her outline, from neck to knees and back again, watching their black shapes wave and roll. Lena gripped his thigh and hooked her foot in the blanket and sheet that covered them and pulled them off the bed and onto the floor. Unencumbered, she stretched under his hand, oblivious to the cold air, and twisted her body to manipulate his touch. Filius was surprised how comfortable she was, forthright and inviting, that she needed this as much as he did, this fusion of limbs and warmth, this reminder of what they both had lost and yet wanted. He looked down at Lena—amazed at how young they both still were, barely thirty, and was suddenly glad that life was long and full of promise.

Mr. Jimmy talked across an entire desert, two hours straight from the moment he'd picked Lew up in front of Miss Williams's until they pulled up in front of the Irataba Hotel in Needles, California.

"She came back six nights ago, Lew. Going to stay a week, make my life miserable the whole time, and spend all my goddamn money on steak dinners and crap games at the club. Comes out on the train from Los Angeles on one day's notice, like my life don't matter, and I got just that much time to move Angie over to the Apache to make room for the wife—and Angie don't like it any more than I do, wants to stay and sock Donna right in the eye, so there goes the rest of my money buying presents to keep *her* from throwing punches or a brick through my window. I send Donna a check whenever she wants, but that ain't enough. No, the bitch has to come here every three or four months to stick her nose down my hole. Left me two years ago and just won't stay gone."

· · ·

The murders at Jilly's diner had made the front pages as far away as Los Angeles and San Francisco, complete with gruesome photographs, police theories and public outrage. But without a motive or suspect and therefore no story, the articles shrank and drifted to the back of the newspapers, and by the end of the week they were gone and forgotten. Frank Strella had done his part. He sent two men to burn down the diner and gas station during a lull in the investigation, and made arrangements for Lew's Lincoln to be driven to Reno in the middle of the night, where it was delivered to an associate who took in cars with histories, glad to repaint and resell them from Salt Lake City to Gallup, New Mexico. He made sure a *Los Angeles Times* reporter got the full story on Kenny Jilly and his brother, replete with wife beatings, child abandonment and—in Lubbock, Texas, where Jack Jilly was still a fugitive—assault with a crowbar. Within a month, the case was all but closed, and Jilly's just another sad and scorched derelict ruin on the California highway, an unsolved desert mystery. Frank told Lew to stay out of sight for a few days, which he did; and to get rid of the gun, which he didn't.

"She asks for a divorce when I'm doing five years in Folsom for bad checks, then changes her mind when I get out in thirty-one. I come back to that shithole on Centinela and she says she's not budging—as if she could. Donna's standing in the doorway when I get out of the cab and I don't even recognize her, got to blink twice and move my head from side to side to take her all in, she's so fat. If you told me before I got out that somebody's skin could stretch that much, I'd of called you a lying dog. But it's true. It's like someone deboned her and poured her full of mashed potatoes. Looked like she had a twin growing right inside of her. Must've been eating six meals a day when I was in Folsom. Standing there on the porch on legs about to buckle, telling me I had to support her or she'd call the police about a couple of houses I sold in Vacaville that was already sold. Something I'd told her back when she was still okay looking. She had me and she knew it. I tried, though. Even offered to take her down to Mexico for a quick little divorce—make a last holiday of it at Tijuana or Ensenada like the movie stars—but just like she said, she wasn't budging."

After they got back to Las Vegas, Shirley went to her room and locked the door, refusing to explain where Cece was to Miss Williams, who knew better than to ask Lew. That same day, early in the evening, Shirley came out—all packed up—and asked for her wages. By that time Miss Williams had heard from Frank Strella, and added an extra hundred dollars to the three hundred that came in his envelope from the Mexico Club. Shirley's hand was shaking as she took all that cash. She had a friend who worked in a house in Phenix City, Alabama, not far from the Georgia line, and she'd go there for a while before moving farther east, maybe to Florida or even Maine, just as far away from that desert as she could go. She didn't say good-bye to anyone as she hurried to the car Mr. Jimmy had waiting to take her to the train station. The only thing she left behind was the dress she'd worn that night in Los Angeles, and Fayette, who was the first to find it hanging sweet and smoky on the back of her door, claimed it as her own. Miss Williams blamed Lew for the loss of yet another girl and wanted him gone, but Frank paid for Lew's room himself and offered to get her some new recruits. Miss Williams never did learn what happened to Cece, deciding it was better not to pry, letting herself believe that maybe Cece found a slick man who took her off to a finer life, and never allowed herself to imagine Cece dead, her bones scattered over the Mojave salt flats.

"So Angie's holed up in the Apache spending every dime Donna isn't, and making a mouthful of demands, but I can't tell her Donna's got me on a real estate hoax out in Vacaville since I made that mistake once before. And don't tell me it's my own bed I made 'cause I'm sleeping on the goddamn couch, getting nothing but misery from both ends, just waiting until I can put that fat bitch on the train tomorrow and my life goes back to whatever it's supposed to be until she turns up again."

Lew had stayed in Cece's room a full week, taking his meals in bed and having George Lenski bring him a newspaper every morning and a casino report every night. He didn't care much about the news, or the beef and peppers and cold chicken that Miss Williams fixed for him, but he made an effort to be engaging, at least in other men's eyes. So when Mr. Jimmy came to say it was time to come back to work, he pretended to be pleased and laughed at his jokes. And when Fayette came to him one night, rank from other men, he took her into his bed and enjoyed her as best he could. But mostly he kept his door locked and thought of Cece as long as he could, covering himself with every blanket in her overheated room until his own smell erased her more precious scent and helped him purge himself of the tenderness he'd felt and the responsibility he didn't want for what had happened in the desert. The pistol-whipped lump behind his ear subsided after a few days, but the searing pain that persisted was like a sharp knife drawn across the top of his skull. It came and went and lasted only moments, but when it did he saw her face and knew he'd failed her.

It was warm enough to ride with the windows open, and when they crossed into California, Lew put his head out and sucked in the desert smell, dry and musty as the back of an old dog. Early wildflowers were beginning to bloom on the roadside, and the bright yellow flowers of brittlebush turned into a buttery mirage as they sped by, the fragile branches curled like open hands over discarded gasoline cans and migrant trash.

Lew and Mr. Jimmy were giving a surprise visit to Haze McGraw, the owner of the Irataba Hotel and a prominent Needles businessman who owed Frank Strella eight hundred dollars in poker stakes he'd borrowed on two consecutive Saturdays the month before. It wasn't a lot of money, but the Mexico Club thought it expedient to set an example now and then. The last few miles of highway followed the Sante Fe Railroad track and took them along the Colorado River, which Lew could hardly recognize—the water so wide and docile, shallow enough for small children to play in, its graduated banks stained with plant life. Ahead, the passive stream disappeared under bridges and into the irrigated green sward that surrounded the town.

Jimmy drove into the center of Needles and turned down Front Street—wide enough to stampede cattle to the feedlots at the other end of town—and parked his big black Dodge a few doors down from the hotel.

Lew got out and looked at the Irataba, a four-story brick building in the middle of the block. Across the street, a park lined with palm trees separated the business district from the rail yards. Down a side alley, Lew saw two horses with fancy Mexican saddles tied to a rail that the hotel shared with Romero's Café. The smaller horse, a pinto, had a hoof cocked, fast asleep.

Mr. Jimmy took off his sunglasses, squinting into the bright sun. "Let's say our piece to Mr. McGraw and get us something to eat."

The lobby was ornate but shabby, as if it hadn't been properly dusted for years, and empty except for the desk clerk and a well-dressed woman sitting on a plush sofa with a baby carriage at her side. Suddenly hungry, eager to get this over with, Lew strode past the woman, as blonde and pretty and peacefully asleep as her baby in the carriage. The clerk, a middle-aged man with a hairline that came to within an inch of his eyebrows, looked up from his newspaper as they glided by. "Can I help you?"

"No." Lew pushed open the office door without knocking. McGraw was sitting at his desk with a pencil behind his ear and a yellow accounts book spread open before him, his shirtsleeves rolled above the elbow and a dark green tie thrown over his shoulder. He was fit and muscular, with a full head of dark hair combed straight back, and sun-etched lines around his eyes. When he jumped up from his desk, Lew could see the fancy western belt buckle that held up his suit pants.

"Frank Strella sent us."

McGraw, recognizing Lew from the Mexico Club, bolted. Lew twisted out of his way but Mr. Jimmy wasn't paying attention, standing in the doorway with his eye on the pretty blonde, and McGraw pushed him off balance as he catapulted into the lobby. Jimmy slid across the floor on the seat of his pants, spinning around until he faced the office door with his head poking up between raised knees, and Lew thought it was the funniest thing he'd ever seen. He jumped over him and ran after Haze, who was fumbling with the lock on the side door.

"Hold it, McGraw."

Haze turned to throw a wild punch, and Lew saw the hard knuckles coming at his ear, and could hear the awful grunt behind it, and it wasn't funny anymore. He ducked and came up with his head in the big man's solid belly and rammed him through the doorway and into the dirt alley. Haze went down backward between the bay mare and the little pinto tied to the rail outside the café. The bay danced as far away as the short rope would allow her, and the pinto almost sat down in panic, both horses kicking up more dust than the man scuttling back and forth between their clicking hooves. Lew got between the horses, and when McGraw tried to get up he cocked him once in the forehead and leaned a knee on his testicles. He pulled out the Hopkins and Allen pocket revolver he'd traded Perry Stubbs a pair of ladies' watches for and stuck it in McGraw's mouth. Lew watched him through the yellow cloud that rose around them, watched his pale lips suck on the short nickel barrel of the gun, watched him send tears and drool down his dirty face. He put more weight on his knee and didn't hear Mr. Jimmy mutter from the curb, "Jesus Christ, Lew. It's only eight hundred bucks."

He heard only the nickering and frightened snorts of the horses pulling on their ropes and trying to get away. He closed his eyes, wishing he could ride off with them, up the shallow Colorado and just keep going—the single thought that prevented him from pulling the trigger.

. . .

Fanny didn't even see it coming when Archie finally proposed. Standing in the window that morning, Lena watched him come around the police car, hat in hand, and when he knocked on the door instead of barging right in she knew something unusual was about to happen. She waved him inside, and his eyes shifted around the empty café, where they hadn't even put the chairs down yet.

"Fanny here?"

"In the kitchen."

When he walked past, Lena could smell an extra dose of Lucky Tiger tonic in his hair, and called through the order window to ask Hi to come out on the floor and help her set up the tables, so Fanny and Archie could be alone. Lena filled the sugar bowls and hovered close enough to the counter to watch Fanny and Archie through the open window. She saw him pull a ring box out of his uniform pocket, and Fanny's eyes widened, her hand shaking as bad as his as he slipped the ring onto her finger. Lena turned away when Fanny threw her arms around him, and she saw Hi grinning by the front door as he switched on the lights.

Archie came out of the kitchen ten minutes later, his face flushed and a smile riding high on his checks, and once he got back into his car, Fanny came out with tears in her eyes and showed Lena the wide gold band with a large pear-cut diamond surrounded by six rubies.

"Archie was the only boy in his family," she said, "and his grandmother's favorite. She promised him since he was twelve that when he was ready to get married, this was the ring he'd propose with. So when Archie told her he wanted to marry me, she said she'd send him the ring. That was in August. In September she lost her husband, in October she lost her mind and in November she died. Her name was Hannah, she was eighty-six."

Lena stood at the counter and poured them each a cup of coffee as Fanny stretched out her fingers and modeled the ring.

"Hannah was married for seventy years to a Russian immigrant from Kremlin, Montana. His name was Gregory Pavlovitch, and he was a farrier by trade, working on all the big ranches from Browning to Ethridge, and he made a good enough living to build them a little house on the Cut Bank River. Then last fall, still working at eighty-nine, he had a heart attack while traveling to a ranch outside Santa Rita. His horses kept walking, and two days later they found him dead on the buggy seat, deep in the Blackfeet Reservation about fifteen miles short of the Canadian border.

"Hannah couldn't sleep anymore for missing her husband, and in her nightly panics she thought the Russians were coming to cut off her head or stick a knife in her heart for taking Gregory away. She was seeing them everywhere. She saw Russians behind trees and in her closet, fishing in the river or riding by in their cars. At night she sat on the porch with Gregory's Remington rifle across her lap, taking shots at the empty road just in case. Got so bad, Archie's mother went to stay with her. But as soon as she fell asleep that first night, old Hannah quietly filled a dozen empty bean cans with all her jewelry and valuables, and Gregory's family treasures—the amethyst-and-gold cuff links his father got for a wedding present in Saint Petersburg, a pair of epaulets his great uncle wore in the Caucasian Cossack army and a small porcelain egg with a portrait of the baby Jesus that had been in the family for over a hundred years. Hannah wrapped each can with a piece of leather cut from Gregory's old shoeing apron, and buried them in soggy ground as the night turned bitter cold. Archie's mother found her at daybreak, crouched over the last two cans and frozen in place, her face the same light blue as the thin ice that covered the river. She carried the old lady back into the house, set her down by the fireplace and called the funeral parlor. The morning after they buried her, a week before Thanksgiving, a blizzard blew in from Alberta to the north and covered Cut Bank in two feet of snow. The cans and the ring inside were buried until an early thaw two weeks ago. Archie's mother got his sisters and the three of them set to work with pickaxes and shovels. That's how I have the ring now, just like his grandmother always wanted."

When Sims Ely came into the café that morning for his usual coffee and two plain doughnuts, Fanny served him herself for the first time in weeks. As he poured a stream of sugar into his coffee, she leaned her elbow next to his saucer and made a fist, holding the ring within an inch of his face.

Sims stirred his coffee, took a sip, glanced at the ring and reached for his doughnut. "Okay, you can stay then."

. . .

Filius and Burr sat in the back of the flatbed truck at the very base of Black Canyon. Below them, deep in a hole between the two cofferdams, men were chipping at the loose gravel and stone with shovels and picks, carefully avoiding the latticework of metal pipes that were sucking out the muddy water welling around their rubber boots, the rank seepage from underground springs that bled through the rocks after every dynamite blast.

Burr looked up when Filius pointed at the railroad tracks that ran along both sides of the canyon, supported by long iron trestles hundreds of feet high, bolted and driven into the rocks.

"Those are the tracks the electric trains will use to bring the cement from the gravel pits six miles upstream to the mixing plants below us. And when the cement's mixed the trains will bring it back along the same tracks, each car fitted with two concrete buckets that will be lifted by those cables overhead and transported to the section of the dam that needs to be poured."

"How long will that take?" Burr asked.

"Two years. Two busy years."

Burr stared up at the cableway that stretched from cliff to cliff. "Can I come watch?"

"Yes, of course." Filius pointed to the gorge in front of them. "We're looking at the exact spot where the dam will be built. It will be locked into place right here, over six hundred feet thick at the base, which is where the greatest pressure will be. Then it will rise over seven hundred feet high, tall as a skyscraper, and it will curve out and taper as it reaches across the canyon, over twelve hundred feet across at the top. It will be the biggest dam in the world and the most beautiful—and this is where it begins, right in this very hole."

Burr remembered the pictures of other dams Filius had shown him, massive structures that held back rivers in forest highlands and on desolate plains. "There won't be any more floods, will there, Mr. Poe?"

"No, there won't be."

"And there'll be a big lake behind the dam, right?"

"They say it will run eight miles long."

"And we can fish in it?"

"Yes, we certainly can."

"And swim?"

"That, too."

Burr could almost see it all, the smooth concrete face of the dam white between the red canyon walls, and beyond it an expanse of bright blue water as far as the eye could see.

She sat on the edge of the bed and looked at the photographs propped up on the dresser. It was one o'clock in the morning, and she tilted the shade on his bedside lamp until the arc of ivory light fell on the pictures. In one, Filius and Addie and Ray stood on a reservation in Montana, among acres of white tents the Cheyenne still lived in during the summer months; she and Filius were smiling directly at the camera while Ray looked skyward, his felt cowboy hat almost falling off his head, his eyes shining brightly. Another picture was of Filius and Addie on their honeymoon in Paris, taken by a stranger as they stood in an open-air market. The last picture was just Addie, in front of a tent pitched in the cottonwood trees on the banks of the Colorado River ten years before. She was sitting next to a campfire with her knees up, barefoot, her short hair held back with a dark band. She was laughing and pointing at the camera, at Filius. Lena could tell she was truly happy, and she envied her.

They were different women, she knew that, but they did have one important thing in common: they both loved this man, though Lena hadn't told him so yet.

They drove out to Uncle Judy's ranch on Saturday morning to pick up the two dozen fryers Fanny had ordered for the café. They had borrowed Hi's pickup, and Burr sat right next to Filius because the front window wouldn't roll all the way up. There had been an unexpected storm earlier that morning, and the quarter inch of fresh snow that coated the valley was already beginning to shrink back from the creek sides and the pastures where Uncle Judy's cattle bunched together and warmed the ground beneath them. Charlie was waiting by the barn, and together they went out to check the four wooden traps he'd placed along the fence lines and in the gullies on the far end of the property, each box baited with carrots and old corn. He checked them every morning, walking the perimeter with an old Ithaca single-shot that weighed only five pounds, not very accurate but good enough to scare off the coyotes or red-tailed hawks that tried to raid his traps. Joe ran ahead of them, nose pushing through the dusting of snow, and reached the traps by instinct, but they were all empty except for the last, which was tipped on its side, the snow around it imprinted with the tracks of a jackrabbit. Joe kept his nose down and his backside up as he snuffled around the door.

Charlie grinned and handed Filius his rifle, then eased the dog away with his boot as he bent to pick up the trap and carry it home.

"He's a rabbit hound, all right."

Back at the ranch house, Uncle Judy made hot chocolate while out on the porch Charlie skinned the rabbit as easily as if he were pulling off his socks. He gave it to Filius to take home for supper, and Uncle Judy provided some of her canned corn and pickle relish to complete the meal. On the drive back to Boulder City, Burr fell asleep with his face against Filius's arm, and didn't wake up until they stopped off in Las Vegas to have lunch at the White Spot Café.

Mr. Jimmy parked next to Rex Bell's Cadillac V16 in front of the Overland Hotel. Lew had noticed the enormous yellow car the night before at the Mexico Club, where the cowboy star was entertaining Lionel Barrymore and a half dozen studio lackeys, all of whom had been staying out at his horse ranch near Searchlight. Bell didn't gamble much, but his company did, so Frank Strella sent over a few bottles of his best French champagne, and gave handfuls of chips to the pretty girls at the table when he made his rounds later that night.

Lew waited on the sidewalk, watching Jimmy try to squeeze out of the driver's seat without scratching the Cadillac with his door.

He finally freed himself and stepped on the curb. "You like big cars, Lew. Why don't you get yourself one of these?"

"I already have a car."

Two weeks ago, when he'd gone back to work, he had Jimmy drive him over to Stan Weiser's on Carson Street, and within five minutes he had bought a three-year-old Studebaker coupe, the most nondescript car on the lot—a car you could vanish in. He walked right past the nice Ford Cabriolet with the rag roof and the older Marmon 78 convertible, and even though Stan said a Lincoln just like his old one was coming in next week, Lew insisted on the drab coupe and paid full price, in cash.

"Not much car, that Studebaker."

"It goes."

"Yeah, and so does my mother's Ford Victoria, but it won't go like this Cadillac."

Lew ignored Jimmy. He saw Speed Owens and Nancy Thayer step out of the hotel restaurant and started toward them. Speed stopped short, like he hit a wall, but relaxed when he saw Lew smile. Lew hadn't seen Speed since Christmas and was surprised by the long scar that ran down the right side of his face.

"Nancy get mad at you again?"

Speed grinned and Nancy frowned and stared off in the opposite direction.

"Shit, Lew. Got it at work."

"How come you're not working now?"

"Pulling nights."

"Tough."

"No it ain't. I'm crew boss." He leaned closer, took Lew by his shoulder and pulled him down the sidewalk. "Making good money. Course I ain't told Nancy that part yet," he whispered, and Lew could smell the morning beer on his breath. "She find out I got extra cash in my hip pocket, it'll be gone and spent before I even get my pants off."

He chuckled into his own fist, and looking past him Lew saw the tall engineer with the long nose across the street, walking out of the White Spot Café. The kid was at his side, Lena's son, and the man had his hand on the boy's shoulder and they wandered, smiling and happy, down the sidewalk. Standing there next to Speed, watching the engineer and the boy, he wondered why happiness always eluded him, why his life wasn't whole and full of the good things he deserved.

Filius stood at the edge of his bed and watched her sleep. It was a warm night, the window open, and he could smell the light orangy scent of the miniature roses that Freda Goodenough had planted next door. The sun was showing on the craggy mountains behind Boulder City, and hazy bands of light fell between the open curtains and across the bed. Lena lay there on her side, the sheets down around her waist, both hands under the pillow that cradled her face. She'd gotten sun the day before; her nose was burnt, her shoulders freckled, and her hair spilled out across the pillow.

She was taller than Addie by an inch or so, and her hair was longer and darker, more cinnamon than gold. Her skin was darker, too, except for the long, narrow scar above her ankle that was almost absent of color and showed pink when her skin turned brown. Some nights when they lay in bed together he gently traced the scar with a finger, and she would stretch her toes and turn to him, much like Addie did when he ran his hand up the back of her leg from her calf to her thigh. They were different, of course, but there was also a powerful similarity, a natural ease, that drew him close.

He wanted to wake her and tell her how glad he was that she was there, or climb into bed and hold her, but he had already done both those things the night before. It was Sunday morning and he let her sleep. He picked up his satchel by the door and headed off to the dam.

She woke up when the bright sunlight struck her square in the eyes. It was only seven o'clock, and still tired, she turned her back to the window, coming face-to-face with Joe, curled in the spot where Filius had slept. The dog was eyeing her suspiciously, as if she'd done something wrong or was about to. She rubbed her cheeks, itchy from yesterday's sun, and glanced over at the framed photographs on the dresser. Still sleepy, it took her a moment to realize that something was different, and she looked again to make sure. It was a new photograph taken the month before, of Burr riding Uncle Judy's old burro, beaming, as Lena sat on the top rail of the corral and watched.

Climbing out of the Studebaker on Sunday morning, he saw George Lenski drop half a dozen gin bottles from the crate he was carrying to the back door. George juggled the rest of the bottles as best he could, and stepped awkwardly through the broken glass at his feet.

Lew was meeting Strella at eight o'clock, to get the payoff money for a Reno judge who'd dismissed charges against one of Joe's bootleggers after he'd killed a drunken Basque outside the Toscano Bar on Christmas Eve. He would drop off the cash at the courthouse on Virginia Street Monday morning, then spend the day in Reno and the next in Lake Tahoe doing minor jobs for Frank. Usually Mr. Jimmy did this kind of run, but Lew decided he needed a break and some time alone so he could clear his head.

He was on his way to the front door of the Club when Victor Lenksi came out of the kitchen looking for his son. When he saw George standing there, he slammed the door and pointed to the broken bottles. "You goddamn idiot!"

When George shrugged, he punched him hard in the ear. The boy stumbled backward, the glass like marbles under his feet, and fell to the pavement, the rest of the bottles smashing around him.

"You goddamn moron!"

Lew stopped and looked at George sitting there in the broken glass, his hands bleeding from where he tried to break his fall. Then he saw Victor Lenski lift his boot. "Hey, Lenski," he shouted, walking over. "Knock it off."

"Mind your fucking business."

"What did you say?"

Now Lenski looked up, the anger rising too fast for him to stop. "I said mind your fucking business, you fucking midget little kike."

Lew's head filled with white space and he heard a terrible roar. He saw Victor standing in front of him, knees bent and fists swelling, and he saw his own hand swoop down and pick up the neck of a broken bottle next to George's bleeding hand. He could smell the juniper perfume of the gin as he came in low under Victor's raised fist and jammed the jagged circle of glass into his belly. He jabbed it three more times and felt Victor go soft all around him, and when he screamed and started tearing at his face, Lew punched him in the forehead with his free hand and stabbed him again in the leg and in the shoulder. Then he heard him moaning and crying on the ground, writhing in the broken liquor bottles, and kicked him in the mouth to shut him up. Sobbing, George pounded on Lew's back with his bloody hands until he shook him off, but George came back again, trying to smother him in his clumsy embrace. Lew hit him in the kidney to make him stop, and saw Frank Strella running toward him and the Mexico Club cook and Perry Stubbs crowding the kitchen door. There was blood all over the ground and on his clothes and on the men who lay before him.

"Stop, Beck! Goddammit, stop!"

The bloody neck of the gin bottle slid out of Lew's hand.

"You want to kill him?"

Lew looked down at George cradling his father in his arms. The deep roar in his head was deafening.

He stood with Filius and Frank Crowe as they inspected the wooden forms. To Burr, these looked like the outline of a giant snake that had crawled into the hole long ago and died, but he knew they would soon be lined with sheet metal and held together with tie irons and pigtails and filled with concrete. The forms ran the entire length of the excavation pit at the very foundation of the dam. High above them strong cables sliced through the clear blue sky, and directly overhead a huge concrete bucket hung from an elaborate set of pulleys and steel.

He liked being down here with Filius, and came every chance he got. He stayed by his side, and watched Mr. Crowe walk to the edge of the gorge and look into the deep hole below them.

"She's going up, Filius," Crowe said.

"Yes, we should be pouring concrete by noon."

Crowe turned to both of them and slapped his hands together. "Gentlemen, it's a good day to build a dam."

He entered Miss Williams's house through the back door, stripped to the waist in the kitchen and washed his face and arms in the deep soapstone sink under the window. When the blood was rinsed from his skin and hair, he ducked his head under the tap and let the cold water run over the aching knots on the back of his neck. Miss Williams came into the room when she heard the water running, but when she saw Lew bent over the sink and the rosy puddles on her counter and floor, she backed away and closed the door. Lew walked through the quiet house to the room he once shared with Cece. He changed clothes and packed everything else into his duffel bag except the fine suits he'd worn at the Mexico Club. He tossed his car keys on the bed and shut the door behind him.

Fayette opened her bedroom door and saw the little man walking down the hallway toward her. She had learned to be meek and respectful in his presence, and stepped back into her room and tried to disappear. When he passed by, she saw that he had his duffel bag slung over his shoulder, and when he shifted its weight she glimpsed the black handle of a revolver in the waistband of his pants. The little man walked fast and didn't even see her, and she was glad to see the back of his head instead of those eyes, and she hoped that he was really leaving and that this time it was for good.

At Nancy Thayer's bungalow on Ogden Street, he knocked until Speed Owens opened the door in his undershirt and half-buttoned trousers, bleary-eyed and angry until he saw who it was.

Walking home from Filius's house that morning, she marveled at the perfect weather. She loved how spring arrived in the desert, bursting out in the most unlikely places. For the last few weeks she'd watched the slender young sycamores along Wyoming Street and New Mexico Street begin to leaf out, and the roses in the plaza pushing out fresh canes studded with buds. All along H Street the sprinkling of Bermuda and rye grass that had survived the winter showed along the sidewalks like the sparse fringe around a bald man's ears, and the Mojave yucca that Pat Simmons planted as a hedge in front of his house was starting to bloom. Lena waved to Sue Howells, kneeling in her front yard to turn the soil around her new tomato plants, and saw the Morgans' sheltie bitch, the poor thing in desperate heat, run zigzag across the street to sniff around every yard, looking for the Randalls' boxer mutt.

The letter was sticking out of Fanny's front door above the knob, bright as a white flag, and knowing it was from him, she took it and sat on the top step, leaning against the railing to read his thick, exact script.

> *Dear Lena,*
>
> *I have become so used to writing down my thoughts rather than speaking them that I hope you will indulge me, just this once, in my need to use this pen as my voice. All my life I've put my mind in the service of practical creation, but in the time since Ray and Addie died, when my life was seized in a heart-beat, held in a void where nothing mattered, I have had no desire to do anything but mourn. All the other feelings that were necessary to sustain my life I was able to squeeze into the margins that took up the hours of my days and left me with nothing but the overwhelming feeling of loss that consumed my nights. But you already know that. You perceived my loss through your own, even though your own was as great. You've had every reason to lose your faith, yet you held fast so you could pass that faith on to your son. In my field, we use tools to arrive at the unknown, to find the distance between two points. For one that cannot be directly measured, we locate some other point and make a triangle. Every angle has a set of corresponding ratios, but of what use is the table of trigonomics to me now? In the past year, I have tried to live by reason alone. I came here, in my arrogance, to change the course of a river. That, in the com-pany of other men, I could do. What I could not do, nor even*

saw the need of doing, was to change my own course. That took
you. It is always women who perceive these things more clearly,
and who show men why and how to save ourselves. I floated in
emptiness, and you found me. But there is more at work here
than a simple formula of rescue and relief, and that is the
absolutely immeasurable prosperity of hope. Our nights together,
our days with Burr, have given me hope for the future, one I
want us to build together. My pen seems to have gone the way of
my voice. What I'm trying to say is that I love you.

Filius

He lay down on the backseat of Speed's Dodge and covered himself with the pale blue blanket they'd taken from Nancy's closet. It
stank of mothballs and peach pits, and Speed's car stank of vinegar
and sweat, and he had both windows rolled down so he could
breathe. Speed complained about Nancy for most of the drive along
the Boulder Highway, and Lew half listened and realized he'd been
half listening to Speed Owens for most of his adult life. He lay there
in the semidarkness under the blanket and thought about where he
would go next—maybe take a train and travel farther east than he'd
ever been before, to Texas, maybe, or even south to Mexico, where
he could start another life across the border, and he wondered if
they would enjoy that, Lena and the boy. When Speed pulled up to
the Boulder gate, Lew pulled the blanket tight around his head
while the government agent looked inside the car, Speed explaining
that he was hauling Eddie Griggs back to his wife so she could sober
him up before Sunday Mass. Lew heard the two of them laugh, then
the agent slapped the rear panel of Speed's shitty car and they
lurched forward. Knowing that he was inside Boulder City, he threw
back the blanket and gulped fresh air at the window.

Even the simple act of turning on the bathwater and adjusting the
tap was strange to her. Everything was different now, and she liked
that, and as she settled in the hot bath and let the water rise to her
shoulders she thought about how these differences would fuse and

blend in the days and weeks to come, and how the three of them would adjust to the new circumstances of their lives. She shut her eyes and heard cars passing down the street outside the window, and Mrs. Fuller whistling for her dogs. It reminded her of when she was a little girl playing at the pond back in Hugo, and how her father would whistle one long note to let her know that he was home from work, and a shorter series of trills to call her in for supper. He would stand by the porch rail until she acknowledged his call, waiting for her to run up the hill and join him. She wished her father could see her now, starting a new life with her son a thousand miles from home; it was everything he'd ever wanted for her.

She climbed out of the clawfoot tub and reached for her towel. She and Emma would walk together to the café, where they would take care of the same people who came in every Sunday after services at Saint Christopher's, the same families circling the same tables, eating the same meals they always ordered, fried chicken, creamed corn and mashed potatoes. She would stay at the café until Filius and Burr came back from the dam, and the three of them would walk home and she would make supper while they sat in the kitchen with her. Her son would be bursting with stories about this momentous day at the site, and she knew Filius would sit back to listen and let the boy tell it. After supper the McCafferty girl would come to mind Burr, and she and Filius would go to his house on Denver Street and walk Joe, and then sit down and talk about where they would go from here.

Lena dressed in the bathroom, the uniform freshly washed and smelling of starch. The bottom of her hair was still damp from the bathwater, but it would dry before she got to the café. She combed it back behind her ears, stepped barefoot out of the bathroom and saw the little man sitting on the couch.

He'd been sitting there long enough to hear the water sloshing around as she climbed out of the tub, the gurgle as she pulled the plug out of the drain, the rustling of her uniform as she took it from the hanger and the slide of the fabric being drawn across her flesh. He felt calm, patient, and like a gentleman he rose and smiled when the bathroom door opened. She looked beautiful, caught in the sunlight that streamed through the parlor windows.

"Lena."

He liked saying her name.

"Hello, Lena."

She was surprised, as she should be, but he knew that would go away. He walked to her, glad that she was barefoot. She was still taller than he was, but so what.

"Let's go."

Her face became hot and she felt a bubbling of queasiness in the bottom of her stomach. She just stood there, trying to think, and watched him approach. Lew Beck. He stopped only inches from her body, and when he cocked his head to look up at her, one of his eyes caught a glint of sunlight; it looked like a sliver of cut glass, and she shuddered.

"Let's go," he said again.

"What?"

"Where's the boy?"

She shook her head.

"Where is he?"

"He's not here."

She watched him nod and smile. When he turned his head to glance behind him, she saw dried blood on the scratches that ran down the back of his neck and below the collar of his shirt.

"He's with the engineer, isn't he? Your friend, right?"

She didn't answer, wanting to get away from him but not knowing how.

He looked back at her. "We'll wait."

He put his hand lightly on her shoulder, and Lena's body went rigid. This, and the look on her face, took his breath away. In her eyes he saw the reckoning of his days. He saw himself, a truth revealed, and it held him fast. He saw his mother's broken spirit and the sadness that rounded her shoulders, and his father's disgust at everything he had ever done and what he had become. He saw all the men who ever mocked or challenged him, and the excruciating pain he'd given to each in turn. Looking deeper, he saw fear and scorn, loathing and dismay. He saw sneers and laughing asides directed at his back, and unctuous submissiveness and dishonest smiles and meaningless nods that were offered to his face. He saw all this in the terror that showed in her wet eyes, as shiny as dark mirrors, and he was sick.

She looked over his shoulder and saw Fanny standing in the front doorway. When he turned around, Lena grabbed him, his small body like a rock exploding in her hands. She fell backward onto the floor and saw him throw his fist, then Fanny crashed against the Radiola under the front window and collapsed. Crawling to her, she saw that Fanny's eyes were closed and there was blood on her lip, but she moaned when Lena reached her. She lifted Fanny's head onto her lap, and through the open front door watched Lew Beck walk toward the Dodge that was parked across the street.

He climbed behind the wheel and jerked away from the curb, the salvation he had hoped for, the plans he'd made for their future, now forgotten. And he blamed Lena for that, too. She didn't know how easily a life could be destroyed, but he did.

It was just before noon when Filius called him to his side. For the last half hour he'd been standing on top of the cofferdam rolling rocks down the sloped face and into the churning brown sweep of the river, or throwing them as far as he could to watch them splash into the current running fast with spring runoff. He'd peered into the water until he was almost dizzy, watching it roil and carry debris to the dark entrances of the diversion tunnels on either side of the canyon.

Now he stood with Filius and Walker Young and Floyd Huntington, and he followed Filius's finger to the top of the canyon and the cable operator who was giving the signal to lower the first concrete bucket from eight hundred feet above the riverbed. Filius didn't want the boy to miss it. The bucket descended almost soundlessly from the steel cables that held it over the wooden forms, and he could feel the quiet settling over the site as trucks slowed and workers watched from every vantage point, from the base of the canyon to its rim. Frank Crowe was standing just above the slot, hands on his hips, posed for posterity in front of the three newsreel cameramen who tilted their tripods under their old Akeley thirty-five-millimeter cameras and opened their telephoto lenses wide enough to capture both Boulder Dam's greatest champion and the massive concrete bucket behind him. The bucket jolted to a stop over the first wooden form, and when it stopped swaying, Filius saw Frank look up at them and smile, then he turned to the puddlers on either side of the form and nodded. They raised their shovels to trip the latches on the bottom of the bucket with their blades and stepped back as fourteen tons of concrete poured onto the exposed bedrock at the bottom of Black Canyon, bubbling gray and viscous over the top of the form.

"Now we're building a dam."

Filius hadn't even known he'd spoken out loud until he looked down at Burr and saw the boy smiling at him.

He parked Speed's car on top of the canyon road and waved down the first truck that came by, a slat-back International loaded with giant spools of wire. Climbing into the cab, he ignored the driver, who kept stealing glances at him as he tore down the twisting road at breakneck speed.

"Beck. Lew Beck, right?"

He leaned his head out the window and waited for his first view of construction below.

"You coming back to work, Beck?"

· · ·

He was sharing an orange with Burr on top of the cofferdam when he heard the siren and looked up. The police car was speeding down the hill, trailing a dust storm in its wake, and he thought that some dam worker's wife had just gone into labor at the Boulder City Hospital or some Nevada politician was trying to make a grand entrance for the cameras.

Burr, shielding his eyes with his hand, watched the police car hit the bottom of the canyon road and speed toward the cofferdam. "That's Archie."

Filius was reaching for another orange when he saw Lew Beck at the other end of the cofferdam, walking quickly and looking directly at them. Filius stood up and put his hand on the boy's shoulder. Beck seemed unaware of the siren or the police car, and everything seemed frozen except for his powerful stride and the dust that shimmered around his ankles. Filius saw him reach into the waistband of his pants. He didn't see the gun, only the flash, but he felt the bullet that struck his shoulder like a staggering punch. Burr was standing there with the orange slice still in his hand. With his good arm, Filius yanked him behind his back. He heard more shots, and men were running away. Looking down, he saw that the front of his white shirt was scarlet. The police siren screamed. When Beck was only an arm's length away, Filius put out a hand to stop him, but he pushed him aside and seized the boy. Archie Swerling slammed on his brakes and jumped out and crouched behind the door of his police car, gun drawn. Beck held Burr in front of him and stepped to the edge of the cofferdam. The boy's eyes locked on Filius. When Beck raised the gun again, Filius lunged toward them and heard the shot and felt the bullet graze his side. He hit the little man with his full weight and grabbed Burr as all three of them went over the side of the cofferdam. He wrapped his body around the boy to shield him from the gouging stones as they rolled down the rough-faced slope. He saw Beck's eyes go wide and roll almost white as they plunged into the water, and felt the immediate grip of the current. He held Burr close as they were pulled under, unable to fight the powerful undertow as it carried them down. He held Burr up as best he could, and for a moment they broke free of the surface and gasped for air before being sucked into the black hole of the diversion tunnel.

. . .

Gliding through the cool water below the cofferdam, Burr felt like he was dreaming. He eyes were open but he saw nothing in the cloudy depths. He felt Filius's strong arm around him, and they tumbled together in the current that took them freely and turned them upside down and pulled them into the tunnel, the water roaring in his ears, a grand and mysterious echo in the darkness as the river swept them along. Feeling the steady pressure of Filius's arm around his waist, his let his body relax. There was comfort in the hands that held him, and for a moment it almost seemed as if he was part of the water, a willing particle in its mad dash through this channel, and he closed his eyes and tried to breathe but swallowed and gagged instead, and kicked his feet as the man beneath him gripped him tighter. He gave up struggling as they were buoyed upward, and when his chin finally broke the surface, he opened his eyes and filled his lungs with air.

The darkness in the tunnel was a soothing and familiar sensation, and Filius let the river embrace them in its black grip and crushing power. He felt numb, but warm. He shut his eyes and listened to the water as it cascaded over him and jettisoned him as easily as a broken stem, plummeting him through all the waters of his life. Waters real and imagined, timid and fierce, mastered and untamed. Waters of all the rivers and lakes and rills and streams, and oceans and seas, all the waters that gave and took so much away. The water was all around him now, deafening as a storm, beckoning him as it always had. It washed the blood from his wounds. It rushed into his nose and mouth. It tugged urgently at his feet. He wanted to join the water, succumb to its demands, its finality, and become part of what it held, things he once had held himself. But then he felt the boy's fists paddling against his shoulders and forced open his eyes, remembering the promises he'd made and the memories he had, then kicked his own feet and broke the water's hold for good. When the river again tried to separate him from the boy, he tightened his grip. When it tried to carry them below the surface, he fought back. He refused to let go. He would never let go. He would not let the river take this boy. And as quickly as they had been dragged into darkness they were delivered into light, borne out of the other end of the tunnel into the blazing canyon, spinning in a gentle current, Filius and the boy and the little man floating facedown, and when he turned Burr's head away he felt the water once more reaching for the boy and he struggled and lashed out until he realized it was only the men who'd come to carry them to shore.

Filius lay on the bank and stared up into the blue-white sky. His body shed blood and water. He heard Burr next to him, coughing, the riverwater rising from the boy's lungs to run clear and warm from the corners of his mouth. A hand applied pressure to the wound on his shoulder, and he took a deep breath and rested, his face sideways on the rocky bank of the Colorado River. In the brightness of the day he thought he could see Lena running toward them, and that was enough.

Acknowledgments

I wish to thank Amanda Urban for
her constant good counsel, and for placing
my unwieldy manuscript into the eminently
capable hands of Gary Fisketjon, whose
surgical strikes and detailed notes are a gift.
And for everything, Suzanne.